Praise for David Levien's

CITY OF THE SUN

"Here's what to expect when reading *City of the Sun*: relentless suspense that will not let you out of its grasp and a cast of characters who are so utterly real you'll forget you're reading fiction. David Levien's novel is moody, riveting, and special."   —Harlan Coben

"Relentless. . . . The truth of the characters— and the intensity of their pain—is as unbearably real as it gets."
          —*The New York Times Book Review*

"*City of the Sun* is hard, mean, beautiful, and touching—a dazzling novel. With this book, David Levien has placed himself among the best writers in the field."   —Robert Crais

"*City of the Sun* is all kinds of trouble. For one thing, it becomes really hard to break away to deal with the rest of the day. Then there's the recurring need to take deep, calming breaths throughout."   —*New York Daily News*

DAVID LEVIEN

CITY OF THE SUN

David Levien cowrote the screenplays for
Ocean's Thirteen, *Runaway Jury*, *Rounders*,
and several other major films. He lives in
Connecticut.

www.davidlevien.com

ALSO BY DAVID LEVIEN

Wormwood

Swagbelly: A Novel for Today's Gentleman

CITY OF
THE SUN

DAVID LEVIEN

CITY OF
THE SUN

A NOVEL

ANCHOR BOOKS

A DIVISION OF RANDOM HOUSE. INC.

NEW YORK

FIRST ANCHOR BOOKS MASS MARKET EDITION, FEBRUARY 2009

The Library of Congress has cataloged the Doubleday edition as follows:
Levien, David.
City of the sun: a novel / by David Levien.—1st ed.
p. cm.
1. Missing persons—Fiction. 2. Teenage boys—Fiction. 3. Parents—Fiction. 4. Private investigators—Fiction. 5. Ex-police officers—Fiction. I. Title.
PS3562.E8887C58 2007
813'.54—dc22   2007028002

Anchor ISBN: 978-0-307-38720-2

www.anchorbooks.com

Printed in the United States of America
10 9 8 7 6 5 4 3 2 1

CITY OF
THE SUN

ONE

JAMIE GABRIEL WAKES at 5:44, as the clock radio's volume bursts from the silence. He rolls and hits the sleep bar, clipping off the words to an annoying pop song by some boy-band graduate who wears the same clothes and does the same moves as his backup dancers. The worst. Kids at school say they like him. Some do; the rest are just following along. Jamie listens to Green Day and Linkin Park. It's three-quarters dark outside. He clicks off the alarm and puts his feet on the floor. Waking up is easy.

In the master bedroom sleep Mom and Dad. Carol and Paul. The carpet is wall-to-wall, light blue. New. The liver-colored stuff that came with the house when they bought it is gone. The blue goes better with the oak bedroom set, Mom says.

It was a good move for the Gabriels, to the split

ranch–style on Richards Avenue, Wayne Township. Trees line most all of the blocks here. The houses have yards.

Jamie walks past his school photo, which hangs in the hall on the way to the bathroom. He hates the picture. His wheat-colored hair lay wrong that day. He takes a pee. That's it. He'll brush his teeth when he gets back, after breakfast, before school.

He moves through the kitchen—*Pop-Tart? Nah*—and goes out the utility door into the connected garage. Mom and Dad love it, the garage on the house, the workbench, and space for the white minivan and the blue Buick.

He hoists the garage door halfway up; it sticks on its track. A streak of black fur darts in and hits him low in the legs.

"Where you been, Tater?"

The gray-whiskered Lab's tail thumps against the boy's leg for a moment. After a night of prowling, Tater likes the way the boy ruffles his fur. The boy pushes him aside and crawl-walks under the garage door.

A stack of the morning *Star* waits there, acrid ink smell, still warm from the press. Jamie drags the papers inside and sets to work, folding them into thirds, throwing style.

He loads white canvas sacks and crosses them, one over each shoulder, then straddles his bike. The Mongoose is his. Paid for with six months' delivery money after the move to Richards

Avenue. Jamie ducks low and pushes the bike out underneath the garage door, when Tater rubs up against his leg again. The old dog begins to whine. He shimmies and bawls in a way that he never does.

"Whatsa matter?"

Jamie puts his feet on the pedals and cranks off on his route. Tater groans and mewls. Dogs know.

"Should've gone to McDonald's, you fat fuck," Garth "Rooster" Mintz said to Tad Ford as he reached across him for a French Toast dipper. Tad's face squeezed in hurt, then relaxed. The smell of gasoline, the fast-food breakfast, and Tad's Old Spice filled the battleship-gray '81 Lincoln.

"You're eating same as me," Tad said back. "You're just lucky it doesn't stick to you."

Rooster said nothing, just started chewing a dipper.

Tad was unsatisfied with the lack of reaction, but that was all he was going to say. Rooster was seventy-five pounds smaller than him, but he was hard. The guy was wiry. Tad could see his sinew. He'd once watched Rooster, piss drunk, tear a guy's nostril open in a bar scrap. The whole left side of the dude's nose was blown out, and just flapped around on his face with each breath after the fight was broken up and Rooster was pulled off.

Tad had plenty of targets of opportunity with

Rooster—the small man stank much of the time. He didn't shower most days. He left his chin-up, push-up, and sit-up sweat in place, only bothering to wipe down his tattoos. His red-blond hair hung limp and greasy as well. Then there were the scars. Nasty raised red ones that ran up and down his forearms like someone had gone at him with a boning knife. When Tad finally screwed up the nerve to ask where he'd gotten them, Rooster merely replied, "Around." Tad left it there.

"You're just lucky it doesn't stick to you," Tad repeated, chewing on his own French toast.

"Yeah, I'm lucky," Rooster said, turned, and looked down the street, still dark beneath all the goddamn trees. "Should've gone to McDonald's."

Jamie Gabriel, rider, pedals. He flows by silent houses, houses dark on the inside. He tosses papers into yards and onto porches. He works on his arc and velocity with each throw. An automatic sprinkler quietly sweeps one lawn, still blue in the bruised morning light. Jamie slings for the front door of that house so the paper stays dry. He works his pedals. A line of streetlights goes dark with a hiss as morning comes. Dad thinks it's great that they moved to a neighborhood that supports tradition: newspaper routes. Mom's not so sure— her boy needs his rest. Few people know the streets like Jamie does. Dark and empty, they're his streets. Jamie wasn't so sure either, at first, when he was still getting used to the work and slogging through the route on his old Huffy. But then he earned the new bike. He read an old story of a mailman who became an Olympic biker. *Why not him, too?* He has a picture. The black man's thighs bulge and ripple. He looks like he's set to tear his bike apart more than ride it. Jamie checks his watch. His time is looking good.

Rooster glanced at the clock inside the Lincoln. Goddamn Lincoln now smelled of an old fuel leak and Tad's farts over the sickly sweet of the aftershave. But the car was clean. Riggi bought it in a cash deal and dropped it off with fixed-up tags. Rooster hated these goddamned pickups. He flexed his forearm, felt the corded muscle move underneath his wounded and roughly healed skin and light red arm hair. His forearm was thick for his stature. He was ripped. He was disciplined with working out, but he was a lazy bastard, he suspected, when it came to certain parts of the job. Yeah, he hated the fucking snatches. Anybody could do 'em. It wasn't like the house work. *That* was rarefied air, sir.

"Start the car," Rooster said low, glancing sideways at the clock again. He scanned out the windshield of the Lincoln. The goddamn thing was like the bridge of the starship *Enterprise*.

"Oh, shit," Tad said, his last bite of hash-brown cake sticking in his gullet. The car turned over, coarse and throaty.

They saw movement at the corner.

Jamie puts his head down and digs his pedals. He's got a shot at his record. He's got a shot at the *world* record. He throws and then dips his right shoulder as he makes the corner of Tibbs. The canvas sack on his left has begun to lighten and unbalance him. He straightens the Mongoose and glances up. Car. Dang. Jamie wheels around the corner right into the rusty grill and locks them up.

Tires bite asphalt and squeal. Smoke and rubber-stink roil. Brakes strain hard and hold. The vehicles come to a stop. Inches separate them.

With a blown-out breath of relief, Jamie shakes his head and starts pushing toward the curb, bending down to pick up a few papers that have lurched free.

Car doors open. Feet hit the pavement. Jamie looks up at the sound. Two men rise out of the car. They move toward him. He squeezes the hand brake hard as they approach.

TWO

CAROL GABRIEL PUSHES a strand of dirty blond hair back behind her ear and sips her coffee, Folgers beans, freshly ground, a mellow roast. Her friends like Starbucks, but she finds it bitter and knows they drink it for the name.

She stands in the kitchen and looks out over the sink through the small square window. She's found herself smiling here most days since the move. Especially since fall hit three weeks back with a burst of color on the trees. There's no smile today, even though the day's a bright, shiny thing. Her second cup of coffee has begun to curdle in her belly, as Jamie usually wheels into the driveway before she's done with her first.

Paul walks into the kitchen, a blue rep tie hanging unknotted around his neck. Because he's got his nose in a pamphlet, he bumps into a kitchen chair. The chair groans across the terra-cotta tile floor and sends a painful report through his knee and up his thigh. Carol looks over at the noise.

Split annuities. Tax-advantaged cash flow and principal protection. How to sell the concept hasn't really stuck yet for Paul, but he's got to get into new products now. He sits, reaches for toast that's gone cold. Variable whole life; yearly contributions to a policy that pays a death benefit but turns into an IRA-type retirement instrument at age sixty-five, is what got him into this neighborhood. He broadened his base, reached a new level of clientele. He made a solid conservative play and bought a house that he could carry the monthly nut on during his worst month, by virtue of his commissions on those policies alone. Now the plan was to have no worst months.

Paul chews toast. Feeding himself right-handed, he presses his gut with his left. It yields. Thirty-five years' worth. It was a cut slab through age thirty-one, but for the last four years he's let it slide. At six-one, he'd been lean, a runner, for most of his life. Then he got a bone spur on his heel. Doctors recommended he get it cut out, but the surgery meant a long recovery, so he decided to run through it. They said it wouldn't work, that the thorny spur would continue to aggravate the plantar fascia, that it couldn't be done, but he'd gotten the idea it could. Mile after grueling mile he kept on, until something changed and yielded, and the thing wore away to nothing. Then his job did what pain could not and stopped him in his tracks. He started coming home tired in a different way from any manual labor he'd done in his youth. A few scotches a week became a few per night, so he could sleep. That, he suspected, added the first girth layer. He switched to vodka, which helped, but he was out of shape and he knew it.

"Paul, I'm worried." Carol stands over him. He looks up. A shadow lies across her face. "Did you see Jamie outside?"

"No. Why?"

"He's not home and I didn't hear him come in from his route."

"Maybe he left for school early. . . ."

Her face radiates a dozen questions back at him, the most pleasant being: What kid goes to school early?

How can a grown man be so damned dumb? It leaps to the front of her mind. She feels guilty for it immediately and pushes it away. But it *had* been there.

"No, you're right," he says. He gulps coffee, pushes together a pile of insurance pamphlets, and stands. "Maybe his bike broke down." Carol looks at him with doubt, not hope. "I'm already late, but I'll drive his route and look for him on the way to the office. Call me if he shows up. I want to know why—"

"Call as soon as you see him. Call as soon as

you can. I'll try the Daughertys'. Maybe he's over there."

"Yeah. That's probably it." Paul gives her a peck and heads for the door. It's like kissing a mannequin.

Mothers know.

Paul's blue Buick LeSabre traverses the neighborhood. Streets that had been empty quiet an hour ago now hum. Minivans tote children to school. Older children pedal in packs. Kids, older still, drive four to a car to the high school. Joggers and dog walkers dot the sidewalks.

Paul coasts up in front of a miniature stop sign held by an aging woman with white hair and an orange sash across her torso. She waves a group of eight-year-olds across the front of the Buick as Paul lowers the window.

"Do you know Jamie Gabriel? Have you seen him?"

"Not by name," she says, years of cigarettes on her voice. "I know the faces."

"Have you seen a paperboy?" Paul asks, wishing he had a picture with him. "His bike might have broken down."

"Sure haven't, just kids on the way to school."

Unsatisfied, Paul nods and drives on. He makes a right on Tibbs. An oil-stained street. Jamie's not there and nothing's out of the ordinary. Not sure what to do next, he drives the rest of the route and then continues to the office.

Rooster sits and sips his morning beer. Overdriven guitar sounds thunder in his head. He'd been playing Mudvayne all morning. He turned it off a minute ago, but can still hear it. He can do that. It is one of many things he can do that others cannot. He's special. He knows he is. But he's not happy. Having gifts is not the same thing as happiness. His mind roils in simulated guitar fuzz—he doesn't want to think about *in there*—until he hears the van drive up outside.

Tad lumbers out of the panel van clutching a sixer of Blue Ribbon and the reload, the day's second round of food. This time it is McDonald's as directed. He approaches the house, the eyesore of the neighborhood. The paint is falling off in flakes and long curls, and only the windows on the side and those of the room down the hall are freshly painted. Black. It is what they'll call their "music studio" if anyone asks. But no one does. This is the house the neighbors wish would just go away so property values could rise.

Tad enters, pulling off dark sunglasses and sliding them into the chest pocket of his flannel shirt. The living room is dingy. Carpet that is lentil in color and texture, and secondhand green and orange sofas that have gone decades without a recovering fill the room.

Fast-food sandwich boxes and wrappers litter a dinette area. Rooster sits on a spindly chair across from a dormant twenty-year-old color television with tinfoil bunny-ears antennae that rests on a milk crate. His eyes are on the dead screen and he rocks slightly in rhythm to music that seems to fill his head from an unknown source. He is shirtless.

"You are one lazy bastard."

Rooster's eyes don't leave the television as he gives Tad the finger.

"You got no work ethic at all."

"You speak to Riggi?" Rooster asks as if Tad has just entered the room and the previous comments had never occurred.

"Shiftless. Look at you."

"I've already been in there two times since you been gone," Rooster says. Flat. His eyes, also flat, turn to Tad, stopping him up. "You speak to Riggi?"

"Two times? Bullshit, two times . . ." Tad gets his breath back. "Yeah, I spoke to him."

"What'd he say?"

Tad puts the beer down among the rubble on the dinette table. He opens one for himself and chucks one over to Rooster.

"Mr. Riggi said he needs it for Thursday."

Rooster opens the new beer and takes a delicate, probing sip. "Thursday. Shit."

"Yeah," Tad begins, enjoying his partner's discomfort, "he's got it arranged for Thursday, so you better get cracking."

"Yeah? *I* should get cracking? Whyn't you take a turn?" This silences Tad for a moment.

"No thanks. You're the pro."

Rooster nods slightly, pleased, then kicks a pill into the back of his mouth, drains off a few ounces of his beer, and wearily stands. Vicodin. When you're in physical pain, it takes away the pain. When you're not in pain, it takes away other things. He gathers himself and walks purposefully down the hall toward the back bedroom door.

Tad occupies the chair in front of the television, leans forward, and turns on cartoons.

The sound of a lock being undone from the outside and the door opens, allowing a crease of light into the ugly, darkened bedroom. The blacked-out windows are nailed shut and have metal grating over them on the inside. A sheetless bed is the only furniture. Rooster reaches up and tightens a bare lightbulb into its fixture, illuminating the room. Balled up between the bed and the wall is a tearstained, violence-shocked flash of skin. The man's face sets in a mask that expresses neither frenzy nor madness. The boy's face forms its own mask of pain, and fear, and incomprehension, and so far below the surface as to be invisible, fury. He doesn't even say no but weakly tries to scrabble away from the man.

"Here it comes," Rooster says. He jerk-steps toward the boy and kicks the door shut.

Out in the living room Tad turns up the volume on the television.

Goddamnit. Where did he put the damned instruction manual for his BlackBerry? Paul sifts through his paperwork-laden desk. The phones outside are busy. He's been programming numbers into the thing for weeks, but now he can't get it to work. His paneled office sports several framed certificates distinguishing him for his efforts as an insurance agent, but they aren't helping him now.

Janine appears at the door. "Carol on three." And she disappears again. He had called Carol on the way to work and told her to start looking for Jamie.

"Carol? My BlackBerry just crashed. Did he show up? 'Cause when he does he has some explaining—" Her answer freezes him inside. It's 10:15.

"The police? We can, but I don't know. It seems a little drastic. . . ." His gaze goes distant. There's a world full of possibilities out there. But he isn't ready to accept them. Fathers may not want to know.

"If he doesn't show up at his normal time after

school . . ." He stops. His stomach has soured. Acid churns in it like he's had six cups of coffee on no food.

"No, you're right—I'll come home and we'll deal with it. . . . Okay. . . . Try not to worry." But as he hangs up, that's what he has begun to do.

Paul and Carol stand static amid the bureaucratic swirl of the busy police station. Things move slowly for them, incoherently, like a warped videotape caught up in the machine.

They stand and gesture with the beefy desk sergeant.

Later, they sit at the desk of a concerned-looking patrolman, filling out forms, giving him photographs.

Now, waiting, silent, on a wooden bench, Paul holds a dead cup of coffee in one hand and Carol's cold palm in his other. Her features have begun to tighten—it's not possible to see it yet—but she's begun to desiccate and wither on the vine.

Finally. Finally, the concerned-looking patrolman shows them into Captain Pomeroy's small, glass-walled office. Pomeroy, a soft, pillowy man with a prominent nose bone, sits behind his desk. His tie has a silver bar across it. A silver pen and pencil set rests in his shirt pocket. His hair is swept back with Vitalis, his face full of Aqua Velva, his mouth full of nicotine gum.

"Mr. and Mrs. Gabriel, I've looked over your paperwork here, and I just want to assure you that this office will do everything it can to assist you in locating your boy, ahh, James."

"Jamie" comes through Carol's clenched jaw.

"Jamie." Pomeroy makes a note. "Thought it was short for—"

"No, that's his name. It's on his birth certificate."

"But before we do, before we open this thing up wide, I just want to be sure that this is . . . That is, that your boy didn't run off for a—"

"He's missing. I know it. You hear about these things."

"Ma'am, most mothers . . . Look, all I'm saying is to be sure. It's just that boys are known to be boys."

"What?" It comes out a hoarse croak, as if Paul hasn't used his voice box for years.

"What I'm saying is, often in these types of situation, maybe he had a math test he didn't want to show up for. Or he got a bad grade on that science project and didn't want you to—"

"Not Jamie."

"Mrs. Gabriel . . ." Pomeroy leans back and shifts his holstered automatic against his hip. He looks to Paul in muted demand.

"Honey, I'm sure that's what everybody says about their . . ."

"Exactly," Pomeroy breathes in gratitude, taking over from Paul. "Hell, he probably just . . ."

Hope is a slim branch, and the men do their best to grasp it, but it's a bit overweighted for Carol. Her expression stops Pomeroy.

"I suggest you talk to his teachers." He manages to start again. "See if everything was jake at school. Ask his friends . . ."

"Fine, we will, but . . ." Paul offers.

"Anything you do along those lines will save us legwork." Pomeroy taps a silver pen against the edge of the desk.

"What are you going to do? What about issuing an alert?"

"We have. We've passed around the information. Okay, ma'am. We'll open it up wide. We'll set up on your house. Your place of business, too. I'll put officers out in the neighborhood canvassing door to door. And I want you to call in the minute your son shows up"—Pomeroy leads them out of the glass-walled office—"because he's going to." Pomeroy smiles reassuringly. "He's going to." And he shuts the door behind them.

"That man is not going to help us." Carol's words come, grim. Paul says nothing.

Darkness comes early this time of year. The Buick drives up. After long hours of looking, of hanging flyers, Paul steps out of the car, the way he has so many times after picking Jamie up from soccer practice. Paul stands on the driver's side. Carol, after an afternoon of waiting by the phone, appears in the front door. She shakes her head. In the setting sun, Paul is a handsome, still-young father. He appraises his home of comfort, his still-young wife before it. A police cruiser is parked at the curb. He walks toward the house and she crosses toward him. They come together and cling to each other in the driveway, neither sure what they're holding on to now. The sun drops below the trees.

Paul eats a bleak dinner of cold cereal. Rigged to the phone is a trace/recording device monitored by the two patrolmen outside in their cruiser. Carol sits in a trancelike state next to him. A scratching is heard at the kitchen door. Carol gets up and lets Tater in. His mouth drips blood. She gets a dish towel and wipes him clean. He is uninjured—the blood belongs to something else—and he rumbles off into the living room, excited at the smell of the police sniffer dogs that have been through the house all afternoon. Paul shakes more Lucky Charms into his bowl and the prize falls out.

"He was waiting for this. I'll save it for him." He puts it aside on the table and breaks down, his shoulders shaking with sobs.

Carol stands across the kitchen. She doesn't go to him. After some time he stops.

"Let's just go up to bed." He stands. *Maybe*

we'll wake up tomorrow and find out this was all a bad dream, he wants to say, but does not.

Paul crosses to the staircase. Carol goes to the wall and turns on the living room and porch lights.

"Let's leave these on in case." She follows him up the stairs.

The door swings open, throwing light onto the mattress, which the boy has pulled off the bed and angled against the wall over himself like a protective lean-to. Rooster offhandedly tosses a grease-soaked fast-food bag into the room and sniffs to himself at the attempted defense. *Never seen that one before. As if it'd work.* He slams the door behind him. Again the room is awash in darkness.

Paul lies on his back in the darkened bedroom, un-feeling of the mattress beneath him. He floats in space defined only by his misery. Grief that he could never have imagined surrounds him and tears at him from every direction. Circumstances pulverize him, sap him motionless in the dark. A dull rumbling sound filters in from the bathroom. There, sitting in a filling tub, Carol thinks of Jamie when he was a three-year-old playing the Down the Drain game, an amusement of his own invention. *Better get the plumber, Mommy, I'm gone. I'm down the drain.* . . . Carol's pale back shakes.

The water pounds and thunders. She realizes the sound isn't the water but her screams.

Rooster and Tad sit at the cluttered dinette table. Heavy feedback music is in the air and Tad drums along to it.

"So's he gonna be ready?"

Rooster looks at his partner. Tad's recently started smoking meth, and he's on it now. Rooster can tell because Tad has that filthy sheen. It's a dirty drug that opens the pores and seems to suck in airborne dirt and debris. He must've smoked up the last time Rooster was in the room down the hall. Disgusting. "Of course he's gonna be ready, bitch."

"Because it's first thing, like fucking dawn on Thursday, you know, asshole?"

Tad has a wild, risky look in his eyes. *Wouldn't be there if not for the meth,* Rooster thinks.

"Yeah, I know, douche bag." Rooster flicks a bottle cap at him. Just misses the fat fucker.

"Watch it." Tad moves evasively and too late. "Just so you're sure, dickhead."

"I'm a professional, fuck face." This taunt catches Tad, and he isn't sure where to go next, how to escalate.

"Listen, faggot," he begins, and then there's a click and a knife blade's at his throat. Rooster's pulled the four-inch Spyderco he carries in his back pocket and locked it back. Just like that. Tad feels the pressure of the blade against his Adam's apple, a hard thin line.

"Don't even say another word. Not sorry, not spit. Hear me?" Rooster's face radiates blood.

Tad Ford nods slowly.

Class has just ended at JFK Middle, and kids stream out toward buses and their parents' cars. Carol Gabriel walks opposite the flow toward the low building and wonders why she's done this to herself and not come later in the afternoon. It has been four days. The police have left her house. Every backpack she sees, every jacket, screams Jamie for a moment before dissolving into a different child. Alex Daugherty walks by her and stops.

"Hi, Mrs. G," he says.

She bends down. "Alex. Hi, Alex." The boy seems to know something's going on but not exactly what. "You know that Jamie's been away for a couple days?" she goes on. She can't hold herself back from touching him. Her hands reach out and smooth the boy's sleeves, his hair. Her hands, disconnected from her mind, need to know that *this* boy at least is real.

"Yeah."

"Do you know if he was . . . upset? Was everything okay at school and stuff?"

"Yeah. Did he run away?" the boy wonders.

"We don't think so." The conversation is already taking a toll on Carol. "He wasn't having any problems that he told you about? He hadn't met anyone? Any secret stuff? Because you should tell me if he did, it's important."

Alex shakes his head and begins digging at the sidewalk with a toe, when a little way off at the curb his mother honks and gets out of her station wagon.

"There's my mom."

Carol straightens up and trades a glance with Kiki Daugherty, who waves. She's told Kiki and Kiki's said all the right things. Carol watches jealously as the other mother collects her child. If there's any accusation in Kiki's stare, any "What kind of a mother lets this happen to her son?," she keeps it to herself so Carol can't see it. Carol hurries toward the school.

Inside Jamie's homeroom, his teacher, Andrea Preston, a twenty-seven-year-old black woman, hands Carol a cup of coffee.

"We have assemblies where we teach the children not to talk to strangers or accept rides. And we had one yesterday to redouble—"

"Yes. Yes." Carol's words echo, disembodied, against the linoleum. "Really, Jamie's old enough to know all that. I just wanted to check again and see if everything was all right here. He was doing fine, wasn't he?" There is panic in her voice now. Perhaps nothing was as she thought.

"He was doing fine. Really well," the teacher says slowly, and gives a pained smile, as if to invest the empty words with hidden meaning. "A few problems with fractions, nothing out of the ordinary. I wish there was something more." Preston's face searches hers.

Carol realizes how young the teacher is and that she is shattered, too. She feels she should try to comfort the woman, but how? "Can I get those things out of his locker?"

The teacher nods.

What passes for lawn in front of the seedy house is purple gray with Thursday-morning frost. Tad sits behind the wheel of a van, an aging Econoline with covered rear windows, listening to wacky morning radio. He's been keeping his distance from Rooster, who's up on the porch walking back and forth and smoking a cigarette.

An immaculate black Cutlass Supreme with smoked windows and custom t-top rolls up to the house. Out steps a stout man in a slightly shiny, several-hundred-dollar suit. He wears gold and sunglasses and has a bald head. He's Oscar Riggi. He's the man.

Rooster stops pacing.

Tad jumps out of the van and crosses through a

cloud of Econoline exhaust. "Mr. Riggi, how you doin'?"

Tad kisses ass, but Rooster doesn't go for that. He knows he's not so easily replaced.

"Rooster. Tad. How are things? How's our package?"

"Everything's all fine and loaded, sir," Tad answers, looking involuntarily at the van and thinking instinctively of the carpet-lined cut in the floor. He pats the van's side.

Riggi looks through Tad as if *he's* an exhaust cloud. "Things went well, I trust, huh, Rooster?"

"Yeah, you can trust, Captain." Rooster flicks his cigarette butt in Tad's direction. Not at him, but in his direction. It's just far enough off so that Tad can't say anything.

Riggi climbs the few steps up to the porch and flips Rooster a fairly thick roll of small and medium bills rubberbanded together. Rooster thumbs it nonchalantly and tucks it away. Riggi cuffs him behind the head, not without affection.

"Hey, I can count on you, huh?"

"That's right, Oscar."

Tad comes up to join them, much larger than both men, yet feeble and intimidated in their presence. Without taking his eyes off Rooster, Riggi reaches into his jacket pocket and produces a packet of papers that he hands to Tad.

"There's the address of the other pickup. Instructions on what roads to take. Your destination is in there, too. Memorize it, write it in code, whatever, then destroy it. There's travel money in there also."

Tad stays with it, endeavors to look keen, on top of things. "Okay, okay."

"Call me every eight hours regardless of where you are. Got it? I want my phone ringing every eight hours."

"Got it."

"Where you gonna call me?"

"Wherever I'm at, eight hours."

Riggi gives a pinched smile, like he's tasting bad jelly. "You get the rest of your money when you're back."

"Yes, sir."

Riggi nods and turns to him. "You're still here?"

Tad hustles into the van and drives off. Riggi turns back to Rooster. "You have breakfast yet?"

THREE

Fourteen Months Later

PAUL GABRIEL POURS a second bowl of cereal. He
reaches in and fishes out the prize. It's a rubber astronaut that dropped in water grows to
eight and a half times its original size. He puts it
with the rest of the prizes he's been saving for his
son. There are more than a dozen now. Paul rubs a
circle at his temple with his fingertips. He's graying
there. He's pale. Tired looking, too.

Paul lowers his spoon. "Carol? Carol? Are you
ready? We should get going." A moment later she
enters the kitchen. Her outfit doesn't do much for
her. No makeup; dark circles under her eyes. She
crosses the kitchen, which is looking shabby. She
pushes a sponge around the countertop and tosses
it into a sink full of dishes. Carol stands next to
Paul as he changes his mind about the cereal and
pours it in the garbage. He has the sensation that

he sees the two of them there, as if from above. They look shitty together, the house looks shitty, everything is shitty.

"Okay, let's go." He sweeps up his keys. She takes a thin folder with Jamie's picture stapled to it, reports and forms protruding slightly from the bottom, and they leave.

The station bustles around them as the Gabriels sit stonelike on their bench outside of Captain Pomeroy's office. Across the room the concerned patrolman who took their statement so long ago looks over at them. He snaps off the sad look and turns away guiltily. Paul and Carol sit inches apart, but it may as well be light-years. They dwell in private capsules now, each alone, unable to reach out for the other. The only thing they share now is great failure.

They can see Pomeroy in his office, feet up on his desk, conversing with a colleague. The colleague is not a cop, at least he wears no gun, and when he notices the time, he gets up. Pomeroy shows him to the door, and as it opens, his hearty laugh escapes into the waiting area. The Gabriels eye him accusatorily; they haven't laughed like that in some time. Upon seeing the Gabriels, Pomeroy claps up.

"Okay, Jase, we'll finish this later. Mr. and Mrs. Gabriel, how are you? Come on in, let's review."

27

They enter his office. Paul and Carol take seats and Pomeroy plunks himself down, wearily now, behind his desk, sighing deeply. "I tell you, things are not quiet around here. Never too quiet."

He riffles through several manila folders and comes up with his copy of the file with a picture of Jamie Gabriel stapled to the cover. Pomeroy dons a pair of plastic-rimmed reading glasses and skims the case much like a merchant reviewing an account. His lips skip and mumble along with his eyes, his volume low. "Case estab'd Oct. 24 . . . Fourteen months . . . Last seen, night before . . . No evidence struggle. Area disappearance: Auburn Manor neighborhood, Wayne T'ship. Exact unknown. Listed: Miss Pers Bureau, Nat Cent of Missing and Exploited . . . Children of Night . . . Proj Shelter . . . Runaway Hotline . . . Angel Find . . . Cross-listed with State Police, Sheriff's Dept., and Federal Bureau—"

"Do you have any new information? Anything?"

Pomeroy doesn't acknowledge hearing the question and continues to scan for another moment. He pushes up his glasses and gives a finger massage to the bridge of his nose. "As you can see by your copy of the report, we haven't been able to develop any hard leads yet."

"What are you people doing about it currently?"

"I want to assure you, the case is still active. In these situations, missing youths, runaways . . ."

"He's not a runaway." Carol's words come out weak, nearly exhausted. Only thin anger fuels them along. "Can't you just understand that? All you've done is send his picture to shelters. He knows his way home if he had run away. But he can't get home, because somebody took him. He's been taken." The last word still cuts through Paul like a dentist's drill finding a nerve.

"We haven't found evidence to suggest that. Neither has the Federal Bureau. Yes, it is a possibility. A probability. These things happen, but often these youths don't want to be found."

"Bullshit," Paul says. He can't believe he's said it aloud to a policeman.

Pomeroy looks at him in surprise. Behind Carol's pain-glazed eyes there is a stirring as she looks at her husband, a spark. She glimpses what she's been missing for so long. But it fades too quickly.

"Look, Captain Pomeroy, I'm sorry. . . . I know you've been working on it, it's just . . ." Paul runs out of what to say.

Pomeroy's mouth spreads into a sickly crescent as his customary control drifts back across the desk to his side.

"I understand what you're going through. We're using best efforts to—" He is cut off by a female detective poking her head in.

"Scuse me, Captain, A-2 task force needs you to sign off on this watch so they can go home."

Pomeroy leaps up, grateful for the interruption. "I'm sorry, folks, this will just take a minute." He follows the detective out into the main squad room.

As he exits, Carol looks after him and then gets up and goes behind his desk. This makes Paul nervous.

"What are you doing?"

She opens Pomeroy's file on Jamie and starts looking through it.

"Carol, honey, what if he sees you?"

"I don't care. I want to know what they're really doing."

"Carol—"

She looks up, raw. "He's our son. Do you remember him?"

He doesn't respond to this, anger freezing his face.

Her head drops down as she reads the file. Then she looks up again. "Oh, god."

"What is it?" he asks, glancing out to see if Pomeroy is on his way back.

She doesn't answer, but as she reads her face contorts, as if she's suffering deep internal bleeding.

"There's some kind of man-hour log in his file. Work hasn't been done on the case in weeks—weeks. Oh, god . . ." Her finger scans the page. The door swings open and Captain Pomeroy steps back into the office. Moving hurriedly behind his desk, he takes the file out of Carol's hands.

"Excuse me, Mrs. Gabriel, but this is department property. And confidential."

She holds up her own version of the Jamie file. "What the hell is this, then?" She slams it down on the desk. "A joke apparently—"

"That's a copy of certain information that you requested, a request that we granted, although we didn't have to. It's not our policy to do so."

Paul moves in his seat. He feels the weakness of his position. If this man harbors ill will against them, then nothing will be done. He attempts to defuse the situation.

"Car, you know we have to be patient. An investigation like this is difficult."

"Exactly," Pomeroy says, retaking his seat in a territorial manner. "You know that from your private efforts. And we know it because the FBI's skunked, too."

"Time? Time?" Carol shouts, starting to unravel. "There have been twenty-two and a half man-hours logged on the case, total. Not even two hours for every month he's been gone."

This stops Paul cold. "What?" he bleats.

Pomeroy looks embarrassed.

All the calculations start to add up for them: Jamie's age when he disappeared. How old he would be now. How little time has been spent looking for him.

"Read it for yourself," she croaks. Carol grabs

the folder out of Pomeroy's hands and flings it across the office to her husband.

Papers fill the air and then settle.

Pomeroy pulls himself up. "Mrs. Gabriel, you may not want to accept it, but there are other cases that this department is dealing with. Right now, for instance, I have—"

At this, Carol loses her composure and rushes out of the office, slamming the door loudly behind her and running through the squad room.

The men look at each other. Pomeroy shrugs. *If the guy didn't have a gun on to show he was a cop, he couldn't sell you on the idea,* Paul thinks.

Paul takes his copy of the Jamie file and exits after his wife.

Patrolman Carriero glanced up at the sound of the door slamming. His heavy brows knit in concern at the sight of a slight, bent woman rushing from Captain Pomeroy's office. He recognized her but couldn't grab her name. A moment later the husband came out. Tall guy. Worried looking. Gabriel. He'd taken their statement . . . a long damn time ago. Missing kid. He sat on their house the first night and remembered it was a nonevent, no ransom call, no nothing. He'd hoped, as he always did, that it'd turn out to be a medical. That the boy had fallen and hit his head, been knocked down by a car, or had taken ill and become disoriented. Then he'd turn up in an emergency room days, or even weeks, later and they'd unravel who he was and return him home. That was the best you could hope for, Carriero had learned in his seven years in uniform. He'd done an initial canvass and a followup that hadn't yielded much, and then he'd been pulled off and put on a string of burglaries.

Carriero was feeling hollow-pitted in the stomach with shame. After the burglaries, he'd moved on to other cases without any further thought of the boy. That never would have happened during his first few years on the job. Now, he knew, the boy's information rested frozen in the cold case file, only to be pulled out and warmed up when the parents made inquiries or visited. The best they could hope for was a body turning up and ending the waiting. He stood without thinking further and crossed the squad room. He caught the man just as he neared the door.

"Excuse me, Mr. Gabriel?"

"Yes?" The man stopped and regarded him. A low-wattage flicker of recognition came to his face. "Oh, yeah, how are you, Officer?"

"I took your statement a while back. Good while back. I've looked into your son's case . . ."

"Yes?" A hunger leaped into Gabriel's eyes. "Have you found out anything about it?"

Carriero chided himself for his careless phrasing. "No, I . . . I don't know quite how to say it without seeming disloyal." He stopped. He knew this wasn't team play, not good for business, as they say, but he couldn't help it.

The father looked at him pleadingly.

"There's a man. He's an investigator. I used to work with him. It can cost some money, but he's . . . I don't know what good it'll do, but personal attention to this might be worth the cost." He held out a worn business card. "He may not even be available," the young patrolman continued, "but you never know."

Paul felt himself deflate. He was hoping for some hard information, but a business card just didn't help right now. His thought was to tell the officer about the two investigators they'd already tried, the sizable piece of their nest egg that they'd gladly spent but which had yielded only monthly meetings at a coffee shop as the investigators tried to pad their lack of results in thickly worded, laser-printed reports. Instead he just took the business card.

"Thanks. I better find my wife." Paul pocketed the card and went off after her.

Carol sat, nearly catatonic, in the darkened living room. Night descended silently without her even noticing. The only light in the room flickered from the silent television. Her fragility was such that any disappointment at all had a gross weight and power.

The door opened and Paul walked in with Tater on a leash. He unclipped the dog, then walked over and switched off the television.

"Carol, let's go on up to bed."

Though she seemed not to hear him, she got up and walked toward the stairs, with Paul right behind her.

At the foot of the steps, Paul clicked on the switch illuminating the front of the house for Jamie, as they did every night.

Carol looked at him and then turned off the lights before going up.

FOUR

PAUL SKIRTED THE CITY and its afternoon traffic, taking County Line until he hit Mitchner. Indianapolis was only a couple hours' drive from where he and Carol had gone to college, and also from where they'd grown up, and he had originally been drawn to the city for its many corporate and technological parks full of businesses and executives to whom he could sell insurance. The chance to buy a house of his own on a tree-lined street was an added bonus back then. Now he worked his way south into Warren and neared the Windemere Homes neighborhood, where the streets had been getting drab for the last several minutes. Lawns were not well tended there during the summer, much less in midwinter. Shrubbery was nonexistent. Most houses were on the one-more-year plan as far as repainting went. Even though the address was all the way out, Paul had decided to drive over without calling first. He couldn't bring himself to go through it all over the phone, and this way, if he changed his mind at any point, he could just drive on.

He glanced over at the copy of Jamie's file resting on the passenger seat. He checked the worn business card in his right hand as he drove. Frank Behr, the investigator's name, had been familiar, but he hadn't been able to place why, so he had Googled the man's name. What came back was a story he remembered reading many years ago.

A man named Herb Bonnet, who worked at a trucking company, had become aware of the smuggling and selling of stolen farm equipment, and money laundering, by the owners of the company. Bonnet had gone to the police, and when the owners were indicted and word got out that he was set to testify, he was beaten badly by two anonymous attackers. It was like something out of the movies. Even though he was put in the hospital for a week, Bonnet didn't relent on his plans to talk in court. One afternoon, while sitting guard duty outside Bonnet's room, a patrolman, Frank Behr, looked down the hall through a glass-paneled door. A man was coming toward him, wearing a black pea coat and looking "all wrong and out of place," Behr had been quoted as saying.

The patrolman leaped up and pushed a swinging door into the man in the pea coat, who turned out to be a gunman coming for Bonnet. Officer Behr put him into a wall, knocking over a cart of housekeeping supplies, as the man drew a .38 with a taped handle. Officer Behr then disarmed him and wrestled him into custody. The would-be gunman, a distant relative of one of the owners of the trucking company who had been paid ten thousand dollars to kill Bonnet, ended up with a broken wrist. Officer Behr had become a local hero behind the incident. There were commendations. He was promoted off patrol to uniformed detective.

A decorated cop, even if it had been more than a decade ago, seemed worth the effort of a drive. A patch of two-story cement buildings with gray facades passed by outside Paul's window, and the cars parked on the streets didn't look like they'd been started lately. He slowed the Buick to a crawl and began checking addresses on the low buildings that looked like double-wide trailers sunk onto cinder-block foundations.

Paul pulled over and parked, taking the file with him as he got out of his car. Number 642 was either a depressing office or an even more depressing two-family residence. A dump truck passed in front of him and hit a pothole with a sound much like an explosion. The truck left Paul in a swirl of brick dust and exhaust, which cleared to reveal a homeless man on his knees, rummaging through several bags of garbage, on a patch of brown grass and dirt in front of 642. Half a pizza, coffee grounds, rotting ribs, a broken jar emitting rancid mayonnaise surrounded the man. Paul could smell it from five yards away. He walked past him to the door and knocked repeatedly, getting no answer. He suddenly saw the downside of just driving over without calling as he turned to look for another entrance. He didn't see one and considered heading back toward his car.

"Who're you looking for?" the homeless man on the ground asked in a clear voice.

Paul turned and regarded him. "Frank Behr. You know where I might find him?"

The man clambered to his feet, which took a long time, since he was so large. He was squared off all over, too, from hands to shoulders to jaw. He had a slightly ruddy face and a bushy mustache. The bridge of his nose showed he had worn a football helmet for several years of his life.

"I'm him. Who're you?"

Paul spent a moment more than a little surprised. "Paul Gabriel. I might want to hire him . . . you."

Behr slung a heavyweight bag of trash over his shoulder and gestured toward another. "You want to give me a hand with this? We'll go inside and talk."

"Bring the garbage inside?"

Behr shrugged. Paul hefted a bag and they walked toward the door.

The place was both office and home to the investigator, and it had all the charm of a brake-shop waiting room. A plaid recliner and a television tray covered with empty bottles were in close proximity to the television. The setup was that of a man who liked to watch sports and drink beer. Across the room, a crowded desk bearing an old computer, phone, and fax, a battered desk chair, and bulging file cabinets gave the impression that Behr liked his work but hadn't gotten enough of it lately.

Behr dropped his bag in the middle of the floor and Paul followed suit. The investigator motioned for Paul to have a seat and left the room. A moment later he returned carrying two cans of soda.

"What's with all this? If you don't mind my asking." An odor of sour milk and tuna fish began to permeate the room.

Behr handed Paul a can. "Trash archaeology. It's Derek Freeman's."

"The Pacer?"

"Yeah, the power forward. I paid a guy I know twenty bucks to get it for me."

"You must be a real fan."

Behr looked at Paul, the slightest glint of humor in his eye. It wasn't a confidential case. He decided to explain.

"The *Trib* hired me. Freeman's suing them for libel over their report of him having an affair. You can learn plenty from someone's trash. Receipts, empty prescription bottles. Discarded papers. Gambling receipts. Phone bills. Strange DNA on Q-Tips. Condoms when their wife is on the pill. They're hoping I'll prove their story. At least enough to keep them out of court. And I will." Behr shrugged and popped his soda can open. If he was at all embarrassed about picking through refuse, he didn't show it. As Behr drank off half his soda, Paul noticed the man's hand was the size of a brick.

"What can I do for you?"

Paul fiddled with his own soda can and took a breath. "I think I need . . . I need a detective. My son. He's twelve. He was twelve and a half. He's almost fourteen now. He's been gone a year and two months."

A darkness came over Behr and seemed to fill the room, as if an eclipse was taking place in the sky outside.

"Gone?"

"Went out on his paper route end of last October. Didn't come back."

"Police?"

"We've been to them, of course." Paul raised the manila file folder by way of explanation.

"Of course. Amber alerts. Neighborhood canvass. They papered the runaway shelters, then

41

pulled the manpower. You don't know if they're incompetent or don't care."

Paul was a bit taken aback at the man's directness and let the file resettle in his lap. "All of the above."

Behr sat back and thought. "Over a year and the trail will be cold. Ice-age cold."

Paul was quiet. He glanced around the place. Bookshelves were filled with nonfiction hardcovers. A glass gun case held several rifles. Law enforcement plaques hung on a paneled wall near the desk. They were awards for community service, distinction in the line of duty. The dates ended several years back.

Behr stared at him and Paul came out and said it. "I'd like someone to look into it. You were recommended."

"I can't do that."

"Why not?"

"The cops aren't incompetent, and they do care. It'd be a thousand to one finding anything . . . and even then you wouldn't like what I found."

Paul couldn't help feeling a foolish sense of rejection and a sudden desperation, a swirling vortex of helplessness threatening him. "But . . ." He gestured at the trash on the living-room floor. "You can't be so busy—"

"It's not about that," Behr half barked. Something close to anger sounded in his voice for a moment, then departed. "Listen, how's your wife coping?"

"Well, I guess. In her own way . . . but badly. Real bad."

Behr nodded with knowing. "What other way is there?"

Silence took over, and neither man seemed willing to tamper with it for a long while, then Behr spoke again. "It'd be very costly, you know. Not just the hourly, but also the expenses. And time-consuming."

Paul shrugged.

"I see. You're willing to pay. Anything you've got."

"That's right."

"Put your house up. Sell everything."

"Yeah."

"But even then . . . Look, Mr. Gabriel, for most people hope's a beautiful thing. For you and your wife it's dangerous. I don't want to take you through anything more than you've been already."

Paul stood. "There's nothing that could be worse than not knowing. Not even . . . nothing."

Behr seemed to understand but averted his gaze.

"I'm sorry, buddy. I can't do this. There are plenty of other investigators and I'm sure you'll find a good one. Now I've got some garbage to sort."

Paul put his unopened soda can down on the television tray and headed for the door.

Behr knelt on the floor and went about his business, not noticing that beneath the soda can rested a manila folder.

FIVE

CAROL ANSWERED THE DOOR late on a Thursday afternoon and found a heavyset woman in her forties with dyed black hair standing outside.

"Hello, Mrs. Gabriel?" she said through the screen door.

"Yes?" Carol caught an almost magenta hue coming off the woman's hair.

"I understand you have a missing boy."

Carol's heart instantly pounded and she felt herself go weak. "Yes. Do you know something about him?"

"I might be able to help. My name is Ms. Raven. I'm a spiritualist. I've worked on these cases before."

Carol's heart began to slow. If this had been last week even, she would have probably said No, thank you. Instead she swung open the screen door. "Umm . . . Why don't you come in? My husband will be home soon."

When Paul arrived, he found them sitting at the kitchen table drinking coffee. Ms. Raven held Jamie's Colts cap. Paul joined them and learned how she had come to them.

"I have a friend down at the station who I confer with on certain cases. He told me about yours and I thought I would try."

"Well, we appreciate it, but . . ." said Paul.

"Do you believe?" the woman asked.

"In what?" Carol said aloud. Paul gave her a look.

"Psychic powers. It helps if you believe. I get stronger sensations that way."

"Oh, well. We don't *not* believe. We don't really think about it, I guess."

"We want to believe." Paul gave it a try. "Is there anything we can do?"

Ms. Raven closed her eyes and sat back, feeling the baseball cap.

Tater, curled up across the kitchen, looked up from time to time.

The kitchen had fallen silent, and just when the quiet threatened to go on forever, Ms. Raven spoke. "I see a van," she said with conviction.

"We have a van."

Carol glanced at Paul, not wanting his talk to mess the woman up.

"And a bicycle. A blue bicycle."

"Yes. Jamie's bike was blue." Paul spoke again. Carol's stomach turned over at the possibility that this woman's vision was real.

"You're on a trip. Down south. Jamie has gone for a bike ride." Ms. Raven became agitated, her breathing short and sharp.

Paul and Carol grew confused.

"The bike has fallen and Jamie seems hurt," she went on. "He's not dead, but hurt."

Carol moaned involuntarily and her face squeezed the way it did before her tears came.

Seeing this, Paul was prompted to speak. "Look, Ms. Raven. I think you've got it wrong. We weren't on a trip. We were right here. We've checked around. The police, the hospitals. It was no bicycle accident. Thank you for trying, but maybe we should, you know, stop."

Ms. Raven sat there for a minute, then two, breathing through her mouth, before she answered. "This is not an exact science."

"I understand that. Look, we appreciate your help, but I think this is upsetting my wife." Carol didn't dispute him. "What do we owe you for this?"

Ms. Raven put down the cap and gathered her coat and bag. "You don't have to pay me. It's quite all right," she said, slight offense in her voice. "If we schedule a time for me to come back, I can look at his room. Try further . . ." She shrugged on her coat.

Paul showed her to the door and held it for her. "Please, let me give you something. For your time," he offered again.

"Well, I'm normally thirty dollars an hour," she said.

Paul handed her some bills. "Here you go. Thanks a lot."

She gave him a flyer from a store where she worked reading palms and tarot cards. "Here's my number if you want to consult further."

"Thanks again." Paul closed the door and returned to the kitchen.

Carol was still sitting there. Tater had left the room.

"Do you think we should have listened to her more?"

Paul said nothing and tried to keep the cynicism off his face, knowing that if he spoke he could not keep it out of his voice.

"She was right about the van. And the bike."

"She's got a friend at the station. She probably read the file."

"We should have her back and try—"

"She took money," he said with finality, "at the door." He crumpled the flyer and fired it in the general direction of the trash can.

Carol began to tremble. A sob started and died within her. Paul moved to hug her. She drew away and into herself and left him standing there, unable to put his arms around her. It was always that way now, the turning away from each other. They didn't touch intentionally anymore. There was a gulf between them in bed at night, and when an arm or a foot crossed the divide and contacted the other, it was quickly retracted in near apology. Their lovemaking was completely frozen over. The day Jamie disappeared was the first of its extinction. They were hardly friends anymore but lived as mere housemates. They were scrupulously polite to each other as they moved about the place.

SIX

TROUBLE CAME IN BATCHES. That was Frank Behr's experience. And he was sure he'd find a fresh lot if he went ahead and pursued the case of this missing boy. It was late in the afternoon after the quiet man, Gabriel, had left and he'd finished with his trash. As Behr sat back in his recliner, he saw the folder on the television tray. His first instinct had been to leave it where it was, to call information for Gabriel's number and tell him to get the hell back over here and pick it up. A man should recognize when no meant no. He didn't call information though.

Instead Behr stretched, his knees and shoulders popping and cracking. He pounded out push-ups and wrestled with the idea of taking the case. Between sets four and five, he bounded up and flipped open the police file that Gabriel had left. He read the particulars, nodding to himself, unsurprised and unmoved at what he saw, until he came to the ranking officer's signature at the bottom of the third page. Even now, nine years later, the cribbed, slanted writing was familiar to him. James P. Pomeroy, Captain Pomeroy now. He had been Behr's lieutenant, his C.O., long ago. That signature, on change of duty orders, on poor performance reports, on demotion sheets, had changed Behr's life.

After reading the file, there was no question about calling the father and chiding him for leaving it behind. He couldn't do that. So he put on gray sweats, tied his running sneakers, and filled a frame pack with a fifty-pound bag of road salt and hardcover books. He strapped on the pack, which now weighed more than seventy pounds, cinched the belt around his waist, and set out for Saddle Hill Road, near the junior high, to run sprints.

As Behr sweated and chugged up the hill, he thought back to the days when Pomeroy had been his commander and personal hair shirt. It had long been his practice, despite the advice of numerous people, to comb through his history as he worked out. Whether it was the department shrink or his ex-wife, Linda, they had all warned him that he'd remain mired in the past if he kept it up. Fighting the burn of lactic acid and sucking in oxygen, Behr went back to the time right after his son, Tim, was born, after he'd guarded the witness in the hospital and been promoted. He'd gotten a pay raise and

Linda had started looking for a bigger house he knew they still couldn't afford.

It wasn't long, a little over a year into his new assignment, when Behr's first partner as a detective, Ed Polk, got lit up. Ed was off duty, as was Behr, and they weren't even together. Ed was out on a roust of an illegal social club, where liquor was served. The club was on the north side, and back in those days, before it was cleaned up a bit, even off-duty cops tried to avoid that part of town. Polk, though, was a graft taker and was trying to shake the club down when words led to a fight and he caught two in the lung from his own backup piece, a .380 auto he wore on his ankle. There was no reason for Behr to have been there backing him up, but his lieutenant, Pomeroy, didn't make this distinction. He said, unofficially but widely, that a cop's always got to have his partner's back. It was also known, unofficially but widely, that Ed Polk was the lieutenant's cousin. Behr became a pariah and things started to unravel.

He strained to the top of the hill for the tenth time, sweat jumping off his brow like grease from a hot pan. Making a hopeless attempt to solve a case his old boss couldn't was just one reason not to take on this kind of work, he thought. What the case would do to him because of his own past was another.

.   .   .

There were days of stillness, stretches of inertia. Sections of calendar passed when Paul felt he hadn't moved one foot in front of the other. The house had become a crypt. He and Carol were mirrors that reflected each other's grief, intensifying the pain and futility until it was almost searing.

They tried to create positive momentum by attending some local encounter groups for the relatives of missing persons. Those in attendance would stand and speak of their loved ones (always in the past tense, as was the rule), giving the details of their particular story. It wasn't so that others there could provide any help or information. The theory was that by intoning the events, one could gain power over them. Denial of the situation, clinging to the idea that the loved one was going to return—these were supposed to dissipate. Healing was supposed to ensue. Paul quickly came to dread the meetings. Withered, they sat in stale church basements, in classrooms after hours, like dead trees or tombstones. They poured coffee down their throats, not tasting it, chewed doughnuts, not tasting them. Everyone was missing somebody. Sons, daughters, wives, husbands, mothers, fathers. Where were they? The reasons for the disappearances were criminal, medical, accidental. But where were they? They were just gone. Carol seemed better after the meetings. Perhaps the sense of community helped her, or perhaps it was the forced talk that made her come alive momentarily. But he had felt it start to work on him, felt his belief that Jamie was coming back start to ebb, and that drove him away for good. He ceased going and returned to stillness.

There were days, too, of motion. Bursts of activity. The yard—mowed, weeded, seeded, watered. After weeks of neglect. The car—lubed, washed, waxed. After months of dirty buildup. He began to stay out of the house, selfish as that was. It had surprised him at first, this instinct in himself. But he pursued it and took to spending long hours at work. He managed to get busy and sell policies with no problem, forgetting the terrible state of his real life. As he gave his regular pitch about being prepared for the unexpected, he could read the faces of those clients who knew his story. The worst *could* happen. The policies sold themselves.

The most unseemly aspect of his behavior, he knew, was his staying away from Carol, but he couldn't help it. To this end he bought and hung a heavy bag in the garage, so even when he was home he still wasn't at home. He began punching it daily, making it swing and shriek on its chain. He pounded out his rage and pain in hourlong bursts. In that bag he saw the faces of anonymous attackers, drunk drivers, predators, who had come for Jamie. He lashed out at the formlessness. The dark leather of his bag gloves grew streaky white with sweat salt and creaked around his fists. After three weeks he felt some of the flab begin to melt away from his once rangy 195-pound frame. Forgotten muscles rose to the surface despite themselves. But most of all he punched to escape the weakness inside of him, a softness he knew was there and couldn't eliminate.

Behr drove his burgundy Toronado toward Dekuyper and the house that had once been his. The neighborhood was modest, but the homes were comfortable in size. It was a place for young families to stretch and grow. He had been a real face on this street once. As a cop, he had been a near celebrity. Everyone had felt safe with him around, and he and Linda had hosted many a barbecue. Turning onto his former street, he saw the old road sign, smashed and dented, the iron pole to which it was connected bent down to the ground the way it had been for ages. Behr thought back half a dozen years to the night he had done it. He'd been on a grief-soaked drunk and had pulled over, half out of his mind, taken out the aluminum bat he kept in his trunk, and beaten the sign down to the ground. No one had stopped him that night. The neighbors had just stood back at a distance and watched with their hands over their mouths. The sign still had not been repaired. It read PLEASE DRIVE CAREFULLY, WE LOVE OUR CHILDREN. Behr wondered what he'd been thinking that night as he rolled up in front of his old house. Number 72. The house was a small center-hall colonial. It had been white when it was his but had been repainted a creamy yellow by the current owners. He could see a swing set around the side in the backyard. Behr looked at the house. Sweat prickled along the back of his neck. He hadn't been by in years and had not stayed in touch with any of the neighbors, his old friends. But the street was still familiar, as if he'd last left it to go to work that very morning. His stomach hollowed out and his throat went dry and stiff. His old life was a relic. He didn't belong here anymore. "Fuck it," he said aloud, jerked the gearshift into drive, and lurched away from the curb.

Carol had taken to thinking about her past most afternoons as the house darkened and she sat looking out the window onto the street. It was the only way to escape the fog of blackness in her mind that was the present. She'd sit and listen to the low thump of Paul punching the bag in the garage and remember the wild times she'd had when she was young, during college, when nothing mattered. She'd gone to school in Michigan and she and her friends had been fixtures on the local saloon circuit. They'd owned the Spaghetti Bender outright. She could still smell the sawdust and peanut shells on the floor in the bar section.

She and her girls would roll in early, around 7:30, in their Champion sweatshirts, their hair up in ponytails, and split dinner specials, not wanting to get too full to blunt the drinking. As the frat boys began trickling in, she and her group would start flirting with them and tag them for pitchers. After the first few icy beers and shots of tequila, accompanied by salt, lemon, and screams, the middle part of the night became a blur. The music they played at the Bender was predictable, and she'd be flying by the time AC/DC came on. Her group would take over the dance floor, mugs in hand, and shout the words to "You Shook Me All Night Long."

The nights would end, often, with young men. Too many. Sometimes they brought the promise of a relationship, other times not. She was no angel, and she didn't want to be. She was learning about life, she told herself. She knew things no angel knew. Oh, those boys and their firm bodies. It led her, as predictably as AC/DC, to a cold clinic one morning her junior year. She'd had an accident, she was pretty sure she knew with whom, and needed it taken care of. She was put on a Valium drip, her head lolling on a stiff sheet, and the sticks were inserted. She'd wondered back then on that lonely morning, if in the future one day, when she was ready, if God would remember that moment, if He would judge her unfit to be a mother. This was the year before she had met Paul and calmed down. Before life was serious. And as she sat in the gloom of the living room, she thought differently about those nights. She knew what they were now and that God *had* judged. They were nights of sin and she was being punished for them.

There was something about the way the man punched. He wasn't trained. He didn't have form. He moved around the bag flat-footed and didn't put his full weight behind his shots. But there was real emotional content in his blows and no quit in his routine.

"You're carrying your hands too low. Your jaw's open for a counter-right."

Paul Gabriel dropped his hands all the way, stepped around the edge of the bag, and saw that it was the detective, Behr, standing in the open door of the garage.

"That happens when you only practice on a bag without leather coming back at you."

Gabriel shrugged, pulling off his gloves. He did throw both hands with commitment, that was the important thing, and Behr supposed that at this point the man didn't much care if he was open to countershots.

"Mr. Behr. I didn't expect to see you. How'd you find me?" Paul stepped toward him.

Behr shook his head. Gabriel nodded. Stupid question.

"Make it Frank. You still want to do this?"

Gabriel did nothing, said nothing, but his whole being answered in the affirmative.

"I read the file. Your son's dead. That's the assumption we'll have to work from."

Gabriel breathed deeply and braced himself against the diamond-hard words.

"I've been coming to grips with that." The truth was, he'd been trying to come to grips with that since the beginning but was unwilling to come any closer to doing so without *knowing*. "My interest is in finding who did it, learning something about it. It's the only way we'll be able to make peace with the situation."

"No promises. No guarantees," Behr said.

"No, sir."

They shook hands, Behr's mitt enclosing Paul's wrapped hand. "Call me Paul."

"Paul."

"My wife's inside. Come meet her."

The abandoned heavy bag swung slowly as the dust motes settled in the garage.

SEVEN

IT WAS WORSE than he thought. Behr was on a comfortable chair in the couple's living room. He had a half-downed cup of coffee next to him and a photo album on his lap. The parents sat across from him silently, watching, waiting, and doing the one thing he told them not to do, and knew they couldn't help: hoping.

"A case like this is a huge slippery wall that's tough to get a grip on," Behr said. He could see that the first time he'd read the file. He selected a batch of photos of the boy, Jamie, spanning a period of years, and carefully removed them from the album.

"The idea is that these might indicate a range, a projection of how he's aged over the past year or so," Behr volunteered. Paul and Carol nodded. He really needed the variety to show to coroners and cops who might've encountered a body in a condition that couldn't be predicted. Maybe some tiny characteristic in one of the photos would correspond to what was left of the boy.

"Now, you two don't have any enemies, people who were looking to hurt you?" He knew it was unlikely but asked anyway. The couple's faces were blank, and they looked at each other and grew even blanker. "Have you fired any domestic help, had a run-in in the workplace? You're in insurance. Any angry beneficiaries who were denied payouts on policies?"

"No. Nothing like that."

Behr nodded. The room went quiet. This was only the first of what was going to be many clipped, unsatisfying conversations. He knew it well, and also knew that there was no way around it.

"I'll need information on what he did. Where he went to school, his teachers. Did he play sports—"

"He played soccer," Paul said.

"I'll need his coach's name, his teammates." Behr spoke to the father, who nodded.

Silence pressed into the room again. Behr realized they'd reached the part of the initial interview he dreaded most. The answer to his next question would reveal whether he was near the beginning or actually closer to a resolution in the case. He had to ask the couple if they were involved in their son's disappearance.

After the question had left his mouth, he would gauge them closely as they answered. There were myriad clues, both verbal and nonverbal, in people's answers to direct, probing questions. Most cops with careers of any length and activity developed powerful abilities in deciding whether or not people were lying to them. For many it was merely the uncomfortable sensation that what they were being given wasn't the truth. The proverbial gut feeling, so often referenced, was a reality according to Behr's experience. For others, distinguishing fact from fabrication was a science.

Behr's approach fell somewhere in between. He had good instincts, but that hadn't satisfied him. After his second year on the force he'd gone to San Francisco on his own dime for a three-day seminar given by an ex-CIA interrogator called Tactical Behavior Assessment and Strategic Interviewing Techniques. His wife hadn't appreciated it, as his dime was actually several thousand dollars that they couldn't afford. It was there that Behr had learned the skills that he would hone over the years. Skills that had helped him make a living ever since. He wouldn't say he was a human lie detector, nothing like the ex-spook who had given the course, but he'd developed a hell of a sniffer. Once he got a hit of deception, he had the tools to run down the truth.

Behr cleared his throat and asked his question. "Did either of you have anything to do with

Jamie's disappearance?" He glanced from husband to wife, prepared for tics or protests or answers that were geared to convince him of their innocence rather than just convey information.

"No," said the father. The mother just shook her head, wept, and then uttered an "Uh-uh" sound.

Behr believed them. He had an inestimably larger amount of work in front of him now. Nonetheless, he felt relief. Later, when he got home, he'd go on the Internet and comb through financial databases. He'd check the family's assets and TRWs to make sure there were no irregularities, no large withdrawals indicating a gambling or drug problem that could've provoked a hideous crime.

"If it's all right, I'll look at his room," he said.

They all stood.

Behr entered the room and paused before turning on the light. Paul and Carol were positioned down the hallway several yards back, afraid to come any closer. Behr slid his hand along the wall and clicked on the light. What he saw hit him low in the gut. He kept his hand against the wall, steadying himself for a long moment. The room belonged to a well-cared-for American boy. A single bed covered by an NFL comforter was built into a tan Formica headboard and nightstand.

There were wrapped gifts on the bed, birthday and Christmas presents for a son who wasn't around to collect them. Two posters dominated the room: Albert Pujols turning on a ball and a red Ferrari F430 Spider. Both were matted on posterboard. A ten-by-twelve photo of a large African American bicycle racer had been torn from a magazine and tacked to the wall near the bed. A basic Compaq desktop computer sat idle on a small desk in a litter of school notebooks. They were next to a large cup from Pizza Pizzazz filled with coins and an old Reggie Miller bobble-head doll. Several Harry Potter books rested on bookshelves next to fairly neatly glued-together plastic model F-15s and battleships.

He turned and opened the closet, pulling a string that switched a light on inside. Jeans hung on hangers next to button-down shirts and several jackets of different weights. A small dark suit was all the way to the left. Along the floor were basketball sneakers, soccer cleats, scuffed penny loafers, Teva sandals, and a pair of winter boots. Behr pulled the light cord and swung the closet shut. He turned to a small dresser, forcing himself to go on. The dresser held T-shirts, socks, underwear. The bottom drawer housed folded dress shirts and two neckties. Beneath them, secreted, was a folded magazine photo of a full-breasted young blond singer wearing a brassiere top and a microphone that fit over her head like an air-traffic controller's mouthpiece. She was covered in sweat and projected sex, youth, and innocence. There were also three packs of Black Cat firecrackers, but no scribbled notes or other information.

Some light dust was under the bed, Behr saw, his mini Maglite slowly sweeping over it as if it were a lunar surface. There was a small boom box and some pop CDs. Eminem, Green Day, Korn, a strange three-course meal. Between the mattress and box spring he discovered a treasure, a Cal Ripken baseball card from his rookie season tucked inside a plastic sleeve. Finding nothing else, he tried to smooth out the bedding the way it had been.

Behr sat on the small desk chair, testing its strength, and flipped quickly through the schoolbooks on the desk. The notebooks were marked "Return to Jamie Gabriel—Room 102, Johnny Fricking Kennedy Middle School." Behr pulled at his chin and looked through them. School exercises, personal notes, top-ten lists organizing and reorganizing the best professional athletes in each of their sports and combining them across sports. Kobe Bryant dueled with Dwayne Wade and Derek Jeter; Behr half smiled at Peyton Manning being crossed out two times and moved right to the top, and at what was written in for tenth place: "Tiger Wood." There was nothing to indicate the boy had met anybody new or had plans to meet someone at the time of his disappearance.

He turned on the computer and searched

through documents, which were school papers on plankton, Paul Revere, and the like. He checked the scrap of paper that the parents had given him and signed on to America Online to review Jamie's account. He found nothing beyond kidlike screen names in the boy's e-mail address book. His favorite places list was made up of movie, music, sports, and car sites. Behr didn't find any links to strange, or borderline, Web sites. Besides spam, there were no e-mails new, old, or to be sent, as they had been automatically deleted by the server long ago after so much inactivity. He made a note to himself to try to get access to the service provider archives. Behr signed off, shut down the computer, and sat back. He rubbed his face with his hand and stood.

Carol and Paul still waited in the hall. They'd been standing there, frozen, for the whole forty minutes Behr had been in the boy's room. As he walked out, they looked up at him, childlike in their anticipation. Behr shook his head and wrote a note in his notebook. They stood uncomfortably for a moment in the close quarters of the hallway.

"Mr. Behr . . . Frank . . ." Carol finally said, her voice low but direct in the tortured air of the hall. "I want to explain how we felt . . . how we feel about our son. How we love him . . ." Time and her pain couldn't completely hide her prettiness, Behr noticed, and when she stopped, unable to go on, he felt the urge to help her.

"No need, ma'am," he began, his voice low and rough. He went on despite himself. "I understand a bit of what you're going through, having lost a son of my own. He died when he was seven."

EIGHT

BEHR CLIMBED into his Toronado and turned it over. The engine woke up hoarse then leveled. He drove away from the Gabriel house, surprised at himself for mentioning Tim to this couple he'd only known for a few minutes, his employers. He hadn't gone into detail when they pursued it, but still, he had brought him up. And now, in the car, he found himself thinking about the events leading up to Tim's death, trying for the thousandth time to untangle the knot they'd become.

Behr crossed County Line and made a left toward Donohue's, where he figured on a skirt steak and a Beck's Dark while he reviewed his new case notes. He hoped the noise and bustle of the low-lit, maroon-boothed, old place would block the path of his memories and focus him on the new task at hand.

Behr arrived at Donohue's, which was just catching fire for the night, barely a step ahead of his recollections of Linda screaming in the halls of the hospital, of the horror of the funeral home. The casket, closed due to the damage. The empty, helpless silence that followed the funeral, which had strangled his heart and slowly killed everything decent in his life. He slid into the last available booth, the vinyl crunching quietly beneath him.

Arch Currey nodded over his white mustache from behind the bar. Behr waved back with a finger that sent Arch to the tap to draw the first Beck's Dark. Behr had been a heavy drinker in the past and it had led to problems, especially around the time of Tim's death, and he'd quit altogether for two years. He was a bit of an oddball now, an ex-abuser who could drink light when he wanted to. It was strange even to him, just another thing he couldn't figure out about himself and the world.

Behr looked toward the corner booth that was Pal Murphy, the owner's regular spot. He'd clocked Pal's Lincoln out back and expected to see him there, thin as a rail, in a crisp white dress shirt and butter-soft leather jacket, tinted shades perched on his nose, hunched over a cup of coffee. But Pal must've been down in his office, as the booth was currently empty. Pal and Behr were something like friends. Pal's age and bearing gave

Behr a comfortable feeling, as if all problems and challenges were temporal, that one could ride it out, that time resolved all situations no matter how confusing. The bond had first been struck when Tim passed, and had deepened when things foundered between him and Linda.

Behr flipped open his notebook and began scanning his notes. The words blurred in front of his eyes for all their lack of information. He pulled out pictures of Jamie and studied them, noting the changes in the boy over time. He was a towhead when he was a toddler. Over the years his hair had darkened, but just a bit. Some freckling came up across the boy's cheeks. His baby teeth fell out; his adult teeth gapped and finally filled in over the course of the photos. In the last shots Jamie seemed poised to grow like a reed. He was four foot ten and one hundred and five pounds at his disappearance.

"Family photos?" Kaitlin asked, placing his Beck's Dark on a paper coaster. She stepped back and stood over him, order pad in hand. Behr slid the pictures under his notebook.

"Not exactly."

"Regular A or B tonight, or do you want to hear specials?"

"Regular A," Behr said, ordering his usual steak and baked. Regular B was his second-most usual meal—the broiled chicken and fries. "And keep these coming steady." He raised the beer and knocked off half of it as Kaitlin walked toward the kitchen.

Donohue's filled up around him. Behr glanced over to see Pal Murphy sliding into his regular spot. He used his hand to smooth the wispy rust-colored hair pasted across his scalp, then nodded to Behr. Pal was sitting with a younger man Behr didn't know, which wasn't a surprise. Ownership of the pub was only the beginning of Pal's business ventures. Several other people Behr knew nodded to him from the bar; several he didn't stared over at him, a lone big man taking a booth that seated four. None of them were going to complain though; Arch kept a shillelagh hanging behind the bar in full view and was willing to use it to keep order.

Behr knew how to cook. It was something he'd had to learn when things ended between him and Linda, but some nights he needed the hum and flurry of a place like Donohue's. The fact was, he needed it more and more lately. Behr worked on his third beer and thought of her. Linda. He hadn't spoken to her since January 6 three years back. She lived down in Vallonia now, near her folks. Behr had gotten out there several times a month for the first few years after they'd separated, but couldn't win her back with anything he'd said or tried. Tim's death was a chasm between them he couldn't leap, no matter how much of a run-up he took. To do that, both of them needed to jump, to meet in the middle, in the dark space between. He knew that now. Knew it even though he'd failed and it was too late and he'd given up. She'd told him on that January 6 that she'd started seeing a man who owned a quick lube shop and a convenience store nearby. Behr had stopped going then, ceased trying. He'd heard they were living together now.

"He's not a better man," she'd told him. "He just doesn't remind me of things." This was intended as consolation, Behr supposed, but it felt like the opposite.

After he'd eaten, Behr drank three cups of coffee to blunt the beers' effect and began to outline a plan of action in his mind.

Step one. After Donohue's, Behr rolled over to Market Square. He trolled through the darkened streets, coasting slowly in the Toronado like a fisherman trying to catch the big one on the first cast. He hoped to run across the boy on the streets, hungry but fine, ready to go home. He looked out his windows at the city that had been his home for two decades.

Indianapolis, the Circle City, was the twelfth largest in the nation. Because of the convergence of important roads, waterways, and railroads, it had long been known as the "Crossroads of America." It was the Hoosier capital, host to the national track and field championships, home of the Indy 500 down at the Brickyard. Taxes were manageable, schools were good, real estate was valuable but still gettable. Behr was aware of the Chamber of Commerce patter, and perhaps it had mattered to him twenty years earlier when he had just graduated from the University of Washington with a degree in criminology and had found openings on the Indianapolis police force down at the school's placement office.

But as he drove, all that fell away and instead he began to see the predators, scumbags, and wasters who populated the city at night. Street cops, if they were going to last at all, quickly developed a sense of what is out there. Where regular people saw a guy in a tight leather jacket, a homeless man panhandling, a nervous woman, a cop saw a monster carrying a gun, a junkie ready to snap, a woman who'd just killed her husband. It was a skill you needed desperately at first, one that didn't seem to come quickly enough. Thing was, Behr thought, you could never turn it off once it was there, no matter how much you wanted to.

He got into the streets named after states: Maryland, Washington, Georgia. He saw long-coated figures standing and talking, sitting in doorways, huddling, but no one whose age or size allowed them to be the boy he was looking for. He cruised past the Fieldhouse, dark and hulking, with no event tonight. He wound around Delaware and South, parked and walked through the Amtrak/Greyhound terminal and

Union Station. The National Guardsmen were there, rifles slung, and some groups of older teenagers heading back to the suburbs. No kids. Behr showed the photos to some of the Reservists, who shook their heads.

He got back in his car and circled the RCA Dome before cutting across West Street. Like most times he'd been fishing, he'd come up empty. Tomorrow he'd have to start a real investigation. It was what the Gabriels were paying him for. It was what the kid deserved.

NINE

BEHR BEGAN EARLY, lowering himself into the blizzardlike maze of details. The Gabriels' bank accounts came up modest and tidy, as he expected they would. He went in and talked to the teacher, Ms. Preston, combed through newspaper archives for reported stories on the case, and then went to interview the soccer coach. Behr sat in his car a distance away and staked out a practice, checking to see if anyone was hanging around near the kids doing the same. He sat for an hour and a half, as the team moved up and down the field, bunching around the ball occasionally, causing the coach to blow his whistle and wave his arms, which returned them to better spacing. Behr raised his miniature Zeiss 12 x 25 and glassed the streets bordering the field; he saw he was the only one in the watcher category. Parents began showing up, and the kids ran, muddy-cleated, to waiting cars. Behr opened his door, swung his feet out, and started toward the field. The coach oversaw the last of his players leaving and was picking up the orange cones that marked the field when Behr got to him.

Coach Finnegan wore plastic-framed glasses, a fleece top, and a flexible knee brace on his right leg beneath baggy Umbro shorts. The guy had coached the Wayne Hornets for six years after moving there from Colorado Springs. Unlike the teacher, Andrea Preston, who was a pillar of the community, Finnegan, according to Behr's background check, was divorced, delinquent on six alimony payments, and had once pleaded no contest to a bad check charge. Fines had been paid.

"Must be cold," Behr said, pointing at the coach's red legs.

"I always wear 'em," Finnegan said of his shorts, "even at the end of the year."

"You're Finnegan?" Behr asked as a formality.

"Uhm-hm. You?"

"I'm here about Jamie Gabriel."

"He used to play for me." The coach nodded. "Sad thing that happened. He was a striker." The man's face didn't give anything away. "Any news?" he asked as an afterthought.

"I work for the family," Behr told him by way of a nonanswer. He wasn't going to tell this guy shit. For many cops and investigators the major obstacle to detecting deception and finding the truth was their own natural tendency to believe people. Behr had no such problem: he'd seen too much ugliness. He couldn't help his prejudice, either. He reserved a little dose of suspicion for men who worked with children. Female teachers had his baseline trust. Male college professors made sense to him. But adult men who worked with young boys chafed just slightly at the part of him that doubted humanity. He knew this was stupid, and he'd seen countless female criminals prove it so. Behr appraised the soccer coach. Could his emotional or psychological issues have led him to do the unspeakable? The guy seemed like a regular ex-jock; he was probably beyond reproach.

"Ever seen anyone hanging around the field who shouldn't be?"

"You mean when Jamie—"

"Anytime. Before or since."

"Haven't. I'd question anyone like that," the coach said, a real solid citizen.

"Ever have a player mention an adult was bothering him?"

"Only their relatives. Usual stuff. 'My father won't let me play because of grades.' 'My mother's boyfriend's an asshole.' "

"Gotcha."

Finnegan toed down a hunk of loose turf. Behr looked over both ends of the field.

"How does transportation work?"

"Parents do drop-offs and pickups. Team van for road games or parents can drive if they want. Anybody who's not a parent who's picking up a player has to be prearranged with me by phone. More than a few times I've had to refuse an aunt or uncle and drive a kid all the way home because the mother or father forgot to call." The coach offered this with a half-smile. He was looking for hosannas for his commitment to youth safety. Behr hated like hell to disappoint him.

He looked down at his notebook, closed it. "Well, that'll do her. Call me if anything occurs." He handed the coach a card and cut across the field toward his car.

Behr drove the paper route before six, as was Jamie's custom, rolling slowly down Richards through the neighborhood. He went down Cypress, around Grace, Sixteenth Street, Perry, and then Tibbs. He passed a jogger as he turned onto Tibbs, a large guy in nylon shorts, high athletic socks, and a thick terry-cloth headband, huffing about a twelve-minute mile. Behr checked his notes as he made the next turn, onto Mooresville, then followed it to Lynhurst. The route was an ambitious one mileage-wise. The kid had carried plenty of papers a good distance.

As he left Lynhurst, Behr passed an old Civic

hatchback coming from the other direction. A Hispanic man was driving while another, the size of a jockey, was crouching in the back and hurling papers toward houses. The kid's replacements, Behr thought, as he drove on to the end of the route. The neighborhood yielded nothing; the houses were blank facades. Behr sat in his idling car and ate a ham sandwich, looking down the street he had just driven. He let his mind wander. Someone leaving for work, so early and as such not thinking about traffic, backs out of the driveway and, boom, hits a kid on a bike. No one else is awake at that time, the boy's down, not moving, so the driver scoops up the kid and the bike and drives out of town to dump him.

Behr shook his head. Chances were that Jamie never even rode his route that day. Any number of things could have distracted him from his usual routine, which would mean that the cops had been looking in the completely wrong place, and he was, too.

Behr flipped through the file he was building on the case. He got to one of the articles he'd printed from the newspaper's online archive. It was from page two, under the fold, three days after the boy had disappeared. There was no picture. Goddamn toddler goes missing for half an hour they're running front-page photos and features on the television news. A kid gets old enough to have his own ideas, it raises too much doubt about what could have happened, renders it unnewsworthy. Behr finished the sandwich, crumpled up the wax paper it had been wrapped in, and drove back to the head of the route to start in on the canvass.

The number of people at home on door-to-door canvasses always surprised Behr. Not just housewives, old people, and invalids, but young, working-age men and women—they were usually at home. At first he figured they should all be at work, but much of the time they were not: They worked the late shift, or the early shift, or they had a day off or were between jobs. Eighty percent of the bells he rang in some neighborhoods got answered. Then there was Mount Auburn. These were working people. Even at a quarter to nine in the morning, almost no one was at home, and that meant no information for him. He checked the police report and saw that the cops had swept three times—prework, midday, and evening—and still owed on completion. Behr got a couple of cleaning ladies, none of whom had worked there at the time of the event, and two home owners with fuzzy recollections of the date, it being so far back.

He went off from Richards, retracing the streets he had driven. He collected contacts and had brief interviews with the few people who answered their doors, but he had no real luck until he reached 3 Tibbs, the second house on the block. The home, according to his street listing, belonged to a Mrs.

Esther Conyard. The house was ill kept compared with those surrounding it, and as soon as Behr saw her through the Plexiglas outer door, he knew why. She was old, nearing ninety, and not a spry ninety at that. She wore a heavy knit sweater over a housecoat over a robe, the type of elderly woman who felt a draft when it was eighty-five and humid. She was past going outside at all, much less doing house upkeep.

"Are you Mrs. Conyard?" Behr asked when she arrived at the door.

"I am. But I'm not buying anything. See, I'm on a fixed income," she told him.

"I'm not selling, ma'am," Behr began. "I'm investigating a boy who went missing around here last year." He appraised her to see if this rang any bells, but she remained blank. He continued. "Maybe you heard something about it? He was a paperboy . . . ?" This seemed to register, and she made a show of nodding, but Behr could tell she was acting. Still, the woman was homebound and he knew many senior citizens kept odd hours. Either they couldn't sleep and stayed up late or they couldn't sleep late and woke up early. And for a woman like this, myopic though she might have been, what else did she have to do but look out her windows? "I was wondering if I could come in and talk about the case?"

Behr watched her fear of strangers wrestle with her desire for company. "I don't know if I should."

He flashed his license, which he kept in a bill-fold with his old three-quarter shield. Then he took out the school picture of Jamie. "This is him. Maybe you saw him riding his bike?" She looked at the picture of the kid, with his cute little cowlick, and that did it. She swung the door open.

"I'm afraid I don't know anything about the case," she said, her voice tremulous with the effort of walking down the hall. "But I'll answer any questions I can." She led him into the living room and a stabbing prickle went down Behr's spine at what he saw there—stacks and stacks of news-papers. The room was filled with them, the *Star*, years' worth of them, unread. Many yellowing. Mrs. Conyard saw Behr looking. "I always mean to read the paper at night, but I end up watching television. . . ." Behr nodded to keep her going. "I like solving the puzzles on *Wheel* and I end up put-ting it off to another day." With the amount of unread papers she had in there, Behr wouldn't have been surprised if she believed Carter was still in office.

"You know, Mrs. Conyard, I wonder if I could look through your papers, see if you got yours that day?"

"Sure, sure, go ahead," she told him. Behr was already kneeling and poring over the stacks for the dates close to the day of the disappearance. "I keep meaning to get rid of the old ones. . . . Maybe they'll be good for something."

There was a loose sort of left-to-right organization to the papers. Within ten minutes Behr had found October of the correct year and saw what didn't completely surprise him. She had all the papers leading up to the day, but no paper from the day Jamie went missing. There was no paper for two days after that, either. Mrs. Conyard remembered the interruption in service. It was disconcerting to her. Then the delivery service resumed, on the third day. "A little brown man. In a car. That's the way they do it now," she told him.

"That's progress," Behr said, looking not at her but through the nearby stacks of papers to make sure that none were misfiled. None were. Her order was fairly meticulous.

"You know what?" Mrs. Conyard told him, memory's light breaking across her face. "Now I *do* remember the police stopping by and asking questions." Behr nodded his support for her recollection, which unfortunately contained no other hard information. She hadn't seen any suspicious cars or people then or since. "It's a very safe neighborhood. That's why I've stayed all these years since my husband died."

She moved across the room to a portrait of her late husband that rested on the television. "This is Mr. Conyard . . . my John . . ." She held it out for Behr's inspection. He looked it over and planned his exit.

Behr spent the next several hours in his car, parked on Tibbs, on the cell phone with the circulation department of the *Star*. It took a good while before he got the right person, a Susan Durant, who had been there many years and had a handle on things, and a memory to boot. She recalled them losing their delivery boy. It was a sad day at the paper even though no one remembered ever having met him. And there was a near mutiny in Circ. when the story only got under-the-fold coverage. She checked the logs and saw that the resident at 5 Tibbs had complained and been credited for no delivery on October 24. Several others from later in the route had made the same call. Susan also confirmed that there was no delivery in place for the next two days. All the customers on the route were credited for those days as well.

"Nope, there weren't any complaints from anyone on the route prior to 5 Tibbs," Susan Durant said from her downtown office, causing Behr to get that prickle down his spine again, as if he felt he was drawing a bead on where something might have happened to Jamie.

"I owe you an Italian dinner, Susan," Behr offered for her time and effort on the phone.

"Oh, I don't do carbs, Frank," Susan said with regret, then added encouragingly, "but we could make it a rib-eye."

"A steak it is, Susan." He promised to call her when things wound down on the case.

Behr turned off his phone and settled in to wait for a Mr. Louis Cranepool, resident of 1 Tibbs Avenue, to return from work. As he waited, Behr ran scenarios in his head. In the case of a missing kid, the parents always got a hard, and often the first, look from police. Behr was sure that within the police file—the official one, not the copy— there was a report showing that the Gabriels had been thoroughly investigated, maybe even poly-graphed. There were circumstances in which Behr would've begun by looking more deeply into the mother and father as well. Veracity of grief was no indicator of innocence in crimes within a family. But having sat with them, Behr recognized the completely blinding condition of *not knowing* what had happened to their son from which the couple suffered. This was much harder to fake. He felt the burled walnut of his custom steering wheel flex under his palms. He looked down and noticed his hands were white-knuckled across it. He relaxed his hands and tried to keep them from becoming fists as he considered what Cranepool's involvement could be.

TEN

IT WAS JUST AFTER 4:00 when a gold Taurus pulled into the short driveway of 1 Tibbs. A squat man in a brown suit wrestled his briefcase from the passenger seat, climbed out of the car, and headed for his door.

Behr strode across the man's patch of lawn, cutting him off before he had his key out.

"You Louis Cranepool?" Behr snarled. He reared up and used his size on the man. There were many tools of influence at the interrogator's disposal when conducting an interview. Beatings and chemicals were the most severe, and usually illegal, though chummy manipulation yielded nearly as much in Behr's estimation. Chances were this guy had nothing to do with anything, but Behr had only this one time to make a first impression. He decided to try to rattle him, to see if anything shook loose.

"I am." Cranepool swallowed, taking in the huge man standing between him and his door. "What do you want?"

"You know what I'm here about." Behr let the words settle. "Jamie Gabriel." If the name *did* mean anything to Cranepool, then Behr never wanted to sit across a poker table from him. "Your paperboy."

Cranepool narrowed his eyes in thought. "The one who used to deliver here? Kid who went missing?"

"That's right." Behr nodded, beginning to modulate his intimidation, already leaning toward the belief that Cranepool wasn't involved. Behr shifted into a more neutral policelike tone, hoping for at least a piece of information. "The date was October twenty-fourth last year. I'm assuming you told the police everything you know about it, which was nothing, yes?"

"Uh-huh," Cranepool said, his fear abating, but only slightly.

"Do you recall if you got your paper on the morning of the twenty-fourth?"

"I did." Cranepool answered too quickly. "I didn't mention that to the police. I didn't think to and they didn't ask."

"It was a long time ago. You're sure?"

"I'm sure." Cranepool nodded.

"How?"

"I trade my own portfolio and I check the stock

page every night. I missed the paper the next day and had to buy it at the gas station for two days running while they replaced deliverymen."

Behr involuntarily glanced toward the street. "Now I'm on the Internet and I get updates throughout the day," he half heard Cranepool continue in the background. Behr refocused and asked half a dozen followups, to which Cranepool shook his head. Behr nodded his thanks and began backing off across the lawn the way he had come. Cranepool hurried inside with relief while Behr made his way to the street.

Behr walked around the corner and imagined himself on a bike. He saw that the clearest shot at Cranepool's front door was from where he stood on Perry *before* making the turn onto Tibbs. Behr brought his right arm across his chest and simulated a cross-body backhanded toss. *This is where you would throw it from,* he thought. Then he continued around the corner. It was another thirty yards to Mrs. Conyard's house. Jamie had never made it that distance. This was the place. It slammed Behr in the chest. The familiar blackness that came with the realization that a horrible crime had occurred rushed up and tunneled around him. *This was the place.*

.   .   .

Behr stood out on Tibbs between the Cranepool
and Conyard houses for a long time. He knelt
down near the asphalt, even brushed it with his
fingertips, and looked into the oil stains like a seer.
Had he glanced up, he would have seen Cranepool
peering at the huge, threatening man from behind
his kitchen curtain. When Behr finally stood, the
cartilage in his knees cracked, and he remembered
the jogger.

ELEVEN

SOMETIMES THINGS HAPPENED QUICKLY on a case, other times not so at all. Usually it was like banging against a slab of rock with a sledgehammer. Tiny chips flew here and there but seemed to lead nowhere, and then *clunk,* the whole thing came apart. That moment was a long way off as Behr sat in the dark and steeled himself to search places on the Internet that should not exist, that would not exist in a decent world. He'd gone late into the previous nights checking the National Center for Missing and Exploited Children Web sites and others. He'd found Jamie's picture posted there among thousands, his just one of the awkward-sweet faces of the missing, though no leads were listed. But tonight Behr was going to a far worse place. Like a predator lurking in cyberspace, he began to locate the sites dedicated to child pornography. Though they were relatively few and hard to find, there were still far too many of them. Some offered censored thumbnails, hoping to entice buyers into the elaborate processes of passwords and protected downloads. Revulsion and sweat bathed the back of Behr's neck as he clicked on sample pictures. They were shot in badly lit rooms, where faceless men penetrated drugged and frail young boys and girls. Black circles and digital buzz-outs did little to mask what was going on. Behr felt his gorge rise but went on as best he could, trying to determine if any of the vacant-eyed youths were Jamie. Cold feverish rage grew within him. It took all of his will to restrain himself from smashing every single thing in his house. He wanted to barehand kill every one of the pale, flabby-bodied men on his computer screen. As a cop he'd encountered all manner of street filth, degenerates, and psychopaths. He'd seen corpses that had suffered grisly fates and living victims who had suffered worse, but none of it had the power to numb him to this. He went later and later into the night, discovering societies that advocated physical *love*—their word for it— between adults and children, until he went bleary-eyed. As he willed himself on, the unimaginable happened at four A.M. His own son appeared to him like a revenant. Tim's face began to appear superimposed over those of the young victims. It made his skin crawl, his scalp boil, and his blood surge in his temples. He found himself weak with rage. Sour vomit filled the back of his throat, and he barely reached the bathroom in time.

Behr was back on Tibbs before six A.M. the next morning, looking for the jogger. His hair still wet from the scalding shower he had hoped would disinfect him, he sat in his car swilling Maalox and praying it would quiet his churning stomach. It was Saturday and by ten he believed the runner wasn't going to show up, but he sat there until five in the afternoon, anyway. He repeated the drill on Sunday, trying to keep from his head the idea that the man could've been from a nearby neighborhood and hit Tibbs by coincidence, not custom. The guy could've been visiting from out of town. Sunday was a bust, too.

Monday, though, at ten after six in the morning, there he came, chugging up the street. He was in his early forties, barrel-bellied on spindly legs. Behr lumbered out of his car and ran up next to the man.

"Sorry to bother you," Behr said, no real apology in his voice, as he jogged along with him like a moving brick building. "I'm investigating a disappearance."

The man stopped his forward progress but kept moving in place, wiping his sweat-soaked sideburns, his breathing coming heavy. "A kid went missing here last October twenty-fourth. You know anything about it?"

"No, I don't," the man wheezed.

"Can I get a name?"

"Brad Figgis."

The man, Figgis, didn't know anything about it. "Time to time I saw a kid whiz by on his bike," he did volunteer.

"Were you ever questioned by the police about this?"

"Nope. I'm not from around here."

Behr looked the man over. He didn't look like he could cover that much ground.

"How far you run?"

"My loop is four and a half. This is about halfway."

"You remember anything unusual back then?"

Figgis sweated and thought, and slowly nodded.

"I remember a big old car out here a few days in a row. Parked right over there so I had to run around it. Then I never saw it again. It was a Pontiac or Lincoln. Big and gray."

"Plates?"

"Nah. Didn't catch that."

"Why'd it strike you?"

"There were two guys in it. I couldn't tell you what they looked like, only that they were eating. I thought they might've been landscapers or painters waiting to start work, but the car was wrong. Those types of guys seem to drive pickups or tiny Corollas. This car was huge. Slabs of gray fender. The kind that drinks gas."

Behr took a number and an address off Figgis, and watched him puff away into the morning. Then Behr went home to hammer away at DMV databases.

TWELVE

MORNINGS WERE THE WORST for the Gabriels, and without coffee Carol was sure she'd have curled into a ball, dried up and blown away. She'd never been the early riser type. In college, she'd worked scrupulously to schedule her classes after ten. Then, when she'd gotten married and Paul had to wake up at quarter to six every day for work, she'd grown to feel so guilty at sleeping past him that she'd forced herself awake to make coffee and breakfast while he took a run. Then she'd sit at the kitchen table and make a pretense at conversation, but all she really wanted was to get back in bed.

That all changed with Jamie. The moment he was born she was filled with energy, a purpose, for which she had never known to even hope. When he was a baby and his crying filled their apartment, and later their first small house, she would get up to attend to him. There was no bitterness, no black exhaustion in her step as she walked to his crib. When he got older and could sleep through the night before popping up to play at six or so in the morning, Carol felt that she barely needed sleep anymore. And by the time Jamie reached school age, Carol was getting up before he was. She faced the morning like a drill instructor, with energy and gusto, with near aggression. She'd rouse Jamie, corral him into the bathroom for a face washing and teeth brushing, get him into appropriate clothes, hustle him down for breakfast and take his lunch order, then putting it together and snapping it into his lunchbox, before he had finished his orange juice. She walked him to school with a bounce in her step. Rain or shine, each day felt like a gift.

But now . . . Now Carol suspected the truth— that the energy had really been all Jamie's. His youth, the relentless brand of spirit unique to young boys, was what had given her her power. Because now that he was gone, she sat at the kitchen table unable to do anything but wrap her fingers around her mug of inky coffee. There was a sense of stagnancy to her life worse than any hangover she'd endured during her partying days. The mornings were a nettlesome chore just to get through these days, a wall she didn't know if she'd be able to climb. Waiting for Paul to leave for work set her teeth on edge.

Carol kicked herself for her irritation at Paul this morning. He was pottering around endlessly, looking for something. She knew, on a rational level, that she should have more patience. Paul had found a way to keep going to work, to keep selling policies so that they could continue paying for the house. For several months she believed that that was the most important thing, because if Jamie ever returned he would know where to find them. If it had been left to her, they'd be living on the streets behind a Dumpster due to her inactivity. But all that didn't matter anymore, because he wasn't ever coming back. And this morning her nerves were unraveling like badly done knitting.

"What is it you're looking for?" she asked, recognizing the overtired timbre to her voice.

Paul stopped and looked at her in surprise that she'd spoken to him before he'd been to work and back and it was dark outside.

"For those cereal-box toys. I had a dozen of them. I was saving them." He stood there holding the latest toy—a small spinning top—in one hand, a bowl of sugared flakes in the other.

"Oh, those. I threw them away when I was cleaning out the drawers the other day," she said, and got the strangest impression that her husband was going to cry.

"Why? Why'd you do that, goddamnit?" he said, as angry as she'd ever seen him. It made her remember: He'd been saving the prizes for their son. Their son, who was never going to return. She'd had something on her mind for several weeks, and now seemed like as good a time as any to mention it.

"Paul?" she said. "Paul, forget about the tops and things." He looked to her. "Paul, I want to talk. There's something I want to do." He was expectant but said nothing. "I want to buy . . . I want us to get a plot. To put up a headstone for Jamie. I want to have a funeral and a place we can go to mourn. To remember him." Everything in her married life told her that her husband would nod and acquiesce to her wish, so she looked on in shock when he slammed the cereal bowl he was holding against the countertop. It exploded in a shower of ceramic and sugared cereal flakes.

"No," he said. "No. No. No. No." Then his face came apart in tearless sobs.

It was pounding rain outside and the gutters were overflowing as Behr banged coffee and scoured DMV databases. Reading the numbers and addresses—dry, desiccated information—was a reprieve from his recent computer use. The sound of the rain brought him back to where he'd grown up, outside Everett, where this wouldn't even be considered a drizzle but more of a light mist. After he'd gotten a criminology degree on a football scholarship, he'd learned that the Indianapolis

P.D. was hiring and that the city had only fifty days of rain per year, which was about two hundred less than he was used to. The odd thing now was that he missed the rain most of the time.

What he'd learned from Figgis, the jogger, had increased his dread about the mission he was on, and Behr buried himself in the minutiae of the task in order to avoid it. A lone degenerate out to grab a kid would be bad enough. But the presence of two men, if that's what they'd been there for, hinted at a more dark-hued thing: organization. Most likely the car that his jogger had mentioned was stolen, and Behr hoped to stumble across a report of a matching model on a motor-vehicle theft list. His hopes remained at low ebb as he covered the databases for Indiana, Illinois, Kentucky, and western Ohio. No old Lincolns and only one Pontiac—an '84 Sunfire outside of Chicago—were reported stolen in the days leading up to the event. The Sunfire was a small, two-door model, Behr knew. There were dozens of reports of stolen license plates during the same time period. This led him to believe it much more likely that the car had been purchased, not stolen, and then had stolen plates put on it. Even if a witness like Figgis had written down the plate number, it would lead nowhere. In the name of thoroughness Behr checked all the title transfers closely preceding October 24. It was a banner sales week for large used sedans. And the pink slips registered at the

DMVs were only a fraction of the cars that had changed hands for cash, he knew.

As far as the two men went—men without description—he realized he'd never figure out the way the car had come into their possession. The car data began to run together until his eyeballs spun like slot-machine wheels. The exercise was a bust. Behr leaned back and let the data wash together on the computer screen and join with the rain on the window. While it had given him a brief jolt of momentum, practically speaking, the car was a dead end.

With all the advances in car theft, Behr considered, *I'd probably have a better time finding the kid's bike. . . .*

"The bike," he said aloud. It gave him pause. Why not try to find the goddamn bike? Behr reached for his car keys.

THIRTEEN

BEHR FELT LIKE A FOOLISH FUCK as he drove out on 65 toward the Southern County Municipal Landfill in the dwindling rain. Long odds had never been his style, and here he was hoping for a lottery-style payout. Still, he drove on, and ahead in the distance loomed the chain-link gate of Southern. Thirty-four acres licensed by the county for the disposal of solid waste, the place was Terry Cottrell's fiefdom. Cottrell had been a thief and a fence when Behr met him a dozen years back on a stolen merch case. Behr had arrested him, and on the way to the station he'd fallen under the man's rap. Many criminals he'd busted had lobbied him in the squad car, looking for special treatment on that last ride to the lockup, but Behr had never had such an objective, almost philosophical conversation with one as he'd had with Cottrell.

Cottrell was a gangly, skinny kid back then. He seemed concerned by his fate, but unwilling, as if bound by an unspoken but tangible code of honor, to question, complain, or speculate about what would become of him. Instead he talked police business with Behr, recent cases that had been in the headlines, and seemed to have a deep knowledge of the life of a cop.

Then, during the trial, on the day he was supposed to testify, Behr found himself at the lunch recess in a diner sitting down the counter from Cottrell and his mother. It was never pleasant facing the family of a guy he was trying to put away. There were usually evil stares, hard words, and often threats. But it was not so in this case. Cottrell's mother, Lana, was an attractive middle-aged lady.

"Good day, sir," she said politely. "No need to feel funny, us all having lunch. We wouldn't be here if not for him."

Behr nodded.

"Mama—" Cottrell began, only to be silenced by her look.

Cottrell had a hell of a lawyer and got a two-year suspended sentence, although Behr had nailed him cold in a storage locker full of high-end audiovisual gear. Behr was a younger cop back then, not yet jaded to the ways of the system, and he felt slapped by the light sentence. After watching Cottrell walk out of the courtroom wearing a fat smile, he couldn't let it go. A few days later he showed up at Cottrell's house to threaten him to not fuck around in the neighborhood at any point in the near future. But Cottrell was out and he ended up sitting with Lana. She was stricken over her son's legal problems and feared that since he'd gotten off, he'd go further down the path of crime. She also talked about how he loved to read and showed Behr the boy's room, which was neatly kept and packed to overflowing with books. Behr was moved enough to give the matter thought and eventually he figured out how to secure the steady, quiet county job at the landfill for the kid.

He and Cottrell had slowly become a kind of friends, and if Cottrell had been fencing or involved in crime these last many years, he kept it small-time enough that it stayed off Behr's radar.

Behr rolled through the gates and caught the acrid smell of the dump. Buried under large berms were millions of cubic yards of waste. In addition to the cars and household appliances quietly rusting into oblivion, there were industrial castoffs like coal tar, iron oxide, and paint, barreled and sunk. Supervising the spreading of earth over the refuse, and generally maintaining the facility, probably wasn't the healthiest job in the world, Behr considered, but it had a hell of a lot more upside than Cottrell's former occupation. Behr pulled up not far from the double-wide that was Cottrell's headquarters.

"Oh, shit, Big Sleep's in the house," Cottrell called as Behr lumbered out of his car.

"What's cracking, Terry?" Behr asked, shaking his hand.

" 'S'up, Philly?" Cottrell asked back, leaning into a chest bump with Behr. He called Behr "Philly," as in Philip Marlowe, half in jest, half out of respect.

"Damn." Cottrell seemed to appraise Behr's bulk for a moment after the chest bump before going back to what he had been doing, which was feeding popcorn to a flock of crows. The big, ugly birds, disturbed at the hiatus, began cawing at him loudly. Their calls knifed through the air. Cottrell drew a few large handfuls of popcorn from a tin at his feet and threw it in the direction of the birds.

"Most sensible people can't stand these damn things," Behr said, massaging his ears against the ringing squawks, "and here you are feeding 'em."

Cottrell shrugged and flung another handful.

"That's why they've got these things called scarecrows, you know, to keep 'em away," Behr said, shaking his head.

"Can I tell you, my man? I always liked these birds. 'Cause they black and they loud. Just like me. . . ." Then Cottrell treated Behr to his signature explosive laugh. "Hah, heh-heh, heh-heh-heh."

Behr smiled and then paused, wanting, for a

moment, to hold off what he knew was coming next. Cottrell picked up the tin and flung the remaining corn at the crows. Behr sighed and went ahead. "If I was looking to buy or sell a stolen bicycle, who'd be the main fence in this area?"

Cottrell was genuinely surprised for a second at the question and then he went with it, spreading a thick layer of additional trumped-up mystification over his features.

"Oh, I get it, I get it. Now I done seen it all. Motherfucking Trouble's Your Business. Philly's working the *big* cases now. Hah, heh-heh, heh-heh-heh."

Behr just shook his head and waited for the cackling to subside. It did eventually.

"Well, well, let's see," Cottrell said, wiping his eyes. "C'mon back to my bat cave."

Behr followed him to the double-wide.

Once inside, Cottrell splashed enough Old Grandad to cover the bottom of his coffee cup and filled it the rest of the way with Pepsi. He knew enough not to offer any to Behr as it would be refused. They used to drink together some days, but that was a long time back when they were nearly a dozen years younger and twenty pounds lighter and when Behr was still on the force before his kid had died.

He watched Behr fall back into an old La-Z-Boy and check out the trailer. The walls, as in his room at his mother's house, were lined with book-shelves. The shelves were filled with crime novels and literature. He could've opened a secondhand specialty bookshop if the books weren't so worn from use and if he weren't interested in keeping them. He'd been a full-on crime-writing buff when he was younger. He'd believed, hoped at least, that a thorough knowledge of how the great fictional gumshoes broke their cases, and the way the famous criminals slipped up, would ensure his success as a fence. In any case he moved on to litera-ture after he found out he was mistaken.

"So, man, what you want?"

"I told you."

"F'real?"

"For real."

Terry Cottrell looked across his trailer at some-one who had done plenty for him and never expected much in return. He'd known Behr as a cop who had worked on violent crimes, important cases, and he didn't know why the hell he was looking into stolen bikes now. The expression on the big man's grill assured him there was a god-damn good reason, though.

"Man, you know how much I hate shouting names," he said. There'd only been a few occa-sions when Behr had asked him to, and no prob-lems had come home to roost based on information he'd given Behr. But still.

"And you know how much I hate asking,

Terry," Behr said, immobile, his arms resting on the chair's arms. He seemed strong enough to tear them clean off at will.

Terry swilled a sip of whiskey and mulled over the names he knew. "At thirty plus I's getting old to clock the streets. Especially since I been retired for so long."

"Uh-huh."

"But I'm retired like MJ was, I still got a few fall-away moves. Problem is, most fences I know deal in bigger items than bikes." He knew Rally Cooper was the one to see if you were looking for a Mercedes. And Earl Powers for rods. Blood could even get you a .30-caliber machine gun. Cottrell figured he could ask Behr why he needed to know and he would probably tell him. But his relationship with Big Philly was based on trust, he decided, and that shit was solid.

Behr sat patiently and waited for Cottrell to work out his answer. The kid wasn't born to talk, and Behr respected that about him. When he gave up a name or a piece of information, he was never rolling over, he was *helping*, and Behr appreciated the difference.

Cottrell finished his thought with a *tsk* of his teeth and spoke. "Mickey Handley. Heard of him? Kid's a wigger from over the other side."

"People still do that?"

"Yeah, man. White kid from up north with a bad case of brother love. Listens to hip-hop, wears the big jeans, thinks he one of us."

Behr nodded. He knew the type. They tried to come off gangsta, though they usually just came off silly. "Where is he?"

"He at Plainfield."

Behr raised his eyebrows.

"Oh, yeah. White boy caught a F. He like me—a fast starter, and quick to get popped. He didn't get himself no Allen Rossum though," Cottrell said, naming the lawyer who'd gotten him off his charges way back.

Behr nodded again. "I appreciate it, Terry," he said, standing. Cottrell nodded. "Reading anything good?"

"Fyodor. The Russians," Cottrell answered. "Shit stands up to repeat. Don't wait till the next big case to stop by." His eyes flashed.

"Sure. We should catch the Pacers."

"A'ight. But I can't be sitting down at Conseco with 5–0."

"We'll watch it on TV then." The men shook and hugged and Behr turned to go, Cottrell watching him. Behr reached his car.

"Yo, Big," Cottrell called out. Behr looked back. "You know where Moses was when the lights went out?"

Behr shook his head.

"In the dark, same as you. Hah, heh-heh, heh-heh-heh."

Behr got in his car and left.

FOURTEEN

BEHR LOOPED BACK past the south edge of the city and got on 40 west. He went past Six Points and drove into Plainfield. On the way he dialed Stan Brookings, an acquaintance from the force who was now a supervisor at the Plainfield adult facility. He asked for and got a hook at the juvenile "campus."

"Have lunch," Brookings told him, "a visitor's pass'll be waiting for you by the time you're done."

"You got a recommend?"

"Try Gulliver's, it's nearby on North Carr."

Behr rolled into Gulliver's and commandeered a booth. They sold antacids right next to the cash register, which was not a good sign, and whether or not the place had had a lunch rush, it was now after 3:00 and dead empty. He scanned the menu and considered his options. The idea of food wasn't a welcome one as his appetite had been a relic since surfing the child-porn sites the other night. Usually he had a cast-iron stomach and could get by on the same fare as the average barnyard goat. Back during his days in uniform, his fellow officers used to joke about his ability to drink coffee at a motor vehicle accident scene or grab a bite of sandwich in the middle of a shoot investigation. But this case had turned his stomach and made his willingness to eat an even-up proposition at best.

"You want something?" the waitress asked, her words in tune with the indecision on his face. She wore a tan uniform with "Darla" on her name tag.

"I think I can do a bowl of chili," he answered, "if it's good."

"It *is* good," Darla assured him, and he nodded that he'd take it.

The longer it went, Behr thought, *the worse the chances of finding 'em.* After about twelve hours, the odds went to shit. It'd been well over twelve months, and that gnawed at him like rats sharpening their teeth on plumbing pipes.

Behr had grown up on a small farm in the Northwest, one where food was basic, if not scarce. The family killed their own chickens for supper back then, same with the seasonal hog. But the chickens had become his job once he'd reached the age of eight. How many hundreds of them had he put on the stump and finished, bringing down the hatchet, then putting all his weight on the twitching birds so they didn't flap around the yard? By the time he had reached his teens, he'd merely taken them by the head and casually swung his wrist in a circle.

Then of course there was the manure shoveling, the slopping, the calving, and the castrations—all the tasks that came along with life on a farm. Growing up, he'd gotten so used to the work and the death that it was only later, into his first ten on the force, that he realized he possessed a stolid, almost bovine endurance for the unpleasant. It was what he relied on to get him through odious, boring, and even hopeless work. It was what he'd need to draw on in order to continue with this case.

Behr, having finished his lunch, which turned out to be only the crackers that came along with the chili, got back in his car. Turning off Plainfield's Main Street, he saw the "campus," a cluster of low cinder-block buildings surrounded by a high fence topped with razor wire. The buildings housed and attempted to rehabilitate some three hundred juvenile offenders. For most of them the place was a stopover before graduation to the nearby maximum-security institution.

Behr entered the admin building and went through a metal detector on his way to picking up the pass. Brookings was as good as his word, and it awaited him. Behr was then directed to building six, where he was wanded and patted down, then shown into an interview room. He wasn't offered coffee or anything else. Packing boxes were stacked in the halls and administrative secretaries made repeated trips, filling them with files and adding to their number. Behr remembered that within the next few weeks the whole facility would be moved down to new quarters on Girls School Road. Ten minutes later a guard wearing a putty-colored uniform escorted in a young man with a cropped head who looked to be about seventeen years old.

"Mickey, thanks for seeing me."

"Make it Mike," he said quietly, extending a small hand. "What's it about?"

"It's about stolen goods. Bicycles."

"I'm out of that. Obviously." Handley gestured to his surroundings. "I'm sprung in eight more weeks and I'm crime-free from here on in." He spoke in earnest, not trying too hard to sell it. After Cottrell's buildup, Behr expected a street-hardened gold-tooth he would have to break down. He was surprised to see Mickey Handley, compact and well spoken. Behr had seen a first incarceration do this to a young person from time to time. The only nod to Handley's prior reputation was the sweatshirt he wore. It was too large, fuzzy, and N.C. Tar Heel blue with ABERCROMBIE written across the chest. His pants were navy blue, institutional issue.

"How'd it used to work, then?"

"Hold up. Where'd you get my name?"

Behr daggered the kid with his eyes. "I'm doing the asking."

The kid hung his head and spoke.

"There was a new and used bike shop over by Range Line, near Carmel, where I'm from, so reselling was easy. I got some cash together and put word out that I was buying." Handley looked up. "The units started rolling in. Bikes are like that," he deadpanned.

Behr's face didn't twitch as he showed the kid there was no audience for the wordplay stuff.

Handley nodded and went on. "Most guys I bought from were either kids or ding heads looking for drug money. These idiots used to walk around with bolt cutters, chop the padlock, jump on, and ride straight over to me. Some guys were fathers, who also had drug problems or gambling debts, and were selling off their own kids' rides."

"You know if you ever bought or sold a near new blue Mongoose BMX?"

Handley showed his palms. "Aw, man, I'm sorry. I did *volume*. Can't remember something like that. Probably did."

"I'm gonna ask you one big one, Mike, and I want you to think before you answer. You're gonna give me a name and then I'm gonna go away and you'll continue with your crime-free life and that'll be it." Behr leaned back and crossed his arms before speaking. "Who's the wrongest bastard ever showed up to sell you a bike?"

Handley hardly paused before speaking. "There was one crankster who sold me about half a dozen units, sometimes two at a time. He'd drive over and take them out of his trunk."

"How'd you know he was using?"

"He had the craters," Handley said, pointing to his face where the telltale sores of a meth smoker showed up.

"What kind of car?"

"Different ones."

"Lincoln?"

Handley shrugged. "Could've been. Anyway, there was no chance he'd be riding 'em over on account of his size. Things'd look like a clown bike he was so big." Handley paused a moment, realizing his audience for the size reference, then looked up at Behr to see if there'd been any offense taken. There wasn't and he continued. "This guy put on airs, you know, like he was *don criminati*—" A flash of the old street talk; Handley caught himself. "I mean he acted like he had bigger things to be doing."

"I get it. What's his name?" Behr asked calmly, feeling the dull thunder of his heart.

"Ted. Ted Ford, I think."

"You think?"

"I'm pretty sure. Anyhow, you could check it."

"How?"

"He was affiliated—maybe he worked there or something—at this titty bar. Ah, what was it called? He was always giving me these cards, these little promo cards offering a free drink off the minimum. Like he was a real businessman. It was . . . it was the Golden Lady. Ted Ford."

FIFTEEN

THE SUN WAS GOING DOWN when Paul rolled into the driveway. Carol grabbed her keys and bag, stepped outside, and pulled the door shut behind her. They had a dinner meeting with the private investigator. Carol brought no hopes with her, assuming there would've been a call if any information had been found.

"Hi," she said, climbing into the car. As Paul backed out, she considered the house. It hadn't changed much since they'd moved in. It had been recently painted then, and it was still in good shape. She hadn't bothered to put geraniums in the window boxes last season. All the same, she hated the place now. Hated it for all that she had once loved about it and for what it now represented—a dream of a happy safe life that had curdled. She knew, though, that she could never move. That

Paul never could, either. Not until they got some final word of Jamie's death.

"Be interesting to see Behr's report," Paul said, breaking into her thoughts.

"Yeah," Carol answered, though she did not agree. Reports full of no information were insults to them and their pain, but that's all they'd gotten from the previous investigators.

The car fell silent as Paul steered toward Curley's, where they always met the investigators. He glanced at his wife and his stomach clenched at the turbulent feeling that hit him there. He cracked the window to let in some fresh evening air and release some of the stale stuff inside the car. Each day had become a series of tasks for him. Getting up, going to work, selling policies, eating, paying bills, keeping up conversations with Carol, checking updates on the missing children Web sites, tending to the house. The tasks were small rivets keeping a lid on what roiled inside him. Rage. Indignation. Helplessness. At different times they would seize him by the back of the neck and thrash him about, until he would force himself to take up a new task and lock things back down. Back at the beginning of his marriage and looking forward to forty, fifty years together with Carol, it didn't seem like enough time. Now the days stretched out ahead of him, a terrifying snakelike monster he couldn't hope to ride down. No amount of tasks could control it.

Behr sat at Curley's, an untouched basket of bread in front of him, having arrived at the restaurant early. The place was white subway-tiled walls with green-shaded lamps hanging low over butcher-block tables. The menu was comfort food, with dessert included. Curley's was an anomaly these days, as it wasn't part of a chain. May as well be, Behr thought, looking around impatiently. He'd shot home after leaving Plainfield and ran addresses, phone numbers, and backgrounds on Ted Fords. There were several and he was able to quickly eliminate most of them based on age and physical descriptions. He didn't find any with records. He had a feeling he wasn't on to much. He knew well enough not to put stock in what Handley had told him. Jailhouse information was like hitting major-league pitching. Even Hall of Famers only connected one out of three. Still, he would've liked to have gone right over to this Golden Lady joint to see if he could find Ford in person. Instead he waited.

Before long they entered. Quiet and tentative, Paul held the door for his wife and they crossed to him. Behr didn't stand or shake hands as they sat, and he felt them glance around at the table and the empty banquette next to him, looking for something.

"Folks," Behr said before too much time could slide by.

"Let's order first, then talk," Paul said, eliciting a look of pained patience but no protest from Carol. Paul ordered Salisbury steak, Carol chose a Caesar salad. Behr passed altogether.

"Where's your report?" Carol asked before the waitress had taken two steps away. Behr showed his empty palms and then pulled out his notebook.

She was surprised but not disappointed that Behr didn't have a typed report to ply them with, and felt the same way about him not donning a suit. This guy was either more good money after bad or maybe something better. He was different anyhow, she thought.

"Did you learn anything?" she wondered.

"Tibbs. Just as he got there. I believe he was on his route and never finished it, and that it was no accident." Behr's words hit them like a thunderhead. The parents didn't move or breathe.

"I think there were two men on the scene, and they probably weren't the only ones involved—"

"Do you know who—" Carol nearly jumped across the table.

"No." He cut her off. "Look, the same assumptions we started with have gotta hold. That there won't be any more information, much less good news." She nodded at him. "I have a lead. A name I can at least ask—"

"Who is it?"

"I'll tell you more as I find it." A stony silence settled. Paul's appetizer salad arrived, small and wilted, drowned in red dressing.

"How will you go about . . . ?" Carol's words petered out as she realized she wasn't about to get a primer in investigation.

"*You* wanted this meeting, folks. I didn't think it was called for, but it was your decision." Behr bristled, not liking their pressure.

Carol blinked, her only movement. The sounds of Curley's, filling up around them, hummed for a moment.

Paul's heart had been thudding since he walked into the restaurant and saw Behr sitting there, put out at having to take the time to update them. He was too busy working to kiss their asses. That was clear from the look on his face and the way he was dressed. When Behr went on and told them what he'd learned, it confirmed the cold, slimy knowing deep within him. When Behr spoke the name of the street where he believed it had happened, Paul recognized that his life had changed—his worst fear had come to pass. There was nothing else the world could do to him.

"I . . ." Paul began, the word catching in his throat, "I want to be involved. To work with you on the case." Carol, eyes wide, looked to him, truly surprised. Paul sounded so set on the idea that for a moment she actually wondered at the outcome.

"No," Behr said. The finality of the answer stole Paul's breath. It seemed that Behr tried to think of something to add, to soften his answer, or at least to make clear the many whys for it. "No," he said again.

"What do you mean no?" Paul asked. "We're the ones who—"

"You hired me to do what I do. That doesn't include you or anyone else coming along."

"I just want to know I'm doing everything I can to help find out what happened to Jamie," the father went on.

"Don't. Don't push this course, Paul. It won't lead you anywhere good. You can fire me if you want, but—"

"No." It was Carol's first word in some time.

"He was our son. My son," Paul continued. "How would you feel?"

Behr banged his palms flat on the table, causing silverware to jump and rattle. Paul's salad bowl capsized and the restaurant went silent for a moment. Behr felt his pulse throb in his neck. He fought for control and for air. My son. Tim's face had flashed through Behr's mind's eye when he heard those words. This used to happen every minute of every day back when it was fresh. It had happened less and less over time, but rather than decreasing in power, Behr was merely left less resistant when it did come. He shook his head hoping to physically knock the image out of it. He looked across the table at Paul and saw a broken, haunted aspect in the man's eyes. Behr knew it well. He wondered if his own eyes featured it at the moment.

Behr considered the place on the continuum of civilized behavior that Paul occupied. No matter how raw he'd lived when he was young, he'd raised his son for over a decade. He'd experienced the softening and respect for life that children bring. Such things did not afflict Behr. Since Tim had been gone he'd been moving steadily the other way. Finally he felt he could speak again.

"If this leads anywhere, it'll be to a horrible place. And you're not prepared for it."

"I'm not a cop, but what I've been through . . ." Paul said, running out of whatever propellant had gotten him this far in the discussion. "And you . . . you're . . . You seem like . . ." he finished, tapping out completely.

"I may seem like a regular guy," Behr said evenly, "but it's a mask."

He sat and looked at the couple looking at him, appraising him anew.

"I'm gonna get back to work." Behr stood up from the table and left them sitting there.

Behr slid behind the wheel and caught a flash of his face in the rearview. How much truth had he just told? More than he'd been prepared to, but not all of it. Tension knotted in his shoulders. He felt sweat running down his sides. It had come to this. How many cases had he been fired off by meddling employers? Most were domestics. Once he started to turn up information, they'd want to come with him on surveillance or to confront their cheating spouse. Behr was clear on that never happening right at the top when he took the cases. Every one of them agreed to the provision, then 90 percent of them reneged when the information came through. This was different. If the average client was ripped apart by a husband or wife nailing a neighbor, or having a workplace affair, or going gay, then this case would have nuclear-level fallout. What he found, no matter how vague, had the potential to destroy whatever was left of the parents. But the truth of it was that Behr didn't work alone to keep his clients out of the line of fire—for him it was penitence. His own conscience bore a debt against him, long from being paid, for what had happened to his own son.

Behr felt worse than bad about it all; he felt like shit. He could Jack Daniel's it away, a bottle and a half's worth. But he didn't do that to himself anymore. Usually he'd drive over to City Club and pound iron until his arms hung limp and lactic acid burned in his chest. Tonight he drove straight for Crawfordsville Road. The Golden Lady.

"What was that about?" Carol asked when they'd gotten in the car, the first time either had spoken since Behr had left them in the restaurant.

"Nothing," Paul said, jerking the car into drive. He felt stupid, exposed in front of his wife. When he'd rehearsed it in his head on the way to Curley's, and then again seconds before he spoke it, things had gone differently. In Paul's version, Behr didn't welcome him on as a partner exactly, but he was supposed to have nodded and agreed. But the guy had been a piece of granite, unwilling to even go into detail. Paul considered calling him and leaving word that he was fired right on his answering machine. He drove, his eyes set on the road, his mind swirling with information and ideas. Could he get Pomeroy to have the cops go house to house on Tibbs, checking for suspicious behavior? Could he go himself, storm the doors one by one and search attics and basements and crawl spaces for Jamie? A shrinking feeling of limitation slowly returned. His limbs went weak and he knew he wasn't going to fire Behr.

SIXTEEN

RENO REMSEN MOVED ONSTAGE to the second song of
her three-song set, "Round and Round" by
Ratt. The blue spots caught her smooth skin.
She glowed. She swung on the pole and dodged
wadded-up singletons and fivers that flew at her
from the rail. Her real name was Meredith. Her
thighs were round and undimpled in the low light
and smoky air. Her tit job was decent and she had
a mane of black hair. She was everything you came
to see in a place like this. But she was no Michelle
Ginelle, the one Tad was in love with. That was
clear even from the second-story balcony where he
sat. Michelle called herself Brandi, with an *i*, and
always hit the stage to "Cherry Pie." Turned out
Michelle had the night off tonight unexpectedly. It
was just as well since he couldn't radiate for her
much right now. He liked to put on his smile and

place a knowing sparkle in his eyes for her. That took energy and he was too worn out. He'd been smoking a lot and not sleeping. The cristy was fine when he was high, but it became a dragon in his head, roaring out of the darkness, when he tried to sleep. It came with its own soundtrack, too. Scary opera blaring out of a tinny loudspeaker, like those strapped to the helicopters in *Apocalypse Now* when they strafed the village. He had tried to quit smoking for a while, to take 'er easy, but he still woke up in the middle of the night; he had started to suspect what it was really all about. That's when he took up the pipe again. Heavy.

He had hurt people. He'd stolen. He'd smuggled cargo precious and illegal. He was a bad boy to be sure. And Michelle was going to like that about him one day when she truly saw it. But of all the things he'd done and done wrong, great and small, that woke him in the middle of the night and chased sleep off from there, it was a strange thing that showed up most often. It was selling those damned bikes. His dirty secret. Six of them before getting out. He'd made twelve hundred bucks from it. The last was eleven months ago, but it felt like a lifetime. He'd basically forgotten about it, then six months ago, after meeting Michelle, it had started to come into the back of his mind, almost like a tickle. He'd burned the addresses, he'd dumped the vans, he hadn't told a soul, but the bikes were a loose end, the *only* damn loose one from his time working with Rooster for Mr. Riggi. In the end he couldn't swallow the work he'd been doing, and despite it paying well enough to make him a free-lance gentleman around the Golden Lady, Tad had ultimately quit and walked. He finally had to just get the fuck away from Rooster, and Mr. Riggi said he understood. He'd had a few conversations with Michelle about it all, every bit of detail cloaked, of course, and she had seemed to agree that Tad shouldn't stay in a bad situation.

This was when he was a customer at the Lady, before his money ran out, and he took the job doing security and door at the club. His idea was that he could work close to Michelle that way, put in the time that a woman of her caliber required. He could also make sure she didn't get too close to anyone else and that no one got too close to her. He never missed a set. She'd come out blasting with Warrant, then take it down to "Mr. Brown-stone," and finish off with something soulful, usu-ally "Home Sweet Home" or Cinderella's "Don't Know What You Got." The way she danced, as if the music was emanating from a place in her belly, moved him. And her body—it was magnetic. It made him want to touch her so bad. She wasn't too thin like so many girls these days. Tad would be in physical pain by the time she finished and he couldn't hear Tom Keifer's searing voice without getting mournfully hard. Before long he became sure that none of the customers meant a thing to her. She made eye contact with them during table dances and that convinced some of the guys that she dug them, but he knew the truth.

"I look right through them," she'd confided to Tad one night as she left the VIP room, tucking a roll of twenties into her little plastic case. As she walked by him, she reached out and touched his cheek. It felt like a kiss. It felt like lightning. "You look pale," she said with sadness in her voice, as if she knew his dirty secret.

Along with the job, he'd gotten the idea that somehow Michelle was the answer to what stalked him. That she could calm his troubled mind. That she was peace. He conjured daydreams for himself. After they'd enjoyed each other, she would lay that cool hand across his brow and he would sleep. Over time he'd leave the smoking behind altogether and get in better shape. He'd be a strong, fit, big man.

The last verse of "Don't Close Your Eyes" by Kix droned on. He looked down at Reno, undulating at the edge of the stage, her legs spread wide, her head thrown back. Tad almost saw her as Michelle for a moment and squeezed his cock hard against his thigh. The song ended and Reno closed her legs. She started scrabbling around the stage picking up her money. Tad hoisted himself out of the chair. His break was over.

. . .

Damn them, Behr thought, cursing the Gabriels as he sat in his car across the street from the windowless building that was the Golden Lady. It was a hulking structure, painted black. By way of a sign there was a halfhearted strip of purple neon outlining a painted dancing girl dipping her bottom into a martini glass. Behr worked on getting ahold of himself and managed to stop blaming the Gabriels for what he was feeling. It was an ancient anger, he realized, that predated them. He prepared himself to go in. He was out near the fairgrounds and didn't have a gun with him. He rarely carried one. His heart thrummed rapidly, a surge of adrenaline coming up the back of his throat. It had been a long time since he'd worked a good case. He leaned over, opened the glove box, and pulled out his bad man's brother—a leather sap, filled with iron shot. Just in case. He tucked it into his waistband and headed for the club. It'd been seven years since he'd gone independent, and he still wasn't used to going in alone. He'd had thirteen years on the force and had never quite got used to going in with backup, either.

Behr entered a small foyer where a man sat in a glassed-in box office. He slid a twenty into the slot and got a drink ticket back. He pushed through a turnstile, went through another door into the club, and was assaulted by blaring metal music and spinning lights that sliced through the darkness. His eyes adjusted and he saw the place was dim and scummy, the gloom merely punctured by neon and strobes. A half-naked young woman in red platform boots slunk across the stage like some kind of feline animal. He scoped the crowd, which was less than capacity, it being early still, and breathed in the smell of jizz, bleach, beer, fruity strippers' perfume, and the low, throat-closing odor of the smoke pumped onto the stage for the feature dancers.

He took a seat at a small round table not far from the stage and his gaze was pulled back to the dancer. Her hair was red, nearly matching her boots, and she was lithe and commanding despite being so young. She couldn't have been much more than nineteen. His desire wrestled with sadness. She seemed to be worldly and expert, a willing courtesan. But he didn't imagine the circumstances of the life that had led her there were good. Between songs an emcee came over the sound system exhorting the patrons to give it up for Lexi. When she was facing away from him, Behr leaned forward and placed a five-dollar bill on the edge of the stage. Another guitar-driven tune began, and a waitress, in a short skirt with a tray glued to her hand, stopped by the table.

"What'll you have?"

"Vodka and tonic." Behr extended his drink ticket. The waitress was a good five years older than the dancer, but it was a wide chasm. Her legs were decent with the benefit of control hose, and it appeared a pushup bra was helping her on top.

"It's a two-drink minimum. The second round is eight bucks. You want both now?"

"Sure."

"You need singles?"

Behr nodded and dropped a twenty on her tray, then leaned back and pretended to be a guy pretending to play it cool. He looked around the club casually instead of staring slavishly at the dancer.

"Just give me five back," Behr said when the waitress brought his drinks.

She smiled and counted out five singles.

"I'm looking for a guy who used to come here—"

"You serving him a summons or he owe you money?" the waitress asked, retreating behind the cool facade built during her dancing days.

"Nah"—Behr coughed, acting embarrassed—"I owe *him* money." He saw this changed things for the waitress and went on. "My cousin, actually. He used to work with him, then moved a while back. Asked me to drop by and pay him if I was in the neighborhood. It's only two hundred forty. But I've got it." Behr pat-patted his pocket. "Ted Ford. He here?"

"Tad."

"Right." Behr locked on the guy's name, understanding why he'd missed him in the databases. The waitress scanned the dark room and bit her lip as she came up empty.

"I don't see him. . . . But he's on tonight." The

fact that Ford worked there settled on him. Behr wondered if the guy had seen him come in, made the remnants of cop that still clung to him, and headed out the back. Then he felt the waitress's acrylic-tipped nails give a squeeze to his upper arm. "Oh, there he is. By the bar."

Behr looked and saw a man wrestle a keg in behind the bar. He disappeared for a moment as he kneeled to hook it up to the line. Tad was young, about twenty-five, with doormat sideburns and dark hair carefully combed into a sort of pompadour. Some kind of brilliantine in it caught the strobes in the club. He was big, but by the way he struggled with the keg, Behr could tell he was soft.

"Hey, I should get a cut." It was the waitress, as if she'd just gotten the idea, joking but full of hope.

"Sounds fair," Behr said, handing her the five singles and dashing those hopes.

As Tad Ford walked back out the side door through which he'd come, Behr waited a beat, then stood and followed him out.

Tad flexed his lats as he walked outside and headed for the refrigerated room for a keg of Busch Light. If he worked here long enough, the kegs would start to feel like quart bottles. He reached for the silver handle of the walk-in and felt himself lurch forward out of control as he was shoved facefirst into the door of the refrigerated room.

"What the fu—?" Tad said, bouncing off the door a little, unhurt, spinning around and looping a lazy right hook at his attacker. Tad's brain flashed that someone—Rudy probably—was jerking around with him, but his eyes went wide when he caught sight of a big man, a stranger.

Behr bobbed the hook by bending his knees. He pulled his blackjack and sapped Ford backhanded across the hipbone as he came back up. Ford squealed and doubled over.

"Goddamn. I'm sorry. I thought you were Rudy fucking with me."

"I'm not Rudy." Behr glared back at him.

"I can see that," Ford whined, straightening up and rubbing his hip. "What do you want, man?"

"What I want to know about, Tad, is you selling stolen bikes." Behr saw Ford's face go ivory with fear. Direct hit. Behr's own pulse raced at the success.

"What?"

"Shut up." Behr pushed him back against the door, grabbing a handful of his shirt. "You lying fuck." He sapped him on the outside of the left thigh, on the peroneal nerve that ran down the leg. He felt Ford buckle and hoisted him up like a flaccid spinnaker. "You sold 'em to Mickey Handley. I want to know where you got 'em."

Tad shook in pain and fear and answered, "I stole them."

"I know you stole them. From who?"

"Kids. They just leave 'em around . . ." Tad saw white and felt his right lower leg burning as if on fire. The big man in front of him had driven the toe of his heavy boot into his shin. It throbbed as Tad's heart pounded.

"Goddamnit, I'm gonna call the cops," Tad whined-threatened.

"No, you're not. Who were you working with?"

"No one," Tad blurted. He'd done the bikes alone. It was the truth and Behr read it as such, confusing as that was. It was only later that Tad thought that maybe the man hadn't just meant the bikes. His answer would've come out different, even though he would never have given up Rooster and Riggi. Behr rolled his wrist flashing the sap for another strike when he heard the club door open with a bang. Behr used his body to hide the sap, then looked over his right shoulder in time to see a bull-necked man, wearing a taut black T-shirt despite the cold, step outside with a wild-haired dancer in tow. He had an air of authority and the easy swagger of a guy about to get blown.

"What the hell's going on?" the man shouted, seeing his trysting spot occupied, the tips of his ears going red in the frosty air. "You better not be selling in my club, Ford."

"No," Tad gurgled, and seemed on the verge of

screaming to Bull Neck for help. Behr knifed him with his eyes, willing him to stay quiet, and somehow he did.

"Selling what? I was looking for the men's room—" Behr tried to fill the silence and wipe away the violence in the air.

"Bullshit," Bull Neck shouted. Behr felt the man try to get a read on him. He considered charging him and cracking his skull on his way to the door. Instead he held his position near Ford and kept cool. "How much does the fat bastard owe you?" Bull Neck finally spoke.

Behr nodded and went with the number he'd used earlier. "Two-forty. He should know the Vikings never cover."

"Do me a favor and take this shit someplace else. I can't be having it here." It was half-demand and half-request, but it seemed like the best out that Behr could hope for in the situation. He cursed to himself, feeling a real chance slipping away. He nodded easily, though, and walked past Bull Neck and his girl and went inside.

Tad, on battered and quaking legs, had nowhere to go but back inside the club as well.

"You look pale, Tad," Reno said as he walked past them.

"You ought to pay your debts," Rudy said to him. Then he heard their laughter.

. . .

Behr had been forced off Ford but he wasn't ready yet to go home empty-handed. The man was connected to foul things. Behr was sure of it. He felt he was on the verge of getting names when they were interrupted, and the idea of walking away now and putting it off to another day killed him. He figured he had a few minutes at least, no matter how sophisticated the girl's charms, before Bull Neck would be back inside to chase him out of the club. He crossed to the far corner and tried to hide in the darkness. A moment later he watched Ford limp in, cast his eyes around, miss him in his hiding spot, and head right for a vestibule by the men's room. Behr saw Ford dial then raise a cell phone to his ear. Even with the distance and the darkness Behr could see it was a prepaid phone— no chance of recovering who Ford was calling. Ford put a finger in his other ear against the noise.

It was like a nightmare come true. Even worse than he had imagined. Tad had almost crapped himself when the huge guy started questioning him. Who the hell was he, and how did he *know*? He seemed coplike but didn't say he was a cop. What other explanation was there? Tad was fucked, that was the one thing he knew for sure. He was screwed blue. The way he saw it there were only two things he could do: Nothing—just squeeze his eyes shut, pretend it never happened, finish his shift, and hope he never saw the huge guy again. Or call Mr. Riggi. It was horrible, but somehow he knew it wasn't all going to go away and that he had to call. There was no sense in waiting, he figured, he might as well rip the Band-Aid off in one shot.

"Yeah." Riggi's voice came through the line, cold and irritated.

"It's Tad Ford."

"Tad," Riggi answered, "I know you're not calling me for your job back or for any kind of favor. Not after you rat-fucked me by walking out."

Tad closed his eyes against the diamond-hard words, the hate, coming through the phone. He pictured him there, in some big modern house—he didn't actually know where Mr. Riggi lived, he had never been invited over—in a silk robe, his bald head gleaming, the sound of ice cubes banging around in a glass of thousand-year-old scotch. He probably had a couple of hot Asian chicks waiting to satisfy his every desire, and now stupid Tad Ford was calling to screw up his night.

"Well, what is it?"

"Mr. Riggi, someone came to see me. He beat me. Fucked up my leg—"

"What's it got to do with me?" Tad could feel Riggi gripping his telephone tightly.

"Maybe nothing, but . . . He was asking about a bike—"

"A goddamned—"

"I know I shouldn't have, but I sold a few, you know, from the pickups a while back." Tad heard a few short breaths of fury, then a quiet voice.

"Where are you calling me from?"

"From work, on a throwaway—"

"Thank god." There was a rush of breath. "This conversation is over. Get out of there. Don't say another word to anyone. You got me, you stupid fuck? I'll call you tomorrow. We'll meet and sort this out."

"I'm sorry, Mr. R., but I swear I didn't say your name. . . ." Tad could've gone on, but he would've been talking to dead air.

Behr slipped out of the club when he saw Ford hang up the phone, figuring his time there was about up. He cast a backward glance on his way out and saw Ford leaning over the rail into the DJ booth. Behr sat in his car, watching the door, wondering if somebody would be showing up for an emergency powwow with Ford, but instead, within three minutes, it was Ford who hurried out. Behr watched him squeeze into an old but well-kept 300 ZX and pull out. He jotted down the plate number and took up a loose and easy tail. He followed him twelve minutes northeast, to a part of town that was choked with low-slung apartment buildings that had units you could pay by the month. The buildings had already started to fall apart and look old by the time the initial construction was finished, and they weren't ever going to look any better before their date with a wrecking ball. Behr nosed toward the curb a half-block back and watched Ford ramble to the lobby door, casting a desperate look behind him. Behr gave it two minutes, saw a light go on in a street-side second-floor window covered by a thin, ratty curtain, then went and checked the mailboxes in the building's foyer. Ford lived in 2-H, and that jibed with the light that had just gone on. Behr walked back to his car, relieved himself on the curb next to it, then climbed in to wait and see who showed for a visit.

SEVENTEEN

THE GODDAMNED MOTHERFUCKING QUIET gnawed at Rooster like a flesh-eating disease. The waiting thing had worn thin on him. He'd had the "just be patient" conversation with Riggi several times over the past four or five months.

This just isn't the kind of thing that's steady, me boy. And in this line you just can't force it when it's not there.

I know, I know.

I've got to find you a new anchor man, and he's got to be the right guy.

I know, I know.

Let it come to you. That's what I've learned you've got to do.

I know, I know.

If you need something, that's never an issue. As

*much cash as you need to get you through, just ask
your captain.*

I know, I know.

But "be patient" wasn't Rooster's stock-in-
trade. Over the past two weeks he'd started to
look on his apartment as a cage. It was a bachelor
style on a street busy with big trucks and whores
on the way out to the fairgrounds. He had a
double bed, a television and a boom box on a
baker's rack, and a chin-up bar in the doorway to
the bathroom. It was supposed to be temporary
before Riggi put him in the next house with whoever would be his new partner. But the weeks had
gone on and he was climbing the walls. He'd been
talking aloud to himself for the past few days.

On the other hand the idle time had yielded
something positive for him: size. Twenty-five
pounds of solid brick-shit muscle. Time in the
gym, supplements that provided hundreds of
grams of whey-protein isolates, creatine, ATP, and
a cycle on anabolics, had made him different
than he had ever been before. Despite his five-foot-
six stature, he now had the musculature of a
slugging American League first baseman. He
could push more weight, for more reps, and
recover faster than ever before. He incorporated a
system called plyometrics into his routine after
reading about it in a weight-lifting magazine.
Down at the gym he'd stack aerobic steps into a

tower that reached his chest and leap up onto it from a stationary position. He'd do it until his legs shook and his lungs were set to explode, then he'd drop and bang out push-ups until his arms seized up on him. After the workouts he'd peel off his sweat-soaked shirt and pace past the mirrors on the way to his locker, taking in his ballooning pecs and the ropy veins cording down his neck. His jaw bulged from having been clenched in effort for the past two hours, and he'd snarl at any fags in the locker room that looked at him too long.

One downside of the program: He had so much damn energy, near aggression, that he was practically bugging. *Have faith, baby,* he told himself, *a change is gonna come.*

Then the phone rang like sweet relief.

"Hello?"

"Oscar."

"What's up, boss?"

"I need you to do something for me."

"Anything," Rooster said, meaning it, because *anything* would get him out of his apartment.

"Tad."

"You want me to do that?" Rooster was not hesitant, only surprised. Tad, the pussy, had quit, because he didn't have a taste for the work anymore and because he was so whipped sick in love with his dancer whore. Not to mention the crank.

He'd screwed up the operation and had now made him and Riggi vulnerable.

There was a quiet static on the line and no reply to his question.

"You know where he lives these days?"

"Yeah," Rooster said, picturing the cheap-ass apartment building just beyond Broad Ripple. Unlike his own dump, which at least didn't pretend to be anything else, Tad's place was supposed to be for the upwardly mobile professional type.

"Only some fucked-up yuppies would live in a place like this," he'd told Tad on the grand tour. Weak-sister Tad had looked like he was ready to cry at that one.

"What's your time frame?" Rooster asked.

"Yesterday," Riggi answered. "Yesterday would've been ideal, in fact. *Before* some guy'd come around asking him questions." Riggi's words brought a cold stab of fear racing through Rooster's chest that was quickly chased by a hot bolt of anger. Oh, he'd take good motherfucking care of Tad.

"What kind of questions? What kind of guy?"

"I don't know. I don't want to know. We'll talk later, in person . . . if you can do this."

"Do this, man?" Rooster said, a luxurious feeling of loose power rolling down through his limbs like syrup. "It's *already* done."

Rooster was half embarrassed at the glow he

knew was on his cheeks at Riggi's asking him to do this important thing. It thrilled him deeply, that he couldn't deny. It was a thing you couldn't ask just anybody to do, nor could just anybody do it. All the same, thrill or no thrill, it surely needed to be done because the idea of going back to jail for a long stretch was unacceptable. Rooster didn't mind his little apartment all of a sudden, compared with the alternative. He climbed up into a small crawl space at the top of his closet. The apartment wasn't so much a cage now as it was a secret headquarters, a base of operations. As bad as the waiting had become, things could be a hell of a lot worse. But he wasn't about to let that happen. Rooster found the hidden plastic box by feel and brought it down. Inside the box, wrapped in an old rag-wool sock, was a stainless Taurus .38. He filled it with soft points, set himself up with two speed loaders, did seventy push-ups, fifty squats, took a piss, and looked at himself in the mirror for a long, centering moment. Then he put on a windbreaker that wasn't heavy enough for the weather but had good pockets, shut the lights, and stepped out.

Tad pressed a bag of frozen Tater Tots to his throbbing shin and tried to control his breathing. He meant to let it out in a calming, hissing growl the way he'd learned in the lone Pilates class he'd taken three months back. He'd gone to the studio after hearing it was where Michelle trained. She wasn't there that day, and by the end of his session Tad was wringing wet with sweat and felt clumsy and stupid. The breath came out a warbling whine. He was scared. He looked around his place and considered running. He had seven hundred in the bank, but he could only pull three hundred from the ATM at one time. The dipshit Indian branch manager had convinced him on this limit when he opened the account.

"This way, if you lose the card, someone can only take three hundred before the card is canceled," he'd said, the push-start, cow-loving bastard. Tad was sorry he even had the bank account and didn't have the cash on hand. He'd needed to open it, though, when he went on the payroll at the Lady. He had a check coming to him in two days, five hundred fifty after withholding. The timing was a bitch. He'd be able to make it a lot farther and for longer if he had that money. He got up and paced the room in a limping gait, wishing he hadn't finished the last of his stash when he smoked up before work. He grabbed a bottle of Wild Turkey from the kitchen cabinet and took a pull that made him shiver. He limped over and sat down on the couch and looked at the phone, thinking of calling Michelle. Things had been going well with her, small steps, a little conversation here, a look there, and he hated to rush it, but maybe he should call her and ask her to go with him. He felt in his pocket for the hand-carved and-painted wooden key chain from Ciudad del Sol, La Frontera. He'd given her a matching one. She didn't know it, but he felt the closeness in their both having the same one. He picked up the phone and dialed her. Rudy from the club, in a rare moment of generosity, had slid her home number Tad's way several weeks back.

Tad tried to control his breathing again. Failed. He wondered what he would say should Michelle answer. *"Hey, 'Chelle, it's Tad. . . . I know we've only been friends around work, but you wanna road trip with me?"* It sounded fucking lame even to him. After four rings, her machine picked up. Her voice, low and sexy, asking for a message while Ryan Adams played in the background. Tad was almost relieved that she didn't answer. He hung up and cradled the Wild Turkey and wondered what to do next.

Sitting surveillance was a mental exercise in calm focus and patience, and knocking a guy around was no way to set up for it. Behr sat still behind the wheel staring up at the lit window that was Ford's apartment, coming down from the electric high the bracing had put him on. It was impossible, he had found, for him to experience physical violence without the adrenaline jag by-product he called the "come-down." To combat it he reached across the front seat and took a Red Bull from the little Igloo that was always stocked with them. It was warm and syrupy, but he downed it and set his mind to the task: watching.

Behr switched on the police scanner he kept in his car. It brought back the old days as it fought off boredom. He looked up at the window while he listened to calls.

No matter how much, Behr talked to himself, which was another thing he did to focus himself and pass the time on stakeout, *you never get used to it.* It was the same with death, he thought, but didn't say it aloud. No matter how much exposure to it, for however long, he never became immune to the hollowness in the pit of his stomach brought on by a dead body. He thought back to his first week on the force, when he was just a kid. He worked Meridian Park then, a nice, quiet section that wasn't known for its action. But he'd encountered two dead bodies within that first week on the job. On his second night there was a motorcycle versus an eighteen-wheeler motor-vehicle casualty. Behr and his training officer, Gene Sasso, a portly vet nearing his pension, were first on the scene. The biker was dead when they got there. His head and legs were twisted at impossible angles, and he was barefoot, his boots blown off and strewn around the blacktop. The truck driver sat on the side of the road, his head in his hands, sobbing.

"Check him for ID," Sasso commanded.

Behr swallowed and reached into the rider's back pocket. He had the momentary sensation that the biker would animate and grab his hand to stop the invasion. But the biker was through moving. The man was dead weight that barely rippled when Behr pulled the wallet free. *Meat* was the word that crossed his young mind. As well as the disquieting sensation that everyone, even he, was headed for that state eventually.

On his fifth day, a call came in from a distraught woman. Her boyfriend had been unreachable for three days. Behr and Sasso were sent to force entry into his third-floor apartment and found the guy, a twenty-six-year-old white male, draped over the arm of his couch. He had overdosed, a strange occurrence in a nice neighborhood where hard drugs weren't supposed to be. Young Officer Behr learned that day that all the fluids drain out of the body in death, creating a vile pooling. The body was rigor mortised in its awkward position, and they couldn't figure out how he would be carried down the narrow staircase.

"Break him," said the seventy-year-old coroner when he arrived on the scene. "Straighten him out."

"Sir?" Behr asked.

"Step on the joints, they'll give."

Behr rolled the corpse to the floor and did as he was told, as only the young are able. It was like crushing corrugated cardboard refrigerator boxes underfoot. Sasso hadn't even helped. It was a question of seniority, youth being served. The older you got, the closer you came to death, the more you wanted to avoid it, Behr figured.

Eight months later Behr was transferred to Haughville, where death was a much more frequent occurrence. He never did get too comfortable with it though. He just learned to put the thought of it away as the body bags were zipped shut.

Rooster arrived on Tad's street and drove it once at speed. The maroon El Camino wouldn't attract any attention in this part of town. Still, after checking the building, Rooster planned on parking a few blocks away and hoofing it over in the shadows so that no one would notice his plates. He wasn't sure how he'd actually do the thing. Maybe he'd push his way through the lobby door, then knock at Tad's apartment. Tad wouldn't be expecting him and in his surprise, since Rooster wasn't a stranger, would probably open the door. Or Rooster could buzz from the lobby and call Tad down for some spurious reason. He could even call him with the cloned cell phone he'd picked up a week earlier.

First he wanted to get the lay of the land, though, and even as he passed Tad's building at twenty-five, thirty miles an hour, something felt wrong to him. He didn't know exactly what he felt. Maybe he was just jumpy. He made three consecutive rights and wound up at the head of the block once again. He killed the lights coming around the last corner and rolled alongside the curb, shutting the engine. From his position Rooster could just make out Tad's building a few hundred yards away. There were a dozen dormant cars dotting the street between him and it. None of them were patrol cars or seemed to be unmarked police vehicles. There were no people out at all. An instinct kept Rooster in his car, though, slouched low in the driver's seat, his fingers drumming lightly on the wheel. He waited. Fifteen minutes. Forty-five. He didn't know what he was waiting for, but he didn't want to hurry, either. It would be an act of extreme ego to walk straight into that building carrying a gun, and ego, Rooster knew, was dangerous. *Better to be smart,* he thought.

It had been five and a half hours and Behr looked ahead to his next move. No one was coming to meet with Ford. It seemed unlikely that Ford was on his way out to meet anyone, either. Behr's pressure tactic was a bust. It had been a slow night for the Indy P.D. as well. A few DUI arrests earlier; an alarm response at a Hooters, but no one apprehended at the scene; a speeder resisting; domestics; the usual drunk and disorderlies outside the bars on Lafayette. Then the low static of the scanner was punctured by a call.

Units respond. Eagle Creek Park. It was a recreational area ten miles northwest of the city with golf courses, boating, archery ranges, and cross-country jogging trails.

Human remains discovered by a dog walker. Advanced decomposition. Appears to be Caucasian youth. M.E. in route. . . .

Icy pinpricks ran up Behr's arms. He turned over the car motor and jerked it into gear.

Son of a bitch. Rooster jolted aware at the sound of the engine. He might've been in a heavy-lidded state of rest and missed it, but he was almost sure that no one had just gotten into a car. He hadn't heard a door slam. No, the driver starting the Olds down the street near Tad's building had been *in it.* For a long time. It didn't seem like a coincidence. The son of a bitch was staking out Tad. Rooster had the idea to drive down the street quick, box the guy in, and do him. But he resisted. Then the car lurched away from the curb and once again the street fell silent. After several hours of stiffening waiting, Rooster felt a charged looseness instantly return to his limbs. His breath came in knifing jabs and he worked to slow it down. He touched the gun handle in his right jacket pocket and felt the outline of the speed loaders in his left. He considered moving his car off the block and walking back to Tad's place.

Fuck it, he decided. He'd already been sitting there long enough to have been ID'd by anybody looking. He reached behind his seat for a faded ball cap and pulled it down low to his eyes. He exhaled hard and stepped out into the cool morning air. His feet hardly made a sound as he walked down the sidewalk. He looked around as he neared the building. Not a soul was in sight. He approached the lobby door and tried it. It opened right up with a slight rattle. The latch bolt had rusted to the faceplate in the unlocked position. Good luck for Rooster, bad luck for Tad.

Rooster went up the stairs toward Tad's apartment door. He'd only been there once, but the building layout, everything, seemed familiar to him, like he'd lived there his whole life. He thought about whoever had been around to the Lady questioning Tad, wondered if it was the same guy who was outside. *Probably was,* he figured. Even dumb-ass Tad would be on his guard after being talked to, Rooster realized, and decided he'd better go into the apartment unannounced. He walked quietly down the hall and reached Tad's door. It was cheap hollow-core, painted builder's white, with six fake inlaid panels. It had a brass knob lock with no extra dead bolt. *That's just penny wise, Tad,* Rooster thought, as he held his breath and listened at the door. He heard some muffled sounds, a rustling from inside. He focused on a spot a few inches to the right of the knob. He flexed his knees and felt his thighs, thick with new muscle.

Tad had reached the dregs of the Wild Turkey and at some point below the label had taken to crying. It was a quiet weeping that had no real direction. The air in the apartment had grown stagnant and close, and not sure what to wear and what to pack, he had taken off his T-shirt and jeans and was down to his skivvies and socks. He touched his stomach, lapping over his underwear band, and felt wretched and cried some more. He was spun out. All his decisions during the past year or so had led him here. Maybe his poor judgment went back even further than that. He had done bad things for money, and he hadn't quit soon enough. Selling the bikes had been plain stupid, and not even that profitable. The smoking didn't improve matters, and he hadn't tried to quit that soon enough, either. Now that he had to leave, he could admit to himself that things at the club—with Michelle—weren't going to work out any better than the rest of it.

"I need help," Tad said aloud, his voice sounding weird and pathetic to his ears. He wasn't religious. He didn't go to church like Mr. Riggi, and he didn't know how to pray. But something about speaking aloud felt right. It wasn't talking to himself. He just felt someone, Jesus, was listening. He put down the bottle and moved out of the chair onto his knees. He moaned as his tender shin met the floor and took his weight.

"I need help," he said again. "Please. I want to change my life. I know I can be good." He thought for a moment, unsure of how to continue, of what words to say. He wasn't exactly waiting for a sign, just a thread to follow. Then there was a loud bang and the front door jumped. A current of fear shot through Tad's chest. There was another bang. A bright piece of brass, part of the lock, broke free and flew through the air. The door swung open, moving through its arc in slow motion, and revealed a stocky man in a cap and a windbreaker.

Rooster, Tad realized after a second, all muscled up. He saw himself there in his underwear and with a tear-stained face. Embarrassment flooded over his skin like hot water.

"Rooster," he said aloud, seeing his old partner's lip curl up in a smirk. Then Rooster's hand went into his pocket and came out holding a pair of scissors. He pointed them at Tad. *It's not scissors.* Tad's mind struggled to catch up. *Gun.* He saw fire.

EIGHTEEN

BEHR ROLLED PAST the entry booth, still unmanned due to the early hour, and drove into Eagle Creek Park. He followed the road around the lake until he saw a string of official vehicles, cruisers, unmarked cars, ambulances, and the M.E.'s meat wagon. A young uniform waved Behr to a stop. He put down his window.

"Officer."

"How ya doin'?" the kid asked. They'd never met, but he read Behr as on the job or retired.

"Frank Behr," he said, sticking his hand out the window and shaking with the officer. "Who's controlling the scene?"

"Detective Petrie for now."

"Don't know him. Is Cale here?" Cale was a lieutenant, a veteran Behr went way back with.

"Vacation, I think."

"Who's down from the coroner's?"

"Gannon."

Behr smiled. "Good. She'll vouch for me."

The kid shrugged, showing fatigue, and pointed. "Pull your vehicle onto the shoulder." Behr did it and got out.

"Have someone radio back that you're cleared or I'll have to come find you."

Behr nodded, then tried to make his last question sound breezy. "Captain Pomeroy's on his way, right?"

"Yep."

Behr made his way to the scene at a more than casual pace.

There was a semicircle of backs standing in tall grass twenty yards from the road. They were ringed around what Behr knew was the body. There were the familiar sounds of a crime scene: radio static, boots on gravel, keys and flashlights swinging on belts, hot coffee being gingerly sipped, the rustle of nylon parkas. Evidence collection kits, looking like orange tackle boxes, were open, tamping down winter-yellow grass at their feet. A few yards off, speaking on a cell phone, was Dr. Jean Gannon, a sturdy woman just past fifty, dressed in cargo pants and a polar fleece top. She began shaking her head at Behr's approach.

"Uh-huh, and send down those dental records,

too. Bye." She closed her phone. "Oh, shit, you're not here. You are *not* here."

"I am, babe, get used to it," Behr said. She smiled despite herself. "Can you make me bona fide?"

"Hal, let 'em know at the perimeter that my guest found me," Jean called out to a cop nearby.

Behr had worked with Gannon a bit when she first joined the M.E.'s office. She'd been a housewife and mother before going back to school and starting her career in her forties. Her husband left her after her first year, thanks to the job and its long hours. "He was leaving me, anyway, the job just gave him an excuse," she'd said when Behr consoled her. She loved her work, and they'd built a friendship over long discussions about forensics.

"So you were out for a morning bike ride and figured you'd say hi?"

"Yeah, about like that. I'm on a case and your rise and shine might have something to do with it."

"Don't tell me you're on a case." Her brows pinched together in regret. "You know you're persona non grata and veal piccata."

"Okay, I'm not on a case, then. Can you tell me what you've got?"

Jean looked up the road in concern, scanning the cluster of uniforms there.

"He's not here yet," Behr said of Pomeroy.

"Oh, all right. C'mon."

Behr followed her over to the body, and Jean shooed away the cops, crime scene photographers, and medical assistants.

Body wasn't quite the word for what lay at their feet. It was skeletal, with brown scraps of flesh hanging off the shinbones and ribs like old banana peels. The hair and facial skin were largely eroded. The eyes were gone, the nose as well. The jaw jutted out and the teeth grinned in a silent scream. The corpse was on its right side and curled, so Behr couldn't tell how tall the person had been, but he or she couldn't have been much over five feet. A wave of dread rolled through him at the possibility that this could be Jamie Gabriel. It vied with a feeling of hope, one that Behr tried to reject, that it *was* Jamie and that he would have his answer.

"Did it happen here?"

"I don't think so. The position shows placement, and the grass has grown up through the body, so he's been here for some time."

"He?" Behr steeled himself for the information.

"Yeah. White male. The hyoid bone shows some damage, so it might be a strangulation."

"How old?"

"Around twenty."

Behr breathed again. "You sure on the age?" Jean shrugged, a gesture loaded with information. It told of her thousands of hours of study and experience in unraveling the secrets the dead hold. It was committed and sure, and yet it surrendered to the utter mystery of her trade. "What's your outside minimum age?"

"Tough to tell. There's been so much weather degradation. Seventeen, sixteen at the youngest." Alive or dead, Jamie Gabriel's fifteenth birthday wasn't until the next year.

"Thanks, Jean."

"Well, I hope that's what you needed to know."

"I should go."

"Yah."

No closer to an outcome in his case but glad of it, Behr took a last look at the remains on the ground and turned to leave.

As he drove out of the park, a gleaming Crown Vic was coming down the one-lane road toward him. It was piloted by a man holding an aluminum travel coffee cup to his lips. Behr and the opposing driver locked eyes through their windshields as they squeezed by each other. The man driving the Crown Vic was Captain Pomeroy.

Numbers streamed through Carol Gabriel's mind as she pulled her running shoes from the back of the closet and tied them on her feet. Awful statistics she'd come to know. More than eight hundred thousand were currently listed as missing persons across the country. Eighty-five to 90 percent of them were children. Two thousand cases a day were logged into the National Crime Information Center. Most of them were family related—a divorced parent violating custody orders—and 90 percent of them were recovered without incident. But there were still so many of them who were kids, and who weren't recovered. Of those, the ones who weren't recovered, 40 percent were determined dead. One was the number of the missing that she cared about. And four hundred and fifty-six was how many days Jamie had been gone. It was a sickening figure that made her feel weak even as she stretched for her run of two miles.

She started at a light trot, about a nine-minute-mile pace, the mottled asphalt passing beneath her. The cold made her breath cloud. Two thousand was the number of flyers she had posted showing her son's picture and listing his height, weight, description, and what she believed he was wearing that morning. Four gross was the amount of buttons she'd had made and distributed, all bearing Jamie's face and their phone number. Zero was the number of calls they had received for the effort. The sweat was starting to come now, despite the chill in the air, sliding down her chest, collecting on and spilling over her brow. She wanted to stop, to double over and gasp already, but she pushed on by force of will. She'd never liked running, it had always been Paul's idea of fun, or recreation, or cleansing. For her it was a chore.

Two-thirds was the percentage of couples that went on to divorce after losing a child. This number bounced around in her mind as she put one heel in front of the other. The shared failure, the constant reminder of grief that the other provided, was just too much for marriages to sustain. She knew she was one of the doomed majority now. The feeling between her and Paul had been shocked and paralyzed in an instant, and then had slowly decayed, and had finally fossilized.

She stopped dead. Blood pounded in her temples. Her breath wouldn't come. Her legs were unable to carry her another step. She lacked the forward thrust to go through with the separation and divorce. She couldn't imagine summoning the energy it would take to have the discussion. She stood there doubled at the waist; the only sounds her gasping and a cold wind blowing across the neighborhood.

Behr dropped the grocery bags on his kitchen counter and set about cooking up his breakfast. It took six eggs, a half pound of bacon, four slices of wheat toast, and a quart of orange juice to lay down his appetite, which had finally made a comeback. As he ate, he tried to decide which way his disappointment over the remains he'd seen at the park was leaning. Like he'd told the Gabriels at the beginning, *an* answer was the best they could all hope for. Still, as fatigue set in after the long night, he couldn't help being glad it wasn't Jamie who was left to rot out in Eagle Creek.

He took a long, scalding shower before getting into bed and set his alarm for six hours hence. It'd be 3:00 in the afternoon when it rang, if he slept that long, and time for him to give Tad, or a few of his coworkers down at the Golden Lady, another try. Behr closed his eyes, hoping that sleep would come quick and that when it did, it didn't bring the dark wraiths of his past. He shook his head on the pillow to wipe away the memory of that skull out in the park, and the image of what his own son must look like nestled inside his mahogany box at St. John's.

It was hours later, in the afternoon, but before the alarm went off, that he heard it. Someone was inside his place. Sleep had come, black and formless, but it was gone for good now. The sounds of tapping and a low cough came from his living room. He slid his feet out from under the sheets and put them on the floor. He eased open his night-table drawer and pushed back a few pieces of paper to reveal a squat hunk of metal: his Charter Arms Bulldog .44. He'd carried a .38 for almost ten years as a cop, and then he'd tried a 9 mm for the higher capacity; he'd seen what those calibers could do and the work they left undone. He preferred the heavier round now. Only five shots, the Bulldog was a belly gun, but most shootings were over in two, and if he couldn't get it done with that many, he deserved whatever was coming back at him. Behr wrapped his fist around the handle and stepped quietly down the hall toward his living room.

There were two of them. White guys. Thirtyish. Short and solid, dressed in loose-fitting pullovers and baggy jeans. They both had similar facial hair: chin beards and mustaches. They were practiced at being quiet and weren't even working that hard at it. One, with close-cropped hair, sat behind Behr's desk looking at his computer monitor, occasionally clicking the mouse. The other sat in the television chair, some of Behr's case files on his lap. The guy wasn't going over them, though, and instead looked bored.

Behr stepped out of the hall and trained his gun on the one seated in his chair, but spoke to the one at the desk.

"Why are you here and who sent you?" Behr's voice was calm, though he knew they were armed. He was really just putting on a show; even at a hundred yards he'd be able to tell they were cops.

The one at the desk leaned back, put his hands behind his head, and stretched, as if the conversation was taking place in the station bullpen. "I'm

Nye, he's Feeley." The guy gestured with his chin to his partner. "Nice nap?"

Feeley, in the chair, snickered.

"That's licensed, right?" Nye asked of Behr's gun.

Plainclothes donkeys, Behr thought, and lowered the Bulldog, though he didn't give an answer.

"Did you break my lock?" Behr asked, surprised at how heavily he'd been sleeping.

"It was open," Feeley piped up in a reedy voice. His partner shot him a look.

"Your lock's fine. Feeley's got a good touch."

Behr nodded his appreciation.

"Look, I know Pomeroy saw me at Eagle Creek this morning, but a call would've done it."

Now Nye laughed a little. Behr knew the way Pomeroy worked. Whether he was corrupt or not couldn't be proved, and was almost beside the point. He did, however, like to have two or three teams who cowboyed for him at all times. Guys willing to do the things a metro police captain needed done in order to keep his department running. They'd deliver messages, administer beatings, find evidence, or make it go away. It was as much a part of American law enforcement as a flag patch sewn on a uniform sleeve. "You're not a friend of the department. And that goes for your friends, too."

Behr flashed on Jean Gannon with regret. "What'd Pomeroy do to her?" he wondered aloud.

"Nothing much. Just tore her a new one."

"And he sent you here to tell me to stay away?"

Nye and Feeley looked across the room at each other. "He wants to know what you're working on." Behr noticed that neither of them had mentioned Pomeroy by name or rank. They didn't blink at the sight of him holding a gun, either. They were well trained as far as Rottweilers went.

"I'm not working on anything. It was an old thing. Just wanted to check if you had an ID on your body." Behr wasn't in the business of helping other people do their jobs, and when it came to Pomeroy, the customer-service window was all the way closed.

"Uh-uh," Nye said.

"No?" Behr asked, mildly surprised his answer wasn't good enough.

"Forget the skelly at the park. We got a bouncer with his guts shot out, and we got you at the Golden Lady making said bouncer nervous a few hours before it happened." Behr took the words like bad medicine. He looked over at Feeley, who just sat there nodding.

"What time was he shot?"

" 'Round near morning. Right in his apartment," Nye said, before glancing back with some interest at something on the computer monitor.

The hairs raced up the back of Behr's neck. It

must have been right after he'd left. The shooter had probably waited and watched him go.

"So what are you working on, man?" Feeley wheezed from the chair.

Donkeys, Behr thought of his visitors and didn't say a word.

"Come on, Frank, you must be working a case . . . unless you've gone perv on us." Nye pointed to the monitor. Behr realized the cop had been checking the Web sites he'd been surfing.

"Don't be a fucking idiot," Behr barked. It had the effect of a slap to Nye's face. The cop jerked the computer's plug out of the power strip.

"You can get fifteen years for even visiting these sites. We can subpoena this and take it in."

"I'll get a lawyer. Illegal search. Breaking and entering. Stuff like that."

"Still, you won't see this for a long time," Nye said of the computer.

Behr shrugged. He didn't care. He hardly needed it now. Knowledge and dismay collided in his chest. While his progress must've been real, had struck a nerve, it was all gone now. His case had fallen apart. He was angry and in no mood for the pair currently in his living room.

"We're waiting," Nye tried again.

"You think *I* did the bouncer?"

"No. But our guy wants to know why you're in it."

"I've said all I'm gonna say."

Feeley stood up from the chair and planted his feet wide. "We're supposed to bring you down for a talk if you acted this way."

Behr put his gun down on top of a bookshelf and dropped into a left-foot-forward stance. "Better get some more guys."

NINETEEN

PAUL LEFT A CLIENT'S OFFICE on Jackson Place, having sold a three-hundred-fifty-thousand-dollar whole life policy, and walked toward South Street, where he'd parked. A small sea of people, mostly parents and grandparents, with their children and grandchildren, filled the streets. They moved toward the Fieldhouse on Pennsylvania, which was lined with an even larger crowd. Paul smelled the fecund odor of hay and animals and urine even before he reached the edge of the crowd and saw it. The circus was in town. He stood and watched the "Pachyderm Parade," a line of elephants, trunk to tail, bearing female riders in red, white, and blue sequined leotards, as it moved up the street. Children in the crowd called out in enthusiastic greeting; the elephants trumpeted randomly in return. The sight stilled Paul. He'd brought Jamie here several years back. Not to the parade when the circus had just arrived, but to the show itself.

He was paralyzed by memory as the elephants' wrinkled brown-gray hulls trundled by. The circus had been a dubious proposition for him and Jamie. When Paul was a kid, he'd never liked them. There was something disturbing about the volume and commotion. He'd loved animals, but there was a frustrated, pathetic quality to the ones in the show. The drugged, impotent cats were sadder than anything else. Only the horses, white with flowing manes, which ran around the ring with riders standing on their backs, were really worth seeing. But he hadn't wanted to project his prejudices on his son. Perhaps his boy would appreciate what millions of other kids did about the circus. So they had come, just the two of them, to the matinee show. Jamie, about five years old at the time, had held Paul's hand and whipped his head about at the crowds and the barkers selling cotton candy, green glow-sticks, and souvenirs.

They'd found their seats and then it started. There was one mad portion, early on in the spectacle, when scores of clowns burst into the ring and began circulating up through the screaming, glow-stick-waving crowd. Many of the clowns carried tall, fake cakes in outstretched hands. Wild music played and the clowns staggered around, comically losing and regaining the balance of the cakes, much to the delight of the youngsters. One particular bald, white-faced, red-nosed fellow, in the classic plaid hobo's outfit, came running down their row shaking hands with the kids. As he approached, Paul felt Jamie curling into him. All of the kids reached out for the white-gloved hand the clown offered, only to have their arm pumped up and down until it seemed the children's laughter would never stop. Jamie burrowed in deeper under his arm as the clown drew nearer, hiding his face completely in Paul's chest when it was his turn. The clown danced around for a second, trying to entice Jamie into a handshake. Jamie was intractable, though, and eventually the clown ran off.

As soon as he'd gone, Jamie peeked back out and looked around.

"It's okay, son, I'm not a big fan of clowns, either," he'd said, admiring his son's stubbornness.

"No." Jamie had shaken his head. "I want one with a cake." None with a cake showed up and the bit ended, and then the tiny poodles came out to jump and flip. Jamie never explained why he wanted to shake one clown's hand and not another's. Paul hadn't asked. He had been content, then, to not understand everything about his mysterious and fascinating boy.

Paul stepped back out of his memories just as the last of the elephants, and an Uncle Sam on stilts bringing up the rear, passed by. He looked at the crowd, at the children bundled against the cold March. The sky was slate gray, as if the sun had just quit. He felt the chill of evil lying over it all and knew no amount of coats and mittens would make these children safe. Despite the cold, he found himself soaked in sweat, his chest heaving with emotion. This was his life now, the sun frozen over and dark as day.

Bullshit and bravado were a quarter of the gig when it came to police work. This was according to Behr's experience. Paperwork and eating shit were another quarter. Taking care of yourself, staying sharp and busy, and sitting on your ass the right way made up the rest, save a sliver for luck. Behr had witnessed it to be true many times in his career, and today was no different as far as the first bit went. Nye and Feeley hadn't wanted a piece of him or his problems. They had left, loudly but peacefully, suggesting he come clean or, better yet, drop off the face of the earth for a while. He had a moment's satisfaction at their frustration as they carted his computer away, but the fact was, his case had gone down the dumper.

He sat motionless in his living room for a long time, until the sound of the alarm bleeping from the bedroom stirred him. He willed himself up, shut it off, and got fully dressed. Thoughts of what to do next were slow to come and sluggish upon arrival. Tad Ford had been shot dead at home. After talking to Behr. And he had missed it. He could try to be heartened, that he'd applied pressure and someone had made a move. But enthusiasm like that was for beat cops in their twenties or detectives just out of the bag. In order to take the next step in this case, he now faced having to unravel a murder. No. Not in this world. Ford could've been popped for a dozen reasons. He and his crimes might have been miles away from Jamie Gabriel's disappearance in the first place.

Behr got his keys and went out to his car. He had never been particularly good at starting over. The problem lay in letting go of the labor and results he'd already put forth. They were gone now. They no longer existed, that time and effort. If the decision was not to abandon the case, then there was no choice other than to pick up the strands and begin again. It was unfair that work done well could come to nothing and had to be done again. But like time and effort, fair only existed in the past. Behr headed toward Tibbs, where he'd gotten on the scent in the first place. He hoped he'd find inspiration there. He didn't know where else to go.

Paul sat on the curb a few feet away from his car. He crossed his arms against the wind. He didn't deserve what had happened. No family did. But he was plagued by a secret knowledge. He hadn't wanted a child. He'd believed that this world was no place for a baby, for any innocent life. He'd had doubts about his own ability to raise a kid. He'd had greater doubts as to why he should. His vanity didn't run toward re-creating in his own image, and that's what having children had felt like back then. But Carol had pushed him on it. She had a certitude he'd envied. It was time, she'd said. He'd held her off, month upon month. He'd dug in and grabbed a season here, a quarter there, using various reasons. A move. The need for more money to come in. A trip that would be easier to take if she weren't pregnant. He'd been waiting for his own sign, an annunciation that he should have a child of his own. Finally, after a good year and a half had passed, he'd realized there was no mystical sign coming for him. He had talked about it with his own father. *It doesn't work that way for men,* his father had said. *You only figure out what's important about it later.*

"How do you know if you're supposed to do it? And when?" Paul had asked.

His father had just smiled. His cigarette-stained teeth barely showed behind his lips, but his eyes had twinkled in a way Paul had never seen before. He knew the answer then though his father hadn't said the word. *Faith.*

Even after they had conceived, after Carol had come out of the bathroom giddy with excitement, holding the stick with the line that had turned blue, the idea of it hadn't clicked for Paul. Even after the doctor confirmed the test, and Carol started to grow and get sick in the mornings, Paul hadn't felt sure about what they'd done. But three months in they had gone for the first sonogram. The room was small and dark. An exam table covered by a paper strip and carts full of equipment awaited them. A nurse came in and moved the sensor over Carol's gel-covered belly and Paul turned toward the monitor. There, in the pitch darkness that was her womb, was a tiny figure outlined in gray, and the hummingbird pulse that was his heartbeat, like a ray of light that came piercing the blackness. There was life. There was Jamie.

Then the nurse put away her sonogram sensor and placed another instrument against Carol's abdomen. This one emitted a washy liquid background noise that filled the closetlike space of the exam room. Sitting there on the curb all these years later, Paul could still hear it, the sound of his son's heart coming through the Doppler, a rhythmic swishing, an insistent hammering. His doubts had vanished in that moment.

This was where Behr had said it happened, Paul thought of the spot where he sat on Tibbs. He looked up and down the street. Could he go door to door knocking, gauging those who answered? If they looked suspicious, could *he* push his way in and search those closets, attics, basements, and crawl spaces for his son or any clue that he had been there? Why couldn't he? It seemed possible and yet impossible at once. The front doors lining the block were like a crooked, mocking smile. They would shut him out for all time.

The sound of a car passing was distant in his ears. In rebound effect he heard a door slam and feet land on the pavement. A dark shadow crossed over him.

"You might not want to sit here too long, we got thunder bumpers coming in."

Paul looked from the large boots that had stopped before him, up the endless legs and broad torso. He tilted his head to see Behr's face. He nodded and looked off over the big man's shoulder at the angry clouds that loomed in the sky. Neither man said anything for quite a while. They merely absorbed the street, the smell of coming rain in the air.

"Why do you do it?" Paul asked, aloud it seemed.

"It's what I know now. One foot in front of the other. Automatic." Behr thought for a moment. "Originally, because I wanted answers, I guess. I knew they were out there, that I could find them if I worked hard enough." He fell silent, and Paul considered what he had heard. "Now I see that I can't know, not really. Especially the why. I see that now." Behr leaned back against Paul's car and looked up at the clouds.

Paul climbed to his feet. It was hard to talk, but he wanted to. "It's my fault, you know. *I* always believed in a work ethic. That it wouldn't serve him well to have it too easy. It was my idea, his job delivering papers." Paul had finally said it, what he'd believed but had been unable to voice since the first moment Jamie had gone missing.

Paul glanced to Behr and saw pain in his eyes and an understanding of guilt that was perhaps deeper even than his own.

"I can't tell you much about fatherhood—my term only lasted seven years." Behr spoke, his voice rough-edged as fresh-quarried limestone. "All I know is that you make 'em and raise 'em. You love the hell out of 'em. But they live in the world and every day it takes a piece of 'em. Until maybe there's nothing left."

The landscape Behr's words created was too bleak for Paul to endure. "But we're their fathers. We're supposed to protect them."

Behr knew he was right. He nodded, a longtime resident welcoming a newer arrival to his neighborhood. The two sonless fathers rested a moment in their defeat.

Paul finally broke it. "Are you here looking for more clues?" he wondered with guarded hope.

Behr shrugged. "A lot's changed since yesterday."

Paul looked to him.

"You want closure," Behr said, his voice harder

now. "But there is no closure, not in something like this"—and he added the rest, perhaps cruelly, but necessarily, he believed—"when a murder is involved."

Paul had mulled the idea already, so Behr's words didn't stop him. "Is that what happened to your son?" he asked.

"No." Fat drops of cold rain began to fall. Paul flipped up his suit jacket collar against it. Behr did nothing.

"I meant what I said. I want to be a part of this thing. I will hire someone else if that's what it takes." Paul's words weren't a threat. In that instant they became a stark reality. And Behr recognized in the same instant that he didn't want off it.

"You're putting me in a position here," Behr said, rubbing his chin. It was axiomatic not to take employers along on cases, on the endless stakeouts and the dead ends, lest they confuse surveillance with just sitting around. A chilly wind joined the accelerating raindrops that now splattered on the street between them.

"I won't bring any expectations, if that's what you're worried about."

Behr looked at Paul and nodded as if that was his concern and not what he had seen on the Web sites. Behr knew those images would destroy the man across from him. "Why do you want to put yourself through this?"

"I can't give him my love anymore. The only thing I've got left is my labor." Paul sounded like a preacher when he said it, and while Behr hadn't known the man to be religious, he understood the flame of loss and the changes it wrought.

The rain began to teem, but that wasn't what convinced him. "Don't wear aftershave. I can't be in the car all day with the smell."

"I don't use it."

"Good. I'll pick you up tomorrow, when you're off work."

Paul nodded and both men moved to their cars to get out of the rain.

TWENTY

THEY SAT IN BEHR'S TORONADO, parked across the street from the Golden Lady. Behr didn't feel great about reentering the club in light of what had happened since he'd been there, especially with a civilian in tow, but something in him had snapped and crossed over. Perhaps his tolerance for the terrible things that can happen to children had run dry, but he knew now he was not going to back off this case. He looked over at Paul, who was staring out the windshield, and considered how much it would be fair to tell him of his dealings with Ford and what had happened since then. *More than I'm going to* was the amount he arrived at.

"Listen, when we interview people, I do the talking," Behr said. Paul nodded almost imperceptibly. "Whatever I say, even if it doesn't make sense, whatever you hear—keep a poker face."

"Poker face."

"Don't try to help. And when I say it's time to leave it alone—we go."

"Okay."

Behr took another look at the club. If anybody inside was upset about Ford's passing, they weren't showing it. There was no black bunting hanging outside in his honor. Just a board announcing drink specials and featured entertainers.

"All right. Go in and sit at the bar. Don't talk to anyone much. I'll come in a few minutes later. We don't know each other unless I say so. Good?"

"Good."

Paul got out of the car and walked toward the club. Behr watched him. His stride was full of purpose, an attempt at concealing his nerves. Behr had him as anxious the minute he'd picked him up. Paul was dressed in carefully selected clothes: khaki pants, trail shoes, button-down shirt under a maroon pullover sweater, and canvas barn jacket. Not too fancy, not too sloppy. He didn't know what he was in for and so had tried to be ready for everything. He hadn't done badly at it, either.

Paul breathed deep as he made his way inside the Golden Lady. He could feel the bass of the music in his crotch even as he paid his cover charge. Entering the main room of the dark club, he felt dizzy and strange. A flash of white and pink flesh tore across his field of vision. He hardly dared to look. Brass and smoke and mirrors and strobes led him to the bar. He sat and raised a finger to a bartender who didn't see it. He left the finger up, then felt like an amateur and lowered it. He didn't go to these types of places. It wasn't that he wasn't allowed, like a lot of the married guys at the office. Carol wasn't that way with him. She'd always trusted him. When they were young, she trusted him too much. Nothing he could think to do in relation to other women could cause her to react jealously, in fact. She didn't take him at all seriously then. Later on, when he'd managed to move things well beyond friendship, she'd started to regard him but still had never worried about his nightlife.

The bartender paid him a visit as Paul negotiated with himself over whether to stare at the young dancer onstage or casually look away.

"What can I get you?" the barman asked.

Paul wasn't sure. He didn't know if he should drink to blend in or abstain to try to stay sharp. "Scotch and soda." He decided he'd just sip it.

"Rail or premium? Whitehall's in the well, Cutty's on the shelf."

"Cutty."

Paul's drink arrived and he took a big sip. Bigger than he'd meant to. It stung the back of his throat and smacked him in the head. He'd watched the bartender pour but doubted it was actually Cutty in the glass. He remembered he hadn't eaten dinner after work. He'd gotten home and changed out of his suit quickly. Carol had walked in and started the "What do you want for dinner?" "I don't know, what do you want?" It was dialogue that had become rote for them, passing for real conversation. She'd been a bit surprised when she heard he was heading out but hadn't said a word to stop him.

Paul picked up his drink and spun around on his barstool, ready to ogle the strippers like a regular customer. He was in time to see a dancer in her early twenties peel out of a leather brassiere. He felt a stab in his chest at the sight of her near-naked body. He also saw Behr make his way into the club. The man moved with a loose, shambling gait that was at once bad-assed and unassuming. Behr sprawled out at a table right by the stage. He tossed some money at the dancer's feet and stared up at her appreciatively, nodding as if he approved of her every undulation.

A waitress was on a path toward Behr's table when something made her try to veer away. It appeared as if Behr snapped his fingers in her direction, his hand shot out, his arm telescoping with incredible reach, and he got ahold of her wrist. She pulled against his grasp for a moment, then sagged and stepped closer to him.

"You're here about Tad. Well, I'm not supposed to talk to anybody about him," said the waitress from the other night, then cast her eyes about the club.

"Yeah? Who said that?"

"The owners. The manager."

"Oh, Rudy," Behr said, confusing her with his familiarity with the name.

"Tad didn't really owe you money," she said accusingly.

"No."

"Who are you?"

"Who do you think?"

The music ended and onstage the dancer collected her tips. She smiled toward him as she picked up the money he'd left her. He smiled back and then she left the stage.

"You're the police?" the waitress asked.

Behr shrugged, then threw a half salute toward Paul at the bar. Paul half raised his drink in return. He watched the waitress watching the exchange. Paul appeared to be the most ill-concealed undercover of all time.

"Do me a favor and get out of my section," the waitress said, and hurried away. Behr didn't move. Paul gestured if he should come over and Behr shook his head not to. Before long the dancer who had been onstage appeared beside Behr's table. She now wore a clingy lavender nightgown over revealing underwear. Her hair was sandy blond and she looked younger standing next to him.

"You want a table dance, big man?"

"No, honey."

"Buy me a drink then?"

Behr pushed out a chair for her with his foot. She sat down. "Sure, but I don't expect the service will be that good." She didn't know what he meant and looked around for a waitress. None were around, so she waved to the bartender.

"You mind?" she asked as she pulled a pack of Capris out of her tiny handbag.

"Nope. Tell me about Tad Ford." Concern passed across the dancer's eyes, but it wasn't fear exactly. She didn't move to get up. She'd been told the same thing as the waitress about not talking, but at ten years her junior, she felt more secure with her place at the club. She crossed one bronzed thigh over the other and pulled the hem of the nightgown to cover a purple-yellow bruise there. "I know you're not supposed to," Behr added. He slid her twenty dollars. She snapped it into her handbag with her cigarettes.

"What do you want to know? The guy was a loser who lost."

"Yeah," he concurred. "Who did he hang around with? Friends, anybody."

"I've only been here like two months. I don't know, *papi chulo*."

"You know anything?"

"Not really," she said, not at all sorry to disappoint him. He waited her out. "You know who would know some shit, though?"

"Who?"

"Brandi."

"She a dancer?"

"That's right."

"Real name?"

"Michelle Ginelle."

"Can you get me back into the dressing room?"

She laughed at him. "Oh, that's the sixty-four-dollar question, as my dad would say. I've heard that one more than a few times since I've been here." He waited her out again. "Anyhow, she's not here."

"No? Where's she at?"

"She hasn't been around much the last few weeks. But Tad used to drool *all* over her. Followed her around like a dog, yo."

"Is that right. Anything ever happen between them?" This really broke her up. Michelle Ginelle, it seemed, was a woman of real standards.

"Hah, not. Michelle says 'you can marry more in a minute than you can make in a lifetime.' She taught me that. So I don't think Tad really qualified, if you know what I mean."

"Right," Behr said as the bartender arrived

with a tiny split of Spanish champagne. He set down a fake crystal flute in front of the dancer and went about opening the bottle.

"This'll be sixty," he said. "You want to open a tab?"

Behr reached out and stopped the man's hand on the cork. "Better not pop that, son."

The bartender scowled, shook his head at the dancer, and walked off.

"Hey," the dancer said, indignant.

"Where can I find Michelle?" Behr demanded. The dancer scoffed, trying to come off hard and unhelpful, but she just didn't have the experience for it.

"Tell me," he barked.

She looked like a startled kid for a second, and then she came back to herself. "She's got a condo off County Line. That's all I know." She wanted the chat to be over.

Behr moved to go, then stopped. "You talked to me. How come you're not afraid of Rudy?" he wondered.

"Why would I be afraid of Rudy?" She opened her hands in a gesture that presented all six feet and nineteen years of her barely clad self. Why, indeed?

Behr crooked a wave at Paul and went for the door.

. . .

Back in the car and heading for County Line, Behr dialed his cell phone.

"Hey, Bobby," Behr began. "Can you get me a home add on a Michelle Ginelle? Vicinity of County Line, I believe."

Behr waited and glanced at Paul. "Guy in my line of work. He's home on his computer most nights. We help each other.

"Hey. Great. Thanks, Bobby," Behr spoke into the phone, then changed course slightly and drove for a while. Paul rode wordlessly. Though it seemed he wanted to ask questions, he resisted the urge. Behr appreciated that. He wanted to remain rapt in his own thoughts but decided to give a few words by way of reward.

"We're gonna go talk to a girl, a dancer from that club. She knew this guy who used to be a bouncer there. He might've been involved."

"*Used* to be a bouncer?"

"Yeah." Behr didn't elaborate.

I'm getting a pooch already. Oh, Michelle, she said to herself and turned away from the mirror. After looking at her body, she had glanced at her eyes as well. Bad news there. She wasn't looking particularly fresh-faced. Twenty-four just wasn't twenty-one and she saw where it was going from here. She'd been sick all day, all week really. Tired and pukey. She knew what it meant. That goddamned

Rudy. He said he'd pulled out in plenty of time. It was her own damn fault, anyway. Rudy had a nice body and a nice car but was not a man of means. He was not a gentleman. That's what happens when you break your own rules: Don't fuck for fun. Play for play, but draw the line if they're in the industry.

She sat down at her kitchen table and played around with a pack of Merits. She wanted one badly. Along with one of the three silver cans of Coors Light in her refrigerator to go with it. But she stopped herself. She was going to go ahead and take the day after pill that would get rid of her problem. It seemed less invasive than a procedure. The decision occupied her room that morning like a dark, threatening figure standing in the corner. It was hours before she could get out of bed and face it. She'd finally decided, though, and knew it was the right choice. The only choice. All the same, she just didn't feel right about drinking or smoking until next week when it was done. Whatever level of being, formed to whatever degree, just didn't deserve to suffer the smoke in her lungs or the alcohol in her blood. *Let it spend its time in peace,* she thought.

She ran her fingers through her hair, appreciating the softness, then her phone rang. She had the momentary instinct to answer it, but she checked that urge. It was the club or her mother, and she didn't want to talk to either. She hadn't had a decent conversation with her mother in a year, since she'd slipped and admitted she was a dancer and not just a waitress at the club. Her mother was a moralist, though it didn't seem to come from any pure place. Michelle believed her mother was afraid of life and embraced what you shouldn't do rather than what you could do, and she just didn't need that negative energy right now. Nor did she want to talk to Rudy or any of the girls from the club. She was in no mood to work, in no state to decide on when her next shift would be. After hearing about Tad, she wondered if she should try to find a new club. There was just a bad vibe around the Golden Lady now. She shuddered and felt like she had a cold, wet bath towel wrapped around her bare shoulders, such was the clammy weight that pressed down on her.

The phone stopped ringing and she had a moment's solitude, then there was a rapping at the front door. Two big dudes were standing there. The bigger of the two asked if she was Michelle Ginelle. Cops, she thought. A pair of them had been by around midday asking a few questions: Had Tad fought with anyone at the club? Did he have any enemies? She opened the door farther. "We want to talk to you about Tad Ford for a minute," he said.

The dancer let them in, and he and Behr followed her down a short hallway to her living room. It was impossible to ignore the grace with which she walked. The town house was cool, the thermostat set low to save money, and she wore loose sweat pants and a tattered T-shirt that was punctured by her nipples. Her hair was pulled back in a ponytail and despite her lack of makeup and the start of faint dark circles under her eyes, she was stunning. She had full lips and soulful eyes, and a tight curvaceous form beneath her clothes. She had a certain energy that he'd noticed before in very beautiful women—as if she were a perfectly fresh sliced orange extended on the palm of the world. Carol used to have that quality. Before. The girl pointed to the couch for them and pulled her stocking feet up under her on a leather recliner. A huge television across the room silently played an infomercial and cast a flickering light along the side of her face. She had the largest CD collection Paul had ever seen, and they were stacked next to the television. He looked around the place. He'd never been inside one like it. The town house was in an eye-numbing development that seemed to stretch for miles. The outsides of the units were dun-colored vertical planks with black slanted roofs, and without the well-lit streets and heavily organized numbering system it would have taken them hours to find her door. Paul had wondered what kind of people settled in places like this. White-collar government workers, computer programmers, and corporate managers, he would have thought. Exotic dancers as well, he knew now. The units were spacious, with two and three bedrooms, but appeared to be inhabited by single people only. There were no bikes outside on the patches of lawn, no toys, no basketball hoops, no multiple cars, nothing to indicate that families lived in the development. Maybe he'd end up in a place like this in the future, he considered, a broken-down, divorced insurance salesman.

The girl was young, in her early twenties. She sat across from them and played with a pack of cigarettes.

"I'm trying not to smoke," she said when she saw them notice. Her voice was low and purring, as if she had glycerin in the back of her throat. She wasn't trying to be seductive, but she was having an effect on him. He was glad Behr was there, because if it was him alone, he would stutter and stumble. "So you want to hear about Tad? I don't know who killed him." Paul shifted as the news of a murder hit him, but he kept himself together.

"That's fine," Behr said. "What did you think when you heard?"

"It freaked me. Totally. I never knew anyone who died like that. But what can you do? It's not something I can think about much. I've got my own issues I'm dealing with right now."

"I understand." Behr nodded. Maybe he did understand. Paul had no idea how to tell how much Behr could read off of people. "He had a thing for you, though."

She took a cigarette out, habitually, then realized and slid it back into the pack. "Yeah, a one-way thing."

"Not your type?"

"Yeah, right," she started with a laugh, then caught herself. "Look, I don't want to talk bad about those who've passed. You know?" Behr nodded like he did know. Paul followed suit. "But you learn pretty quick when you're a dancer not to date inside the industry." She said the last part with considerable bitterness. "His, uh, attention . . . it just got kind of uncomfortable after a while. Anyway, that's about all I've got to say. That's what I said to the other cops who were here, too."

"We're not cops," Behr said, and Paul saw her eyes flare, angry and betrayed. "Hey, I didn't say we were—"

"Yeah, but—"

"We're private. Hired by Tad Ford's family," Behr told her. Paul watched her try and catch up with this.

"His family?"

"Let's just say they're prominent." Behr let this land. It seemed to reverberate off the chalky white walls. "They have a big family business you may have heard of. In Detroit." He waited as she put it together. Suddenly it clicked, and what might have been went across her face so clearly that Paul could've reached out and touched the thought.

"Tad never told me he was . . ." Her words trailed off in a whiskey-voiced puddle of disappointment.

"Jeez, you think he would've mentioned it," Behr shot across the couch to Paul. Paul gave him a shrug back. "I guess that's just the kind of guy he was."

"I guess," the girl said. She sounded sick about it.

"So you think you remember any details about him? What he did before starting at the club? Any friends or associates you might've seen?" Paul admired Behr's style with her. He was neither friendly nor heavy, more like an immovable object that would not be leaving until he got his information.

Now the girl spoke to them from a faraway place. Her own troubles had magnified and were making the room crowded. Paul expected Behr to give her a line about how Tad's family would be grateful for any information, how they might pay for it. That's what he would've done. But Behr didn't. Paul made a mental note to ask him why not. Then he saw why. A change had come over the girl. Tad's having been special made her special in kind, and now she wanted to talk.

"Tad used to be a customer, starting a while

back. That's how we met. He was a regular. I was his favorite. He didn't spend money on any of the other girls. . . ." She smiled. It was like a cold knife in Paul's chest. He could imagine how powerless men at the club were in her presence. He was aware of how this bouncer had gone from an object of revulsion to a mysterious man of good taste in an instant when she thought he was from a wealthy family, and still her smile pierced him. "Come to think of it, he did spend plenty back then. And he used to come in with a guy back when he was a customer, then it tapered off when Tad started working at the club and I didn't see the guy anymore." Paul caught himself leaning forward on the faux leather sofa and tried to ease back into a more staid pose.

"What kind of guy?" Behr asked.

"A wiry little guy. Called Rooster."

"Rooster."

"That was his nickname, obviously."

"Uh-huh."

"Kinda sexy, but a little weird. What's the word . . . ?" She fished around in her mind for a minute, then gave up and continued. "He had kind of an Axl thing going, but with a little shorter hair. Spent lots of time in the gym. Would always leave the club to go and do late-night workouts. He was religious about it. He was pretty uncomfortable sitting and talking with the girls, too." Behr absorbed the information, making a mental note to ask Terry Cottrell and other sources for help in running down the associate, but she wasn't done yet. "I always knew Tad was in love with me. He was kind of shy and clumsy around me, but I thought that's just the way he was all the time, then I realized how much worse it was around me. . . . Then he started working at the Lady and that disqualified him."

"Do you know what he was doing before?" Behr wondered in a voice so soft, Paul would have never thought he possessed it.

"He said he was a driver."

"A driver. Like a chauffeur or a trucker?" Behr wanted clarification.

She shrugged, her breasts moving upward against her T-shirt. "Just a driver of some kind. Long hauls. He had that left-arm tan." She demonstrated the arm hanging on the windowsill of a car door. "He used to try to impress me by promising trips. I thought he was trying to impress me." They watched while she rethought her dealing with the dead man.

"Where'd he want to take you?"

"He knew Mexico. He said he could take me down to this or that amazing beach where nobody was around. Totally private. To villages where you could hire a native to cook you the best chicken you'd ever tasted for like seventy cents. But all the girls know: There are only certain guys that you go on a trip with. The ones who give you a first-class ticket or have their own plane."

"Right," Behr said without judgment.

"Makes sense," Paul added, because his saying nothing was starting to feel conspicuous.

"Oh. Hold on," she said, and bounded up and left the room with alarming speed. They heard her in the kitchen rustling around. A drawer opened and closed. Paul looked to Behr. Behr gave him nothing back. She returned and held out her hand to Behr. He took a small, carved wooden key chain from her. It had letters painted on it and a sun setting between palm trees.

"He gave it to me."

"Ciudad del Sol."

"Yeah."

"This where he wanted to take you?"

"No. Someplace else. Jalisco or something." Then she shuddered and hugged herself. "You can keep that, I don't want to remember what happened to him. It gives me the creeps."

"Okay," Behr said, and palmed the little key chain.

"Recently he was talking all about how he had to distance himself from Rooster, which was strange because the guy hadn't even been around much for a long time. I thought maybe he was jealous because the guy would get all the attention from the dancers, but Tad said he was a bad person."

"Really." Behr nodded. "Anything else?"

She bit her lower lip in thought, causing it to whiten. Then she stopped and it reddened to the point of near bursting. "No. Guess not." They all stood and started for the front door.

"Menacing." She stopped. "That's the word I was looking for. That guy, Rooster, he was menacing."

TWENTY-ONE

AFTER MIDNIGHT Sebo's Gym was populated almost exclusively by fags, bodybuilders, and psychos. If anyone had any misconceptions about Rooster belonging to one of those groups, he'd be glad to straighten it out for him. Anytime. The place shimmered under banks of fluorescent lights. Barbells and iron plates sang out in harmony with violent grunts. The air smelled of disinfectant and steroid-laden shits that wafted out of the men's locker room, where juiced-up lifters dropped them in between squeezing the boil-size pimples on their backs and shooting their next dose.

Still, it was the only option in town for guys in serious training. Not pumped-up buffy boys with their show muscles, but those looking for power. Rooster had tried to stick to morning workouts for a while, in the hope of avoiding the degenerate crowd. He'd learned of a method: Do the most important task of the day first, that way you can focus on it, do it to the highest level of your ability, and there would be little chance of putting it off or skipping it. He couldn't stay with the plan though. It just didn't work for him. Daylight left him cold. He couldn't generate the intensity required for power cleans before nightfall, regardless of how many Turbo Teas he drank first. No, for Rooster, the only way to find the purging, heart-pounding, iron-pounding force was late night. He was never one to skip his workouts, anyway. Especially now.

He was on the bench. It was an indulgence he rarely afforded himself. Most guys in the gym threw down on bench press every single workout, skipping more important stuff like legs and core strength for the ostentatious chesty look that benching gave. Rooster knew doing a series of rows and sumo squats would serve him a lot better in the long run. But at 1:00 A.M., a few days after a piece of business like that with Tad, nothing suited mind movies like bench press. Rooster crashed the bar, loaded with plates and memories, down on his chest. The stupefied look on Tad's face when Rooster was suddenly standing in his living room was one that he would never forget. Rooster pushed his reps as he relived the moment.

The first shot had entered just below the sternum and it shook Tad all over. Rooster gave him the rest of a five-pack to the torso, taking the trouble to line up the front blade through the rear ramp sight between each shot. He saw Tad shimmy and fall forward, blood all over his tightie whities. He considered putting the last one in his dome, but stopped himself. Tad already had Xs for eyes by that point, and Rooster figured he should keep an extra, without taking the time to reload, in case he ran into a looky-loo in the hall on his way out. He hadn't, though, he hadn't seen a single person, and now he regretted saving the round. *Oh, well.* His chest burned. His arms quivered. He racked the bar, ran a hand through his recently cropped hair, and breathed. He sat up and looked across the gym to the front desk.

Behr and Paul parked out front of a large corrugated-metal and cinder-block building that took up a city block. The place housed several businesses, a self-storage facility and a car wash among them.

"When she said the guy was the night-owl workout type it rang a bell," Behr said, his words whitening the dark, frosty air. "There's only a couple of places open all night," he went on, entering the building, climbing the stairs ahead of Paul. "And this place is pretty special."

Behr swung the door open and cleared the doorframe, allowing Paul his first look at Sebo's.

"Je-sus," Paul uttered softly. He felt like a high-order extraterrestrial discovering a strange savage Earth custom. Flesh, barely covered by tank tops, writhed on purple-covered workout equipment under harsh lights. There were guttural sounds and clanging, as would accompany a dog fight in a blacksmith's shop. The air was bleachy and fetid, the humidity high enough to grow ferns. Paul's eyes adjusted and he saw the place was merely a gym, full of muscled men applying themselves to force/resistance training.

They walked a small distance over black rubber flooring to a reception desk, where they faced a squat man with a neck tattoo. He worked a battery of screaming blenders, mixing pink and brown protein liquids. Another man, deeply tanned, in workout clothes, waited for his beverage.

"Membership cards?" the squat man said loudly over the blenders, revealing a hint of an Irish accent.

"We're not members," Behr answered.

"Single workout pass is six dollars," the deskman said, his voice dropping as he cut a blender and began pouring a drink for the tanned lifter.

"We're not here to work out," Behr tried to explain.

"Hell, it's not a fooking bathhouse—"

"Close enough," Behr snarled back.

The man cut another blender and a bit of quiet crept over the counter.

"What do you cunts want, then?" The man folded his arms, trying to maximize his biceps, which were fairly maximal. Still, in Behr's shadow, the man seemed shrunken. Paul wondered how handy Behr was with his fists or if he was merely a size-reliant big man.

"Us cunts"—Behr leaned forward over the counter—"want to know if you have a member here who goes by the name Rooster."

"You're the cops?" The man wilted a bit, rubbing his neck tattoo. It was a spider or tarantula on a web, as far as Paul could tell. All black. Badly done. There was a matching one on the man's elbow, too.

"You want the police? Because that's where we're headed if you don't stay with me. Rooster. He's supposed to work out nights," Behr said, his voice flat and uncompromising. He put his hands down on the counter with a meaty thud. Several of his fingers were bent and gnarled, his punching knuckles raised like acorns under the skin. The gym monkey crumbled some more at the sight of them. He finished pouring the drink and handed it to the tanned man, who hurried away.

"Look, I'm usually not on nights. Do you have his proper name?" The man rubbed his neck tattoo as if it would come off.

Behr nodded once at the new demeanor and backed off the counter. "No. He's not tall. Red hair, longish. Wiry."

"I dunno. You can check the member profiles. But they're just names and addresses. We're going to photo cards next month, but—"

"That's all right. Mind if we look around?"

The man waved a hand toward the gym, giving them the run of it, relieved to be done with them.

"Some attitude on that guy," Paul said as they stepped onto the floor.

"You run into all kinds in my business. The ones having bad days are real generous about sharing 'em with you."

They stopped near a rack of barbells and scanned the area. No one fit the description they'd been given. And then their eyes landed on someone familiar. Coincidence stopped them cold.

"Hey, that's—" Behr began. He was looking at a bearded guy wearing baggy Umbro shorts and a knee brace, grinding out a set on the leg press.

"Bill Finnegan," Paul said. It was the soccer coach. Behr beelined for him, but Paul was with him stride for stride. They were making their way across the gym, picking their way through equipment and burly men, when Finnegan saw them. He slammed the weight home, hopped off the leg press, and half ran for a door marked Exit on the far side of the dumbbell area.

They went after him, picking up their pace to a

fast walk. When Finnegan hit the door and disappeared down the stairwell, they broke into a run. Paul considered himself fleet of foot, he'd been a runner for close to twenty years, so he was stunned to see Behr burn by him and reach the door first. Behr took the stairs, which were divided into switchbacks every sixth step, a full landing at a time. Paul covered them in threes and hoped he didn't break an ankle. He reached the ground floor in time to see Behr cuff Finnegan in the back of the neck and send him sprawling into the door to the street. The coach's shoulder and elbow echoed off the hollow metal door.

"Ah," Finnegan said in pain, but managed to keep his feet.

Behr caught him by the collar and spun him around. Finnegan raised his hands, closed his eyes, and turned his face away. Paul was relieved he didn't resist and that Behr pulled up short of beating him. He was now satisfied with the answer to his earlier question of the detective's physical proficiency.

"What the fuck are you doing here?" Behr asked, speaking the question in Paul's swirling mind.

"Nothing. Nothing." Finnegan breathed, high and reedy.

"Why're you running?" Behr snarled at him.

"I . . . Nothing. Just working out. And I . . ."

Paul stepped forward and spoke in as even a voice as he could manage. "Hey. Bill. Hey. What's going on?"

Behr let go of him and the soccer coach shifted around uncomfortably. "Hi, Paul. I come here. To stay in shape."

"Uh-huh." Behr appraised him.

"It has nothing to do with . . . anything. Really."

"Bullshit. Give," Behr barked. He put a hand forward and held the coach by his throat. He shifted his weight back as if he would punch.

"I'm gay. All right? I'm a gay man." Silence fell in the stairwell for a moment as they absorbed the statement. Apparently, Finnegan felt compelled to go on. "But I never touched a kid. Not in my life." That seemed to be all there was to the bombshell.

"Jesus, Bill, what the hell are you running for?"

"I coach *youth soccer*, Paul. This isn't New York, you know? People around here wouldn't like it. Goddamnit!" he shouted, his last word reverberating through the stairwell in frustration and humiliation. Paul looked to Behr and shook his head. Behr stepped back.

"I don't want to lose my job."

"Nobody's gonna find out, Bill," Paul said with reassurance. The coach's breathing began to calm and he nodded and went out the door into the night. Paul and Behr walked back up to the gym and looked around for anybody fitting Rooster's description, but no one was even close.

.   .   .

Rooster drove too fast and checked his mirrors every three seconds. Those guys at the desk had been cops, clear as day, and they'd been looking for him. He didn't know how the hell they didn't find him in the locker room, either. He took his chance when they were jawing with the desk guy. He grabbed a ten-pound plate and slipped inside the locker room, around the corner, next to the urinals, ready to lay out the big one first. But they never showed. He waited two minutes and then booked out the front door, and they'd missed him. They hadn't been thorough, or he was damned lucky. He didn't know which. He couldn't imagine how they'd gotten on to him for the little visit he'd paid to Tad in the first place, but they sure as hell had.

Now he needed to regroup. He needed to chill and get in touch with Riggi. "Wait," he said aloud. He couldn't just call Riggi, get him rattled, too, or he'd be facing his own little visit from someone else. Riggi was always bringing in new help, looking for the proper situation in which to prove their chops. Maybe he'd better just keep the whole deal to himself for a while, Rooster thought. A sickening sense of the mundane traveled in the car with him. He'd prided himself on being a professional, and now one simple piece of trigger business and he'd come away dirty, like a two-bit gangbanger. He coursed through the intersection of June and Prosser, trying to outdistance the damp feeling of failure, the car's shocks bunching as he hit a swale in the road. He caught a glimpse, through the top of the windshield, of the traffic signal going from amber to red.

Officer Stacy Jennings dropped the radar gun, hit her lights, and went after the El Camino doing fifty-seven on June Road. *Fifty-seven in a forty.* Stacy loved being a cop. She was twenty-four years old and had been on the force for eighteen months. She couldn't believe how right the job was for her. Her friends were all secretaries or worked in banks or were in law school. All that seemed like slow death by boredom to her. Even though nothing beyond a DUI had happened to her so far, she still got all jacked up on traffic stops, each and every one. She knew that things could turn without warning and stuck to the procedure she'd learned at the academy. She'd move up on the driver's side, keeping in his blind spot as long as possible, and stop about a foot and a half back of being even with him, so he'd have to crane around to see her once he'd opened his window. This way, she stayed out of the line of fire if the motorist pulled a gun. She knew danger rode in every car. It was this knowledge that made her blood surge, that amped her up, so that even after a routine shift she'd have to put in a hard half hour on the stair-climber her father had given her for Christmas just to wind down and tire out for sleep. Daddy was so proud of her, though he said he'd never stop being nervous now that she was on the force.

The El Camino neared Clairmont before she'd reached speed and for a moment it pulled away from her. She felt her pulse hum and her stomach elevator-dropped halfway before she caught it and stepped on the gas. She wondered if she had her first runner and grabbed for the radio to call for backup. But she began closing ground on the El Camino and its speed dropped below fifty, almost as if its will had flagged. The driver made a show of drifting into the right lane, as if carefully looking for a good place to pull over. At least she knew he'd seen her lights. Growing impatient, she fluttered the siren, two crisp chirps, and he finished pulling over. She stopped about ten feet back of him and put it in park. Her patrol car was rigged with a dash-mounted video camera that automatically taped her traffic stops after the flashers were activated, for her safety, for a review of her performance, and to protect motorists' rights. She focused her mind for a moment, then got out.

Inside the El Camino the feeling of failure was gone. What replaced it was a bubbling lava river of self-disgust. Rooster was acting like a teenage redneck stick-up man on a losing streak. Now he faced a license check and worse if they put together who he was and that other cops were looking for him. He sat stone still and peeped his side mirror as the officer drew close. The cop stopped a few feet back of him, and he could see that it was a woman. She was pretty. Young. She had sandy blond hair pulled back in a tight ponytail and not a stitch of makeup. Her coat collar had white fleece lining that rode up around her chin and she looked cute in it. She tapped his window, which he lowered, then craned around for a straight-on look at her.

"License and registration, sir."

He made her name tag in the glow of the streetlight. Officer Jennings. He felt his stomach quiver. She was a beauty.

"Aw, come on now, that light back there was yellow all the way," Rooster said. He smiled. The smile came easy, clean and fresh as she was.

"License and registration," the cop repeated, her voice flat.

Rooster half moaned in frustration but kept it low as he reached for the glove compartment. He handed over his papers. They linked him to a long-gone address with no forwarding information. The car itself was pristine, too, nothing—no weapons or substances—in it that could get him hauled in. His problem, however, was twofold. He had a hell of a lot of old parking tickets he hadn't paid that had *poof* turned into bench warrants, and if she punched in his name, it might come up that her brother officers were looking. *Can't let that happen,* he thought, shifting around again, trying for another look. She checked the license against his face, the registration against the car.

"Any chance of a warning on this one, Officer?" Rooster tried.

"You were going pretty good there, you know," she said back. A little humorless, he thought, but he kind of liked it.

"I guess."

"What's the hurry?"

"Nothing. Just coming from the gym. I'm all jacked up after my workout, ya know?"

This penetrated her shell. She became present for a moment. "Yeah," she said. For a moment he could see her racing a mountain bike or running, covered with sweat, like in a sports drink commercial. Then the job came back into her. "But still."

"I'll take it slow from here. You can bank on that," he offered. He tried to put some friendly in his eyes, unsure of how it came across.

She narrowed her eyes and looked at him for a moment. She didn't say yes or no to the ticket, just stared. He felt unable to stop himself from drifting. It was the sight of her patrolman's shoes; shiny cap toes that were small, barely sticking out from under her trousers. *This Officer Jennings, this pretty young thing, is the kind of girl I should be with,* he said silently to himself. *Could be, too. Why not? It wasn't a great way to meet, but there'd been worse.*

He imagined them together, a few months in. Long enough so that they were comfortable, not so long that it had become routine. He pictured her coming home after work. She'd toss her cap at him on the couch and pull out the ponytail doodad that held her hair back. She'd walk up to him and he'd unclip her gun belt, removing it from her slim hips. He'd begin to unbutton her pants, revealing a flat, hard stomach and the top of her fine white cotton underwear. He would've just gotten home before her, too. Because unbeknownst to her he'd have followed her on her patrol, making sure nothing bad had befallen her. He'd lay back and scout her patrol area for threats. He'd be her invisible backup. He pictured himself living clean. He'd drop the "Rooster" and go by "Garth." Garth Mintz and Officer Jennings. *Damn, what was her first name?* It brought him out of his reverie just in time to hear her speak.

"Wait in the car, please, sir. It'll be just a minute."

A sense of gloom came down on Rooster like a heavy wave crashing over him. His movements felt thick, distracted, as if he were swimming through gelatin. He swung his car door open and put his feet on the ground. Officer Jennings, on the way back to her car, stopped. He stood and stretched, as if his arms and legs were tight. And they were tight—with disgust, for where he'd ended up and for what he had to do.

"I said, wait in your vehicle, sir." He heard Officer Jennings's voice, tight, come back at him.

"Just grabbing a smoke," he said, bashful, making a show of looking for his cigarettes.

She took a few steps back toward him, reaching for her radio as she came. "I'm gonna ask you to place your hands on the side of the car." Now her voice was commanding. If she had any fear, she'd put it down and locked it away.

He began to comply, turning toward the El Camino, stretching his hands out toward it. As he turned he saw her key her radio, readying to use it. He took a sip of night air, the gelatin hesitation gone from his limbs, and spun back the way he had turned. He threw a lead right with everything he could put on it that would still allow him to retain good balance on the tail end.

What's he doing? Stacy Jennings wondered to herself when Mintz, the traffic stop, climbed out of his car. It was her last clear recollection. The rest she got from the dashboard videotape. Months later, after the surgeries, she'd watched the tape and could hardly comprehend it. She couldn't believe the way the first punch landed, dead solid, that she didn't slip it at all. She pretty much walked into it, in fact. She'd been a damn good boxer at the academy, and before, when her father had taught her. She could trade with any of the male recruits, and often got the better of them because of the way she could bob and move in the ring. But that was in the ring, with headgear and mouth guards and gloves and rounds. She could hardly believe the way she went down on the street: like a bag of beans. The first punch broke her jaw. She still couldn't process the weird distance, the remove she felt as she watched the man kneel on her chest and begin pounding her face. Even though she recognized herself on the tape, acknowledged the face she used to know, the one she'd never have again, it seemed the whole thing was happening to someone else. The back of her head hit the pavement with each blow, blows that messed up her teeth, cut her cheeks, smashed her nose and orbital bone on the left side. Blood, dark and colorless due to the video wash, ran back and soaked her hair, blackening it. She saw the man jump up once she was unconscious, look around, pause oddly over her, then climb into his car and drive away. She lay still for just under a minute, her cap sitting in the lower left edge of the frame. Then her hands began to move, touched her face, then found her radio, and a low gurgling voice called in, "Code one-five-four. Officer down, past intersection of June and Prosser," before the radio, shiny and slick with blood, fell from her hand.

TWENTY-TWO

THERE WERE HOME MOVIES on videotape, more than ten years old, but Paul found them. It had been years since he'd seen them, months since he'd even considered watching them, but after returning from his night with Behr, he felt he had the strength to look. He sat downstairs in the living room in front of the television and slid a tape into the VCR. He kept the volume low, more for himself than out of concern for Carol. Jamie's first day home from the hospital, his first bath, his first solid food, oatmeal spread all over his smiling face, an episode of him objecting to being on the changing table. Two minutes of tape, his stupid narration over his own bad camera work. The subject: a tiny faultless being who gurgled and cooed in a language that spoke pure happiness.

There were other special moments to come—Jamie crawling and then walking, using finger paints—all too exquisitely painful to watch as they were now, preserved within digital grain and the impossibility of time. Paul rolled forward out of his chair, landing on his knees in the thick carpet. He stabbed at the VCR stop button, causing the image to vanish and the plastic tape to croak out of the machine. He knelt there staring into the blackness of the screen and drew on the dead air for breath.

Carol lay in bed. Through the darkness she heard Paul enter downstairs. She felt the electric hum of the television being turned on, a palpable high-pitched whine. She heard the muted sound of voices, the poor-quality audio, and couldn't tell what he was watching. Then Jamie's cry reached her in the night. His cry as a baby, an abject bawl like the rest in the hospital nursery, was distinct and piercing to her then, and was familiar even now. That cry had instantly brought her to a new understanding of love. It made milk weep from her breasts. The response was nature in all its force and glory. That cry no longer caused her to weep. She seemed to have cried her final tear some months back and now there was hardly even feeling, just emptiness. It was then she realized there was something even more horrible than the agony caused by the cry of one's child—and that was a total lack of sensation at that same cry. She turned on her side and tried for sleep.

Behr arrived home after dropping Paul off and switched on the lights. As he moved about, squaring himself away for the night, he saw the empty spot on the desk where his computer customarily sat. His eyes found the space like a tongue exploring where a tooth had been pulled. He slid into his armchair, flipped open his notebook, and considered what to do next.

He drew a line connecting Jamie's name to Tad Ford's. He hung a question mark beneath the line. He drew another line connecting Ford's name to Rooster's. He drew still another line that went off toward the edge of the page. He dangled still another question mark from it, one that threatened to fall off into white space. He tapped his pen rhythmically on the spot. This moment came along on most meaningful jobs. The time when the beginning was far behind him, the chance to abandon the matter long gone, and yet there was no end, no resolution in sight. It made Behr feel physically weak in his core. A sense of formless fear filled the room as water would a sinking boat. His familiarity with the moment did little to lessen the feeling. A horrible quiet settled, one that allowed silent questions, about his lost family and what lay at his essence, to echo in his head. This was the moment for courage, Behr knew. More than facing an armed suspect, more than preparing to ram a door and enter a room, back when he'd been a police officer—at least then there was action and adrenaline to cover the fear. This was the moment for which Behr was paid, what little he was paid, to face and endure. The rest was just running down the details.

A sense of clarity returned as Behr managed to control his breathing. Quiet confidence throbbed from a distant, nameless place deep within him. He'd find this son of a bitch Rooster and he would discover his relationship to the rest, and he'd find the next piece of information after that, and so on until Jamie Gabriel's fate had been laid to rest. Behr would get to the end of it. He knew it once again. It was all he had, but he felt rich for a moment knowing it. Then his telephone rang.

"Yeah?" he said, looking at his watch, noting it was late, too late for a call.

"Hello? Oh, jeez, hi. Is this Frank?" It was a woman. He recognized her voice.

"Who's this?"

"Sue. Susan Durant." Silence hung on the line. Behr grabbed her name just as she added, "From the *Star*." It was the woman from the circulation department who'd helped him a while back.

"Yeah, sure, how're you?"

"I'm fine. I'm feeling silly now, though.

Thought I was reaching your office. I was just gonna leave a message."

"I work out of the house. What's the message?"

"To call me. We were supposed to get together. You think I'm letting you slide on that dinner?" The shyness was gone now, and the snap he'd appreciated the first time he spoke to her was back.

"What're you doing up?"

"Watching television."

"What?"

"*ER* reruns. They show 'em back to back. And nerving up to call you. A few hours slid by. Then it got to be, you know, ridiculous. And just 'cause it was late, I couldn't just go to bed without doing it."

Behr found himself smiling. "Uh-huh."

"You were gonna call me. You could've saved me a lot of trouble."

"I see that." There was a moment of quiet on the line as Behr nerved up himself. "So what nights are you free?"

They went ahead and made their plans: Dono-hue's next week. He could take her somewhere fancier, but it'd be better to see how it went at a regular place.

Before they hung up she asked, "Any luck on that case?"

"Some, Sue," he found himself answering, "maybe some."

Rooster sat in a Denny's on Kentucky eating a
Grand Slam that had devolved into him just
pounding coffee. He thought the greasy food
might calm him, soothe his churning gut, but in
the end he couldn't eat that shit. He put in too
much time in the gym to waste it on fried eggs and
hash browns. Truth was, his appetite was gone
anyway after what he'd done. He wasn't proud of
himself. *No, sir.* He knew he had to dump his car,
that he should've done it already instead of leaving
it in the parking lot like a lighthouse beacon. But
he felt a fatigue in his limbs that was outsized to
the physical effort he'd just put forth. He considered whether the cop would live and whether he
should send her something by way of apology if
she did. There'd been a moment there, damned if
he could explain it, after he'd beaten her. He
should've jumped in the car and hauled ass, but he
stopped and stood over her instead. It wasn't with
pride, no way. He had the strongest urge to lean
down and kiss her, and to wipe the blood from her
broken face. Of course he couldn't. Of course not.
He finally *had* jumped in the car and hauled ass.
Now he hardly recognized himself. He looked at
his arms and counted the scars up and down them,
poorly healed cuts from this most recent and other
incidents. *Fuck it,* they were the scars of war.

He continued on and drank coffee for what felt

like hours, and eventually the glass panels of the windows in front of him lit up in a strobe of red and blue lights. Four patrol cars slid into the parking lot, two circled around back, with lights but no sirens. He sat and finished his coffee. Even as the first two teams of uniforms hit the front door of the restaurant, Rooster just sat, letting the pulsing lights wash over him. It was almost soothing.

TWENTY-THREE

STAY WITH IT, Behr urged himself early Friday morning as he humped up Saddle Hill, a road-salt-and-book-filled pack on his back, for his first rep. The middle of his week had consisted of further attempts to chase down Rooster's real name, an address, or known associates. He'd come up empty as a bucket from a dead well. He'd put the question out to friends and acquaintances all over town and wondered which of them might come through with something. He'd toted Paul along for several hours over several evenings, and they'd gone through the bars in Hawthorne, where parolees and future cons drank, and the West District, where it was only safe for them because he used to patrol there, but even so, he didn't linger for long. Nothing had come back to him, and the only conclusion Behr ended up with was that this

Rooster kept to himself. He was on the verge of begging out of taking Paul along after the first few nights, feeling uncomfortable about having his employer watch him fail so consistently. Then, when he'd been dropping him off, Paul turned to him and thanked him. He'd said, "I appreciate how hard you're trying, Frank. I know you're doing everything you can. I'll see you tomorrow." The acknowledgment meant more to him than he would care to admit. He realized that he didn't mind having Paul along with him. Beyond that, he liked it sometimes. Even when they weren't talking, just having another body along for the ride tempered the isolation of the job. He also realized that though in the beginning finding the boy was his sole motivation, after these weeks with this staunch father, Behr knew he was doing it as much for Paul, so that he should at least know some peace.

Stay with it, Behr urged himself again on his second and third trips up the hill. For some men it was the stock market or the box scores, for others the racing form, some even found it with the weather channel, but most men, Behr thought on his way back down, engaged in the habitual consumption of some form of information. They weighed this data and considered the ramifications of it in quiet, almost Talmudic study. The result was a mastery of certain facts and sometimes a glimpse at an order, or an understanding of the larger world beyond the numbers. Behr's vice wasn't rotisserie league sports but rather the weekly arrest reports, the rundown on all police apprehensions that had been made, their locations, and the pertinent details. He used to read the sheets on a daily basis when he was on the force, compiling his own knowledge and sense of the city, like an instinctual human crime-tracking computer. Now the daily approach was impractical and there was little point to it, but he hadn't been able to give it up altogether. He had a buddy, a young cop named Mike Carriero, who fired him a once-a-week fax through which he sifted like a medium. He still felt connected to the dark web of crime in the city when he did, as he considered the potential relationship between car thefts on the north side, drunk-driving stops on I-74, and domestic disturbances down in the mobile home parks by Stringtown. Over the course of working on the Gabriel case, however, nothing he'd seen on the reports seemed to hold any kind of correlation. Besides Ford's killing, only the body in the park, which had quickly proved to hold no connection, and the recent beating of a female cop, had even proved newsworthy.

Stay with it, he urged himself on trips four and five up the hill. Now he referred solely to the run. Thoughts of the case momentarily dropped away as his lungs burned and his legs sizzled and he fought for the will to continue. No matter how many years he trained and to what degree of shape he banged himself into, this question never went away: Will I continue? He fought against it anew each time he worked out. As he crested the hill on his sixth trip up, he stopped. Not because the answer to his question was no this time, but because Terry Cottrell stood there waiting for him. Behr gave him a nod and proceeded to double over and suck wind for a minute. He stood up when he was able, a question on his face.

"I got something last night, Big," Terry said without much crackle in his eyes or voice, which wasn't a surprise considering that Behr had given him a few hints about the case he was working. "Had to give it to you straight, baby. Face-to-face."

"You know to find me over at Donohue's."

"Not a friendly joint for me to wander into by myself."

"Come on, Terry, it's fine and you're not shy."

"Whatever, bro. Anyway, I might could've got a last name on the dude with the Rooster tag and that's Mintz," Terry said. Something about the name felt awfully familiar to Behr. "And I don't know where he is, but I found out what he does." Cottrell stopped talking, not the type to pause for effect, seemingly unable to say the rest.

Behr stood there sweating, his heart pounding. "Fucking tell me, Terry. Don't make me beat it out of you."

Cottrell's face grew more serious. "Dude's a handler. They also known as 'breakers.' " His words caused Behr's sweat to go cold. "I'm sorry, man."

Behr was already unclipping his pack belt and shucking the shoulder straps. The thud of the heavy pack hitting the ground covered his "Thanks." He was already sprinting for home. He knew where he'd seen the name.

"You have to take the day off," Behr told him when he called at 7:15 A.M. "The morning at least, if I can get things set by then. You're coming along with me." Paul could practically hear Behr's mind churning through the phone.

"Okay," Paul said, mentally noting the appointments he needed to reschedule or cancel.

"And wear what you usually wear when we're riding. Don't suit up on me."

"All right. Where are we headed?" Behr didn't answer for a moment. Paul could hear him breathing, low and measured.

"Marion County Jail." Behr hung up.

Paul hadn't expected that answer, just as he hadn't expected to ever visit County. He stood in front of his house dressed in navy chino pants, hiking shoes, sweater, and windbreaker. He didn't know what was coming, only that it was unusual and important. That much was clear from Behr's tone. He guessed that whomever they were going to see in lockup knew something about Jamie, and he tried to keep his hope in check. It was surprisingly easy to do now that he'd seen what was behind his worst fears in the middle of the night. The reality there leered at him from the darkness. It stripped the meat off the bones of his expectations and had sucked the marrow from all he'd planned in life.

Behr rolled up and he got in. The inside of the car was brisk, the leather seat stiff and cold beneath him. Behr's hair was still wet even though his place was a good half-hour drive away. He wore jeans, work boots, and a thermal shirt that was stretched tight over his forearms. Paul stayed quiet during the ride. Behr was far away; there was no one really to talk to. Finally, Behr turned toward him and said, "Rooster's real name is Garth Mintz."

"This is about Rooster?" Paul asked, anticipation flooding his chest.

"Yeah, it is," Behr said. Paul puzzled over the ramifications of this news. They covered a few miles and were in the heart of downtown before he spoke again.

"What's the deal with him?" he asked.

Behr's hands clenched the steering wheel and his eyes didn't leave the road. "In child trafficking docility is at a premium. For obvious reasons. Drugs are often used. But over the long term they cause sickness, you know . . ." Behr said, his tone strangely academic. "One method is to send in an adult who'll . . . commit . . . acts . . . until there's very little will or resistance left. They're called 'breakers.' That's what Rooster does."

Paul felt he'd had a railroad spike nailed through his chest and into the car seat.

"But we don't know if he ever met Jamie?" Paul heard the meek, horrible plea in his own voice.

"No, we don't."

Sights and sounds became muted and washy as they drove down Alabama past the blond-stone jailhouse. They circled on one-way streets around the fortresslike building for a little while—Paul lost track of how long—and they eventually found a spot and parked. Paul wondered if he was in some kind of shock, or if he was actually more acutely focused on the reality at hand than usual and this was what extreme clarity felt like.

They entered the building through the service entrance on Delaware, held open by a man in a custodial uniform, and a strong smell, foreign and unpleasant, hit Paul with force. He followed Behr, their shoes squeaking softly on polished linoleum. They passed through a door into an employee area, Behr entering without pause. Behr shook hands and then shared a back-patting hug with an older gentleman who had brilliantine-slicked steel-gray hair and emanated an odor of tobacco. He wore a brown sheriff's uniform with a name tag that read SILVA. Behr and Silva stepped away from him a few feet and had a short, quiet conversation.

"Couldn't believe it when you called, Frank," Silva said, his voice rough with past nicotine. "The guy's in here suspected of beating on that female officer. There's videotape. You know how many requests I've been getting for alone time with him?"

"Every single County employee?" Behr asked back.

"You know it. I could be in Florida golfing and fishing on odd days with the gratuities I've been offered." Silva allowed himself a moment's departure at the image.

"Why am I so lucky?"

"I let a cop in the room with him, that cop can call it a career. State of civil liberties these days." Silva let out a snort of disgust. "But with you . . ." He trailed off.

"With me, what?" Behr asked, suddenly on edge. "What do I have to lose?"

"It's not that way, Frank. I'd be costing someone his badge if I let 'em in there. I couldn't live good with that. Besides, I don't want to get well off of the situation. And then you called. I can give you five minutes."

Behr nodded. "Been a long time coming."

Silva nodded, too. "Been a real long time. Coming to even."

"Yep. That's where we're at."

Behr rejoined Paul, Silva didn't speak another word, and they were led through a pair of man-trap doors and into a cinder-block interview room.

"We only have five minutes," Behr muttered low as the door was unlocked. The hurry in Behr's voice made Paul feel unready. He wondered exactly what kind of monster would come walking through the door. It didn't take long to get his answer. The door was swung open by a guard and a red-haired man dressed in a faded County jumpsuit, rubber shower thongs on his feet, and listening to a CD Walkman, sauntered in. The guard removed handcuffs and the door closed behind him, leaving only the three of them in the room.

He's small was Paul's first impression. *Muscled up,* his second. That was all there was time for, as Behr was up out of his chair. He cuffed the man in the head, hard, slapping his headphones off.

"Hey," the man protested. "Who the fuck're you—"

"Shut up," Behr grunted, and grabbed at him.

The CD player, knocked loose, clattered to the floor and got kicked into a corner. Behr wrapped the headphone cord around the smaller man's neck and choked him, snapping the wires and leaving red and white stripes across his throat. Behr threw the broken headphones aside and pushed Garth "Rooster" Mintz into a chair. The man rubbed his throat and wiped away the water that had come to his bulging eyes.

"You know why we're here?" Behr began, anthracite hardness in his voice that Paul hadn't heard before, not just from Behr but also from anyone else.

Mintz kept rubbing his throat and shook his head. "That cop thing?"

"Not the cop." Behr slid a picture of Jamie across the desk toward Mintz, who didn't even acknowledge it.

"Look at it," Behr ordered. Mintz only held his gaze for a moment before tilting his glance down over the photo. Then he looked back up at them, his face betraying no signs of recognition.

"Okay, I scoped it."

"Have you seen this kid?" Behr demanded.

"I don't know." The answer wasn't taunting; if anything, it was respectful. For Paul's money the guy actually didn't know.

"You're gonna come across, you son of a bitch," Behr breathed close into the man's face, causing him to blink twice.

"What do you want me to say? Cute kid."

Behr stuffed Mintz into the chair back, moved

around behind him, and pinned his arms. He looked to Paul.

"Give him one."

Paul's scrotum tightened and his bladder threatened to release. He knew what Behr was asking but couldn't believe it.

"Hold up. Are we sure he even knew Jamie?" The situation felt all wrong to Paul, like he was on some insane quest and Behr had roped him into meting out punishment on a guy who'd hurt a cop and had nothing to do with him.

Then Paul flashed on his one fight, the only time he had hit a man in anger. It was back in college. Senior year. He and his friends were juiced up on pitchers of Milwaukee's Best. They were at the Spaghetti Bender off Washtenaw, a place Carol liked to go just after they'd started dating. A guy from the football fraternity had touched Carol's hair as he walked toward the men's room. The guy ran his hand down her blond ponytail before continuing on his way. It was a proprietary gesture that caused Paul to go white-hot with anger. Despite his size, the guy never made it to the john. Paul clocked him in the side of the jaw and followed him, swinging, as he went down. He landed two or three more clean punches, then he was pulled off by the guy's friends and his own. They all scraped and tussled before being thrown out by bouncers and braced by the local authorities. His friends started calling him "Clubber," after Mr. T's character in one of the *Rocky* movies, and Paul had felt guilty for what he'd done for a long time.

Behr's words cut through his thoughts.

"This guy's done unspeakable shit. Whatever he gets he deserves." Behr wrestled the smaller man up out of the chair and held him. Paul stood.

Nothing smells like a jail, Behr thought when they'd entered—floor wax, bad cafeteria food, sweat, human filth, and hate. He'd been wondering if bringing Paul Gabriel there had been his biggest mistake to date. Although the man had showed some nerve so far, he had no experience in these matters or places. Or people. The second Rooster Mintz entered the interview room Behr's old cop radar blipped and bleeped and bonged. The little grease ball was radioactive with bad energy. He seemed to be riding high on the respect that cop killers and cop hurters received in the joint. One look told Behr that the man in front of him lived in a world of foul darkness, and that beating the female officer nearly to death wasn't the ends or depths of what he'd done.

Behr had hoped the unexpectedness and intensity of the father of a victim would help extract information from Mintz in a way no organized professional pressure might. At the least, Paul deserved a moment of indirect payback. Behr's wisdom, or lack of it, was about to be seen. Paul got up from his chair and moved awkwardly, his arms stiff, and threw a tentative right that landed with a clop to the left side of Rooster's chin.

"Not the face," Behr corrected, and watched with growing concern as Paul redirected his attack to the body, the punches brittle and weak. He swung for a bit, to no effect, then stepped back, panting. Mintz took the shots no problem and seemed to be smirking. Paul was nervous, afraid, and Behr knew well what fear did to punchers: It sapped them of power. It made them feeble. Behr had seen it before many times, in overworked cops on high-pressure cases who suddenly began to function at a quarter of their capacity and then started to fail in important ways. He'd seen it in the ring, at the Police Firefighter Smokers. Strong, fit men who were suddenly unable to stop their opponents even when landing clean shots, while their respective departments cheered rabidly for them. He'd felt it in the ring himself, at the same smokers, but had managed to overcome it and stop the Kelly brothers two years running, one on cuts, one by clean knockout. Now Behr grew concerned. They weren't getting to Mintz, and it would soon ruin their play. He was tempted to spin the con around and chop into him personally. He certainly had enough bad feeling for the task. He didn't want to, though. It wasn't how he figured they would succeed.

"Drop your shoulders . . . see your son . . . and hit this bastard," Behr said sternly.

Paul's eyes went distant. He swallowed a gout of air, rolled his shoulders, and waded in close. Now his blows came with more fluidity. He punched with controlled intent, with anger so old and compressed it didn't flame but rather glowed like burning coal. Paul stayed with it as if he wanted to carve through Rooster's abdomen and tear out his organs, which is exactly how it's supposed to be done. Behr felt the man in his arms, who had been loose and active in his defensive posture at first, go tight with pain and then, finally, start to sag with damage. Behr could see that the fury had started to flow in Paul and it just kept flowing.

I can take this, ran through Rooster's head, *all damn day.* It was a stroke of luck that the big fucker was just holding him and not beating on him. *Hells, I'm lucky,* he mused as the other guy's peashooter rights and lefts rattled off his stone abs. *Always been lucky.* It didn't look good for a minute there, when he'd walked in and Big Fucker had jumped up on him. He recognized them from Sebo's, and then the big one had looked clean through him and fixed him with a glare of hate that made his guts slide. He felt the man's power when he stretched the headphone cord across his larynx and felt it again when the man's viselike hands pinned back his arms, fingers of iron squashing his biceps and cranking down on his brachial nerves. If that guy had started in with the trimming, it might've been trouble, but this shit he could handle. He took a moment to decide who they were and what they had on him. He'd thought they were cops, and there was something vaguely copish about them, but the way they were going on about other things and beating on him had him confused. As far as the picture went, there *was* something familiar about the kid in the shot— he looked like every kid he'd ever worked. And he looked like none of 'em in the same way. How the hell was he supposed to remember? They were all just bodies once he was in the room. He didn't bother trying to keep track. And even if he did remember, he sure wouldn't tell them about it. He wasn't here to make the world some better place. Nuh-uh. The world had taken a big shit on him and the way he felt about it was: *Pass it on.*

John B. Good stepped back off him, winded already, and it was only Rooster's experience that kept him from smiling outright. He didn't want to inspire them, for god's sake. Then Big Fucker started coaching his buddy and things went south. B. Good rolled his shoulders like a cruiserweight when he came back in for round two. The next punches were different. The man had his weight planted and his arms were firing like pistons.

Rooster felt his obliques begin to cave, and the blows started to eat him up, and then panic flooded in. He felt the breath get knocked out of him. He fought to keep down his peas and carrots. He found himself wishing it was over, silently crying out for it to *Stop*, just *Fucking stop*. But it didn't stop. His abs failed him. They gave out like hammered copper. The punches were landing straight on his liver and spleen now. The blood rushed from his head and he got dizzy. If Big Fucker wasn't holding him, he'd be weaving and staggering around the room. He'd give 'em what they wanted now, whatever he had, which was nothing, if they'd just ask. *Just please fucking ask.* But they weren't asking. He felt the foamy remnants of his breakfast shoot out of the corners of his mouth and his legs started to go. He sagged in the big man's arms and then, *Thank fucking Christ,* it ended.

"Okay," Behr said, and deposited what was left of Mintz in his chair. Black bile was running out of the guy's mouth and he wasn't even trying to wipe it away. Behr was tempted to allow the beating to go on until there was a knock on the door, let Mintz go to the hospital after they left, but he saw how spent Paul was. He didn't want his partner passing out in the room, and he had questions to get to.

Mintz retched, two, then three times, but they were just spasms and he managed to hold his mud. Now Behr made the picture of Jamie reappear. Mintz looked at it and just shook his head weakly.

"You're not protecting anything. We know who you are. We know your business."

"I don't . . ." Mintz's head bobbed slightly in surrender. "I don't . . ."

"We know about you and your old buddy Tad Ford." Behr saw Mintz's Adam's apple bob and constrict. *Son of a bitch,* he thought, *he's got the dirt on Ford's killing.*

"We don't give a crap about that. We want to know about the kids. This boy." Behr pounded Jamie's photo with his index finger. "Do you know him?"

"I don't know," came the answer.

"You'll give or I'm going next." Behr saw blank fear shoot across Mintz's face.

"What are you fucking with me for? Huh?" Mintz asked, his voice a high whine. He was crying. His tears and snot were mixing with the bile and sweat on his face, making him a total mess. There was a sharp knock on the door. Time was up.

"Hold that door, Paul," Behr snarled, glad to see Paul jump up and head for it. "I know you break down these kids so they make for better companions. Now tell me something I can use or you'll never leave this room." Behr shot his hand out, grabbed Mintz around the throat, and squeezed. The sounds of a key in the lock and a hand on the knob could be heard. Paul gripped the knob, holding it still. Behr throttled Mintz as if he'd kill him and thought maybe he would.

"What the fuck am I? I never kept track of what I was doing. You want the guy who matters, right?" Mintz croaked. "You want Riggi. Oscar Riggi."

The knocks had turned to banging. Paul looked back to Behr, who nodded. Paul stepped away from the door and it opened. Silva was standing there, a pissed-off look on his face.

"It's time, goddamnit."

Behr let go of the man's throat, took out a notebook, and wrote down the name, doing his best to control a hand that trembled with adrenaline and disgust.

They all stood, looking around uncomfortably. Rooster was recuffed and they exited the room single file. Waiting in the hall was the room's next occupant, a bald middle-aged lawyer holding a large briefcase. The interview room was soundproof, but the lawyer gave them a knowing look. The ugliness that had just occurred inside poured out into the hall, as palpable as a shit-house odor.

Being led down the corridor was the lawyer's client, a big, strong black man with a shaved dome. Behr recognized him. Earl Powers. He could put a hand to whatever a buyer wanted, which was often guns. He was Terry Cottrell's friend.

"Earl," he said in greeting.

"What you doing down here, Behr?" Earl nodded.

Mintz turned back as he was half led, half carried away. "That's your name? Behr? I'm gonna sue your fucking ass."

"You know this bastard?" Behr said to Earl. "The guy *'guls* kids." Behr spoke in a moment of rash anger, sentencing Rooster Mintz with his words.

Powers's face changed. His eyes enlarged in their sockets with fury. Anyone who'd been inside, as Earl Powers had, knew the term. It came from Italian, from *fungulo,* and it meant to take someone by force.

"Bullshit," Mintz screamed, more animal than man, because he knew how child rapers were treated inside, and now he was branded. He was still screaming his denials as he was prodded on down the hall by the guard and they turned the corner out of sight.

Behr and Paul left the jail. Troy Silva at County sure didn't owe him anymore.

TWENTY-FOUR

THE BLOND WOOD GRAIN of the floor at Samadhi Yoga Center was close to Carol's face as she lay on her stomach and then arched up into *bhujangasana*, cobra pose. The sound of Indian music was in the air, harmonium, finger cymbals, and sitar, in addition to the faint traces of sandalwood incense. She dreaded what came next and struggled not to anticipate, but to remain in the moment. The instructor's voice came, soothing, encouraging, and directed the class through downward dog and into pigeon pose. Carol placed her right leg in front of, and folded beneath, her and puffed her chest out like a bird. She held for a moment before folding over toward the floor and opening her hips. An advanced student in front of her moved into *eka pada rajakapotasana*, one-legged king pigeon pose, the sole of her rear foot bending up to touch the back of her head. Carol couldn't imagine the flexibility required to do that when the preparatory position she was in already flooded her body with something approximating searing pain. The ancient wounds of her pelvis, which had spread wide to birth Jamie, began to open.

She had taken up yoga two years earlier and had hardly been a devoted student, stopping entirely when Jamie disappeared, until a few months back when she was standing in line at a supermarket checkout and saw a yoga magazine featuring a model in an extended side-angle pose. The image spoke to her heart and called her back to the mat. Now she practiced five days a week and had felt physical stability slowly returning to her through the motion and focused breathing. At first, for many months, and even now, the stilling of the mind, the quiet, was terrifying for her. Memories of sounds and images, of Jamie's face, his smile and laugh, would launch in her mind when she was completely defenseless in the midst of class. The agony was profound. Where her emotional nerves had once been dead, they had begun to spike with sensation. She had, one moment and one breath at a time, found a way to not give up. She continued to attend class, unrolling her mat and lying down before it began, participating silently, and then rolling up her mat without saying a word to fellow students or the teacher. She had made progress, but still there were obstacles in the way of her body's opening and she wondered if she'd ever develop the confidence and ability others in the class had. The teacher's voice came again, urging them.

"Breathe deeply and soften your edges to the vast sea of divine grace around you."

Carol glanced left, trying to empty her mind, and saw the large brass Dancing Shiva statue. The god stood under the flaming arch, with his right foot resting on the back of a dwarfish figure that personified illusion and ignorance. She had learned this all at a meditation seminar months ago. Shiva had two sets of arms, and in one of his right hands was the small drum on which he beat out the rhythm of the universe and creation, while the flame in one of his left hands represented the burning, the destruction and purification, of all things worldly and temporal.

She looked up toward the god's head, focused on his third eye, in the middle of his forehead, center of omniscience, and suddenly her psoas muscles, then lower back and hamstrings, released and opened. What felt like a wave of warm liquid poured through her hips. Her torso settled flat and she melted into the floor, going further than she'd imagined possible. Her every cell spoke to her now as she felt an onrushing of deep emotion breaking free from her hips. The pain of childbirth, every sickness, fear, and disappointment Jamie had faced in his life, washed over her. And then a great soaring of joy in her motherhood, the agony of her loss, it all seemed to spring forth from the seat of her being. Overwhelmed, she felt her stomach seize up and she began to sob quietly. She'd heard that this emotion-body connection was possible in deep practice but hadn't imagined she would ever find herself weeping in class. But finally the tender pain was of a magnitude that she could not, did not even want to, stand in the way of any longer. It all just flowed.

Paul knew he'd run into Carol if he went home to change. It was unfortunate, but he had to. He had popped sweat the moment he and Behr had entered the jail and was drenched, sodden, by the time they'd left. He needed to wash off the filth of the day, and Behr had to go run down information on the name they'd gotten before they'd meet up again to go talk to this Oscar Riggi. He flexed his swollen hands and rolled his wrists. He'd learned some things about hitting a man that day that he wouldn't soon forget. Distance was the enemy. Short punches, the way. He felt he was wearing stiff gloves, several sizes too small, so sore were his wrists and hands now. Wrong as it may have been, landing the blows had brought a measure of satisfaction. He'd have to thank Behr for that.

. . .

Carol got back from her class around midday and realized Paul was at home. When she had seen that he wasn't wearing a suit that morning and that he didn't go off to work, she felt sure he was having an affair. She wasn't surprised that he was, considering the state of their life together, only that he'd waited so long to start one. He'd been out most nights for the past few weeks, with no explanation. For her part she hadn't asked for one. It seemed he was unconcerned about hiding things. This hurt her in a place she didn't know could still be hurt. The pain was brand new to her, and not unpleasant, but rather enervating. She went upstairs, expecting to find him with someone, and wondering what she should do about it. She hardly had the indignation or the energy for a scene. But in the bedroom she found Paul alone. He was uncommunicative and on his way to the closet after a shower. She was sitting on the edge of the bed when she got her next surprise—his hands.

She looked up from them, all puffy and red, to his towel-clad waist, across his naked torso, to his face. "Were you boxing again?" As far as she knew, the heavy bag had hung dormant in the garage for some time.

He didn't meet her eyes. "Yeah. That's right." He went to the closet and dressed. Her eyes were clear and she recognized the lie immediately.

Something is going on, she thought, but she didn't know what.

Paul left the room and went downstairs. She could hear him in the kitchen making something to eat. After a moment a car horn sounded. The front door opened, then closed behind Paul. She felt the house empty. She went to the window in time to see him, carrying two sandwiches, cross to Frank Behr's car and climb in. Then they drove off. *Something is going on* repeated in her head.

O Loving Jesus, meek Lamb of God, I miserable sinner, Oscar Riggi incanted, kneeling in the mottled light of St. Francis Church, *salute and worship the most Sacred Wound of Thy Shoulder on which Thou didst bear Thy heavy Cross, which so tore Thy flesh and laid bare Thy Bones as to inflict on Thee an anguish greater than any other wound of Thy Most Blessed Body.* The church smelled of stale frankincense, an odor that brought him back to his youth, to his long hours spent in service as an altar boy. Mass had become routine for him on those endless, repetitive mornings, and it was only the old habit that kept him worshipping these days. He said the words to himself, but there was no longer any connection to what they meant. In fact, the words would hardly come anymore. He was a long way from the Church. Further than he'd ever been. *I adore Thee, O Jesus most sorrowful; I praise and glorify Thee, and give Thee thanks for this most sacred and painful Wound. . . .*

As he stared up at the image of the mournful One in black brass hanging crucified before him, Riggi imagined their faces: the boys', bright and innocent. He only imagined them, as he'd never met or laid eyes on a single one of them, even after they'd fallen under his control. He wondered idly if he'd ever happened to have unknowingly seen one of them in passing *before*. He tried to calculate their number now, so far in, but could not. It had been twelve years, three cities, since he'd begun. There had been quite a few. He had encrypted records that held the answer and kept an accounting of all the amounts, but he had not consulted them in a long, long time. . . . *beseeching Thee by that exceeding pain, and by the crushing burden of Thy heavy Cross to be merciful to me, to forgive me all my mortal and venial sins, and to lead me on towards Heaven along the Way of Thy Cross. Amen.* The ancient cadence of prayer ground to a halt inside his head.

He stood and felt the blood flow back through his knees. He couldn't keep his thoughts on what he was doing, and lack of focus was the earmark of a poor manager. Tad Ford was dead. His main man, Rooster, was unreachable. His business was off the chain, and not in the way the niggers meant it—to describe something incredibly good. Rather the machinery he had painstakingly built was no longer functioning. It had seemed like a minor thing when Tad bowed out a few months back.

The guy had been half a lummox, a burro who had merely followed orders, but replacing him had become surprisingly difficult, before he'd made himself an outright liability and had to go. It was the first killing Riggi had ordered. The only other death on his tab had been ten years back, a beating he'd assigned that had gone wrong. Now he'd closed the regular office, too, given everyone their two weeks' pay just to keep things nice and tight. As far as restaffing went, Riggi knew plenty of young men willing to do just about anything in order to get a wad of cash pressed into their palms. Several of them, two guys in particular, Wenck and Gilley, who worked together as a team, had proved sure enough to steal some cars and dump some others, but he'd found himself hesitating when it came time to broach the subject of making a run. Maybe he was getting too old and too cautious. He'd always listened to his instincts, though, and in turn they spoke to him in a clear, nearly audible way. Lately they'd been screaming *wait*. His heels rang off the stone floor as he headed for the door, pausing to bob and make the sign of the crucifix across his chest as he passed the font of holy water.

Outside, the air was steely with cold. He buttoned his cashmere coat, twisting his silk and cashmere muffler up around his throat to block any stray wind. The winter felt never-ending and he longed to get away to the Bahamas, to Paradise

Island. His joints craved some warm, humid air. He envisioned a massage on the beach, tropical drinks and a bit of time in the casino at night, smoking the Havanas that were abundant down there. He could call the travel agent and head out for a couple or three days, the only decision being which young lady to take with him. He could afford it. He still had plenty of rental income from his properties, but it just didn't feel like the right time. His work ethic was such that when things were faltering, his first reaction was to buckle down and apply himself until they were running well again. Of course, when things were cooking, he felt the urge to push the advantage and was reluctant to break the momentum with something so indulgent as a vacation. The result was accumulated tension that at the moment was beating him. He was a workaholic and he knew it. He slid into his car, the leather seat cold as a marble slab, and kicked over the engine. He drove out of the lot and headed for the office as if on autopilot.

"I've got two addresses so far. An office and a residence," Behr said when Paul got in the car. He spent some rubber pulling out and drove across town. "This guy, Riggi, he comes up as a real estate broker. I've got his home on Heatherstone in Carmel."

"He must be doing well," Paul said, handing him a sandwich.

"Yeah. I say we try the office first."

They finished their turkey and Muenster on seven-grain sandwiches by the time they reached the small stand-alone building of a faux Tudor style that housed Hemlock Point Realty. They approached the thick brown wooden door, which was locked. They peered in through a small glass square in the door. A main room held three desks, which bore computers and listings books, but were currently unoccupied. The whole place, in fact, including the waiting area, and what they could see of some back offices, was empty.

"It's around midday. The office could be out to lunch."

"They could be closed for the day. Or longer."

"Yep." There was no sign informing them as to which.

They returned to the car and sat there, the ignition turned off as Behr had been taught, breath clouding the cold air.

"We could chase around to the home address, but we could end up missing him all over the place. I say we invest a few hours in waiting."

Paul nodded his agreement.

They sat for a quarter hour in attentive silence, both scrupulously avoiding the events of the morning, Paul's methodic flexing and rubbing of his hands the only tangible reminder of what had gone on. Then Behr spoke.

"It was a chance I took bringing you to County. Lots of guys would've collared up in that situation"—Behr put a hand near his throat in a choking gesture—"but you did good."

"If lots of guys would've collared up, why'd you risk bringing me?" Paul asked.

"You're not lots of guys."

Paul nodded his thanks. "Neither are you, Frank."

They fell silent again and watched midday slide through to early afternoon. Before long Paul's breathing deepened. His eyelids began to flicker and he drifted off into a light sleep.

Paul felt his bones go to rubber. His mind released to a place without thought. A golden darkness surrounded him. He walked down a beach of powdery sand. He was in Destin, Florida. They had gone there as a family three years ago Easter, but he was there now, in a time out of time. A parasailer floated by him, towed by a boat, black in silhouette against the sky. As the canopy cleared it, the sun shone bright in his eyes. He did not look away. He felt his thudding footsteps absorbed by the sand, sucking his feet downward. He knew he was dozing, dreaming, but the images were more real than any reality he'd known. He kept walking and began to come up on the figure of his wife. She was in a bathing suit, her body young and firm. His eyes traveled down her arm, with aching slowness, to her hand. Hers held on to the small hand of a boy. Jamie. His son's feet moved in a youthful dance, like a colt's, light sand kicking up around his ankles. Paul walked faster, his legs feeling incredibly heavy. Still, he gained ground, one step, two steps closer. Suddenly, his wife's and his son's hands broke free. Jamie skipped down the beach, nimble, free. Paul had no hope of catching him. His legs were rubber. Jamie wasn't fleeing, though; he turned where he was, as he used to when he was a young child, exploring the boundaries of independence but wanting to be sure his parents were still there. Paul's wakeful mind rose up and he asked himself the very clear question of whether this was a mere dream or if he was being visited by the spirit of his dead son.

His eyes snapped open and he was back in the cold car. There was no time to revel in or mourn the vision, as a man was crossing from a gleaming sedan toward the Tudor building. Paul looked out at him and saw with the fleeting, penetrating clarity that the edge of consciousness brings. He'd believed he'd faced a difficult, ugly fact of the world that morning at the jail, but in that one look through the windshield he recognized that there were layers upon layers of filth and meanness, and he'd only been at the surface.

Behr was already halfway out of the car when Paul went for his door handle.

"Yeah, Mr. Riggi, how are you?" The eyes of the man in the expensive coat darted and revealed they had the right person. "We're interested in some property—"

"No, you're not," Riggi said, stopping and squaring, cutting right through Behr's little pretext. "What do you want?"

"You're right, it's not about property. It's about your side business—"

"Side business? No. I'm a Realtor. If it's not about property, there's nothing I can do for you."

"We spoke to an associate of yours, a nasty guy in a nasty place. He says different."

"Oh, yeah? Who was that?"

"Garth Mintz." Behr watched Riggi's jaw work, his face going a bit more florid than even the cold demanded.

"I don't have any associate by that name. What is it you want?"

"Yeah, you do—"

"What, exactly, do you want? It's the last time I'm asking."

Behr recognized that they had reached the point where there was nothing to do but plunge forward. "We're here about a boy named Jamie Gabriel, who went missing."

Amazing things happened on Riggi's face. Several complex emotions began and were then reined in, no single one allowed to reach full bloom. The net effect was a vacant sort of expression that revealed nothing. The guy was harder to read than a Chinese Bible. Behr realized he was witnessing deception on a very high level. He would need hours with the man, in a controlled environment, applying an array of interrogation techniques, if he hoped to be sure of a truthful response. When Riggi spoke, his voice was even and unhurried.

"Never heard the name. Don't know anything about it. If this Mintz said I did, I should probably go talk to him about it. Where's he at?"

Behr respected the man's effort at turning the inquiry into a question of his own. "Don't worry about that," he countered.

Riggi's chest practically heaved under his overcoat as he asked his next question, though his voice remained level. "Who are you, then? You know, in case I think of something that'll help, so's I can pass it on to you."

Behr stared across the short distance into Riggi's eyes. They were porcine, black and cold, but intelligent. He reached into his pocket and drew out a business card. It was a smart move by Riggi, putting Behr in a position to give information about himself.

"Here." Behr handed him the card. Riggi looked it over.

"Okay, Mr. Behr." Then Riggi's eyes tracked over to Paul. "And how do I reach you, quiet guy?"

Behr answered for him. "Quiet guy's *my* associate. He doesn't have a card. You can reach him through me."

Riggi nodded as if the answer told him much more than the words seemed to. "I see." He tucked the business card away and made to move toward his office. "I'm going now. If you two ever plan on coming back, you better make an appointment first."

"We'll do that," Behr said, matching Riggi's stare. The man before him was no pervert wrestling with his desires. He was an organized man, a businessman. If Behr had thought he'd been in the presence of evil in the interrogation room at County, he knew he had now witnessed a much more evolved version.

Riggi sat in his vacant office in the dark. He'd locked the door behind him and drawn the blinds. A bottle of Lagavulin was in easy reach of one hand, the business card rested in his other. FRANK BEHR, INVESTIGATIVE SERVICES. There was a telephone number, a cell phone number, and a fax number. All the information he could possibly need. He'd read bad news off the guy as soon as the fucker and his mute friend had rolled up on him. And now, a few hours later, as he thought it over slowly, carefully, he was sure Behr was the same man who'd put the bitch-slapping on Tad Ford. He was certainly big enough to do it, and he must have had plenty of drive to end up on his doorstep. Riggi had assumed, or perhaps hoped, that Tad hadn't given anything up the night he'd been braced, that there hadn't been time before Tad was no more. He had half talked himself into believing that was the case, as time had passed since the incident and there'd been no further ripples. But he saw now that he'd been wrong. He had deluded himself. Believing what he wanted to, rather than seeing what was, was no way for a serious man to operate. There had been an article in the paper about a female cop being beaten. Police hadn't released the name of the assailant. He had his guess. Either that, or Tad had spit out enough for this detective to have found Rooster, and the man had found some damn way to make Rooster talk. Riggi took a swallow of scotch against the chill that this thought delivered. Now it was all pressing up on him. He didn't like that. It was time to make ready for war.

He reached across his desk, picked up the phone, and dialed.

"Wenck?" he said. "It's Oscar. Is Gilley with you? Good. It's time we did business."

TWENTY-FIVE

BEHR SAT IN PAUL'S OFFICE using the computer late into the afternoon. He began by checking Riggi's name with various search engines and newsgroups. No mention appeared. Most people were referenced in some fashion, by wedding, funeral, or various other announcements that invariably found their way onto the Internet. Behr considered whether he was dealing with an alias or a changed-name situation. He leaned back and noticed the plaques that hung on the office walls around him, proclaiming Paul's achievements in sales, completion of seminars, and qualification in various financial instruments. He glanced at the photos on Paul's desk—Carol, Jamie, the three of them—smiling in testament to the family they'd once been. The images sent him back into the stream of data that filled the computer screen before him. Paul stepped in and out from time to time to retrieve documents from his file cabinets for the next client meeting, which he took in a conference room down the hall as Behr continued on into a more exhaustive background search. Paul's secretary also popped in and out of the office, fetching and dropping off papers, giving him a quizzical look each time, but Paul had her trained well and she asked him no questions. Behr entered into the Indianapolis municipal records database and searched property titles. It was there that he began getting hits. Riggi owned more than half a dozen commercial properties. There wasn't much information beyond location, assessments, and the fact that the taxes were current. Behr wrote down the addresses, and when he looked up, he realized it had grown dark.

They left together, Paul locking up the office behind them. They crossed to the parking lot. He'd been riding with Behr all day and would need a lift home.

"What did you come up with?" he asked.

"So far Riggi's story is true. He owns rental property all over town. You got a minute before I drop you?"

Paul was drained after the long day, but he nodded. They headed toward the first address, Behr referring to a handwritten list as they drove.

The first property was a small strip center off Binford Boulevard. It housed a taco joint, a watch shop, a dry cleaner, a pediatrician's office, and a frozen yogurt shop, which was the only business still open at the time. They looked at it for a moment from across the street, then drove along the storefronts, the dark glass reflecting the pinpoints of streetlights back at them. They continued on, looping around the back, where they found a row of Dumpsters and two parked cars. Behr paused to write down the license plate numbers. The back door to the fro-yo place swung open, a peel of light spilling out from the inside. A diminutive dark-skinned man dragged an industrial-size trash bag out. He rocked back and forth from foot to foot for a moment, gaining momentum, then slung the garbage up and into a Dumpster. The man paused, dusted off his hands, and stared at them in the car for a few long beats. Paul wondered if Behr would go and question him. Instead he put the car in gear and slowly pulled out.

The second location was a minimall similar to the first. There was a tanning salon, a Subway shop, an herbal health-food store, an out-of-business independent video store, and a beauty salon. They stared for a while, and then Behr shrugged and drove on.

"These addresses mean anything to you?" he asked, handing Paul the list.

Paul looked it over. "These street numbers

don't, but if this one is at the intersection of Shade-land and Forty-sixth, I do know it," he said, point-ing at the fourth location down the list.

They had reached the third center, Behr trolling slowly along past more nondescript businesses. "That's the second pediatrician's office," Behr noted, the air seeming to hang still in the car. "What's the address you know?"

"It's where Jamie went to the dentist," Paul answered.

Behr goosed the accelerator, causing the car to leap out into traffic.

They continued through the rest of the dozen properties, the collective adrenaline level rising at each stop. All but two of the properties housed doctor and dental offices that were pediatrics-based or family practices.

"Frank, my stomach's churning here. This is no coincidence, is it?" Paul asked.

Behr shook his head slowly. A sense of knowing emanated from him even as he pulled over, turned, and removed a thick file folder from the backseat. "I've researched the other missing children in the area who fit the profile. This is my case file," Behr explained.

"You're checking if any of them were patients?"

"Right." Behr turned the pages of police records. "There were seven cases in the past three years of boys who went missing in greater Indianapolis under circumstances similar to Jamie's. There were actually nine total, but two turned up. One visited a shopping mall on the other side of the city, got lost, feared trouble with his parents, and stayed on the streets for close to a week before returning home. Case closed. The other is dead, the body discovered ten days after the disappearance, having been struck by a car and dragged into a wooded area. Again, case closed." It was as much as Paul had ever heard Behr speak at one time.

Behr began writing down a list of the names of the other seven boys.

"The police reports don't list their doctors and dentists, do they?" Paul asked.

"Not usually, unless there's a reason," Behr said, glancing over the documents on the odd chance that they did. "And no, not in this instance." He closed the folder.

"Are the doctors involved?"

Behr seemed to turn the question around in his mind like someone playing with the old Rubik's Cube before he answered.

"I've never seen a connection between the missing kids. I've been working under the assumption that the abduction was related to the newspaper delivery route. I was wrong. I'm guessing Riggi, or someone who works for him, follows certain patients home. Or they case the offices. Maybe they access the practices using passkeys to get names and addresses."

Behr turned around with the case file and

dropped it in the backseat. He looked at the list in his hand. The names of seven boys, ages eleven to fourteen, all gone. "There's nothing else to be done tonight," he said.

"Shit," Paul breathed.

"I'm at the first doctor's office at 8:00 A.M. You with me?"

"Hell, yes." Paul nodded.

Behr went into Dr. Milton Howard's practice minutes after it opened and found it already busy. Walk-ins, mothers with sick infants and toddlers, were in the waiting room. He'd left Paul in the car, as numbers didn't help in this kind of task. He approached the desk, where an attractive Latin woman wrestled with patient records, the ringing phone, her morning coffee, and the tremendously large hoop earrings she was wearing. When Behr reached her, she didn't even look up.

"Put the child's name on the sign-in sheet," she instructed.

"Yeah, excuse me," Behr began, "what's your name?"

She looked up. "Gloria. What you need?" She didn't have the time or the inclination for a smile.

"I'm an investigator," Behr said, passing her his card. "I was hoping to get a patient list for the past two years or so." He smiled at what he imagined was the likelihood of his request being granted.

"Honey, you can subpoena that. Otherwise, never gonna happen. Anything else?"

"What's the least busy time of day? Maybe I can come back when we could talk a little more—"

"Baby, you looking at it," Gloria told him. "It only gets worse."

Behr heard a wet cough, glanced back, and saw a mother holding a red-nosed child behind him.

"Lunch?" he tried.

"With you? Uh-uh, no. Move over, let the patients through."

Behr edged to the side and allowed the woman to sign in. She then retreated to a small plastic seat near a fish tank. He leaned back over the desk before two more women, one with a boy who'd just begun to walk, the other with a daughter who was about nine years old, could squeeze in on the list. Gloria sighed at the fact that he was still there.

"How about this? I ask you a name, you tell me if he's a patient. Then I get out of your face."

Gloria tapped a fingernail on the desk before her. It was long, probably acrylic.

"Fine. Go."

"Aaron Barr."

"No," she said, almost before he'd finished speaking.

He paused, hating to push it, but he had to ask. "You want to check the patient rolls, maybe?"

"No. I don't need to. I know the patients and I

got a good memory for names." She tapped her temple with an acrylic spear.

Behr shot through three more names before he hit the number. "Adam Greiss."

Gloria nodded, her eyes growing large and her throat working as she swallowed. Tough as she was, she had to talk when she heard the name. "He used to come here. He disappeared two years ago. He was about twelve."

Behr felt his heart banging in his chest. "Did he ever turn up? You know anything else about it?"

"No. It was sad what happened. Weird. Scary."

"That it is," he agreed.

"You on his case, looking for him?" she wondered.

"Yeah. Indirectly," he answered.

The line behind him was three or four deep now. He rattled off the last two names but drew blanks from her.

Paul saw Behr leaving the doctor's office at a near run. When he drew close to the car and came around to the passenger side, Paul put down the window. "Get something?" he asked.

Behr nodded. "One hit. A patient. You drive to the next place so I can just hop out. It'll be faster."

Paul slid over behind the wheel and pointed the car toward the next location. The car wasn't smooth like his LeSabre, the transmission changed gears in a jagged way, but he was surprised at its power, which he used to get them where they were going faster than the law permitted.

He waited, fairly going out of his skin, in the idling car, while Behr checked each office systematically. He found that four other missing children were former patients of the doctors and dentists. One doctor, who specialized in pediatric oncology, refused to give any information, even a confirmation, regarding his patients and threatened to call the police on Behr if he continued to press the matter. They were both in a lather by the end of the day, with only one address to go. The last office was that of Jamie's dentist, Dr. Ira Sibarsky, and Paul led the way.

"Hey, Karen," he said to the receptionist-hygienist who was up front, seated at a computer desk beneath an oversize toothbrush mounted on the wall.

"Paul," she said, surprise and dismay registering on her face. It was the expression of helpless pity that everyone who knew about Jamie gave him. If he'd ever appreciated the sympathy, he sure couldn't remember when. "How are you?"

"Good, good. Can I talk to Ira for a minute?" She nodded and disappeared in the back. Paul looked at Behr and they stood and waited, breathing in the faint mint and medicinal smell of the place. Soon the dentist, a smallish man with curly gray hair and a rounded rabbitlike nose, appeared in the doorway and beckoned them to the back.

The dentist's office was decorated in muted plaids. X-rays of teeth and bite molds littered a scarred wooden desk. Paul remembered the other times he'd been in the office, when the biggest problem in his life was a pair of Jamie's cavities that needed filling. Sibarsky sat back in a threadbare office chair and took off his glasses.

"What's up, Paul, and . . . ?"

"This is Frank Behr. He's a private investigator who's helping us regarding Jamie."

"Oh, I see," Sibarsky said. "Any word?"

"What can you tell us about your landlord?" Paul said, unwilling to discuss details.

"My landlord?" the dentist asked, concern spreading over his face.

"That's right. I'd tell you if you had any cause to worry, Ira," Paul said with assurance.

"Hemlock Point Realty. I don't have much contact with them. I leased the space from Polly someone or other seven years ago. She's the one I call if need be. I send in a check on or about the first of the month. The roof leaked once. They put in a new bathroom three or four years ago. Why?"

"Have you ever dealt with Oscar Riggi?" Paul asked. He'd learned from watching Behr that this was a probing exercise, not a conversation, and as such he was best served not wasting time answering the other person's questions. It may have struck Sibarsky as a bit rude, but Paul was well beyond caring.

"No. I don't think I know him. Something about the name is familiar."

"He's the principal of Hemlock Point. Midforties. Expensive clothes. Bald-headed. Stronglooking," Paul elaborated.

Sibarsky nodded. "Sure, sure. I've seen him. He inspected after the new bathroom was installed."

"He ever come by at other times?" Behr asked, joining the proceedings for the first time.

Sibarsky's glance swiveled toward Behr. "No."

"Does he have a key? Could he access the office when you're closed? Have you ever been robbed or suspected that your records or files were disturbed?" Behr continued.

"No. You don't think . . ." Sibarsky considered, seeming to grow nervous at the idea of it. He stared at the two blank faces and stuck to answering the questions. "I suppose the company has keys in case of emergency. I've never seen evidence they were in here. Do you think he's involved—"

"What about other employees of Hemlock Point?" Paul cut him off.

"Have you ever met or heard of Tad Ford or Garth Mintz?" Behr added.

"No, I haven't," Sibarsky said, raising his hands off the desk slightly.

Paul glanced at Behr and the look he got in return told him they were done there.

As they got up, Ira Sibarsky's lips moved silently for a few seconds before he spoke. "I'm . . . we're all real sorry about the situation. . . ."

Paul snapped off a curt nod and walked out the door.

They stood outside the car and looked over the list of the places they'd been to, the names.

"There's one more stop," Behr said.

"Besides Riggi's house," Paul clarified.

"Right." It wasn't a medical office or a strip mall. It was a house, a rental property, on Kellogg Street. "I'll drive this time," Behr said.

They drove over to the Hawthorne area, the environs going seedy as they neared their destination. It looked like some blight was killing the trees along Lynhurst. They drifted slowly down Kellogg, which was lined by houses that were trying hard to maintain their dignity. Most were white or gray, recently painted, but with thin coats of cheap paint. Then they saw number 96. It was painted a sickly green color and appeared to be abandoned. The paint had given up and was peeling off in long curls, and the weather had been getting at the wood underneath. The lawn wasn't tended. If it'd been summer, the grass would have grown over a foot high since its last cutting. As it was, it was weedy and brown. There was a drooping narrow porch leading to a pitted front door. Behr pulled over to the curb and put the car in park. They observed the house for any signs of life, of which there were none.

"At what point do we involve the cops?" Paul wondered out loud.

"At some point. But I need to get into this house first, and the police will prevent that from happening."

"We're going in then?"

"I am."

Behr leaned over and reached across Paul, opening the glove compartment. He fished around in it for a moment, under registration and insurance papers, before he found what he was looking for: two small pieces of black-painted metal, one twisted like a drill bit, the other L-shaped like an Allen wrench but flat at the end.

Behr got out, looking up and down the street for any neighbors. No one was around. Paul stepped out of the car as well and followed as Behr walked up the few steps and onto the porch. He pounded on the front door, then put his ear against it. Both of them listened.

"Nothing," he said, walking down the steps

and around the side of the house. They peered in the windows and saw darkened rooms, mostly devoid of furniture or anything else. There was a side door with a corroded brass knob. Behr tried it, and though it turned a bit in its casing, it was locked. They continued on and reached the windows of what would have been a back bedroom. They were unable to see inside, as the windows were painted black.

After a full orbit around the outside, Behr led them back to the locked side door. He took a knee and produced the two pieces of metal he'd taken from the glove compartment. He slid the one that looked like a drill bit into the keyhole on the knob. He jiggled it around for a moment and then inserted the Allen wrench–looking piece next to it. For the next five minutes Behr's hands worked as if he was conducting a miniature concert. He seemed to make progress. The knob rattled a bit but didn't yield.

"I can only get one pin and there are two others," Behr said, removing the tools and standing up.

"Lock's too strong?"

"Lock's a piece of shit. This small tension tool and pry bar won't get it done, though. The pins are too far apart along the shear line for it."

"What next?"

"Cough."

It was mostly symbolic, but Paul hacked loudly

as Behr put a shoulder into the door. The jamb exploded in a geyser of rotted wood chips, and they were in.

The house was silent and near empty. The door they'd broken through led into the kitchen. Aging appliances in a shade of green rested on cracking linoleum that was curling up in the corners. They checked the refrigerator, which was turned off and devoid of provisions. It emitted the faint smell of ancient dairy products. The oven was empty and hadn't been cooked in for quite a while.

They stepped into the living room. A plastic milk crate was the only furniture. There were marks in the crusty shag carpeting that showed where couches and chairs had once rested. The walls were pocked with holes of various sizes and shapes. There was nothing to look at in the room and they moved on quickly, a sense of anticipation rising in them. The house had no basement, just a dead-end crawl space they peered into, and they moved down a short hallway.

When they reached the end, they found two bedrooms separated by a bathroom. One bedroom was carpeted, an old shaggy brown, and had roller shades on the windows. The room and its closets were empty. The other bedroom was empty as well. It was uncarpeted. Other details were diffi-cult to make out because of the darkness caused by the black-painted windows that they'd noticed from the outside. They moved close to the windows and found deep screw holes along the windowpanes. Behr ran his fingers over them, wondering exactly what they signified. Paul moved his foot along the floor, sliding crumpled fast-food wrappers from various chains down the baseboard. They turned around, surveying the area, inspecting the empty closets, then moved on to the bathroom.

The bathroom was both filthy and empty save for one item. On the stained tile floor in front of the toilet was a copy of the *Star,* folded back to the sports section. It was sodden from a slow leak at the base of the toilet. Behr knelt down and looked at it, the newsprint bloated and spreading due to the water. He picked it up gingerly, the pages heavy with water, and checked the date.

"October twenty-fourth?" Paul said aloud. Behr nodded his head, then carefully rested the paper on the toilet lid and folded it to the front page to check for a subscriber address. But the upper-right-hand corner of the page had been torn away.

TWENTY-SIX

HE HAD PLANS TO MEET Susan Durant for the first
time, and it took a nearly physical effort for
Behr to put aside the case and focus on the
evening. He and Paul had agreed to meet early the
next morning, to go and take a look at Riggi's
house. That moment seemed a long way off and he
felt pulled in two directions. While he drove over
to pick Susan up, he tried to concentrate on the social occasion at hand. He had long ago learned to
relegate his hopes to a modest place when getting
together with a female whom he'd never before
met. It had become a necessity after many blind
dates and acquaintances made over the phone that
hadn't panned out. He'd gone too many times for
dinner or a drink with a woman with whom he'd
had good phone rapport, hoping for a looker or at
least someone who stirred him, only to find some-

one he couldn't even get started with. It was a superficial way to view things, he couldn't deny it. He suspected that the essence he'd encountered over the telephone was the important thing, but he wasn't much for faking it when it came to romance. It was a two-way street anyhow. He'd clocked enough disappointment coming back across the table at him over the years.

Susan's voice was bright and animated when he called from downstairs to say he'd arrived. Still, the best he'd allowed himself to anticipate was someone who gave good phone but was on the edge of pretty or just plain. When she came through her building's door, moving fast, her hair a yellow slash against her black coat, he saw she was well beyond that. She was tall, nearly six feet, with swept-back blond hair and pure white teeth. She was broad, a few important degrees from big, though. One of his first thoughts was that she was too young for him. He got out to greet her.

"Susan."

" 'Lo, Frank." Her grip was firm and her hand was soft, as he knew they would be. Standing closer, he saw the faint laugh lines at the corners of her eyes. The age gap wasn't as wide as he'd thought. She was in her midthirties, but with great energy, and he was heartened.

She shimmied out of her coat and threw it down on the front seat. She wore a black boatneck dress that gave him a moment to appreciate her smooth, powerful swimmer's shoulders before she slid into the car. He closed the door behind her and they drove toward Donohue's.

Wenck put the Gran Torino in gear and followed the Olds about a dozen car lengths back.

"Keep back about ten cars," Gilley said unnecessarily.

"I know," Wenck responded as they entered into the light flow of traffic on North Cooper Road, where it was easy to stay with him, but there were still enough cars with which to blend. They were just another pair of headlights. The investigator would never see them coming. They'd finally got their audition. They'd heard several rumors over the past year about what working for Riggi could yield; mainly money, plenty of money. And support. A constant flow of employment, from a boss who was in a position to supply jobs, proper tools, and even lawyers in the event they were needed. Wenck and Gilley had been fairly somber in their agreement not to fuck up this chance. They crossed through Knolton Heights with no sign they'd been made.

"Date," Gilley had said when they'd pulled over down the block from where the detective had stopped and they'd witnessed the pickup.

"First date," Wenck advanced. The stiff, formal way the man had gotten out of his car and the handshake greeting were what tipped him off. The shamus had done well for himself. "All he's probably wondering is if he's gonna get some slit."

"Guy's got no idea he's ending up in the hospital tonight," Gilley said aloud, allowing himself one half-snort of laughter.

"Hospital at best," Wenck said, pulling out once again. They'd agreed to play it loose as to whether they would take him going to or from his destination or on the way home, depending on the best place for the move. Riggi had warned them to be careful, that the investigator had put a hurting on some of his other men. "Brought down enough big boys to know how to do it," Wenck had said, though he planned to heed the advice nonetheless. The investigator turned and pulled into a lot behind a brick building on Belmont. Wenck nosed the Torino just past the opening of the alley to take a look. A stark bulb shone above a green door and was the only light in the area. It was ideal.

"It's a shame she's gonna have to be part of it," Wenck mused aloud of the woman. Gilley ventured a nod. They readied their arms and set to wait for Behr to come out.

Riggi valet-parked at the Westin on South Capitol and headed into the steakhouse's bar, where he planned to wait while it happened. It was best for him to be seen in a public place, to make purchases with a credit card, to perhaps be photographed by security cameras. It was preferable to meeting an associate, letting it all rest on him or her if questions started being asked, just to see that person squeezed into recanting the alibi. He sat at a cocktail table in the middle of the room and didn't even attempt to signal a waitress. He had nothing but time. He'd considered his options and decided on Wenck and Gilley and an extremely bad beating for Behr. The kind of beating that would distract and discourage and require major recovery time. He was willing for the detective to die but couldn't risk having him shot. Most detectives were ex-cops and there'd be too much suspicion and outrage over a shooting, not to mention the fact he was sure to have notes on his recent interviews that could name Riggi. No, a beating could look like something else, a street crime or a fight gone wrong, and would be harder to follow up.

"If he dies, he dies," Riggi had said when Wenck asked how far they should take it.

Wenck and Gilley. Gilley was tall and rangy, a skate punk who'd grown too old for half-pipes and rail grinding. He could've been an electrician or a plumber, made a regular life for himself, if only he could stand people. He'd punched out enough foremen, with his big hands and long-distance right, that Riggi started hearing about him around the real estate office. He looked a little further into the stories and learned that Gilley ran with a guy, Wenck, who'd been arrested a dozen times on assault, stolen property, and extortion beefs. Wenck had served three stretches in prison ranging from thirty days in lockup to eighteen months in the state facility. He was as wide as he was tall, with a thick, smashed-down brow and a low forehead, and could only have been what he was—a piece of grease for hire. It would have been the same for him no matter what era he'd lived in. If he had been around in 1800s New York, he would've been a perfect Plug Ugly. When Riggi asked himself if he had the right men for the job, he could only conclude that he did.

Paul sat in his car down the street from the fine house, aware that he was in exactly the wrong place. A few lights shone in various parts of the home, but he had been there for forty-five minutes and hadn't seen any movement or other signs of life. He was beginning to think the lights were on to create an impression but that no one was there. He felt his heart thudding; he thought he could even hear it. He and Behr had left the abandoned rental house after deciding that there was nothing else, besides that newspaper, to be gleaned from the place. They'd done their best to smooth out the broken jamb and pull the door shut behind them. Behr drove Paul back to his car, and as he had something else to do that night, they'd agreed to go and look at Riggi's residence the next day. Less than an hour later Paul found himself sitting at Riggi's, wondering if he had the stomach to do what he intended.

He had seen the list of addresses several times over the course of the last few days and Riggi's street and number were burned into his brain. He'd pointed his car toward his own home in earnest after leaving Behr, had even reached the outskirts of his neighborhood, before succumbing to the raw urge that wouldn't allow him to let it go for the night. Riggi was living well, that much was clear. The house was a whitewashed brick job, a modified Georgian with a great room squared in by large leaded windows. If the addition was a bit out of the style of the rest of the house, the place certainly looked rich and comfortable. Well-kept grass and some boxwoods surrounded it. Up and down the block lights were on in other expensive houses. There was the occasional figure passing by a window, a garage door opening and a car pulling in or out. Paul assumed there must be signs beyond that, a process or method by which a trained individual could tell if a house was occupied. But Behr wasn't with him. He was alone. He decided on his own method: He'd wait two full hours and if there were no signs of movement, he would do it.

. . .

Rooster hung from the horizontal crossbar that stretched across the top of his cell door jacking out pull-ups. He was on his fifth set of fifteen, his forearms pressed against the vertical bars, but something was wrong. He hadn't been able to conjure a song, not even a guitar riff, in his head all day. He thought back and realized it was before he'd been roughed up when he'd last heard music in his mind. Danzig's "Ashes." Then he'd been knocked around and he'd lost the music. He squeezed out his last rep, feeling the blood flow into his lats. He smacked his hands together after lowering himself to the floor, trying to summon energy, then hit the ground on his back and began his last set of one hundred sit-ups. In the past day he'd gotten to a thousand. There was no telling how long he'd be inside and he'd set his mind to staying hard. It was the only choice. If he let the mind go, the body would follow, and he'd be chum the second he was dropped into general population. He was meeting with his court-appointed attorney the next morning to prepare for his arraignment. In the meantime he was being kept in special holding. It wasn't bad so far: no roommate; two hours optional in the television room, which he skipped to work out in his cell; fifteen-minute private shower at the end of the night before lights out. The food was rough—salty, fatty, carbed up. That was the biggest problem he'd faced in the short term. He didn't hold much hope for Mr. Free Lawyer, either.

Those guys tended to be pretty bottom of the barrel, and he found himself considering whether he should call Riggi for a hook or not. If the private investigator–fuck had shown up on Riggi's doorstep, it'd be a suicide call. If not, it'd be what was referred to as a lifeline. He finished his set, his abdomen seizing and burning with the effort, and decided he'd wait and see what the public defender guy had to offer tomorrow before he'd make the call. He slid his feet into shower sandals, got his soap, razor, and towel, and shuffled down toward the shower room.

"I considered Pinnochino's, but, you know, I thought maybe it was too romantic. Didn't want it to look like I was pressing," Behr found himself volunteering after Susan had complimented Donohue's.

"Cool place," she'd said. "Clubby."

"Also, you go all out on the first date, how do you know what she's coming back for, right?" he added, wondering why in the hell he was acting so gabby.

"C'mon, Frank. How 'bout a little confidence in what you have to offer?" She smiled.

"Sorry, I haven't been out much lately."

"Yeah? That case you're working on?"

"That. And my line of work. I never meet—"

"Me neither."

"You? No—"

"Who'm I gonna date, the inkblots I work with? Nah."

She drank Johnnie Black on the rocks and ordered a flank steak right along with him.

"I'm not a salad girl," she offered without much apology, starting in on her food.

"Good," he said.

"Ah, you're probably right. Pinnochino's, the candles in the wine bottles and all, might've reeked a little like desperation," she allowed, then asked, "Ever been married?"

"Once. You?"

"Close one time. Kids?"

"Had a son."

"Had?"

"What say maybe next time we talk about it?" Behr said, trying to keep any edge out of his voice.

She gave him the eye, trying to decide what she was dealing with. Then she nodded and went back to her food.

"Who's that?" she asked of Pal Murphy, who was, at the moment, sitting and holding court with six young men in their early twenties standing in a circle before him.

"The owner."

"Oh, he's Donohue then," she concluded.

"No, Murphy."

"He bought the place from Donohue?"

"Uh-uh, Maguire, I think: Must've been a Donohue somewhere down the line, though."

"Yeah."

They smiled at each other.

Oscar Riggi's left knee bounced in a rapid rhythm beneath his cocktail table. He was tired of the taste of scotch and salted nuts and had twice gotten up to leave, only to grab ahold of himself and ask where the men's room was once and where the telephone was the second time. He'd had his credit card swiped through and had had a tab open for the last hour and a half. He'd made sure the waitress knew him, and the bartender would remember him, too, now that he'd asked the brace of questions. There had been a dozen random patrons in and out over the course of the last hour, in addition to a wave of conventioneers whose panel discussion had just broken, and more than a few would recall the well-dressed man with the shining dome who'd sat alone in the middle of the bar. "He seemed to be waiting for someone or something," they'd think, not knowing that it was a call to his cell phone from Wenck and Gilley to tell him it was done. Time was crawling, though, and he couldn't keep the doubts in his mind at bay. He'd told the boys to take their time, to pick the right moment and location, but they were eager and he'd expected them to call already. He couldn't make himself wait anymore. He held up his hand for the check. He'd head home, make some calls, and sign on to the Internet from there. Not as good as waiting in the bar, but he was out of patience.

Paul drummed his fingers on the wheel and calmed his breathing as he came to his decision. His thoughts had been of Jamie during the past hour and a half. It was unusual. He had taken a disciplined approach when it came to musing about his son. When he let himself go for more than a moment or two, the memories flooded in and threatened to wash him away altogether, so he preferred to keep them at bay. But sitting in the car with nothing else to distract him besides the large white house filling his view, he'd been powerless to stop or even organize the images in his head. He pictured Jamie as a young boy, wearing his choo-choo train pajamas, sitting in his lap, the soft weight of him in his arms. He remembered him standing in right field, half bored, his mitt hanging low at his side. He recalled the smile on his boy's face when Paul pretended he couldn't find him and he had popped up from a cardboard-box fort in the basement after Paul had said, "I give up. I just don't know where the heck he is." The memories were like a jab to the stomach that left Paul half gasping and sickened. He rubbed his face and got out of the car.

The night air had a late-winter bite to it, just a

promise of spring off in the distance. He approached the house, leaving the flagstone path and cutting across the lawn. He didn't knock or ring the bell before trying the knob. Locked. He circled the house in a replay of what he and Behr had done that afternoon. He found this to be a house with sturdy doors and bolted sliders, not to mention armed alarm panels glowing inside behind small, thick windows in both the front and back doors.

Paul performed a full loop of the house and discovered nothing close to a way in. He knew he should get his ass back in his car and speed it out of there, but he sat down on the back patio on a piece of lawn furniture to think. It was peaceful in the back, only the sounds of the neighborhood, distant and muted, floating in as a reminder of where he was. Deep inside him a faint voice was urging: *leave, leave*. But still he didn't move. During his wait he tried to conjure up cover stories as to what he was doing there should Riggi get home and discover him. When he came up with absolutely nothing plausible, he began to consider whether he could handle the man physically should it come to that. He wasn't sure. He played two scenarios in his head—one that had him kicking out Riggi's knee and pouncing on him, the other beginning with a hard cross to the man's face before he was ready for it. Neither seemed too definite.

Finally the sounds of the night began to intrude and Paul realized he'd stayed too long and it was time to clear out. As he got up and headed back around front, he saw a small hutch that protected the garbage from raccoons and other vermin. He looked around and crossed to it. He opened the hutch doors and found three large Rubbermaid trash cans. Two were empty, but one held a pair of kitchen-size garbage bags. Paul half held his breath before pulling the bags out, closing the hutch, and hustling back toward his car. He opened his trunk to put them inside when a pair of headlights washed him with blinding white.

Behr had enjoyed the feel of having a young, pretty woman at his table. Her scents changed the familiar booth to an exotic place. There was the light mint, remnant of the gum she'd chewed for a minute after her coffee and then wrapped in a sugar packet, a citrus he clocked as hairspray, and an exotic floral that was her perfume. It was time to leave, however. He didn't want to stretch a first date's conversation to the point of uncomfortable. That didn't seem to be a danger as Susan knew how to alight on a subject just long enough before moving on to the next and to sit quietly for pleasant moments as well. Still, though, when something had gone as well as this dinner had, Behr was loath to kill it by dragging it on too long. He raised his hand toward Kaitlin, who was standing by the service end of the bar, and she headed right over with the check she had ready.

"Anything else, Frank?" the waitress asked, her voice husky from a lifetime of nights spent working in places like Donohue's.

"No, we're good," Behr said, looking to Susan, who nodded. Kaitlin moved on as Behr reached for his cash.

"Can I . . . ?" Susan said, picking up her purse.

"No, you definitely can't," Behr answered, counting out bills, "but you're a peach for asking."

"I knew you'd say no." Susan smiled, causing his blood to rush to his stomach.

"Ready?"

"Let's blow this joint," she said, collecting her bag, coat, and scarf and sliding out of the booth.

Rooster be-bopped into the shower room, silence inside his head and out. He'd mastered a confident walk his first time in jail. He'd learned it was paramount, even if one wasn't feeling confident. He steered clear of two big dudes who were just finishing up, moving down the row of showerheads to the end of the line. He flexed his lats a little and realized he was bulked up but not truly big and never would be at one eighty-five, one ninety tops. The two guys, turning off the water and toweling dry, each had forty, fifty pounds on him and probably didn't work too hard to get it. The County towels barely went around their trunks. Rooster felt his own somewhat heavy steps on the tiled floor and recognized his own size change was a sham. He was jacked but still not truly big. And he'd lost some speed and quickness, which used to be among his primary weapons. If he could manage to get out of this place, get back to a diet of his own choosing, he decided he'd cut down, go high rep, fast twitch, until he was wire and sinew like an Asian shoot fighter. He'd give up the bull and become the cobra.

He kept half an eye on the guys down the way as they collected their stuff and drifted out of the room. He adjusted the water and stepped under the needle spray of the water-saver head. He worked his cheap soap into the best lather he could and began washing. He was rinsing off when they came in, three of them now, big and thick. Rooster felt them move down the row, heard their steps under the shower's sizzle. He saw shoes on the first one, out of the corner of his eye, and that was a bad sign. He played it cool for another second, girding to turn to them and start the ritual of proving he was no bitch. But they weren't circling and testing. They were on a direct course.

The first blow landed on his lower back with a wet slap just before he was ready. He felt a moment's smug confidence at the lightness of the blow, the lack of pain it caused, and turned to kick some ass. Fighting naked wasn't his first choice, but such considerations fled his mind as fury rushed in. Then his body realized it wasn't an open-handed smack. He'd been stabbed. *Fuck,* he breathed, as his kidney went cold. It felt frozen over. Then the shivs started landing like a flurry of bee stings. His fists went out in a feeble combination that caught nothing but air. The attackers' jabs produced bright red starbursts of blood against his pale skin. His legs turned to lead, then went taffy soft. He didn't drop, more melted to the floor near the spray of the shower. His three attackers stood over him for a moment, towering black men he'd never seen before, blank looks on their faces.

"Welcome to County, short eye," one of them said in a low voice.

They extended their bloody metal points into the flowing water, and once they'd been rinsed clean, turned and left the room. Rooster felt his eyes go clear. He wasn't seeing anything now. He squinted and fought for focus. The tile floor came into view. His blood ran in a brown stream, with water, down the floor drain a few inches from his face.

I could have been special echoed in his mind, then evaporated. He sighed, the last oxygen he'd ever breathe seeping from his lungs.

They were crossing the short expanse of Dono-hue's parking lot when they heard the staccato thump of two car doors closing. Behr glanced toward the street. A car was there, motor running and lights on. Two men approached. *More of Pomeroy's terriers,* Behr thought. Their appearance caused him to keep walking toward his car, in an attempt to look unworried, rather than turn back inside the restaurant.

The men, Mutt and Jeff in size and vibe, started coming faster. They didn't say anything, and Behr saw the blood in their eyes and realized they weren't cops.

"Get around the car," he said to Susan, flipping her the keys. It was then he made out in the darkness the length of pipe each held alongside his leg.

The shorter of the pair, a stout bastard, led the way, stepping like a crab, pipe raised, other hand up around his face, ready to rock. But Behr was ready, too. He dove toward the incipient violence with abandon, the way he knew he must.

The side kick of a strong, trained six-foot-six-inch man is a weapon for which there is very little answer in the street, and the stout man ate one full bore. Behr loaded up and stepped into the kick, sending it right up the middle below the man's defenses. Despite the fact that Wenck weighed north of two hundred and thirty pounds while standing only five foot six, he was lifted off his feet. He landed hard, sitting down on his ass, behind a great out-rushing of air from his lungs, a look of befuddlement on his face.

Behr regained his stance, left foot forward, and squared just as the tall guy swung at his head. Behr understood, when he managed to block it, that the pipes they carried weren't hollow but solid-core cut-down rebar. He took a glancing blow off his forearm that would swell and bear a bruise for months, but it didn't catch bone. As bad as his left arm felt was as good as his right did when he pivoted and connected to the lanky man's chin. A shiver ran up Behr's arm, all the way to his shoulder cap. The man crumbled back and sagged to a knee, the rebar dropping from his hand. A broken jaw for certain.

Behr glanced over his shoulder to see that Susan had gotten behind the car and was crouching at the fender. He turned back to locate the recipient of his kick, expecting the man to be back up in his face or pointing a gun at him. Instead the man was on hands and knees, his abdomen heaving for breath, ropes of saliva hanging out of his mouth. Behr swept up the piece of rebar and stepped toward the man, who stood, then took a half-step forward, before he lost his will. He turned and fled from the parking lot toward the street. Behr would have chased him if not for Susan and the screaming freight train of agony that was only now rushing into his forearm. He looked back to the tall one, who had managed to scuttle a good ten yards away on his hands and heels. Now he got up and ran, in dizzy, loping strides, after his partner. They got in their car, which Behr made as a Gran Torino, though he couldn't see any license plate, and it backed out of the alley fast. The car shot into the street, lurched into forward gear, and disappeared.

Behr doubled over a bit, cradling his wounded arm, when a hand landed on his shoulder. He flinched and shrugged it off, then spun to see who else was coming after him. It was Pal Murphy.

"I heard the noise," he said.

"What noise?" Behr wondered. He had experienced the fight in complete silence. He received a quizzical look from Pal, and even Susan, who had emerged from behind the car. As he replayed the encounter in his mind, he realized that all three combatants had screamed unconscious war cries as they attacked. His *ki-ai* was as instinctual as it was loud.

Pal put his hand back on Behr's shoulder, and his other on Susan's lower back. "Come in. Have something to drink until the cops come."

"No cops," Behr said.

Pal looked him in the eye, then nodded. "Okay, just the drink. And something for that arm."

TWENTY-SEVEN

BEHR DROVE FAST. He had allowed Pal to lead him and Susan back inside. Twenty minutes later, after a pair of Tullamore Dews, Behr's arm was wrapped in a bar towel full of ice. Susan was recovering from a slight case of the shakes, and the color began to return to her cheeks.

"Hell of a date you put on, Frank," she said, smiling over the rim of her glass. He'd imposed upon Pal to take Susan home. They'd hugged each other tight and promised to see each other again, and Behr prayed she didn't have second thoughts about it.

There was no connection between him and Paul. Riggi had made a play for Paul's identity, which he had shut down. All the same, Behr took out his cell phone, hesitating for only a moment before dialing his employer. It was odd, he didn't think of Paul in that way anymore. Though the man was paying him, their relationship was unlike any he'd ever had with a client. They weren't partners and they certainly weren't friends. A tether that went beyond compatibility and personality now joined them. They weren't soul mates, for the silly romantic connotations that term held, but they intersected at a place in the soul. They were joined, in this moment in time, looking for a single answer, simple or complex, and wouldn't be pulled apart until they had it.

He tried the Gabriel house and got no answer. He hung up after four or five rings, before an answering device picked up. He tried Paul's cell phone, and this time when the voice mail picked up, he left a message.

"It's Frank. Be aware tonight. If anything's out of the ordinary, you hear a doorknob rattle, a branch scraping a window, call the police first and then me. Call me either way when you get this."

He called the house again, ready to leave a similar message, when Carol answered.

"Hello," she said, sounding distant. He wasn't sure if he'd woken her, or if this was just the way she seemed now.

"It's Frank Behr. Can I speak to Paul?"

"He's not home. I'm upstairs, but I haven't heard him come in. What's wrong?"

"You okay?"

"Yeah, what do you mean? Are you?"

"Is the house locked?"

"Yes—"

"Keep it that way. I'll be there in five minutes."

Paul's cell phone had been ringing, but he didn't bother answering it. It was all he could do to keep his car on the road and in an approximation of the standards of speed and safety. He felt like he had a dead body in the trunk. There was the accompanying clunk and shift as he cornered too quickly. Paul couldn't remember ever doing anything as reckless as this, and he'd thought he was about to pay for it when he was caught in the high beams. He'd expected the car to stop and for Riggi to come at him out of the glare. Instead the car slowed, the baffled face of the driver just staring at him as it passed by. The car continued down the block and turned into a driveway, but Paul was in the LeSabre and out of there before anything else could happen.

He pulled into the garage, leaving the door up behind him, and turned off the car, the adrenaline finally easing off in his system. He picked up his cell and saw the call had come from Frank and that there was a message waiting. Instead of checking it, he opened the trunk and removed the garbage bags. He was bent over at the waist, untying the first bag, when the door to the house opened. Carol, dressed for bed and wearing a robe, stepped into the garage.

"I thought I heard the car," she began, looking with curiosity at the bags.

"Hi, what's up?" Paul said.

"You tell me," she answered.

They were illuminated by the sweep of head-lights as a car rolled to a stop in the driveway just outside. Behr got out of his car and walked toward them, a towel wrapped around his arm.

The separate pieces of the night came together as the three of them picked through Oscar Riggi's trash. Carol, for the most part, was silent in her surprise. She'd had her ideas about her husband's and the detective's comings and goings, but none as to how far things had gone. Paul bowed his head while Behr chastised him for his surveillance of Riggi's house and for taking the garbage. Both of the Gabriels fell silent at the telling of Behr's assault.

"We must've pushed his buttons," Paul said of Riggi.

"Oh, yeah," Behr answered, "and he tried to push mine in return."

Carol was aghast when Behr rolled up his shirt-sleeve, wet from melted ice, and showed his swollen forearm.

The garbage bags didn't yield much: old utility bills—cable, electric, and water, no phone—all shredded, and various food packaging, both frozen and fresh. There were magazines: *Sports Illustrated*, *Indianapolis*, *Money*, and *Playboy*. They learned that Riggi drank scotch, good scotch. There was an old pair of sneakers, along with a bunch of worn-out socks. Riggi wore size eleven. There were plastic and stickers from CD or DVD purchases. They all kept half an eye out on the street in case a strange car showed up.

They stood back from the pile of refuse.

"I guess that was a lot of risk for nothing," Paul said. Behr clapped him on the shoulder in encouragement.

"It's late," Carol said. "Either I fire up the coffee maker or it's time for bed."

"You gonna head home?" Paul asked.

"Why don't I stay here, make sure nothing exciting happens tonight?" Behr offered.

Paul and Carol looked to each other. Paul nodded.

"You can stay in Jamie's room," Carol said.

Behr understood the significance of the offer. He cleared his throat, then said, "I should be closer to the front door. The couch is fine."

"Okay. I'll get you a pillow and blankets," Carol said, heading through the door into the house.

Behr spoke quietly to Paul alone. "Do you have a gun?"

"No. You don't?" he answered.

Carol stopped. "Oh, Jesus."

Behr adjusted his tone for everyone to hear. "I don't generally carry one. It would've just been a precaution."

"What about Jamie's baseball bat?" she asked.

"That'll be fine." They continued on inside.

Carol had rested Jamie's bat against the couch and had gone up to sleep. Behr was scrolling through numbers on his cell phone when Paul hesitated at the foot of the stairs before going up for the night. He had something to say that seemed to be bothering him. "After what happened tonight," he began, "is it time to . . . Are you going to back off?"

"That's not the way I play, Paul," Behr said.

Riggi was jumpier than he ever remembered feeling. He'd been crossing the hotel lobby when he got word from Wenck and Gilley—Wenck on the phone, Gilley slurring through a cracked jaw in the background—that things had gone to shit. He'd made a hard left to the front desk and checked in. He asked that a bag containing a few things be brought from his car up to his room. He asked to be registered in complete privacy, that no calls be put through, and no messages taken on his behalf with no acknowledgment made by the desk staff to any visitors that he was there. Fifty-dollar bills all around ensured his wishes were carried out.

He passed a long, unpleasant night unlike any he'd ever spent in a nice hotel, places in which he usually enjoyed room-service dinners and flowing champagne in the company of young women. It was only when the morning light came burning around the edges of the curtains that he realized he hadn't slept for a moment. He forced himself into action, ordering eggs, toast, and cappuccino from room service. Then he took a shower, alternating the water temperature from scalding to freezing for a good twenty minutes until the food showed up. He sat on the edge of the bed in his hotel robe and felt his mind start to settle and his calm return. His exposure was fairly limited, after all. He decided he would stay at the hotel for a few more days, for good measure, and would risk a quick swing home to pick up some clothes and other things he'd need. He also decided he would no longer allow himself to think about how things had recently gone wrong. What he needed to do was to focus on a positive future and a rebuilding. Once he finished eating, he dressed, turned on the television, and put the Do Not Disturb sign on the door. He'd let a chambermaid in to do her business only once he was back to supervise. Looking both ways down the corridor and seeing no one and nothing, he headed for the elevator.

He could've sent someone, but after the job

Wenck and Gilley had done, he suddenly felt there was no one he could trust, and the truth was, he wanted to clap an eyeball on his house himself, to make sure there was no activity around it, police or otherwise. He figured if everything looked clear, he'd go in, get his things, sanitize certain papers, lock it down, and be gone in ten minutes. As he was driving up his block, his recent return to calm deepened. The suburban street was quiet, almost silent but for the birds. Putting his money into a nice house in a desirable neighborhood had been a great investment and an even better quality-of-life choice. It seemed to his eye that nothing out of the ordinary had, would, or ever could happen on his little street. It was by dint of discipline alone that he drove past his house and around the corner at speed. He then circled around and passed more slowly. On the third pass, all was still quiet and he turned into his driveway. He pressed the garage button while he was still at a distance and slid right in. He left the garage door up, the car running, and headed for the interior door. As soon as he entered the small hallway that the real estate agents like to refer to as "the mudroom" and had closed the door to the garage behind him, he realized something was wrong. There was no beeping of the alarm. He turned to the panel and saw the light a steady green. He was sure he had armed it before leaving the night before.

TWENTY-EIGHT

IT WAS STILL DARK and Carol was sleeping when they left for Behr's place.

"Do me a favor and make the coffee while I shower," Behr asked when they arrived. He crossed to his answering machine and played the lone message; it was a woman's voice.

"Hey, Frank, Sue. Wanted to thank you for last night. Do me a favor: When you call, don't forget to tell me again how that kind of thing never happens. Well, that's it. Oh, and do me another favor: Watch yourself."

Behr wore a faint smile as he headed toward his bedroom.

Paul was pouring his second cup of coffee when there was a rapping at the door. Behr, hair wet, pulling on pants, emerged from the bedroom and went to answer it. The man at the door was thin, dark-skinned, with black hair that would have been curly had it not been cropped close. His nose was prominent, like the prow of a Viking ship.

"This is Toombakis," Behr said by way of introduction. The man shifted his battered mason bag from right to left and offered a work-callused hand.

"Paul."

"How are you?" Toombakis replied. Paul detected an East Coast accent, New York probably, not New England. The man's voice was fairly bright, but he had dark shadows under his eyes that hinted of a difficult past.

"Coffee," Behr offered, and went off to finish dressing. As he did, Paul saw not just Behr's injured forearm, which was swollen and blackish-purple, but welts, scars, and cuts, including a starfishlike magenta pucker on his lower back that wrote a story of a life battling in the streets across Behr's large torso.

They drank their coffee, and Toombakis didn't volunteer why he was there and Paul didn't ask; rather they talked dispassionately about the Colts and the Hoosiers.

A half hour later the three of them were sitting just around the corner from Riggi's house, where they had a view of the place across a lawn. The night before, Paul had set up farther away but on the actual street. His was a more conspicuous spot, he acknowledged to himself. Toombakis was in the backseat, his head leaning forward between theirs; his car was two blocks farther away.

They sat and watched the house for a mere quarter hour. There were signs of morning activity beginning in the other houses nearby, but none in the one in question.

"Well," Behr said rhetorically, then pulled out his cell phone and dialed. He put it to his ear, and in the quiet of the car they could hear the muted ringing on the other end. It rang and rang before voice mail picked up. Paul felt a sharp dose of embarrassment over the obviousness with which Behr probed whether or not someone was inside the house. Behr hung up on the voice mail and redialed.

"Is he listed?" Paul asked, hoping to mitigate his feeling like a dunce.

"No, but I've got a reverse directory that lists every number by address. It's very comprehensive." This made Paul feel better, but only by a little.

"All right, we're a go," Behr said after a final ring, closing his phone and getting out. Just like that, a short wait, no excruciating period of hours.

Toombakis fell in next to Behr, Paul a few steps back.

"Locks aren't my thing, you know," Toombakis said. "I could give it a try, but . . ."

"Let's just have a look," Behr said. They contin- ued past the house, and Behr pointed at a security company sticker in a front window.

"Ah, fuck, I see it," Toombakis said as they crossed around to the side door. "The blue Valiant crest."

"Problem?" Behr asked.

"We'll only have thirty seconds instead of a minute once we're inside," Toombakis answered. "And we can't lean on the door until we're in. Pressure strips."

"Hmm," Behr breathed as they reached the door. His eyes scanned all around the frame, then came to rest on the knob and lock. He moved quickly. There was a zipping sound and a black leather case folded open in his hands. An array of almost dental-looking equipment was fastened to the velvet lining of the case: Allen wrenches, awls, tiny screwdrivers, and a dozen of what Paul now knew were pry bars and tension wrenches.

"You sure you don't want to try?" Behr offered Toombakis.

"Nope. Not even. Unless you want me to drill it," came the response.

Behr gave the man a look and then kneeled and went to it. Toombakis and Paul did their best to appear casual, as if waiting for a friend, and used their bodies to try to shield Behr as he worked. A few minutes later, with no unusual activity on the street, Behr stood. "Okay."

Paul glanced at the lock, which looked as if it had undergone acupuncture, with several thin metal tools protruding. Behr had his hand on a short, corkscrewed piece of metal, holding it in place.

Toombakis opened his bag, drew out a few pump-ratchet bit drivers of different sizes and several tiny two-ended alligator clamps connected by red wire, which he draped over his neck like a tailor's measuring tape. He handed Paul his bag, which was surprisingly heavy.

"Keep this close to me," he instructed, then nodded to Behr.

"If we need to head for the car, do it fast but don't run," Behr instructed, then turned back to the knob. He snapped down with the hand that held the tool, causing a clicking noise in the lock and a grimace to cross Behr's face. It was his bad arm. He turned the knob with his other hand. The door opened and they stepped inside.

The house felt vacant around them, the only sounds that of their shoes on the tile floor and the high-pitched beeping of the alarm's warning signal. Toombakis approached the panel. His hands moved like rising doves as he tried several sizes of bit drivers on the screws holding it in place. He dropped the drivers that didn't fit onto the floor with a clatter. When he found the right one, he pumped hard and popped off the alarm plate within seconds.

Paul bent and collected the discarded bit drivers, glancing up to see exposed wires behind the panel. The alarm's beeping sounded increasingly insistent with the panel off, but he wondered whether it was his imagination. Toombakis worked, clamping off wires, to restore the alarm's circuit. The time seemed to be growing extremely long, well over half a minute, and Paul braced himself for the alarm's scream when Toombakis placed a last clip, raised his hands like a rodeo roper after tying off a calf, and stepped back in a new, complete silence. He gingerly tipped the hanging panel out of the way so they could see the light was now a steady green.

"Take care of the panel, then let yourself out. And thanks," Behr said, offering a hand to Toombakis, who nodded. "You can forget about that thing," Behr added.

The statement seemed to brighten Toombakis's dark eyes a bit. "Don't worry, I won't forget that other thing," he said.

Behr nodded and said to Paul, "Come on."

"Are you going to try and open it?" Paul asked.

They had moved slowly about the house, through rooms that were furnished well if sparsely. Couches were dark leather, the rugs and walls of standard solid colors. The home was conscientiously decorated, but by a man. The living room was dominated by a big-screen television, DVD player, and stereo all rigged up with surround sound. They looked briefly through Riggi's music and movie collection. It was mundane, certainly not depraved, and consisted largely of classic rock: Seger, the Who, the Stones, and up through Guns N' Roses. The films were mostly dramas: *The Godfather* series, *Scarface, Wall Street,* and everything by Tarantino.

"It's not a real safe," Behr said as they stared at the wall safe, hidden behind some dress shirts on hangers that they'd pushed aside.

"No?" Paul asked. They were in the main bedroom closet, a huge, neatly made California king bed visible in the room beyond the doorway.

"It's real, but it's not for actual valuables, know what I mean? A guy like this, careful, puts a safe in the master closet? I don't think so. That's the first place anybody looks." It was true, it was the first place they had looked upon entering the bedroom.

Behr tried the handle. "Just for good measure," he said. The safe didn't open. "Cheap box like this, burglars just rip it out of the wall, take it home and work on it there." He straightened the shirts to their original positions. They moved through the bedroom and master bath and a few guest bedrooms; one held old furniture, stereo equipment, and golf clubs, the others just beds.

"Let's go downstairs and check the study," Behr said. As they moved down the stairs, they heard the sound of a door opening. Paul froze, his heart rate jumping by a hundred beats. "Toombakis,"

Behr said in reminder. They heard the door shut. Paul nodded and they continued on.

The study walls were covered by bookshelves that held mostly nonfiction bestsellers and a few coffee table–size histories of European car manufacturers: Mercedes, Porsche, and Maserati. A blotter covered with indeterminate notes, dates, and phone numbers topped the dark wooden desk. There was another television, VCR, and DVD player in a cabinet. There were prints of African animals framed on the wall that didn't hold bookshelves: an elephant, zebras watering, and a lion on a kill. Behr sat for a while behind the desk in a new-looking burgundy leather chair, then began going through the drawers.

He pulled out a ledger-size checkbook and opened it on the desk. It showed a healthy mid-five-figure balance. He combed through other drawers and came up with statements from a few brokerage firms. Behr held them up for Paul to see; they showed low to middling six-figure balances.

"He's doing real well," Behr muttered to himself.

Paul checked out the titles in the bookshelves while Behr replaced the documents and leaned back in the chair. He glanced over his shoulder at the window and a look of puzzlement came over his face. He looked at a wall holding bookshelves, then the door. He stood and moved around the room, trying to assess its dimensions. He left the room, peeked around in the living room, and then reappeared in the study, his brow knit in thought.

"What?" Paul wondered.

"This room."

"What about it?"

"It's too small. Look." Behr pointed to the window and then the bookshelves. "This is the side of the house, right? The living room shares a common wall, so it should end here."

"The bookshelves are built-ins," Paul said, not quite understanding the layout in his mind but feeling the thread of the thing and urging his brain to catch up.

"But they're not that deep," Behr said.

"Yeah. They should end there, not here," Paul said, pointing to a space beyond the shelves. "Could it . . . ?" His question hung in the air as he was unable to fully ask it.

"I've seen this before," Behr said, facing the bookshelves and pulling on them. Nothing happened. He pushed on the front of the woodwork as well. Still nothing. He pushed harder, throwing his shoulder into it, and there was a click. Behr stepped back, pulling the front of the bookshelves again, but this time they hinged out and swung free. Behr and Paul looked at each other. There was a space between the bookshelves and the outer wall of the house, perhaps two feet deep, and in it a series of three two-drawer file cabinets.

Behr crouched, Paul fell in next to him, and they tried the drawers, which were locked.

"Can you pick them?" Paul asked.

"Fuck that," Behr said, pulling out a Leatherman tool and selecting a blunt blade. He jammed it into the crack between drawer and cabinet and pried. The drawer came open with a pop.

Behr pulled folders out of the drawer and began thumbing through the papers inside. Paul moved in close to read over Behr's shoulder, trying not to block the light. The documents were both handwritten and typed and consisted mostly of columns of initials and numbers. There was a clear pattern to it, which Paul struggled to make sense of.

"It looks like records."

"Yeah, I have 'em as records, too. It's written in some basic code." Behr jiggled a few of the other cabinets. "Maybe there's a key to it in one of these drawers." The drawers were still locked and Behr must not have wanted to waste time with them. Instead they turned the pages and began to intuit the system.

"These have got to be initials," Paul said, and Behr nodded.

"Dates," Behr offered, and it seemed to make sense.

"And these?" Paul wondered, a sick feeling coming to his stomach.

"That's the money," Behr said in a low voice, just a shade from completely sure. "Two-part payments. The lower numbers look like some kind of monthly accounting."

They sifted through a few more folders when Paul fell back a few steps.

"Oh, god," he uttered.

"What's wrong?" Behr asked.

"Bottom of the page," Paul said. The letters "JG" were there, in lowercase. Behr glanced at it, then back at him, a current of knowing and confirmation flowing between them. That's when they heard the garage door open.

Riggi inspected the alarm panel and saw a few slight gouges in the plastic near the screws holding it in place. He did his best to remember whether they had always been there or not. Then he recognized a difference in the usual energy of his house. He felt a presence, a stirring within it, and realized someone was there. A feeling of indignation welled deep within him, a black territorial violence, and he headed deeper into the house. He heard a footstep, a depression of weight on a floorboard coming from the study, and went toward it. *I'm gonna crack whoever's in my place* went through his head. He moved through the kitchen, glancing toward the knife block and considering whether to take one. His gun was in the safe upstairs. If he faced an armed man or men, the knife wouldn't do him a damned bit of good. He decided he'd take them barehanded.

He passed through the other side of the kitchen and moved into the foyer and saw them. Two figures, one good-sized, the other even larger, emerged from the darkened hall and were silhouetted in the doorframe. He knew who they were right away, and their presence froze his blood.

"What the fuck are you doing here?" he snapped, hoping the anger masked his fear.

"Just so you know, we knocked and the door pushed open, so we entered," Behr, the investigator, said.

"Bullshit," Riggi practically shouted. He could see down the hall that the bookshelves in his study were swung out from the wall. The quiet partner stood behind Behr, one hand balled into a fist, the other clenching one of his folders. A wave of panic hit Riggi low in the gut, and he fought a sudden dizziness.

"Time to talk, Riggi."

"You sick son of a bitch." The quiet one finally spoke, his words a snarl coming from deep in his throat. The man stepped around his partner toward him.

Riggi began backing away toward the kitchen. "I'm calling the cops," he said, his last word hanging in the air over the sound of his feet scuffing over the floor as he turned and ran.

He flew through the door into the garage and slid into his car. He barked the tires against the painted garage floor and chunked the car into gear, ripping out of his driveway. He turned right onto the street, made another right at the corner, checked his rearview, and saw them running across a lawn after him. He glanced back at the road in time to miss a gardener's truck that was double-parked by a neighbor's. He sped onto Bay-hill Drive. He had no idea where he was going.

The way to catch somebody, Behr reminded himself, *is to stay calm and remain objective.* It went for running down evidence, same as it did for a car chase, and while breaking into Riggi's house might have showed judgment affected by emotion, he was determined not to let it interfere now. They ran across the lawn toward the car, Paul clutching a folder. It would have been better to leave it behind, but there was no time to go back and return it. They couldn't afford to wait for Riggi to go lawyer up and use the cops against them. When they got in and he turned the engine over, Behr spent the extra five seconds it took to buckle his seat belt.

"Put it on," he instructed Paul, not waiting for him to do so. His injured arm throbbed as he spun the wheel and gave chase down Heatherstone.

Behr kept his car up well and the automatic

transmission shifted smoothly, pressing their backs against the seats. He could see Riggi up ahead, maybe six hundred yards away, just making the turn onto Bayhill. The important thing when chasing someone in a car is to drive faster than he or she does on the straights, and for longer, then brake harder going into the turns in order to take them at the same speed. Behr had learned and practiced the technique in weekend driving courses over the past decade of his life. He was driving with both feet now, left on the brake, right on the accelerator, so he could keep up his RPMs even as he was finishing braking on the turns. The net result was a gain of two hundred yards on Riggi's car. They were on the same block now. Behr cut his eyes left and right as he crossed an intersection, as much looking for oncoming cars as for police on patrol. If the cops got involved, it would be trouble. There was no good way to explain what they were doing and it could result in an arrest. He didn't look forward to it for himself, and it would kill what was left of his reputation in the business if Paul was brought in, too. He looked over at his passenger. Paul was sunk low into his seat, one hand gripping the armrest on the door, the other braced against the dash. He didn't utter a sound, nor did he look frightened. He peered out the windshield with the intent eyes of a hunter. Riggi's car went loose on the next corner, the rear end swinging wide as he took the turn.

Riggi did not know what a thirty-second lead meant in a car chase. He thought it'd be enough time to turn a few corners and leave them completely behind. Moments later he saw he was wrong—a maroon Olds filled his mirrors.

"Damnit," he said, slapping the wheel and mashing the pedal, asking the Cutlass for speed. The car was a beast on straight shots. The thing quartered in some ridiculous time—fourteen or fifteen seconds flat—but corners weren't the American car's strength. He made several turns as fast as he could, glancing back to see Behr's Olds getting closer, looming larger after each one. He tried to think of where to go. He could head for his attorney's office, but it was a good half hour away even at this speed. His thoughts narrowed, as did his vision, and he was unable to think ahead. Destinations left his mind, as did any plan, as did a good choice of route, as did the next turn, and everything else but the blacktop streaking underneath his tires.

The back end swung out going around the corner onto Hazel Dell Parkway. Riggi oversteered in correction and swept the side of a parked Explorer. It changed the angle of the front end and sent him up over a high curb. He felt the front tires blow as he hit the curb, then the car got air and began a yawning roll. White sky filled the front windshield. *I'm going* passed through his mind, and then there was brown tree and green grass. The caustic smell of radiator fluid filled his world. The sound of crushing metal and glass seemed to catch up a moment later and washed over him. Then there was blackness.

TWENTY-NINE

BEHR PULLED OVER and left his car idling. Paul was
a step behind him as they crossed to Riggi's
wrecked vehicle. The car was upside down,
dripping colored liquids, the tires slowly spinning
down. A broken and bloodied Riggi lay half out of
the driver's-side window, the steering wheel lodged
in his midsection. The windshield was blown out.
From the looks of things, Riggi hadn't been wearing a seat belt and his head had done that work.
Drivers began to pull over and gawk at the carnage. Behr took out his cell phone and dialed 911,
wondering if Riggi was dead already, when he began to stir. Behr asked for an ambulance and gave
the address, then shut off his phone just as Riggi's
eyes opened and rolled around a little, struggling
for focus. Then his right hand reached out across
the torn-up grass. Behr tracked what he was going

for, but Paul saw it first: a crucifix attached to a rosary that had been flung free of the wreck. Paul kneeled and picked up the beads, clenching them in his fist out of Riggi's reach.

It was clear the man was dying, and Behr girded himself for what he had to do. He squatted close to the man's bloody face.

"You use the medical offices in your centers to target kids?" he asked.

Riggi shook his head weakly from side to side.

"What do you do with them?" Behr asked, insistent.

Bad. I know it. I'm dying. Things were broken and winding down deep inside of him. His thoughts were disconnected from his words. He didn't feel he could work his mouth. If only he could've reached his rosary, perhaps he wouldn't pass on to damnation. He looked up at the quiet one, who held them, and mouthed the words, "Who are you?" No answer came, and he wondered if he'd spoken at all.

Light clouds moved across a pale sky. Blades of grass near his face stirred in a faint breeze. His mind drifted to Ramon Ponceterra, to the recent and future orders that would remain unfilled. He was slapped across the face a few times and he felt himself returning once again.

"Do you kill them when you're done with

them?" the big one asked, breathing old coffee in his face.

No answer came from Riggi, just shallow breathing.

"C'mon, it's over for you. Give," Behr said, demanding information even though it caused his stomach to churn.

"They're gone," Riggi rasped.

For some reason Behr didn't think he meant that he'd killed them. "You keep them somewhere to use, is that it?"

Riggi shook his head again and spent a precious breath saying, "No."

Behr felt weak and wondered whether he could do what he had to do. He reached out and grabbed Riggi's jaw. "Do you want me to make this last moment painful for you?" Riggi was probably beyond pain, but Behr squeezed up under the man's trachea hard, wondering the whole time if it would do any good besides causing him to relive the deed for the rest of his life. Riggi's eyes changed, though, and the act dislodged a statement.

"They're worth more to me than you could pay."

Behr and Paul looked at each another in horror at the words.

The tumblers in Behr's mind clicked like a series in a combination and understanding came to him. "Because you sell them," he said.

Riggi blinked. The lying went out of his eyes. It was a yes.

"You used Rooster Mintz and Tad Ford," Behr thought aloud. "Ford was a driver. You ship 'em out."

Riggi's mouth opened but emitted no sound, and Behr realized how hard his grip was on the man's throat. He forced himself to relax it.

"You send them away. To where?"

"South . . . to Mexico," Riggi said as the life began to seep from his eyes.

Behr shuddered at the thought of the cold transit. Then he remembered the small wooden key chain he'd been given by the exotic dancer, which had been given to her by Tad Ford. It was in the Stor-Box that housed all the paperwork and meager evidence he'd assembled so far.

Paul was right there. "Ciudad del Sol," he said.

Riggi blinked and panted. His eyes began to lose focus and color.

Behr slapped him on the cheek harder to bring him back. "They're taken to Ciudad del Sol. I don't want to hear you fucking deny it. You only say 'no' if I'm wrong." There was no response, only the labored and scraping sound of Riggi's breathing. Behr and Paul looked at each other over the bleeding man, understanding the enormity of what they'd heard.

"What'd you do with him, you bastard?" Paul demanded, spittle flying out from between his teeth. Riggi's head just rolled from side to side in response. "What did you do to my son?"

"Don't know . . ." Riggi croaked.

"Where's his body?" Paul practically screamed in the man's face.

"I'm . . . I'm a businessman," Riggi gasped in faded defiance. ". . . *in nomine Patris* . . ." He said no more.

Only the wind rustled the thin branches high above them. Paul looked at Behr, then down at the dying man, and then at the rosary and crucifix in his own hand, the beads making a quiet clicking sound. He closed his eyes for a long moment, then opened them and, with a look of pure disgust, reached out for Riggi's open hand and dropped the beads into his palm.

Riggi closed his eyes like an old man taking a nap. His body stopped moving. A vibrating sound escaped his lungs, which caused Paul to jump back.

"Death rattle," Behr said to the question in Paul's wide eyes.

Behr stood, his knee joints cracking in protest, and walked off a few yards. Paul moved back several feet, sat on the grass, and hung his head.

"When they ask, you waited in the car," Behr said. Paul just nodded. "You don't know how I got inside. There was no Toombakis."

. . .

The police were first to arrive, a cruiser and then another. They spotted up on Behr and Paul and made radio calls for half a minute. The ambulance was next. Paramedics climbed out, and while the driver got a box from the back, the other, a Latino with a pitted face, crossed to Riggi.

"Ho, Doc," the Latino called out to his partner as he checked for vitals, "zeroes across the board."

"Ho," the partner called back, putting the box away and closing the doors. He approached the body with a clipboard and began filling out paperwork.

The responding officers photographed the scene and then began asking vague questions. Before long a silver Crown Vic rolled up.

Captain Pomeroy climbed out and surveyed the scene for only a moment before crooking a finger at Behr. Behr nodded and crossed over to him.

"I thought I was done with you when I fired your ass," Pomeroy began, loud enough for a few officers to hear. Behr bit down hard on his tongue against the insult.

"Get in." Pomeroy gestured to his car, and Behr did.

The dove-gray velour was plush, but the fabric seemed to hold on to Pomeroy's cologne. Over time it had gone sour. Sitting in the car gave Behr an immediate headache. He sat there as Pomeroy moved around the scene and oversaw Riggi being zipped up in a body bag and placed in the back of a coroner's van. Then he crossed to Paul and they had a brief conversation. Pomeroy had gained weight in the few years since Behr had seen him. The flesh under his chin had gone soft and would double in a few more years. Dark command circles had formed under the captain's eyes as well. Behr felt the changes he himself had undergone reflected in his old superior. But the captain still had the look of a hawk—piercing eyes over a prominent nose bone—while he recognized himself as a failure. Behr may have been full of promise as a young officer. He may have added knowledge and experience to that promise and for a moment been on his way to becoming a fine policeman. But then things got in the way. An ill-fated partnership, poor political skills, too much drinking, and then Tim's death, topped off by a busted marriage and more drinking. He could've viewed any single one of those factors as bad luck, but taken together he knew it was less a question of chance and more one of limitation or even destiny.

Pomeroy got in the car and slammed the door, bringing a fresh wave of cologne with him. There were no pleasantries, as Behr expected.

"Time for the eternal questions, Frank. Why am I here? Why are you here? What the hell happened?"

"That's my client." He pointed at Paul.

"I know him."

"I've been working his son's case. It led me to Riggi—the DB."

Pomeroy just grimaced.

"I was looking to talk to the man, get something firm, then turn it over. I'd been in his house waiting when he showed up—"

"Is that so?" Pomeroy cut in. Behr figured he may as well put it out there. It could be found out later and then there'd be problems.

"The door was open."

"Uh-huh. Was your client with you?"

"He was out in the car. Then the guy ran and we followed him and he jumped the curb."

"Motherfucker. And why didn't you come in with this at the start?"

"I didn't have anything firm then."

"Well, is it firm enough now? What'd you get?"

"He targeted kids who frequented medical practices in strip malls he owned. He had people grabbing them up. Selling them, I believe."

"Selling them? Jesus Christ."

"That's right. I have reason to believe my client's son was one of them. There's a file of his in my car. Records."

"How'd you . . ." Pomeroy began. "Don't tell me that. How many are we talking about?"

"About seven in this area, a thirty-mile radius the best I can figure, over the past few years. Boys of a certain age. Many more before that."

Pomeroy's complexion grew ashen. "Shit, this is going to be a major followup investigation. I'm gonna need this all on paper."

Behr nodded. "I'm gonna need time."

"Why didn't you give when I sent my guys around?"

"I didn't have any of this then. It just came together," Behr said convincingly.

Pomeroy rubbed his face, massaging in the aftershave oil, Behr imagined. "I've heard rumors. You were behind a prisoner getting a pretty severe trimming in County. Same prisoner is now dead." Behr felt Pomeroy study him for a reaction and did his best not to give one beyond his natural appreciation for the swiftness of prison justice.

"I don't know anything about that—"

"Don't bother. Just don't bother, all right? The prisoner was stabbed to death. Do you have any information on it?"

"None."

"Where? What the hell does he do with them?"

"I don't know, Captain." It was a grand-scale lie, and one Behr had planned on telling since the moment Riggi's car had flipped and hit the tree. If he gave up Mexico, the department would contact local authorities, there would be tipoffs, and the resolution he and Paul had been looking for would vanish forever.

Behr watched Pomeroy chew over questions in his mind and either answer them or realize there were no answers. A wrecker arrived on the scene and the driver began to hook cables to the rear axle of Riggi's broken car.

"You always were a fuckup, but you were also honest to a goddamned fucking fault," Pomeroy said, half as if talking to himself, half for Behr's benefit. It was a tone all good leaders possessed. "You got anything else for me on this steaming pile?"

Behr brought together his inner resolve. If he could sell his next response, he felt Pomeroy would give up on him and attack the endless paperwork that followed such a situation. If not, he'd be sitting down at his old station with a lawyer for the next several weeks dealing with questions.

"Negative," he said.

Pomeroy looked at him and finally gave a nod that was tantamount to pulling on the car-door lever. A momentary détente settled between them.

"Have I mentioned I'm gonna need all this on paper?"

"Yeah, you did."

"Make sure you're easy to find, next little while," Pomeroy said.

"Will do."

Behr got out and Pomeroy spoke before he'd closed the door. "An arrest would've been better, but this son of a bitch is done and gone. That's a result, Frank." Pomeroy pressed his lips together in approval.

"Can I get my computer back?" Behr asked. Pomeroy jerked the Crown Vic into motion by the time Behr had shut the door.

THIRTY

STRENGTH OR WEAKNESS, Paul didn't know which it had been. He'd granted his mortal enemy, the source of all pain in his life, a moment's comfort in death. He'd sent the man to eternity with a symbol of God. He hadn't done it for Riggi, that much he did know, but for himself. He was filled with regret for the action, even as he knew it was what he had to do. He was not a religious man in the conventional sense. He'd left the observance of his Episcopalian upbringing long ago. But he believed in God. He had a real faith that the power existed. And he knew in that moment that in order for God to grant him any relief in the search for an answer regarding his son, he must be worthy of it.

They'd gone to a Chili's after the police had finished with them and silently ate Southwestern Ranch burgers without tasting them. He'd told lies to the police when they'd asked him questions and he'd lied by omission as well. Despite the jeopardy, it was easier than he thought it'd be. It was like anything else, he supposed: simple once one had moved past caring about the outcome. They finished and paid and were set to go when he realized they hadn't talked about what was next.

"The department's gonna come down on this and all the related cases with both boots, just so you know," Behr said, draining his Arnie Palmer.

"What'll be the time frame on that?" Paul wondered as they rose.

"Days. Weeks. It's a question of them catching up," Behr told him.

"I'll drive," Behr said as they walked outside into a day the color of a battered tin pan and crossed the parking lot. It was a strange, unnecessary statement as they'd been in Behr's car all day and he had the keys.

Paul thought about home and Carol and how much he'd tell her. "I'm not waiting for the police. I'm going," he said aloud. "To Ciudad del Sol. To find out what happened to him."

"I know," Behr said. "I just told you: I'll drive."

Behr bought flowers and was waiting in front of her building when she got home from work. She drove up in a Miata, parked, and climbed out, slinging a leather bag across her shoulder. She hadn't expected him, that was clear, but it wasn't just surprise that spread across her face with her smile.

"He returns," she said, stopping for a moment, then walking toward him.

"It's me," he said back. "How are you, Susan?" She had looked beautiful all made up on their date. Today she was wearing her work clothes—a jacket over a blouse—and her makeup was lighter or had worn off, the slight lines by her eyes more visible. But he saw her more clearly without the layer, and with her hair pulled back as it was. She was beautiful.

He'd felt idiotic sitting there, the bouquet filling his car with a wet earthy smell. All the hesitation left him when she smiled.

"Pretty," she said, accepting the flowers.

"They were closing and were out of roses."

"Would you stop?" she said, her eyes flickering up over the tops of the flowers as she smelled them.

"So . . ." he said.

"So, what's up?"

"I'm going away for a while."

"You are?" It seemed to sadden her a bit. "That case?"

"Right." He felt his heart beating hard under his shirt.

"Where to? If it's not confidential."

It wasn't, but he didn't want to get into the

details. He didn't want to bring that part of his life to her.

"A bad place."

"Uh-uh," she said.

"No?" he asked.

"I'm the in or out type, Frank, and I called you after the other night 'cause I'm in. Which are you?"

"I'm going to the border, to Mexico," he said, and moved toward her. "I'm in." She reached her hand behind his head and pulled him to her, and they kissed.

The night had been almost unreal, and now it was nearly over. Blue light glowed around the edges of the shades and told them it was time. She didn't lie next to him as usual, but instead across him, like in the old days, her head on his chest, her hair spread over his torso. Paul's heart beat steady and implacable beneath her ear. It was a sound she hadn't heard in so long. Neither of them was asleep but in a waking state that was nearly indistinguishable. They'd talked half the night, until Paul had talked himself out, relating all the facts of the case. She wondered if she knew everything now. She felt she did—all that mattered, anyway. He'd told her what he'd learned. Horrible things. They'd begun the conversation standing in the kitchen, then moved to the bedroom. Then they'd sat on the edge of the bed. She'd found herself moving closer and closer to him as the hours progressed. Her husband was brave and unrelenting, she saw it now, and didn't understand how she'd missed it for so long. At a point in his story their hands found each other in gestures of comfort. When he told her where he was going, she grasped him in fear.

The hour had grown late when she felt it: The current that had been dead between them for as long as she could remember, half of which she considered extinct within her, switched on once again. She reached for him just as he leaned toward her. She met his kiss and felt herself fall into his open mouth. He was tentative at first, touching her as if she were a fragile thing, as if she were made of mist and he might fall through her. But she responded and the touches grew. The room was dark. They shed their clothes. They pressed their bodies against each other in need and relief and love. He moved on top of her and she was solid beneath him, substantial. His smell and the weight of him on her were familiar and intoxicating. Tears of bittersweet joy rolled from the corners of her eyes. For a moment Jamie was gone completely. Not in the agonizing way that he had been for all these months, but in the way he used to be even when he was safe in his room and they went to the special world that husbands and wives occupy for precious moments. They talked in tongues, garbled sounds of passion flying from their mouths.

"Carol," he said into the darkness.

"Yes?" she answered.

"You're right, we should do a burial for him: a headstone, a memorial service. I can wait until after that to go."

She squeezed his hand. "When you get back," she said.

It wasn't all he wanted to say.

"It's no death wish. I'm afraid I'll get hurt, that I won't come back. But I'm more afraid of not going."

She found his strength contagious and she remained infected with it now. "First go and find out what happened to our son, or someone else's. Then come home to me," she said.

She felt him smile. Her hand slipped into his in the coming dawn. Their hands began a familiar, playful wrestle that was their lost ritual in moments of intimacy. Their thumbs danced together, brushing softly, speaking silently their love.

Behr sat outside in his idling car. He saw a few lights on inside the house piercing the morning semidarkness. He wondered why he was even there, when driving on alone and leaving Paul behind was the smart move. It was out of allegiance, he realized. And then there was the fact that Paul would show up on his own if Behr left him behind. He considered honking the horn despite the hour. All the times he'd picked up his employer in the past he'd never needed to do that, for Paul would be waiting for him outside or would come out within an instant of his arrival. And of all those times he'd only seen Carol pass by a window once or twice. She was either out most of the time or moving about the depths of the house like a spirit.

Today, though, the screen door swung open and she appeared, in the flesh, wearing sweat pants and a faded sweatshirt, her hair pulled back in a ponytail. Her face was fresh and clean of makeup. She looked both young and ravaged at the same time, and the combination was a beautiful one. He lowered the window as she approached. He half expected to hear that Paul wouldn't be going, that the trip seemed too dangerous, and that he shouldn't come around anymore.

"Come in," she said, "I'm going to cook you two a hot breakfast before you go."

THIRTY-ONE

THEY DROVE TOWARD A HORIZON of gunmetal blue. As they crossed out of state they passed the custom cutters working their way north on the harvest run. They were out even though it was just past dawn, as there was no dew and the wind was blowing from the south. Formations of combines swept across stands of red clover. In the distance, the massive machines trembled under dust clouds of their own making, as they cut and gathered the standing crop, threshed the seed from the stem, separated the chaff, and spit the stem back to the ground.

The radio was tuned to AM and pulled in a broadcast of a farm report. The familiar cadence brought Behr back to his own youth, to his father's pickup truck as they listened to news that was vitally important to their survival. "Though acres and yield will be down," the local elevator man informed, "late winter conditions were ideal. Wheat broke winter dormancy and went into its final growth cycle early. Moisture level is fourteen percent now, perfect for a young harvest and a chance to double crop . . ."

The station didn't last much longer before it lost reception. Paul switched off the radio and they rode in silence, looking out the windows. Cutting was fast work, and before long the fields they passed held only stubble. They continued on over featureless plain under an empty sky.

Behr nearly detoured past Linda's out of habit as he did anytime he drove south. It was an automatic response whenever he was near Vallonia. There had long been an ache inside him, a throbbing sense of emptiness in the place she used to fill, like the phantom pain people claimed after they'd lost a limb to amputation. It was a feeling he took for granted for many years, and he had developed an almost perverse familiarity with it. But as they blazed past the exit he would've taken to get to her, the ache was only a brief, reflexive thought that didn't occupy nearly the amount of space as his thoughts of Susan. As they drove on, though, she, too, was pulled from his mind, replaced by speculation on what they would find and face in Ciudad del Sol and of what he'd packed in the trunk under a piece of carpet in the large spare tire well.

The sun was high in the sky and sliced through the windshield like an acetylene torch when they crossed into Missouri, and almost by force of momentum they started talking.

"What went down between you and Captain Pomeroy?" Paul asked.

Behr drove for another mile or so looking for a comfortable way to rest his injured arm while he considered how best to answer.

"When you're a cop," he began, easing the car around a road-killed possum drying in the sun, "the city you work in becomes *your* city. It's your concern. You give yourself to it. Accidents. Emergencies. Fires. Riots. Shootings. Whatever. If it happens, you show up, whether you're on duty or not, even after you retire. And you expect something back for that. Something small. You expect to belong to it as much as it belongs to you." Behr told Paul about the relationship between his partner and Pomeroy, the shooting, the grudge. "The way he ran me," Behr finished, "Pomeroy took that belonging away from me."

They filled up in Sikeston and Behr stayed behind the wheel. They approached the next topic like swimmers entering an extremely cold mountain lake.

"He was full of contradictions, Jamie was," Paul said. "Shy, but also self-possessed. It would take him a minute when he walked into a new situation, the first day of school, or a kid's birthday party, or whatever. He'd just take it in quietly, start figuring out his place there. Before long he'd start picking up volume and speed. Then he'd become himself again, like he was at home, running around, laughing, and talking. . . ." He tapered off, not used to the subject despite it all. As much as they discussed the details of the case, Paul had never ventured to discuss personal memories with Behr. But the man's simple recollections pushed him to his own.

"Tim was laughing all the time. He was a big boy."

"Not a surprise."

"A bruiser. A lineman in a diaper even when he was a baby. The world seemed to bounce off him. He broke everything in the house at least once." Behr smiled and grimaced as the humor still carried an edge of pain.

"How come you didn't have more?" Paul asked.

"Couldn't. Linda, my ex-wife, had complications with Tim. You?"

"Should've. Thought we would. But as the years went by with Jamie we just seemed . . . complete."

They had waded in ankle-deep, the water's temperature seizing their breath and discouraging them from going further. But they braced and continued.

"I know . . ." Paul began, and then adjusted his words. "I mean I try and tell myself . . . that every minute with him was a gift to be appreciated. I keep waiting for the sense of failure to lift so I can do it that way."

It was a partial question and Behr's answer was wordless, a shift of body, a sound related to a sigh from which only an unfortunate few could draw meaning. Silence reigned for another sixty miles. The dark greens of the blooming deciduous trees gave way to a more faded landscape of pale yellow and sage.

"I wish I would've just been happier every day, with my wife and son, back when I had everything," Behr said as they passed by a sign advertising the turnoff to Jesse James's birthplace several miles ahead. "I found myself always looking forward to another time, though, to a vacation or a promotion or the summer, when things were gonna be perfect. I didn't realize it was already those times every morning or at the end of the day, depending on the shift I worked. And during the Little League games . . . the shit he'd come home from school having learned—"

"From his friends, not in class—"

"Exactly." Both men's smiles slid away.

Paul's head nodded slowly, as if the inside of the car was a space capsule at zero gravity. "Luck always seems like it belongs to someone else," he said. He thought of the breakfast before they'd left. Carol had cooked the bacon and eggs just right and the coffee had been the proper strength. Though there had been little talk, it had been abidingly pleasant between the three of them, as it might've been if he and Behr were setting off for a day of fishing and not into the unknown. He'd once heard an idea that at the end, one didn't remember life as a whole but as just a string of moments. If that was the case, then that morning's breakfast was one of them.

"All we have are moments," Paul said aloud, as if Behr were privy to his thoughts.

"Yeah," Behr agreed, sounding complete in his understanding.

They drove through the night, a blanket of blackness pierced only by the headlights of big rigs and the bright gas station signs along the highway, as Arkansas and Texas passed beneath their wheels. They pulled off the interstate to buy chips and sodas and to switch drivers, but didn't stop for the night. The distance was twelve hundred miles and they'd figured on it taking twenty-five or twenty-six hours. They made it in closer to twenty-two.

They were south of Austin when the night had run out. Morning had come and the landscape had gone from high steppe to desert by the time they reached Laredo and the border. They bought ten gallons of drinking water and finally reclined their seats for a few hours' sleep before they headed south and west into a notch of land that was sand, scrub, and chaparral, where they finally joined a line of cars waiting to cross over the river bridge.

Ciudad del Sol. A sickening sense of dread covered Paul along with a thin coating of dust as they rolled in from the U.S. side with barely a glance from the Mexican border guards. Paul caught Behr's eyes absorbing the details of the checkpoint and followed suit, scoping the American guards on the return side who, even now, took only slightly more care than their Mexican counterparts. Traffic had snarled among tired coils of rusted wire and chain link that halfheartedly secured the area. He wasn't sure if there was any significance to it, or which details he was supposed to remember, but he attempted to catalog it all nonetheless.

"We're just tourists. On vacation," Behr said. "If they search the car, we're thinking about doing a little wing-shooting and target plinking." Paul understood then that there were guns in the trunk.

There was a knock on the passenger window.

They turned. A slender man in his midtwenties was there, having made his way along the rows of stopped cars. He held a bag of dirty oranges.

"We don't want any. *No, gracias,*" Paul said putting down the window halfway.

"*No queremos,*" Behr added from the driver's seat.

The man threw the oranges to the ground. "Ah, you speak Spanish. Good, eh. What you want? I'm Victor. I be your travel agent here," the young man said in decent English. Behr and Paul considered him, then traffic cleared ahead of them and they drove on. Paul put up the window against the swirling dust.

The border behind them, they passed through what resembled a demilitarized zone of broken bottles, smoldering garbage, and burned-out vehicles. They drove past young people who pushed old bicycles heavily laden with cargo. They made a loop around the outskirts of the town, which was ringed by muddy fields attempting to pass for farmland. Groups of *braceros* lay in the shade of ancient stake-bed trucks taking lunch that seemed to include little food, merely rest. On the east side of the town they passed the *maquiladoras*, long, low cinder-block factories dotted by tiny broken windows that could not admit much light or air for the young women who worked there assembling goods for slave wages.

They reached the city center, as it was, a bit tidier than the outskirts, and parked the car. They began walking among Mexicans and other Americans— fraternity boys wearing southwestern college T-shirts starting off on tequila benders; older middle-management types, pale and pasty under their polo shirts and khakis; young bohemian travelers on their way farther south; and aging married couples, huddling together in groups, who might have been better advised to try a cruise. They passed booths selling cheap merchandise that filled both sides of the streets, narrowing them, forcing pedestrians together in choking foot traffic made dangerous by the dusty vehicles that occasionally rumbled by with bleating horns. Shoddy guitars hung in dense rows outside music stores. Sombreros, plastic sunglasses, bottles of mescal, suntan lotion, woven blankets, and T-shirts of every color lined the way. There were what appeared to be small zebras, actually little donkeys painted black and white, hitched to carts. Pictures with the animals cost a dollar, rides in the carts cost two. Nobody seemed to be buying.

They came upon a plaza, boxed in by a large, run-down church on one end and a neglected government building on the other. Sun-bleached dogs ran around a dry fountain. Old men congregated on benches and stout women pulled children around by the hand, many carrying infants in their free arm. Standing under a large tree smoking were young men in thin leather jackets and worn-out sneakers. Paul had no idea what they'd do next.

"Hungry?" Behr asked. Paul shrugged and they left the plaza for a side street, where they found a small, tin-roofed building that was both a grocery store and some type of restaurant.

They were eating stringy chicken and yellow rice doused in a flaming-hot sauce they hoped would kill the bacteria when Victor walked in and approached them.

"*Hola* once and again," he said, and sat down at their table. Paul looked to Behr, who didn't object. "You are on vacation?" Victor asked.

"Yeah, sure," Behr answered.

"Buy me beer," Victor said. Behr nodded and Victor shouted to the woman who had brought them the food. She arrived with a can of Tecate a moment later. Victor took a sip and smiled, putting pointy elbows on the table. He was tall and thin, with a downy black mustache and improbable blue eyes.

"So what you want? A tour? A party? A fishing charter? I get it all for you." Behr shrugged, noncommittal, at the offers. "Maybe you want women? Pretty girls . . ."

Paul saw Behr perk up at this and attempted to look interested as well.

"*Sí, sí, señor, lo que quieras.* I take you to a good place."

Behr pushed his plate away. "Sounds good," he said.

As they left the restaurant, Behr said, "We're kind of choosy. We're looking for a special place, just so you know. Don't take us to the usual."

"*Sí, sí,* you choose," Victor assured them. It was unclear whether he'd understood.

The day grew impressively hot in the afternoon, the air suffocating. Everything and everyone moved about at a choked, languid pace. The first brothel was a low mud building connected to a trailer that was up on blocks. There was a canopy creating shade tied to the structure and a half dozen women sat around on plastic chairs beneath it. They wore polyester tube tops and loose skirts. They drank Coke out of sweating bottles and didn't move or bother putting on a presentation as Behr and Paul walked up behind Victor. Victor greeted several of them and then a slight, dark woman with forbidding eyes emerged from the trailer. Victor addressed her as Marta, then must've spoken of them, as she looked them over with a piercing gaze.

She walked toward them boldly despite her not being over five feet tall.

"*Como están,*" she began. "You want pretty girls?"

Behr and Paul each shrugged a vague yes, and she took Paul by the hand and dragged him closer to the women. A few of them smiled at his obvious discomfort. As a group they came off as medium plain. Some were taller than others, some meatier, others prettier, but particular characteristics seemed to blend together.

"We have fun," invited one of the younger girls, who possessed bright white teeth and shining black hair. She had chosen not to dye it blond as had several of her compatriots and so was one of the more attractive members of the group.

Marta looked to Behr and Paul for their decision, and when none came, she turned to Victor.

"You like these girls?" Victor asked.

"No," Behr said. "Are there any others?"

"Others maybe later tonight. But they are like these," he answered.

"We want something different. Younger. Different," Behr said.

Victor and Marta spoke karate-chop Spanish at a speed they were unable to follow. Marta glared at them some more and muttered, "*¿Que quieren, el rancho de los caballitos?*"

"*Ya basta,* Marta," Victor said, and then Marta and Victor spoke too quietly for them to hear.

Victor turned to them. "She thinks maybe you're *policía.* I tell her no."

Behr turned to Marta. "No," he said. "*No queremos.*" He broke a hundred-dollar bill off his bankroll and gave it to her. She took it as if he'd offered her a toothpick. The rest of the women seemed amused if anything at the rejection.

"*No importa,*" she mumbled before drifting inside.

"Come on," Victor said, pulling them away by their arms. "There are many places."

Behr stopped. "Victor, we don't want this. Find us something more *interesting. ¿Comprende?*"

Victor did his best to understand. "*Más interesante. Sí. Claro.*"

They spent the next several hours visiting whorehouse after piss-smelling whorehouse until they all became a blur. Some were in the middle of the town in cramped apartment buildings; others were farther out in mud farmhouses. They expended upward of a thousand dollars on madams and steerers, attempting to buy goodwill and loose conversation, and almost that much getting rid of the steerers who wanted to follow them around to the next place. After a while they couldn't tell if the customers, mostly Americans, some of whom they saw at more than one place, were getting older or the girls working in the houses, parading in front of them, were actually getting younger at each stop. Perhaps it was the sheer number of available young women that overwhelmed them. Behr and Paul played the part of somewhat wealthy Americans, sexual tourists, looking for a certain kind of debauched experience. At several of the places they had drinks and perused the hookers, then declined and talked to some of the girls and the madams in cryptic terms about what they were really looking for.

At dusk they stumbled on a live sex show. They stood in the back of a room that was mostly empty except for a few standing patrons. The room had a heavy, fetid smell of chickens and blood that brought Behr back to his boyhood on the farm.

"They hold cockfights here?" he asked Victor, who seemed impressed with the question and answered yes.

A rail-thin man entered and strutted about the stage to a poor, crackling recording of traditional Mexican music. Then a woman no older than twenty walked onto the stage in a sheer red coverup, which she dropped without fanfare. Her body was mocha-colored and supple but bore purple keloid scars on one side of her abdomen. Her hair was wavy and fell past her shoulders, where it obscured some amateurish tattoos. She lay down on a bed and the thin man mounted her without much preamble.

An unseen emcee prattled on loudly in Spanish over the speaker system to the delight of the three or four other men in the audience.

The couple went on for a good while, changing positions several times. Behr and Paul exchanged a glance and headed for the door. Victor had one eye still on the show even as he followed them out.

Outside, the arrival of night had taken some of the weight out of the air, or maybe just being away from the performance enabled them to breathe easier.

"You no like the show?" Victor asked, his faith in his clients seeming to waver for the first time.

"Not much," Behr answered.

"It was fine," Paul said, as if Victor was the impresario behind what they'd seen and he didn't want to offend.

"We're gonna go eat dinner," Behr said, walking away.

"I come," Victor offered. "There are other places—"

"No," Behr said. He gave Victor one hundred and fifty dollars. "See you later." The tawdry day had worked on his nerves and had built a well of sickened frustration in him. He needed a break.

They left Victor standing behind them looking bereft despite his smile.

Behr and Paul found a grim motel that had a room with two double beds and a mildewed bathroom, where they washed the day's grit off their faces and necks. Behr's arm had recovered to the point where he no longer needed to ice it and just kept it wrapped in an Ace bandage, which was a good thing as the motel had no ice machine. They were tired, but sleep was out of the question. The hotel clerk pointed them to a restaurant down the street. They'd traded perhaps fifty words all day. There was nothing to say.

They sat and ate carne asada with rice and beans off large ceramic plates. They washed it down with half-cold beer and waved at fat and greedy flies with their free hand.

"I had to come here, man," Paul said, apology in his voice.

"I know," Behr responded.

"It was a waste of time. Of everything."

"No," Behr said without much behind it.

"I'm not even his father anymore."

"It doesn't end just because your son is gone." Behr pushed his plate away.

"We can leave—"

"We'll leave when we're done."

It was then that they saw Victor across the restaurant coming in the door. Paul threw some bills on the table and they got up. He followed Behr's lead, which was to walk past Victor right out the door. The persistent young man followed them, even as they walked out of the pool of light produced by the restaurant and on into the darkness of the rest of the street.

"Ay, wait."

"This kid doesn't quit," Behr said to Paul, stopping and allowing Victor to reach them.

"I take you someplace else?" Victor said hopefully.

"We're done with you," Behr said.

"Come on, man."

"All right," Behr said, turning and stepping closer to the slight younger man. "Take us to the place where the rich gringos go. The place where the real young ones are. *Chicos.*"

It registered with Victor. He studied them. "You're not *jotos.*"

Behr grabbed him by the shirt and jacket and jerked him forward off balance. Paul glanced up and down the street, which was clear.

"No, but we're looking for what happened to someone important. Someone who may have ended up there. So where would you take us if we had a taste for young boys?"

"You are cops—"

"No."

"Fuck off."

"I like you, Victor. You've been decent to us. You're just a guy trying to get ahead. Right?"

"*Sí, sí.*"

"But I will start breaking things on you if you don't help us."

"No, man. Fuck off."

Behr drew back in a blaze of motion and delivered a short, chopping punch to Victor's liver. The young man gasped and keeled, and Behr held him up.

"More is coming," Behr warned, and Victor's head set to nodding. After a moment he regained the ability to speak.

"My cousin is a *pollero*."

"What's that? A chicken cowboy?" Behr wondered, as his Spanish was rudimentary.

"*Coyote?* Maybe you know that?"

"Border crosser." Behr nodded with understanding.

"*Sí.* One thousand U.S." Victor sucked at the air. "He help with other things. ¿*Entiendes?*"

"Where is he?"

"He gone now. He back tomorrow night. Maybe the next."

"Fuck that," Behr said.

"For true. You meet him then."

Behr let Victor loose and then stepped back and ran his hands through his hair. Victor probed around his midsection with his hands.

Paul moved over to him, handed him two hundred-dollar bills, and patted him on the shoulder. "Bring him to us when he's back, then. If he takes us where we want to go, you get the rest of the thousand," he said.

"And don't fuck around with us," Behr added.

"I no fuck," Victor assured them and moved off into the night.

"Damnit," Behr breathed when it was just the two of them.

"Let's get a drink," Paul said.

"Eh—" Behr began, as much defeat in his voice as Paul had ever heard. From some men the tone of voice wouldn't have meant much, but from Behr it was unacceptable.

"I need one," Paul said.

THIRTY-TWO

FINDING A PLACE TO DRINK wasn't difficult. They didn't know Ciudad del Sol well, but all cities were the same basic mixture of humanity. They all had aspects of beauty and ugliness. All had at least one church and one jail. Paul and Behr had been there long enough to start to understand the geometry, and they found a bar on Calle Maria del Monte that served the local tequila out of clay gourds. It was a clear, fresh-tasting distillation that had salt and lime undertones, as well as some flavor of the clay in which it came. The first drink was had in silence. Paul quickly repoured.

"I tell you, I don't like doing that shit."

"I know, Frank."

"You get to the point where you're tired of being fucked around."

"I can't tell if you're talking about the case and this trip, or life in general," Paul wondered.

"I'm not sure, either." They both laughed.

"I don't know that the kid has information and was holding back," Paul said over the rim of his glass.

"He knows something. Everybody does. And when they hold back it's not always conscious."

Paul realized that he was getting a lesson learned of years. They drank more. Behr had a distant expression in his eyes.

There was a row of men at the bar who wore paper-thin T-shirts streaked with ground-in dirt. Long hair shot out from beneath ball caps and straw hats. Their fingernails were ringed with black earth. They drank quickly and talked among themselves, and began drifting out before long.

Behr ordered another gourd of tequila. Paul started to go hazy, between the liquor and the fatigue, a more tolerable distance from the hard edges of reality. He let out a deep breath. It felt like it went on forever, like he'd been holding it in for a year. He reached for his wallet, but not to pay. He pulled out the photo of Jamie that he carried now. It was one of the last taken before he went missing. It was shot in their backyard. Jamie wore a red polo shirt and a half-smile. Paul felt his eyes burn into his son's eyes in the photo. He wondered at the face, at what it would have become. After a while it was enough; he put away the photo and looked across at Behr.

Behr finished his glass and set it on the table. He reached for his own wallet. He flipped through several credit cards and business cards to where he kept it, his photo of Tim. He didn't keep it on top. He couldn't handle that kind of thorn on a daily basis. He looked down at his son, handsome in his blue sweater over a pale blue button-down shirt, standing in front of a felt background cloth, his hand posed unnaturally by the school photographer on a fence-rail prop. Behr looked at the photo for a long moment, then passed it to Paul, whose head bent over it reverentially.

"Tim, right," Paul said.

Behr nodded. "His first-grade school portrait," he began. "I still remember the day, even though he's been gone longer than he was alive." Behr poured himself another drink, his hand steady. "Linda had taken extra care in combing his hair and getting him ready. The class pictures were at nine thirty in the morning, and that was a good thing. By lunch Tim's shirt would have been untucked, rumpled, the sweater in a ball at the bottom of his cubby, his hair a mess. By the time he came home he'd be grass-stained at best, if a piece of clothing wasn't ripped outright. Linda told him every day to keep himself nice. It didn't work. The day of the picture she'd told him at least twice and maybe because of that we ended up with that good a picture."

Paul smiled and handed it back. Behr put it down on the table between them, unwilling as yet to return his son to his wallet crypt.

"You never told me how he died," Paul said.

Behr straightened and spoke in a measured way. "I'd been on night watch. I was sleeping during the day. At the end of shift we'd go to Loader's. A cop bar. They'd be opening for the day and we'd have a few pops. I'd been pulling overtime and it added to the exhaustion." He knew he sounded like he was on the witness stand or giving a deposition; the dry facts were what he drew on to get through it the few times he'd told it aloud.

"It was funny, because I didn't feel so tired that day when I got home, so I sat down on the couch and started watching sports highlights," he continued. "I fell asleep there. The gunshot woke me up, and by the time I made it into the bedroom, blood was everywhere." Now he had to pause, because the memory was twisting in him like a rusty knife. Bitterness overtook his measured testimonial.

"You don't put your gun up proper one mother-fucking day, your lockbox isn't closed tight, or your boy's watched you open it one too many times and knows how to do it, and that's what you motherfucking get." Behr reached for his drink. They both saw the tremor in his hand then, and

Behr pulled it back and put it under the table. "He was in a coma for three weeks before he died. Three goddamned weeks." Horrible images played in his mind while he fought his uneven breathing.

"It would've ended quick with this." He placed a hand, now stable, he thought, onto the tabletop. Beneath it was the black silhouette of his gun, the Bulldog .44. "In case of accident, or if you have to use it, you don't want there to be any question. That's my takeaway. How's that for stupid?" Behr made the gun disappear and then his tequila. He tapped his wristwatch, a stainless steel Omega Speedmaster. "So this is the sum total of my family. Wife gave it to me for our fifth anniversary. It's all that's left. Guess it was better made." There was a mad look on his face that he could feel and was sure Paul could see.

"Ah, Frank," Paul said, unable to offer anything else.

"I'm drunk enough." Behr stood.

The night was dark black. Whatever streetlamps there were in the town must have been uniformly broken or extinguished at a set time, as none of them threw any light. They made their way intuitively back toward their motel, turning down one street, rethinking it, turning back and going down another. They rounded a corner and walked along a long chain-link fence that surrounded a used-car lot they recognized from earlier in the day. Suddenly, a blur of black fur and white gnashing teeth came smashing against the fence. A pair of yellow-eyed guard dogs, growling low and throaty, had come out of the darkness and went after Behr and Paul. The animals bounced off the fence, only to lunge again. Paul had jumped back out of instinct while Behr had turned to face them. He hooked his fingers through the fence and let out a growl of his own, which was lower and more menacing than what the dogs had mustered. Behr's hands on the fence gave the dogs ample opportunity to snap at him, but instead the dogs shrank back. They shimmied down on front paws and tried to put up another wall of growls. Behr began barking at them. He sounded like a deranged human mastiff. Paul stepped up next to him and grabbed the fence. He started barking, too, his sounding like a frenzied hyena's. The real dogs, fear-ridden and confused, let out squeals and disappeared back into the darkness of the lot.

After their fingers had gone white from gripping, Behr let go of the fence and started laughing. Then Paul started in laughing, too. It came in waves. They snorted and howled, doubling over at the waist. Eventually whatever was funny about it petered out and there was only silence. They straightened and headed back to the motel, where sleep awaited, black and dreamless.

THIRTY-THREE

DON RAMON PONCETERRA TOOK LUNCH ALONE on his tiled veranda, the quiet bubbling of a small fountain and the occasional bird the only accompaniments to his meal. The *camarones* had been excellent, and as he forked sliced mango into his mouth, he considered the liver spots on the backs of his hands. When fall came Don Ramon would turn seventy years old, and while most of his contemporaries had gone fat and sedentary and bald, he was still slender and vigorous and had a fine head of silver hair. It was only the cursed spots on the backs of his hands, thickening into a brown pattern like the belly of a brook trout, which reminded him of his years. The sight disturbed him and conjured visions of the dark labyrinths of oblivion that awaited him if he did not act.

In his life as a businessman he had made countless acquaintances. He had known landowners, merchants, traders, manufacturers, cattlemen, and the like, and each group thought Don Ramon a mere entrepreneur like them. Until he was in his midforties, that perception was entirely accurate. He *was* financially well off and scrupulously polite; an immaculate dresser; he had daughters and a son; he owned land, donated to the church, and was a sponsor of the fiesta.

But then the change came, his awakening. It coincided with his rereading of the classics and coming across the concept of the "philosopher-king," as Socrates had put it. While that term was a bit grandiose for a modest man such as himself, Don Ramon recognized the truth in it. He discovered that a man could live his life by the highest precepts, even if a deteriorated society could not grasp them. Now, very few in the world truly knew him or understood how he remained so youthful in aspect. It was this secret of his that drew his thoughts to the *rubio*.

Many *potros* had come to him over the years. It would be impossible to remember all the boys. For most, the brevity of their stay, and their inevitably failing health, made a lasting relationship unlikely. It was quite sad. Still, there had been three who had become truly important to him. They had gone from the occupation of a few weeks to that of a few months to several years. Those three alone had had the potential to become true acolytes. As the ancient Greeks knew, the intellectual inter-course between learned men and the young boys in their charge, and the physical consummation of said relationships, was superior to any other bond. While many men thought women and the off-spring they bore were the path to immortality, Don Ramon knew that the vitality that sprang from his *mentorships* was the true road.

But those three opportunities had passed bit-terly. One of the catamites had perished by his own hand. Even now Don Ramon could remem-ber the pale morning light in the room when he discovered the young man hanging by his bed sheet. The second, regrettably, had been a discipli-nary accident. And the third, perhaps the most regrettable of all, had merely disappeared, escap-ing into the wind, never to be heard from again. He had probably perished in the desert. The dis-tress these endings caused Don Ramon had almost been enough to discourage any further attach-ments. But then he felt the march of time and the cobwebbed fingers of death reaching out for him, and he knew that he needed to continue. The call to become the evolved, the truly *Platonic* man, would not quiet within him.

So a few years back he had begun the lengthy search for the next in a line of magical consorts who would keep him forever beyond the grave. Despite the establishment of a complex infrastruc-ture (for the truth was that his gift in the organization of businesses was real, and even in this, a profit-generating enterprise was of paramount importance), and despite the dozens of spiders he had crawling all over the earth on his behalf, each working with great energy to bring him the special individual he sought, he had nearly given up hope of finding him. That is, until the *rubio* had been delivered unto him.

Don Ramon sipped his rioja. It was a bit sharp. He didn't prefer his wines so young. Though he didn't know the *rubio*'s name, as he never learned their names, and he didn't know where he was from, that information did not matter to him, either. He only knew that this one glowed. Some might have suggested that Don Ramon was blinded by the fair hair and fair complexion, but that was foolishness, the kind of superficial assumption that an uncomprehending world was all too happy to make. It was another, inner quality that this one possessed. Don Ramon had spent long hours sitting in the dark with the *rubio*. Conversation was difficult due to their languages, but beyond that, words were wholly beside the point. There was an aura one could feel from another that told the whole story. In this case the tale was one of eternity. Even when sitting in the same room, simply sharing the same air, he could feel the *rubio*'s healing youth. Remaining chances were few, though. This time there could be no mistake. And so Don Ramon had been exceedingly cautious with him, saving him, waiting for the sign of acquiescence that would signal the beginning of the physical union that would heal him. It had been many months and he didn't know how much longer he could wait. He had turned to several of the others for relief of his corporeal urges, and as always that had left him feeling incredibly youthful and vigorous, yet disgusted. He hadn't wanted to spoil the *rubio* with that. No, with the *rubio* he needed nothing less than complete acceptance. If he could achieve this, Don Ramon felt he could truly live forever.

Don Ramon's musings were interrupted by the arrival of another on the veranda. There was the telltale cough, whether an attempt at politeness or a chronic condition, Don Ramon was unable to tell. Then came the shuffling of feet on the tile, the sound of thin, cheap shoes. Don Ramon could only put the choice down to poor taste, as he certainly paid his employees well enough for them to buy quality goods. It was Esteban.

Esteban Carnera stepped out from around the potted plant and, seeing that the meal was finished, advanced.

"Don Ramon," he began, his raspy voice scraping the adobe walls around the courtyard. Whatever he lacked in social graces, Esteban made up for in utility. He was tall and stringy-muscled like a fighting bantam and walked on the balls of his feet. His face was deeply pocked and scarred so that there was little value in his protecting his looks when it came to physical matters. Over time, Don Ramon had come to learn that this was of great advantage.

"Yes, Esteban."

"There are men in town, going to all the places."

"Yes?"

"They do not buy, they just look, and ask for other things."

This in itself was not worrisome to Don Ramon. There were many kinds of clients and many ways in which they behaved.

"What kind of men? *¿Clientes?*"

"*No sé, Don Ramon. Ellos son gueros.*"

THIRTY-FOUR

IT HAD BEEN TWO MORE DAYS of looking around, two more nights of drinking. They figured they had seen the last of Victor. Now Behr and Paul passed the day flat on their backs in their dingy motel room, drinking the dwindling water they'd brought, considering their diminishing funds, and watching a national soccer game that seemed to go on for hours and hours and hours on the minuscule television set. Their stomachs rumbled, but food was not an option.

"That mescal's got some kick," Paul said, not for the first time.

"Like a damn mule," Behr agreed.

They sent a halfhearted maid away and went in and out of sleep, interrupted by the chants and shouts of college kids across the motel engaging in a drinking game, turbo quarters or beer pong, it sounded like.

Finally the light coming in through the patchy curtain started turning color from bright yellow to pale and they began to stir.

"I'm hitting the shower," Paul said, standing.

"I'll go after you."

There was a hammering at the door. They looked at each other and Behr got up. He put his gun at the small of his back in the waistband of his pants.

"*¿Quién es?*" he said.

"*Policía*," came the answer. Behr swung the door open. There was a stout man in his mid-thirties standing there. He chewed tobacco and wore a straw cowboy hat, and he had a .45 on his hip. His partner waited back in the distance in a dirty patrol car.

"*¿Sí?*" Behr asked.

"We speak English," the cop said, "it's more easy." Behr nodded.

"I am First Sergeant Guillermo Garcia. They call me 'Gigi,' or also, Fernando." He patted his big gut and smiled. "Now tell me what are you here for in the *ciudad*?"

"For the tequila mostly, it seems." Behr smiled, blanking the cop with his eyes.

"Tequila is good, huh?" It was clear Fernando wanted more.

"And to see the sights, of course," Behr added.

"Maybe the girls, too?" Fernando said.

"Maybe. We haven't decided," Behr said. Now Fernando's face changed.

"Ah, you know prostitution is illegal here? This is an important thing."

"We didn't know," Paul said, from the bed.

"Is that a fact?" Behr asked.

"Yes. A big crime," Fernando said. "But it is possible to get a license. Then you do what you want."

"Huh. Sounds like we need one," Behr said, already reaching for his money roll. He kept it in his pocket as he peeled off a hundred-dollar bill wrapped around the outside. He handed the bill to Fernando.

"This is good. Now you have no problem," Fernando said. "My boss will get his *mordida*—you know what I say?" Behr did, and it wasn't because of his Spanish, but rather that almost everyone in law enforcement was familiar with the term. It translated to "little bite," as in everyone up the chain took his. Behr had often wondered at the productivity that would result if all the organization and effort that went into the systemic corruption were applied to a useful enterprise. "Oh yeah, but this license," Fernando held up the bill, "it expire tomorrow. Understand? If you stay, I got to come back."

Behr just nodded.

"So then, have a good night," Fernando said, and stepped back. Behr closed the door.

After a moment, Behr turned to Paul. "I was wondering when we'd have to deal with that. It'll cost more next time. We're pretty much out of time here."

Paul absorbed this and hurried to the shower.

Around evening time they went to the café, which had become their usual place. They ate and then ordered coffee and waited. After a half hour Victor appeared in the doorway. If he held any ill will over the roughing he'd received, it didn't show. Instead he whistled and waved, and Behr and Paul followed him out.

They walked quickly through the streets, cutting down a few back alleys. No one said anything, and they soon came upon a worn, mud-spattered Toyota pickup with a man resting on the hood. The man popped up at their approach. He was lithe and wiry, like a punk singer, an orangutan without the hair.

"This is Ernesto," Victor said, "*mi primo*." Ernesto wore silver-framed glasses with blue lenses despite the darkness. The man slid off the truck and landed solidly on his feet. They shook hands with him.

"*Qué tal,*" Behr offered. "You have something to show us?"

Ernesto shrugged.

"You can make your fee without carrying anyone across," Behr said. The *pollero* looked at
them. Maybe he smelled cop. But he wanted the
money.

"You hit on my cousin," Ernesto said. Behr
bristled and met his eyes in time to see that the
man thought it was more funny than anything
else, but then he added, "You no hit on me or else
problems." Behr glared back at him but said nothing. "I show you a place. Get in." He gestured to
the back of his truck.

"We'll get our car and follow you," Behr said,
not liking it.

"Then no come." Ernesto got in the truck and
started it. Behr and Paul looked at each other and
then climbed in.

They rumbled out over crumbling asphalt road
that gave way to dirt track, and the air changed
from thick and fetid with the smells of the town
and outlying factories to cool and fresh. Dark
hunches of juniper and sagebrush stood out in the
blue of the night. They sat low in the truckbed,
backs against the wheel wells, heads down against
the wind. Every rut shot through the truck's metal
frame and up their spines.

Behr spoke as quietly as he could and yet still be
heard over the wind.

"This guy, the cousin," he began, "watch him. He's a blade man."

"Yeah?"

"If something goes down, you won't see it coming. Knives are meant to be felt, not seen. If he shows it to you, look for what else is on the way."

"How did you . . . ?"

"I noticed when we shook hands, a callus at the base of his first finger hard as a rock. You ever meet a chef? They always have a callus there, where the heels of all the knives they use rest. And this guy doesn't seem like a cook to me."

Paul nodded. There was nothing else to say.

After a few miles of rough travel, they drove off the track onto the open plain and the truck began to jostle and buck hard. Behr and Paul held on to the gunwales and ate dust. A few painful minutes passed and the truck began to slow. It came to a stop and then crept along again for several hundred yards before stopping once more. This time it was for good. Behr and Paul climbed down as Ernesto shut the engine but left the headlights on. Ernesto walked forward to where the lights illuminated a low berm, and Victor got out of the truck.

"What's up?" Paul asked.

"Don't know," Behr answered.

"You see?" Victor said.

"You see?" Ernesto echoed from his place near

the berm. "I show you something very dangerous." And then he began kicking at the ground.
He went on for a few moments, going deeper into
the soft dirt, and then stopped and stepped back.

Behr and Paul looked at each other and walked
forward. They saw it there, covered in brown
earth, a human rib cage. Behr pushed at a nearby
pile with his foot and uncovered a lower jawbone
complete with teeth.

"Ah, shit," he said.

"What is this?" Paul wondered.

Behr thought back to what he'd seen at Eagle
Creek Park and knew. "The remains of a teenage
boy."

"*Sí,*" Ernesto said. He seemed vaguely proud to
have shown them.

Paul moved forward and began kicking hard at
the ground. Behr joined him. They uncovered
femur bones, arms, clavicles, and skulls, evidence
of perhaps half a dozen bodies. The remains
weren't fresh, but still an odor became present—
that of decomposition.

"This is where they dump them," Behr said.

Ernesto nodded. "I don't go more far," he said.
"Or we all be killed."

Paul realized he was in an unholy burial ground
and doubled over, his hands on his thighs. He fell
to his knees and began raking through the debris
with his hands, looking for what, he was not sure,
only something that would tell him what he

needed to know. His breathing became ragged and shallow. He fought against a rising nausea and finally ceased with the digging.

Behr stopped his digging, too. There was very little sound above their breathing. "Why did you bring us here?" Behr asked.

"He hope you be satisfy," Victor piped in. "And you pay him."

"We're not satisfied," Behr said. "Where are they kept before?"

Ernesto just shook his head.

"You think I'm going to pay you for a graveyard?" Behr asked.

"This is where they end," Ernesto said. "I no can take you where they are before."

"Then you're not getting any money," Behr said with firmness.

"You see this place. I know from my cousin you no customers. I know if I take you there, you make trouble. Then trouble find *me*. So you gon' pay me now and then go away." Ernesto smiled, the rhythmic clicking of a butterfly knife opening in his hand.

"For this? No," Behr said, allowing himself to face Ernesto full-on but quartering away from Victor so his right side was shielded. "We want more. We need answers."

Ernesto nodded at Victor, who was standing at the edge of the pool of the truck's headlights. Behr's assumptions proved correct as Victor raised both arms and in his trembling hands was a Ruger .357.

Paul saw it and slowly stood. Perhaps he had come all this way to die among what might be the bones of his son.

Behr eased his hand into his pocket and gripped his own gun.

"Don't fuck around, Victor. *¿Comprende?*" Behr said evenly. "Put that thing up before this goes to shit."

"You no pay him. You hit me. No good," Victor said.

"You're not shooting anyone. And I'm not shooting you." Behr slowly took out his gun and kept it pointed low, but in Victor's general direction. "We'll pay, and we'll pay plenty if you take us to where the boys are kept when they're alive."

"Maybe we kill you and take all your money?" Ernesto suggested. "Safer for me than to take you there."

"You do that, you'll have the FBI up your ass," Behr said with conviction.

"Bullshit, FBI." Ernesto tried to sound brave and convinced.

"Bullshit if you look in my wallet and don't find a badge there," Behr said firmly.

Ernesto showed no inclination to check badges or anything else. Instead he yelled harshly at Victor in rapid Spanish. The words *policía* and *federales* popped out from the speech. Victor struggled to keep the gun up and under control. It was an uncomfortable stalemate, one Paul anticipated Behr breaking with gunfire at any moment, and it motivated him to speak.

"Do you have kids?" Paul asked the men. Out of the corner of his eye he saw Victor look to Ernesto, giving him away.

"*Sí*, my son, Keke, is two years," Ernesto said, his voice losing its sharp edges.

"I believe *my* son, Jamie, could be one of them." Paul gestured to the bones at their feet. "He'd be fourteen." His words hung like dust in the desert air. "I need to find out what happened to him. To see where he was, how he may have ended up here. That's all I want now." He swallowed. "I hope nothing bad ever happens to Keke. You can make a lot of money for him right now. It can be easy." They watched Ernesto chew it over.

"I want two thousand. It's more danger than to bring people across." He finally spoke.

"Forget two thousand," Behr began.

"Two thousand," Paul agreed. Ernesto nodded to Victor to lower the gun. Victor seemed relieved to do it. Paul went right to his pocket for the money. There wouldn't be much left after he paid.

THIRTY-FIVE

WHEN THE DARKNESS COMES, *so do the noises. The
sounds of cars and trucks arriving, of men
laughing, the thumping of doors open and
shut, the dogs barking, and sometimes music,
other times a lone squeal. The night is the time of
dreams for the world, but not for him. For him,
the night is a time for work. The cinder-block
shavings come slowly together in a pile by his
knees, which he blows away from time to time.
Once, a long time ago, a meal had gone back without a spoon and it had not been noticed and now
the spoon handle heats from friction, its point
sharp and mean. He's bent the rounded part of the
spoon back toward itself, and after holding it for
so many hours it fits smoothly into his palm. The
point and edges of the weapon have long been*

sharp enough. He knows this by his blood, which he's drawn from his own hand. He stops at a sound: footsteps in the hall. He tucks his weapon behind him. Then the footsteps continue on and he returns to his work. . . .

THIRTY-SIX

THEIR HEADLIGHTS WASHED OVER what looked like a lunar landscape. The stark desert dirt, dried to chalky powder by the day's sun, puffed up from the ground and filled the air inside the car. They had driven back to town, riding uncomfortable and alert in Ernesto's truckbed. They had picked up Behr's car and then followed Ernesto out into the night. They drove for a long time into the desert, beyond roads, paved or otherwise, in a direction they calculated as south and west of where they had been before. They passed giant saguaro cacti, standing silent like ominous sentinels, and caught sight of a fleeing jackrabbit, painted white by their headlamps. Finally the pickup ahead of them slowed and doused its lights. Frank did the same and followed as they rolled slowly, finding their way in the darkness for a half-mile. Their eyes adjusted to the night, and eventually they came to a stop in what they saw was a swale in the desert floor. A tall rise of sandstone and rock a few hundred yards distant blocked any view farther on. All four men climbed out of the vehicles. None seemed eager to speak.

"So . . ." Paul ventured.

"Over that hill." Ernesto pointed toward the rise. "*El rancho de los caballitos.*"

Something about the phrase was familiar to Behr. "Over the hill? That's it, then?" he asked. "Take us there."

"Hey, *pendejo,* you just visiting here, but we have to live," Ernesto said, and then spat. He got in the truck.

Victor hesitated, seeming unwilling to part from them.

"I sorry," he said, looking down at his feet uncomfortably, "about the gun. I didn't know for what you were here. I didn't know about your son. I just think—"

Ernesto rolled down his window. "*Cierra la boca.*" He spoke with disgust. "*Hijo de puta.*"

Victor fell silent.

"It's okay," Paul said. "Don't worry about it."

Victor began moving toward the passenger side with resignation and then stopped. "If you try to go there, don't go without the word."

"What word?" Behr asked.

Victor thought for a moment. "Password. If

you go without the password, they shoot you at the gate."

"What is it?" Behr asked.

"*Cállate, burro,*" Ernesto called, causing Victor to flinch.

"*No sé.*" Victor sighed deeply and slumped into Ernesto's truck.

The Toyota pulled out, kicking up considerable dust, and drove back from where they had come. When the dust and the night silence had settled once again, Behr edged their car up just beyond where Ernesto had ventured. They went the rest of the way on foot. They climbed the rise, perhaps seventy vertical feet at a steep pitch, their feet sliding in the soft sand as it gave way in miniature avalanches at their every step.

"You think there's anything over this hill?" Paul asked, grabbing at roots and rocks to help pull himself up.

"Either way we've seen the last of those guys and that two grand," Behr responded.

"It didn't seem like the time to haggle."

"You're probably right about that."

They scrambled up the last of the hill, taking care not to profile themselves against the ridgeline. They flattened on their bellies amid the sagebrush and saw the place for the first time in what remained of the darkness. Down in the bowl beneath them a quarter mile in the distance was a series of low buildings, some constructed entirely of cinder block, others of fiberglass but propped up on cinder-block foundations that rose a few feet out of the desert floor. Floodlights mounted on ten-foot-high poles cast stark light on the compound.

The structures appeared sturdy enough, but the place seemed temporary, like an army encampment. The only nod to permanence was a dark, moatlike band of vegetation that had been deliberately planted and wrapped around the far edges of the buildings. A hurricane fence topped with coiled razor wire wrapped around that. A single dirt road led in from the darkness, and a tired-looking man leaned against a sturdy gate. A quarter mile beyond the cluster of buildings was a large propane tank and a small shed from which they could hear the low clatter of a generator. Occasionally, quiet bursts of Spanish escaped one or another of the buildings and reached them on the hill.

Behr produced a pair of field glasses from his jacket and scoped the place in detail. "Off the grid," he said. He turned the binoculars on the man leaning against the gate. "That big boy's on guard duty. He's got a sidearm strapped to his hip." Behr pointed out that the band of undergrowth around the buildings was horse crippler cactus, planted close together, deterring anyone from crossing it to get to the buildings or vice versa.

There was a row of four cars parked to one side. A dust-covered Bronco, a shiny Nissan Armada SUV, an aging Ford sedan, and a Japanese car, perhaps a Honda Civic. Another few cars protruded from around a building, but they could make out neither model nor license plate. Paul watched as Behr pulled out a notebook, removed a pen cap with his teeth, and wrote down the license plate numbers of the other vehicles.

Paul hoped Behr's professional eye was picking the place apart for weaknesses, because he didn't spot any gaps in the place's defenses.

At the main building, a door opened and a rotund man emerged walking two large-barreled dogs that strained against their chain leashes.

"Rottweilers?" Paul asked, squinting into the distance.

"Worse," Behr said, recognizing the breed. "Presa Canarios. Portuguese fighting dogs." After a time the dogs squatted by the cactus patch until they'd done their business, then the man took them inside. They did not reemerge.

Behr passed the binoculars and Paul took a long look. At the sound of another door opening, Paul whip-panned to the largest of the structures in time to see a pair of men exiting. The men, Caucasian, apparently Americans, in their late forties and dressed in casual clothes, wove slightly, as if pleasantly drunk. They did not speak before they got into the Armada and drove out. The guard swung the gate open and raised a hand in farewell as the SUV exited. The guard resecured the gate as the Armada drove off into the night, and all was quiet again, until another pair of men, smaller in stature than the gate guard and the dog walker, appeared from inside the main structure as well. Between them was a tallish but slight boy dressed in a tracksuit, perhaps sixteen years old, with dark hair and features. They led the boy, who showed no signs of resistance, toward a long, trailer-style building. They paused. One of the men lit a cigarette and he and the boy waited while the other one pissed into the cactus. When he was done, they crossed the interior of the compound and then disappeared one by one into the long trailer. A snatch of Latin music leaked out the door when they entered. Over the next three-quarters of an hour, several lone men left. Then all became still and quiet. After a long time looking, Paul lowered the glasses.

"Something wrong's going on down there."

"Yep," Behr breathed. Cold descended on them and they stiffened on the hard, dusty ground, where they lay.

THIRTY-SEVEN

DON RAMON PONCETERRA LAY NEXT TO his wife in the large hand-carved wooden bed that had been in his family for generations. Though the air was cool, the bed was soft, and he felt the comfort of all of his ancestors who had rested in it before him, sleep was far off. He thought of his father, the stern presence who had shaped his life, in large part in this very bed. There were nights when his mother had left the *finca* and gone into the city, and Señor Ponceterra had called young Ramon into the darkened room. *There are many things you must understand,* mijo, *in order to become a man,* he would say, his rough hands grabbing at the boy's nightshirt. But Ponceterra had become a man and built his world around him as all men must do.

He had received a few more reports and checked

with his sources in town earlier that evening. They had made inquiries at the various brothels and learned that, indeed, two *gueros* a bit unlike the rest had been seen. They had spent money and previewed but hadn't partaken, not that he'd learned so far, anyway. This was not unheard-of, but it was not usual, and now it concerned him. He'd learned that they'd spread cash around, had also paid cash at the motel, and though they seemed to have left, he didn't take for granted that they actually had. Other than that, there was no real information to be gained. Only that they had been seen in the company of a young local named Victor Colon. He'd asked Esteban to try to find Victor, to see if he had anything to volunteer on the subject. Esteban had not yet turned up this Victor. But he would. He always did. He had never let Ponceterra down. This thought eased his mind. He listened to his wife's steady, ignorant breathing and finally the hold of the day relaxed, and he began his own drift toward the territory of sleep.

THIRTY-EIGHT

THE NIGHT WAS HALF SPENT when Behr spoke.

"We have a couple of choices here, and I've got to set them out for you."

"Okay."

"We can drive back and notify the U.S. government, see what they say. Plain and simple, this is the high-percentage play and I'm honor-bound to advance it."

"Uh-huh," Paul said, but he was concerned about the time it might take to involve U.S. authorities. He felt that leaving their spot, even breaking his gaze, would cause the compound to disappear like a mirage, and he was afraid to risk that.

"We could go back to town and call the Mexican police," Behr went on, "but we don't know for sure what the fuck is going on down there. We've seen some remains in a different location. And we don't even know whose. It's clear people are paid off left, right, and center out here. If they get word about us, they'll arrest us or kill us, or move or kill everybody in that place and burn it to the ground." This hung in the dark air for a moment as the light around them turned from purple to gray with the morning's approach. "It might be time to pull back and hire some help," Behr finally continued.

"Other detectives?"

"PIs, private security. I've got contacts, but again it'd take time."

"And I'm out of money."

They kept looking.

"Or?" Paul said.

Behr couldn't bring himself to answer for a long time. In his mind was the notion of the great mistake. One in a lifetime was enough to ruin a man and he seemed to be trading in them. His first had destroyed his son, the second his career. There had been others, and this last one upon which he was on the precipice would likely kill his client and himself. But as he looked down on the compound he realized that unspeakable things happened inside it, that he'd been living in an unspeakable world since he'd started on the case and he was unable to go one more day without changing that.

"We can go in and try to find out for ourselves," Behr said. "We've confirmed four guards.

Dogs. The place can only be reached by crossing an open expanse. We'd have to drive straight in. I could try and do it alone, but it'd be senseless."

He fell silent.

Paul was unable to answer. A wave of panic broke over him, causing him to sweat and chill at the same time. Fear of what might happen down there, that he wouldn't make it back, and that Behr himself was afraid, hit hard against his lower abdomen. Paul flipped over onto his back looking for air, sucking in great gulps of the cold stuff, as if his goal were to swallow the night sky. He flashed on the last breakfast at home, and on his last night with Carol, and the hope it gave him for his return, whether with answers or without.

Paul felt Behr looking at him, but the detective didn't say anything and eventually turned his gaze back down to what was in front of them. Paul didn't belong out here in the desert. Nothing in his life had prepared him for what he was contemplating. He had once thought of his existence as a neat package. Then he had watched that package explode. He knew now that life was never the tidy thing he had imagined it to be, that he had just seen it that way. He had come to learn that the horrible could happen, and when it did, there were things more horrible still that could occur. But when the power that ran the universe, whatever it was, had decided to lay him low, it had reached out and touched him, it had singled him out and had become intimate with him. He understood then that even if his existence had become warped and misshapen, it was life nonetheless, and it was worth everything. He knew now that anything was possible. Maybe he'd even survive.

"We need to tell the FBI, you're right about that," Paul said, his words floating away into the darkness. "But after. If that was my son out there rotting in the desert, then I can't leave this spot until I know. I've got to go in there, Frank. I've got to. But I won't ask you to. I can't do that."

"We'll do it together," Behr said without pause. "You stay here and watch. I'd better go work on that password." He pulled himself to his feet.

Sometime just after three the floodlights in the compound went out and the whole bowl below Paul was cast into darkness, thick and absolute. Moments later the generator cut off, and silence joined the dark in a chorus of isolation for Paul on top of the bleak hill. He had no concept of where he was. He would have no idea how to even locate himself on a map. His only tether to civilization, to his life, was Behr, and there was no guarantee of his return. He felt his heart beat into the hard ground beneath him, scarce evidence of his own existence. Fear, as he had once known it, no longer existed. He had passed beyond such an earthbound condition. He was eye-to-eye with his oblivion now. Only a sense of logic, feeble and habitual, suggested that the morning would even come.

Behr looked out the windshield, thick with dirt, as girls in groups of two and three left the hybrid adobe-trailer building. Nearly a dozen in all, they made their way to a battered pickup that quickly drove off. Another few walked down the road into the night, perhaps to a bus stop, he considered. Lights went off from one end of the building to another, until only one remained on. Where the kitchen would be, Behr thought, based on most of the double-wides he'd been in. The screen door opened, and the woman, older than the others, small and slight, exited smoking a cigarette. That was when Behr got out of his car.

The woman was the one he had heard Victor call Marta. The one he had heard mention the *rancho de los caballitos*. She was frightened as he stepped out of the darkness into the trailer's weak ring of light, but she hid it quickly and well.

"*Buenas,*" he said.

"We are closed, eh. *Cerrado.* Girls gone home." If she remembered him from his last visit, she was trying to keep it from him. But he knew she knew. There was a flinty intelligence in her black eyes. It had made an impression on him during his last visit, and it gave him hope for coming back now.

"I'm not here for that, Marta."

"*No hablo*—"

"Yes, you do."

"It's late. I go to bed."

"Wait. Finish your cigarette." She stared up at him with malice. He supposed in that moment that he was every man that had made her a commodity in her day and currently did so to all the girls in her charge.

"What you want?"

"I need the password to enter the *rancho*," he said. Now she glared at him outright. He saw genuine fear behind the expression she was trying to mask with the anger.

"They look for you," she said. "They gon' kill you."

"Who?"

She made a *tsk* sound with her teeth that told him she would probably die before telling him that.

"Then give me the password."

"No."

A moment of quiet passed.

"Come inside," she offered.

"No thanks," Behr said. She was five feet tall, but Behr was reluctant to share a space with her where she undoubtedly had a weapon.

"It won't come back on you," he went on. "Others must know it. Plenty of others."

"Go ask them," she said.

"I'm asking you."

"Nothing here is for free. You know?"

"I know." Behr dug the ground with the ball of his foot. "I have very little money to pay you, and I don't guess you take credit cards."

She squared up with him for the negotiation. He looked at her. She flicked her cigarette away and crossed her arms. Her hard eyes shone back at him, black and cold as the night.

THIRTY-NINE

WHEN THE DARKNESS goes away, along with the cold of the night, and all is thick with heat and quiet, like now, he dreams of touching his mother's face. He isn't sure how old he is anymore. A long time has passed. His birthday has as well. At least one, he is sure. But he remembers her face well. The soft, thin skin of her cheeks . . . the slight circles under her eyes . . . of pressing on her full lips with his fingertips . . . of knocking his forehead against hers as he did when he was a child, the code for their love when he felt he had grown too old to speak it. It is a dream of peace out of reach. The dream visits him almost every time he sleeps. It haunts him, and drives him to try to run. Even though he doesn't know where he is—only that he thinks it may be called *Cuando Tiempo*, for those are the words he hears most *often. And even though he doesn't know how far, he knows it is a great distance from anyplace else. They have taken his shoes. It is their practice to do this. He has been left alone for a long time, but he feels that something is about to change. His visits from the guards are more frequent now, their checks on his condition more focused. They had given him more food for a time, the occasional Coca-Cola, but not so much recently. He looks out the window and sees the cactus just outside. Low, flat plants with clusters of spines that shine in the sun lay around the building in every direction as far as he can see. He has seen others from time to time. And then not for a while and he knows they are dead. Like the one who was inside the van's well with him, cloth sacks over their heads. Chris Something. The other had said a last name, but he can no longer remember it. He only recalls the moment when he knew Chris Something had died, lying heavy on top of him, the smell building up in the small space as the van drove.*

FORTY

PAUL MUST HAVE FALLEN ASLEEP because when he lifted his head the pink of morning was in the sky and Behr's boots filled his eyes. He glanced up to see Behr crouched below the ridgeline, peering down on the compound.

"You get the password?" Paul asked.

"I got it," Behr answered.

The brief fresh cool of morning burned off minute by minute, and by the time it was ten o'clock, the sun was high and striking down on them like molten lava.

"We don't know what to expect during daylight hours," Behr had said. "The high-percentage play would be to do it late night, when we know the routine. But I sure don't feel good about going in there when it's dark. Do you? We'll keep on with the recon, go around dusk."

Paul nodded.

"We go in there, there's no guarantee of our safety. If it comes to it, can you shoot?" Behr asked.

"Yes," Paul answered. They said no more.

They retired back to the car in shifts for shade and water but didn't want to risk the sound of running the engine for air-conditioning, so if anything the car was even hotter than the outside air. The water, too, was warm and oily and tasted of plastic, but they drank it because they knew they needed it. By noon they'd eaten the last of the beef jerky and the other snacks they'd bought at gas stations on their way. Sweat rolled down their faces and stung their eyes, and even though they covered their heads and arms with extra shirts, they felt their skin burning. Their eyeballs ached and their heads were splitting, and while several men had left early in the day, and for a time only the Bronco was parked below them, they had yet to see any further sign of what went on inside. Later on, well after noon, a pickup with a canvas over a payload entered, but it pulled in behind one of the buildings out of their sight.

.   .   .

Don Ramon Ponceterra took great care in dressing, as he always did, although he was moving more quickly than usual. This day was unusual in the extreme, but he was loath to abandon his habits. He had gotten the phone call from Esteban that Victor Colon had been located and that surely there would be something learned within an hour or two. Don Ramon had said that he would meet them out at the *rancho*. Then he set about choosing a white linen shirt, cream-colored trousers, fine socks, and light tan suede shoes. Lastly, he tied a short silk scarf around his throat, for though he wore a sturdy twill shooting jacket, he always made allowances, regardless of his dress, for at least one piece of silk against his skin. As Plato taught, "all physical objects are mere shadows of their ideal forms." Except for silk. Silk was the apotheosis of fabric, in Ponceterra's considered opinion.

A light coating of Bay Rum on his smooth cheeks, the citrus scent pleasantly piquant in his nostrils, and he was ready. He went outside to where his Cadillac Eldorado had been pulled around. He'd be driving himself today. It was not something he liked to do, but there was good reason for it, as Esteban was otherwise occupied. He got into the well-kept car, the interior cool enough from being parked inside the carriage house that he needed only to keep the fan turned low. He pulled out of his property and made his way to the *ruta*.

There had been screams. They began after lunch and seem to go on and on. They belong to a grown man, not a boy, though at times they resemble those of an animal. Something is happening. Something different. There has been a sense of waiting. It has gone on for so long it has given way to deadness. He dreads the visits from the Fancy Man. Though the man never touches him beyond a pat on the leg, the back, a hand on the cheek, there is a feeling that something is coming, and not knowing what is the worst thing he's ever tasted. The Fancy Man wears suits that smell like moth-balls underneath the odor of flowery aftershave.

There is a lull in the screaming and he hears the sound of a car arriving. This is strange, it being so early, and also because a small truck has arrived already and has pulled around the far side of the building, where he cannot see it. Now he goes and peers out from behind the vinyl shade that covers the small window, too small for him to slip through. He glances down and sees the cacti they had forced him to plant. "Since we can't make you 'work,' " they said, "you will work." He had dug and planted for endless hot days, the spiny needles tearing at his flesh, as he secured his own prison. Now he sees the car enter the compound—it is the Fancy Man. He stands, looks a last time out the window at the arrival, and then crosses to the cinder block to finish his sharpening. . . .

Paul had been staring through the binoculars for much of the day, the rubber cups on the eyepieces cutting into his face, when he finally saw it. A car, an older Cadillac, was approaching, and he'd just looked away from it when he saw a figure flash by a window. The person's coloring stood out from the dark-skinned, dark-haired background that Mexico had come to be in his mind's eye. The familiar rose up through all improbability and grabbed him by the throat. He knew what he'd seen. Before he realized it, he had climbed to one knee and was in the process of starting to run straight down the hill. Behr's hand shot out, gripped Paul's calf, and yanked him back down on his belly in the dust.

"You have heat stroke?" Behr asked.

"Frank," Paul gasped. He felt Behr looking at him, saw with his peripheral vision that Behr's hand was extended for the field glasses.

"What is it?"

"He's there—"

"What?"

"He's there. Jamie."

FORTY-ONE

PONCETERRA'S ELDORADO MOVED through the gate in a dust cloud of its own making. Paco had swung the gate back into place behind him by the time he'd gotten out of his car. Ponceterra regarded the air of the compound. *Is something different today?* he wondered.

"*Buenas tardes, patrón,*" Paco said.

Ponceterra ignored him and moved toward the main house, his mind occupied with two things: whether or not Esteban had been successful and the *rubio*. He had been limiting his visits, staying away so as not to push him too hard, but considered if he should look in on him today. Perhaps all the waiting and careful cajoling would finally cause the boy to yield. And then he thought of Esteban's project: the *gueros*. Were they merely new customers or could they be trouble? His people were armed with meticulous instructions for avoiding the wrong kinds of clients. And they knew the punishment for failing to follow said instructions was utterly severe.

Suddenly Don Ramon stopped. Why not be safe and make a new password today? He called out to Paco, "*Hay una nueva contraseña hoy . . .*" Then he quietly spoke it. "Let them know in town."

"*Sí, jefe.*" Paco nodded.

Don Ramon entered the main house. The lights were off and all was quiet, as it would be for at least two more hours. Fat Miguel jumped up from a sofa, his magazine falling to the floor, at Don Ramon's arrival.

"Esteban?" Don Ramon demanded.

"*Oficina.*" Miguel bent and picked up his magazine.

Ponceterra swung the office door open to find Esteban in the middle of his work on the young man from town. The man was slumped on the floor, wedged against the wall in a heap, his head hanging forward, hair and face a mess of sweat and blood. Esteban turned, the look on his face that of a patient butcher.

"*¿Qué pasó?*" Ponceterra asked.

"*Un ratito.*"

Four men on the premises had always been enough. Management of the working boys was simple, and no customer had ever given any trouble. Then of course there were the dogs. But seeing the violence in front of him made him wonder.

"*Todos saben—*" he began, asking whether the guards knew to be vigilant.

"*Sí, patrón.*" Esteban quarter turned, ready to go back to his work.

Ponceterra could see that Esteban had everything in hand. The *policía* would stay far away, as arranged, and on the off chance the men who had been inquiring found the *rancho,* his security was well ready for them. Beyond that he knew that Esteban would learn who these men were, even if they never came, and he would hunt them down. Esteban would follow their trail over road, over river and rocky ground, and even across borders, until he killed them in their own beds if Don Ramon so ordered it. He nodded for Esteban to continue and closed the door. He would wait at the *rancho* until Esteban was done, but he felt the pull from the room down the hall. *Perhaps just a short visit, some quiet time together,* he thought, *since I'm here.*

The screams had just stopped, and the silence was more horrible than even the noise. He gripped his weapon, scraping the edge more quickly on the cinder block. Then he heard footsteps and stopped. He stood and looked at the sharp point he had created. It seemed there was no more time. It would have to do.

FORTY-TWO

THEY DROVE IN SILENCE. The coming dusk finally brought promise of cooler air that spilled in the open car windows. The final period of waiting had passed as a painful, nearly physical trial. They had handed the binoculars back and forth between them many times, Behr trying to see for himself what Paul had witnessed and Paul trying to see it again.

"You're sure?" Behr had asked over and over, until Paul had stopped answering. Paul had checked the repeated urge to rush down on the place. He put his trust in Behr's judgment that dusk was the best time for them to make their move.

"It won't work, us just rambling in and kicking up dust as we go straight at the place," Behr said.

They had used the cover of the rise, driving

behind it until it ran out and then tracked north and east in a big loop that kept them out of sight of the compound. Once they had traveled perhaps a dozen miles they tacked left and began looking for the dirt road that would lead them in the conventional way they'd seen other vehicles arrive.

Paul's mind raced and his heart hammered as they drove. He had a thousand questions fighting in his brain and the result was that none reached his tongue. He looked over at Behr's left hand gripping the steering wheel as he stared intently out the windshield, only turning occasionally to check their coordinates in the desert by instinct like a seasoned mariner in familiar waters.

"Frank," Paul finally asked after a moment, "how did you get the password?"

"It's not important," he said.

"No?" Paul's eyes were on Behr's left wrist, now naked of his watch. Behr saw this and switched hands on the wheel.

"It's not important," Behr said again.

The car bounced low into the ditch that ran alongside the road, then the suspension gathered and they surged up onto the surface. It had appeared like magic, a line dissecting the empty wasteland that stretched endlessly in all directions. Behr spun the wheel and made the left turn as if he was pulling into his driveway. They drove on, nothingness ahead of them, until it seemed they would continue on forever into an endless void.

And then, sticking up out of the desert like antennae, they saw the light poles. Paul swallowed. Behr's hand tightened on the steering wheel like he was trying to wring an elixir from it. The coiled wire atop the fence came into view next, and after that the whole place. They could see the two vehicles they had seen arrive from their vantage point: the pickup and the well-kept Cadillac Eldorado. Wandering over from one side of the entrance came the gate guard, the day man every bit as large as his nighttime counterpart.

"Hopefully he speaks some English and we can use this password. Otherwise . . ."

Paul nodded. He glanced at the backseat, where a .12-gauge pump shotgun rested beneath a beach towel.

"Smile. We've been here before."

They stuck wide grins on their faces and Behr raised a hand in greeting.

Ponceterra entered the room where he'd been keeping the *rubio*. He was already shucking his shooting jacket as he kicked the door shut. The room was at least twice as large as any other and easily the nicest one in the place. He was losing potential profits by not having the room in use, his concession to his heart, but it would be worth it when finally things had begun. He felt his own inner clock racing and wondered how long he would be able to remain patient. He looked at the *rubio,* who took a single step toward him. Hope sprung alive in him and he felt his mouth wet with anticipation. The boy crossed the room toward him. Perhaps his patience had paid off. The *rubio* was finally coming close.

"*¿Qué pasa?*" Behr said to the gate guard, a large man with narrow, suspicious eyes.

"*Buenas, señores,*" the guard answered. "*¿Qué quieren ustedes aquí?*" He had only opened the gate enough for himself to step up to the driver's window.

"Ah," said Behr. "*Quiero visitar . . . Hablas inglés?*" The guard shrugged. Behr, running out of Spanish quickly, went on in English. "We're sportsmen. Clients. *¿Entiendes?* Our friends brought us here before." Behr produced his last hundred-dollar bill. The guard took it, his eyes narrowing further. But he didn't open the gate for them. Instead he put his hand on his pistol. It was clear the man knew someone unwelcome might be coming.

"Get out the fucking car," he said, and when Behr hesitated, he kicked the door.

"Easy. Easy there, friend," Behr said, slowly pushing open the car door to step out. "*Pajarito.* That's what we said last time. I should have said that first. *Pajarito.*" Behr waited for the password to have an effect. It was not the one he expected. "¿*Problema?*" he asked. As he spoke, the guard began to draw the gun.

Paul saw the sap Behr shielded with his body as he got out of the car. He had not yet risen to his full height when he swung the sap and connected. The guard's teeth flew through the air like popping corn. The man sagged back a few steps, ropes of blood falling from his mouth to the dusty ground near where he'd dropped his gun. Most men, inexperienced in these matters, would panic and crumple from the pain of the blow. This man gathered himself, turned back toward Behr, and advanced.

Targets. Behr's mind's eye went wide, seeing the man as a whole, not looking at any part of him in particular. Knees. Groin. Bladder. Ulnas. Saphenous. The man drew into range and Behr flew at him, closing the rest of the distance, allowing him no space. He raked the man's eyes. It was not a hard blow, but his fingers made contact with an eyeball, gouging deep. The guard's hands flew up to his face. Behr went up the middle with a swinging kick and caught the guard full in the testicles with his shin. The man was suffering involuntary spinal reactions now, and no amount of training or practical experience could help him. He doubled over at the waist, hands going to his groin, his chin extended. Behr passed on the chin and instead delivered the sap to the side of the guard's neck. It sounded a dull *thwack* as it caught the vagus nerve. The man shut off and landed heavily on the ground. Behr stepped over him, rolled him to the side, pushed the gate open, and headed back to the car, where Paul had slid behind the wheel.

The time was now. All sound and thought fell away. He felt small and weak and that it would be easy for him to die. But he did not care anymore. Across the small expanse from him the Fancy Man babbled in Spanish and smiled. He wanted more than anything to erase that smile. He forced his feet and body to move in a single direction. The smile bloomed bigger on the Fancy Man's face but froze when he saw it coming. His hand rose up from behind his thigh, where he'd hidden it. He drove the sharpened spoon handle into the Fancy Man's heart. Or what would have been the heart if he'd had a proper weapon. As it was, the sharpened spoon handle lodged in bone and the remnants of muscle that covered the Fancy Man's wretched organ. The man screamed the high-pitched shriek of a woman that dissolved into pained snorts.

Esteban heard the shriek from inside the room down the hall and it stopped him from what he was doing. He wiped his bloody hands on the front of his pants as he ran down the hall. He tried the knob and found the door locked.

"*¿Patrón?*" he called out and banged on the door. "*¿Patrón?*" He put an ear against the door and finally heard Don Ramon's voice.

"*Está bien. Todo es tranquilo. Tranquilo . . .*" came through the door.

"*¿Necesita algo usted?*"

"*No, nada*" was all that came back. Esteban waited there for another moment, but on hearing nothing further, he returned down the hall to continue his work.

Ponceterra rested on his knees for a moment and slowly realized that the blade hadn't killed him and was not going to, that it was a flesh wound. He peeled open his shirt for a closer inspection, the fine linen shredding around the embedded metal. He stood and felt a surge of power run through his body. Whether it was seeing his fresh blood or his own inner clock, he decided the wait had gone on long enough. Circumstance had brought him here *today*. And today it would begin at last. He worked at the cravat around his neck, his fingers fumbling at the knot in their excitement, and he realized he had been right, that he could live forever. *I CAN LIVE FOREVER.* He heard the words in his head. He felt triumph and confirmation, and also desire. He looked toward the *rubio*. The veil of the special had been lifted. After all his kindness and patience, this is how the *rubio* had repaid him. The boy was a piece of meat to him now, and it was time to feed. He moved toward the boy, speaking low.

Eres mi posesión, mi tesoro. Eres mi carne. . . .
And that's when the noise started.

Behr held the shotgun at port arms and twice kicked the front door hard near the knob. The fiberglass door bowed but didn't open. He'd have it with another half-dozen tries, but he didn't have the time. The car waited behind them, and beyond it the body of the guard lay motionless. Behr leveled the shotgun and fired, spending a shell blowing away the knob and chunks of the jamb. The door swung open. He handed the gun to Paul.

"Four rounds left in it." Behr could scarcely imagine a scenario in which Paul would get the chance to reload. "Don't forget about those dogs."

They entered the building. Behr pulled out his pistol and led the way into a fussily decorated parlor. Someone had made an attempt to create an elegant old Mexican look but had succeeded only in making it cheap and tawdry. Behr nodded down a hallway lined with closed doors and Paul advanced that way while Behr continued on into a sitting room.

Paul kicked the first door open, falling to the ground for cover as he entered. A man wearing a holster, his gun already drawn, shot a naked, dark-haired teenage boy twice in the back and then turned the gun on himself, putting a round through his own temple before Paul could get to his feet and do it for him.

Behr registered the shots as he had made his way through the empty sitting room and went through a closed door. He found himself in a large dormitory-style room with three or four sets of bunk beds. A warm breeze greeted him as a metal grate had been peeled back and a window smashed. Looking out, Behr could see the lithe bodies of four or five dark-haired teens racing over the horse crippler and, as their feet were bare, hopping in pain, before making it through the front gate, which was swinging open and still abandoned. They continued on, around sagebrush and tarbush, and into the distance.

He left the room and reentered the main part of the house when behind him he heard the clink of a metal chain, then a growl, and turned to see the dogs coming at him in a staggered pair. He let them come. Their teeth bared and eyes mad and black, they were a tableau of fury. He raised his .44 at the lead animal's open mouth and fired. The dog slid to his feet in a heap, its face blown off by

the hollow-point round. Behr heard the word
"*Mierda!*" through the ringing in his ears caused
by the shot. Out of the corner of his eye Behr saw
the man who had released the dogs turn and run.
Before Behr could redirect his weapon, the second
dog leaped. Behr leveled a forearm and the dog
went for it like it was a training exercise, colliding
with Behr and taking him to the ground. He felt a
bolt of lightning shoot through him as the Presa's
teeth went through his jacket, shirt, and then the
flesh of his bad arm. The dog, a writhing mass of
power, ripped its head from side to side, threatening to dislocate the arm. When it had and the arm
was dead, Behr knew the dog would release it and
move for his groin or his throat and he'd be done.
He gouged the dog's eye with his thumb, but the
animal ignored it, so Behr took to fishing around
in space with his right hand. Behr realized that
when the dog had brought him down, he'd
dropped his gun. . . .

Paul continued on through two other rooms that
contained shag carpeting, neatly made beds, and
temporary-looking fiberglass sinks but were empty
of people. He pushed the last door open. A slim,
aged man came toward him, shirtless, covered in
blood and wailing incomprehensible Spanish. A
silver piece of metal protruded from his chest. And
against the wall, partially obscured, was Jamie. He

413

was taller now, very thin, and with blood on his hands. Their eyes locked in a split second's recognition, which Paul broke by gun-butting the wailing man in the side of the head as he tried to barrel out of the room. The blow contained more than seventeen months' worth of frustration, agony, and fury, and the man went sideways, his skull yielding to the shotgun's stock like an overripe melon, then collapsed to the ground and didn't move again. The man's breathing became a gurgle, weak and irregular, and then grew inaudible. Paul moved jerkily across the room. It seemed his legs would hardly function, and his knees wouldn't bend. He looked into his son's eyes in wonder at the brokenness he saw there. He reached out and felt his boy's shoulders, thin but strong under his hands. He was alive. Paul grabbed his son in an embrace.

"Dad," the boy said, the word muffled in Paul's chest. "They stole my bike, Daddy. . . ."

"Jamie, shh," Paul said, then disengaged and spun toward the door as he heard someone enter.

Get up! Behr commanded himself. *Get the fuck up, Frank.* He could squat four hundred pounds easy, and though the dog weighed a third of that, having the thing swinging from his arm changed the equation. He managed to roll to a knee and drove the animal against the wall. Thin wood paneling buckled and snapped free, but the dog didn't disengage. Behr tried to drop his weight on the dog, to crush it, but the thing writhed and squirmed and endured no damage. Behr's feet were beneath him now, and moving. Improbably the image of a blocking sled flashed in his mind from his high school football days. He continued on a few steps and the struggling pair crashed through a temporary bar setup. Broken bottles rained down around them, and Behr felt his hip grinding in broken glass. He found a bottleneck with his loose hand and drove it into the underbelly of the dog. The glass just crumbled and could not penetrate the dog's thick hide. Finally the Presa let go of his arm, but there was no relief. It lunged for his throat. Behr tucked his chin. The dog's skull slammed into his jaw, and he was almost knocked out by the blow. The dog sunk its teeth into Behr's upper chest and hung on. Behr threw himself down on the animal again, beginning to lose hope. They landed among the broken glassware once more, and also on a cutting board and a half dozen limes. And a paring knife.

The shotgun was leaning against the wall where Paul had rested it, and it may as well have been in the car for all the good it would do him, for coming at him quickly, with smooth, assured steps, was a sinewy man with blood speckled all over his shirt and face and smeared on his pants. That was all Paul had time to register as he was grabbed around both arms and had his feet swept out from under him. He went down hard on his shoulder and ribs, the air crushed out of him. A tunnel of blackness swallowed him for a moment and then opened back up into a searing flash of white light.

Paul felt the man atop him, lifting, driving sharp knees into his midsection. Paul struggled and rolled from side to side, but found his every movement checked by the man's weight. The man rose up, the violence on his face making it piglike, and drove a punch down at Paul's chin. A slight turn of his head at the last moment was all that saved Paul from having his jaw crushed. The punch still landed, though, causing Paul's head to bounce off the floor and his vision to swim. Paul felt his breath choked off as the man jammed a forearm across his windpipe. Paul was utterly unable to move, as if a vise secured him to the floor. Out of the corner of his eye he saw Jamie kicking his attacker in the side, but with no effect.

"Run, Jamie," Paul said, or hoped he had managed to say aloud as he felt his strength slide away and his vision dim once again. He recognized unconsciousness and death coming at him from the near distance. He bucked his hips and clawed out in desperation, but to no avail. Then there was a thud, repeated, then repeated again. Paul felt it more than heard it, the basslike vibration coming through the man who was killing him and into his own body. The man relaxed over Paul, his body dead weight now, lurching forward and going slack.

Paul took in a huge gout of air and then, with a great effort, pushed the man off him and looked up to find Victor standing there, covered in blood.

"Victor?" Victor held the shotgun in bleeding hands and appeared to be missing a few fingers.

"*Yo lo necesito,*" Victor said through broken teeth, and held up the shotgun.

Paul nodded, took Jamie by the arm, and exited the room. Victor, standing above the fallen man, swung the door shut.

Paul and Jamie came upon Behr, bleeding and big-eyed, in the narrow hallway.

"My god," Behr said at the sight of the boy he'd stared at a thousand times in photos. "Is he . . . ?"

"We're gonna go, Jamie," Paul said. "Can you?"

"Yeah," the boy answered.

"Can *you*, Frank?"

"Follow me," Behr said, gathering himself and raising his handgun. They followed him down the hall and out through the carnage of the house. Furniture was turned over and broken in the main area. The smell of gunpowder and the thick copper stink of blood were in the air. There were bodies.

Paul saw two dead dogs sprawled on opposite sides of the room. They encountered one last guard, who was in the process of stealing something from a lockbox. He might have been the night gate guard, though neither Behr nor Paul could be sure, having only seen him through binoculars. Behr leveled his handgun. The man looked up and then ran out through a back door at the sight of them.

The sound of one, then another, shotgun blast reached them from inside as they made the car. Behr looked to Paul and gripped his gun.

"Victor," Paul said.

"Victor?"

Jamie slid into the back and Behr lunged into the passenger seat. Paul started the car and began to drive. He expected the crack of a bullet from some unseen guard to tear his head away at any moment.

"Get down," he said to Jamie, who did, lying across the floor in the back. Behr slumped lower, too, kicking off a shoe and peeling off a sock, which he pressed against one of his wounds. Paul rooster-tailed the car out of the gate, which hung open and still abandoned. No shot came. Paul fought to control his breathing, his sides heaving for oxygen, overloaded with adrenaline. He spit up in his mouth and let it go out the window, not taking his foot off the accelerator. Tears slicked his face.

"Jamie, get up now. I need to see you."

His boy, impossibly, appeared in the rearview mirror. Paul thought for a moment that he himself had been shot back in the house and he was dying, and this was his death-moment fantasy image. But the moment went on and on. Paul got control of the car. Jamie was really there. Paul flashed on Carol, waiting at home for him, *for them*, to return. In his mind burned an image, of her face exploding with light, a light he could barely remember, in the instant when she saw her son again. Paul reached back with a hand and Jamie took it.

The dirt road gave way to gravel, and finally they were on asphalt again. They merged onto the main route, joining other cars and large trucks heading north. Mexican wind blew in the open windows. A cordon of federales' cars passed them going southbound with lights and sirens rending the night. Paul glimpsed Jamie in the backseat, staring out the window, incomprehension and barrenness on his young man's face. They used dirty T-shirts and what was left at the bottom of the water bottles to clean themselves up. Behr wrapped a shirt around his tattered forearm. They kept driving, looking out every window and then at one another. It wouldn't be long now. They'd be at the border soon.

For the missing and those who wait for them

ACKNOWLEDGMENTS

The author would like to thank Dale Wunderlich, Michael Levien, and Arthur Nascarella for generously sharing their insights on law enforcement and private investigation. These are three men who always go after the truth, and their contributions were invaluable.

An excerpt from

WHERE THE DEAD LAY

by

DAVID LEVIEN

Available in hardcover from
Doubleday in July 2009

THE MORNING WAS gray, and a cool that wouldn't last. Frank Behr steered his Toronado across East Prospect, and appreciated the empty streets at 5:45 a.m. His neck still throbbed from a guillotine choke he had barely escaped a day ago, and he was having trouble turning his head to the left, but at this hour the city was his. He had a jump on the world, and that felt good. As he drove, he tried to leave his mind distant and unfocused. Better not to dwell on the soft bed he'd just left, or on the physical challenge that loomed ahead of him. In twenty minutes time he'd be soaked in sweat, his heart hammering, arms and legs turned to molten lead, as he attempted to gain limb-breaking position on a man who was basically impossible to achieve this against.

Pummeling, clinches, fire-feet and sprawl drills, takedowns, guard escapes, and technique work. Topped off by lunge walks with a hundred-pound ground-and-pound bag on his shoulder. It was enough to cause a replay of last night's dinner, and that was just for openers, before they began to "roll," which was what they called sparring at Aurelio Santos's Brazilian Jiujitsu Academy.

Behr cut right on Sherman. There wasn't much traf-

3

fic, but whatever cars were out at this hour would be along 74, so he avoided it. Behr trained alone with Aurelio himself, and because of that made damn sure he was on time for their 6:00 a.m. starts. It was a matter of respect. Behr had tried the normal group classes in the evenings at the academy, but leaving the hardest thing of the day until the end was exactly the opposite of how it worked for him now. The specter of it tended to hang over his day and mess with his mind. It was a concession to his age, which was just on the wrong side of forty, but nowadays he needed to clear the physical effort first.

Aurelio charged him the regular fee of a hundred-fifty bucks a month despite the private lessons that should have cost at least a hundred an hour. For that, Behr figured, he owed Aurelio plenty. He had to consider, though, that it might not be a straight-up favor. Behr had a habit of accidentally breaking people. Six-seven and two-fortyish was a handful for the recreational martial arts practitioner, and Behr had caused plenty of unintentional injuries to various training partners during the decade and a half he'd studied karate, boxing, and kickboxing before taking up jiu-jitsu. Regular-sized, civilized, often white-collar folk, plying techniques on someone of his mass and dimension, tended to lose faith in a system when the moves suddenly didn't work. Even those of a much higher belt rank weren't immune. It wasn't unheard of for someone to quit outright and not come back after practicing with him. Plain and simple, Frank Behr could be bad for business. Maybe Aurelio had gamed that out.

Behr hit a string of green lights along Campbell, letting the big car drift around some potholes, and then steered toward the academy on Cumberland Street. He felt it before he saw it, as he rounded the corner and clicked his right-turn blinker: there was too much activity in the parking lot, which should've been quiet. His eyes zeroed in on a pair of patrol cars, done up in graphite and black, the color scheme for Indianapolis Metro PD since the consolidation with the Sheriff's Department, that still wasn't the norm in his mind after all those years of taupe and brown. There was also an ambulance in the lot. The ambulance had its flashers on, no siren. The patrol cars were split, and parked in a wedge, one directly in front of the academy, the other at the door of the neighboring check-cashing place.

That doesn't make much sense, Behr thought, as he pulled in and parked and saw that the metal grate over the door to the check-cashing place was securely closed and the lights turned off. Then his eyes found the door to the studio, which was swung wide open.

Who the hell robs a martial arts school? he wondered. *That is no kind of score.* Anyone who's ever been to one has to know the office would only contain disorganized paperwork, out-of-date liability waivers, moldy addresses; and as for a safe to break:

that'd be a petty cash envelope holding small change amounting to less than fifty dollars maximum. Not even worth the trouble.

Maybe somebody hit the studio hoping to go through the wall into the check-cashing place, Behr considered, shutting off his car.

If that was the case, and Aurelio had arrived to discover some thief with the bad fortune to not be finished . . . Well, Behr supposed, that would explain the ambulance. He opened the car door. He wore sweats over shorts and a rash guard top, and automatically grabbed for his gear bag, which contained mouthpiece, towel, and dry clothes for after, and walked toward the studio. *No workout today*, it occurred to him, knowing too well how long the bull-shit paperwork with the cops would drag on, until the morning class started to arrive. Then his experience reminded him that robberies didn't happen at 6:00 a.m. very often. He quickened his pace.

The air inside the academy was thick with it. It was unmistakable. Behr stepped through the door and saw it in tableau. Two EMTs sat back on their haunches, idle and staring at the walls. A pair of cops stood, arms crossed, heads down. Silence. Between them, on the ground, was Aurelio, his face and skull blown away from his neck like a snapped-off match head. The once supremely powerful and intelligent body lay there, simply turned off, just a pile of bone, sinew, and other dumb tissue now. Dark blood spattered the blue mat.

Behr edged closer. What stared up at him from the ground made him go cold: death, still and final, that which had recently been his friend, now gone for good. He felt his stomach knot and threaten to turn over. He bit back on it hard and held his mud. It was the least he, the living, could do.

Then, even as he stood there, stunned, not saying a word, his eyes began to work, undirected. Aurelio's fists were clenched, the knuckles raised and purpled, as to be expected after his fourteen-year Mixed Martial Arts career. There were damp patches on the mat. Water or sweat? The few pieces of furniture in the studio—chairs and a table—were upturned. A chunk of drywall was caved in. On another wall were a few small, round holes, buckshot pellets lodged in them. The blood streak on the mat grew chunky with solid matter as it neared and stopped at the body.

It came together in an instinctive rush in his mind: Aurelio had been shotgunned under the palate. It had been an interrogation finished by an execution, but not before a struggle. No *two* men he'd ever met could've held Aurelio down. A gun changed any equation, to be sure, but Behr's gut reaction was that there had to have been three, at least. The body had been dragged a distance, but then abandoned.

"Ah, goddamnit," he breathed. It just slipped out. Behr cursed himself for the words. He could have used an extra few seconds to take in the details.

But now one of the cops turned to him, REGAN printed on his nameplate. "This is a crime scene. You can't be here. Who are you?" The kid in uniform was blond, maybe twenty-five, but his blue eyes were already going flat and probably only lit when his son or daughter was around. It was what happened.

"Frank Behr. I train here."

"Behr. You used to be over on the Near North Side?" the other cop, a dark-haired, dark-eyed thirty-year-old said. His tag read DOMINIC. "My uncle Mike's said your name."

"That's right. A while back," Behr said, and tried to think. "How'd the call come in?" They gave him the courtesy.

"Bread truck delivery driver went by on Cumberland. He saw a flash in the window. Didn't think much of it at first, but it stayed with him enough to call 911 further on along his route," Regan said.

"Don't suppose he saw anybody or any cars in front?" Behr wondered.

"Nah. Course not. Detectives are on the way to question him anyway."

"You know *this*?" the second cop asked, gesturing to the body.

Behr bristled, but nodded. "Aurelio Santos."

"Like the name on the sign."

"Yeah. It's his place." Behr heard the defeat in his own voice. He'd seen enough of them to know that this was one cold crime scene. It looked icy. How many dozens of prints and partials would be all over

the place thanks to the student traffic? And no wit-
nesses either. A grim, hopeless feeling looked for a
place to grab hold in his belly at the waste of it, at the
empty hull that was now all that remained of a man.

Then anger settled on Behr, hot and familiar. His
jaw set and he knew in that instant that whatever the
police did or did not do, no matter how much or how
little they threw at the case, no matter how quickly
they might try to clear it, that *he* would invest the
minutes, the hours, the days, the months it would
take to hunt down the scum, the animals, the
maggot-motherfuckers who did this. He felt his
breath come in short stabs, a bellows of fury working
deep within him. He tried to control it, to not be a
"belly breather," the way Aurelio had taught him
when an opponent had a knee on your chest and was
going for full mount and every cubic centimeter of
oxygen left in the lungs meant the difference between
light and blackness.

A random killing? Behr tried it out in his head.
Not the norm for Indianapolis. There'd been too
many murders in the city lately, but they all had a
crime-on-crime connection and Aurelio was the fur-
thest thing from a criminal. It wasn't right. He felt it
again: *someone had wanted something.*

Behr's eye fell on the office in the far corner of the
main room. *Information.* It wasn't a mere idea but an
imperative that pulsed deep in his cortex, like a rep-
tile's desire for food. He figured Aurelio's Rolodex
would be on the desk, and his best hope of a lead

would be found inside. But it would be a matter of moments before the officers threw him out, regardless of whether he'd once been on the job, and went ahead and locked down the crime scene. Like the cop saying went: *when you're in you're a guest, when you're out you're a pest.*

Taking a chance, Behr started for the office, going wide around the body and blood trail, staying on the edge of the mat. His movement seemed to stir the others into action. As he passed the high shelves holding tall, elaborate trophies from Aurelio's wins in the Mundials and Abu Dhabi and Tokyo, the EMTs started closing their unused medical kits, and the cops looked to one another.

"Ho, buddy. Where you headed?" asked the dark-haired officer, Dominic. Behr felt them starting after him.

"You guys are gonna need to notify next of kin, I'm gonna get the number," Behr tossed back over his shoulder.

He reached the office, nudged the door open with a toe, and in the half-light saw an address book with a plastic cover on the corner of the desk. Leaving the lights off, Behr dropped his gym bag on top of the book, covering it. Then he took a paperclip off of a file cabinet and used it to gently click on the light switch without disturbing any possible prints.

"He's from Brazil. Unmarried. No family in state. Are Homicide Branch and Crime Scene on the way?

No one's touched anything, right? You guys seem like you know the dance steps. Goddamn, he was a great guy . . . " Behr used the patter to distract while his eyes darted around the office looking for something he could use before they clocked his bag on the desk. The cops filled the doorway.

"Look at that, huh?" Behr said of a calendar sponsored by a Brazilian beer called Brahma featuring beautiful copper-skinned girls in dental floss bikinis playing volleyball on Ipanema Beach. The young cops glanced at it for a long moment and then Behr saw a sheet of notepaper tacked to the wall over the phone. It was covered with scrawled Portuguese first names, and digits with the +55 prefix needed to call Brazil. Aurelio was from a large, close-knit family, and the list was his frequently dialed numbers back home.

"There you go," Behr said, stepping back, letting the officers move in. "If there isn't a family member on that list I'd be real surprised, and there'll at least be a close friend."

"Thanks," Regan said. Dominic just grunted. Then the pair raised their notebooks and started copying down the names and numbers. Their backs to him, Behr took the opportunity to pick up his bag, and the address book under it, which he made disappear into the waistband of his sweatpants, pulling his shirt down over it. It didn't appear that the office had been disturbed by whoever had killed Aurelio, and the worn, cloth cover of the book wouldn't hold a

print very well. The risk had already been taken anyway. There was no going back now.

Behr stepped into the main room again. The blond
cop, Regan, followed him out, on point now.

"Okay, Behr, Frank," he said, writing.

"B-e-h-r," Behr spelled it for him.

"Phone numbers, home, office, cell."

Behr supplied them, and his address.

"We train four days a week here, for an hour, hour
and a half. Then the other instructors, some private
students, start to arrive. There's a morning blue-belt
class at eight most weekdays," Behr went on. He
began to feel his emotions beating at the door of the
cold methodology. He didn't know how long the bar-
rier would hold.

"Blue belt, what level's that?"

"Fairly beginner, but guys who know their way
around."

"What belt are you?"

"We weren't doing it that way."

"So, no wife," Regan shrugged. "He got an ex-
wife?"

"No. Had a girlfriend but they broke up maybe
ten months ago. No one steady since then."

"Uh huh. I'll need that name."

"If I can think of it. Maria something."

"This guy have any beefs?"

"None that I know of. Everybody loved him."

"Teachers he'd fired? Pissed-off student? Creditor?"

"I'm telling you, everybody loved the guy."

"Someone didn't fucking love him. Or had a strange way of showing it," the dark-haired cop, Dominic, said as he rejoined them.

"Why don't you shut your mouth?" Behr bored holes in him with his eyes. The one EMT who remained, writing notes on a clipboard, froze.

"Oh," Dominic turned. "What're you gonna cry now?"

"Be a professional, asshole," Behr said.

"*You* be one." They stood nose to nose, or thereabouts, since Behr had four inches on him. The truth was: he didn't mean anything by it and Behr knew it. It was just the way cops talked to one another to get through their shift. That didn't make Behr let off any though.

"Look, you've been helpful, but you're gonna need to fall back for us," Regan said. "Watch Commander's coming to set."

Behr broke off with Dominic, nodded, and took one last look at the scene, drinking it in with his eyes. Aurelio wore a green satiny warm-up suit that could've just as easily been his dress from the night before as it was for that morning. He was wearing Puma track shoes, which he wouldn't have stepped onto the mat with ordinarily, but under the circumstances that didn't seem to mean much. The body still appeared supple. Rigidity hadn't yet set in. The blood was wet. He couldn't have been dead for very long.

Behr was turning away when something struck him as wrong. He turned back and tried not to be blinded by the obvious, and then he saw just below where the wound started, Aurelio's neck.

"You didn't remove anything from him, did you?" Behr wondered. The EMT looked up at him.

"Yeah, a mole from his left butt cheek—" Dominic started in.

"Like what?" Regan said, his voice sounding tired.

"You gonna give us a lesson—" Dominic tried again.

"Jewelry," Behr said. The EMT shook his head.

"Nah. There was none," Regan said. "Why, you thinking robbery?"

Behr shrugged, he wasn't in the mood to volunteer it but Aurelio wore a thick gold rope chain around his neck that held a figurine of Christ the Redeemer, like the one up on Corcovado in Rio. He only took it off when he went out on the mat, but like the cop said, it wasn't there. The EMT finished and exited. The detectives would be showing up within minutes and it would be better if he wasn't around when they did, especially with a piece of evidence tucked into his waist.

Behr kneeled, almost in communion, near Aurelio's feet, and the room got quiet. Even Dominic gave him the respect. Behr made a final, silent promise, then stood and headed for the door.